THE LONG WALKABOUT

Jane Paul

Matchstick Literary
1-888-306-8885
www.matchliterary.com
orders@matchliterary.com

*This book is dedicated to all those who choose
to make the bush their home.
These people are courageous, big-hearted and unbelievably generous.
To my colleagues, the nurses, who work out there,
sometimes under, trying conditions.*

*To the magnificent Royal Flying Doctor
Service, which I have been privileged
to see in action during my time in the bush.
You truly are a national treasure!*

*To the many Indigenous people, especially Shirley, who so readily
shared their culture and their wisdom with a 'New Chum'*

*To my Children Joanne & Michael. My reason for being. My brother
Andrew, and to Bill – always there for me in those days. I miss you.*

THANK YOU

CONTENTS

FOREWARD

When Patrick O'Hara fled from Ireland, following a bar-room brawl, resulting in a death, he could never have imagined the effect his decision would have on his descendants.

From his arrival in Australia, as a seaman on the 'Irish Rose' to his chance meeting with Sam Kingsley from Walkabout Creek, the fates of the two families were forever intertwined in the small outback town and the Imperial Arms hotel

Separated and traumatised by war, the families struggle to maintain their relationships and trust in each other.

Daniel O'Hara takes over running the Imperial Arms Hotel, and turns it into the hub of the district.

Goldy, who is Patrick's granddaughter, sees the best and the worst, the outback has to offer as she learns to love the country, in her role as a Community Nurse in Walkabout Creek. She works with the Royal Flying Doctor Service as she attempts to meet the needs of the Aboriginal settlement.

She will have her heart torn in two by the charming Charlie Wentworth, who dreams of owning his own spread one day, and the enigmatic and arrogant, Guy Kingsley, heir to the rich Brolga Hills station.

When murder shatters the peace of the bush, the families are again, called upon to support each other in unimaginable ways, culminating in a cruel, unexpected twist, as each of them live out their destinies.

ACKNOWLEDGEMENTS

As always, there are many people to thank. My family is always a great source of encouragement. Joanne, my daughter, who advised on matters equestrian, and who was the inspiration for the character of the spirited Jo Kingsley.

Bruce, who shows such faith in me, it is humbling. He never fails to assist me with research, this time on the Kakoda Track, and who gives me good ideas and food for thought.

My son Mike, for believing I can do anything!

Sarah, my granddaughter, who kindly let me use her race horse's name as the title for the book.

Glenn, after a chance encounter, for his encouragement and assistance, regarding firearms and police procedures. Forgive me if I have made mistakes and some bits are wrong!;

Hanne, who is always there, looking up things for me and generally assisting with practicalities. For calming me when my computer stops loving me, and for rescuing my flagging spirits, by organising great holidays!.

My friends, Jan, Natalie, Margaret, Marie, and Jennifer, who never give up on me, and constantly encourage me to 'Get on with it!'.

I would also like to acknowledge Peter Fitzsimons' book 'Kakoda', which gave me a greater understanding of the conditions Australian soldiers endured.

CHAPTER ONE

IRELAND

Under the dim street light, outside the Brazen Head Ale House, two young men stood in stunned silence. Finally, one said softly, 'By God Patrick, I think you've done for him. I think he's dead!' Daniel O'Hara looked across at this brother, who was staring in disbelief at the crumpled heap in front of him. 'We had best be getting out of here before the Gardai arrive!' He grabbed his younger brother's hand, and together they fled into the darkness.

It was Saturday evening in Dublin, and the O'Hara brothers had been enjoying a quiet Guinness at their favourite watering hole, after a hard day's work. Daniel had a day ashore from his job as a seaman on the Irish Rose, a steamer which regularly sailed from Ireland to the Far East. Patrick worked on the docks on the Liffey river, loading and unloading cargo. With many of the population unemployed in those troubled times, it was a blessing that they both had jobs and were able to contribute to the upkeep of their small home, their long suffering mother and five siblings. Their father had not worked since an accident on the docks some years before, and the combination of poverty and drink had made him a bitter man, old before his time.

Now the two young Irishmen ran for their lives down the dark narrow alleys to their home.

Their mother Ellen gave a cry of dismay when she saw the vicious cut on Pat's face, and as she bathed and dressed his wounds, he told her haltingly of what had occurred.

He and Daniel had been drinking quietly at the bar, when they heard raucous laughter further up the bar and had pricked up their ears when they heard someone mention their sister Ann's name. He recognised one of the men as a young suitor who often called on his sister at their home. Then he heard a stranger say in a drunken slur, 'Good sort your Ann. I wouldn't mind a night in the sack with her meself!

Before anyone had a chance to say anything, Paddy had leapt to his feet, grabbed the stranger by the jacket. 'That's enough of that! You'll no be talkin' about my sister in those tones. unless you want your face rearranged!'

'What! Are you wantin' to keep her at home for yerself?' he laughed drunkenly as Paddy took a swing at him, and landed a blow on the chin, knocking him backward against the bar, where he continued to pummel him. From nowhere, one of the man's companions grabbed a bottle from the bar, smashed it on the edge and slashed at Patrick, catching him unawares, opening up the left side of his face, narrowly missing his eye.

At this point, the barman intervened. 'Outside the lot of yers!' he shouted. 'I'll no be havin' this behaviour in my bar.' and he forcibly pushed the young men out into the street.

Pat continued to rain blows on the young man and his companions until they slunk away, leaving the brothers standing over the inert body of the offensive stranger.

'And that,' he told his mother, 'was what happened. I never meant to kill him Mammie, honestly I didn't. I just couldn't let him say those things about our Ann!'

'Good Lord, what will happen now? They'll hang you for sure!' cried Ellen O'Hara as she broke into paroxysms of weeping. Daniel was sitting quietly nearby. 'He'll have to get away Mam,' he said softly. 'I'll see what can be done, and I will be back shortly.' He slipped out of the room.

Ellen continued to weep, 'I don't know what it is will ever become of you Patrick O'Hara, the devil will take you for sure'!

He winced as he tried to smile. 'You needn't be worrying mammie. The devil will never catch me.'

About half an hour later, Daniel returned. He spoke softly to his mother. 'You'll be needing to pack a few things for him, Mammie. Our Pat will be going away for a time. Don't you be worrying. He'll be in good hands.'.

Ellen rose slowly to her feet and went to do her son's bidding. Patrick was her youngest son and how she loved her recalcitrant boy. A strong youth of 16, some 5.10" of strong, sinewy muscle. His curly black hair, sparkling blue eyes and profoundly good nature endeared him to all. He loved to play the fiddle and to dance with all the pretty girls. He was as much a favourite with all the young women in the district as he was to his mother. He was, she reflected, so like her husband had been as a young man. Not like he who now snored drunkenly in the next room. She had always held such high hopes for her son, now this. She wept again. Patrick was as honest as the day was long, he had a strong sense of justice, which meant he often stood up for the underdog, the weakest, and the underprivileged. He worked and played hard, but with his exceptionally fast reflexes and uncertain temper, could easily be provoked to fight. Although well known to the local constabulary he was never in serious trouble, as they took his misdemeanours as youthful jousting, but this time it was different. He would feel the full wrath of the law and probably hang for murder!

Patrick sat with his head in his hands. Daniel put an arm around his brother's shoulders.

'Now then young Pat,' he said gently. 'I have been down to the ship to see Captain Fitzharding. I told him that something has come up at home and I won't be able to sail this trip. He knows nothing about what happened tonight but as it is such short notice, he is prepared to take you on as a seaman on the trip to Australia. They sail on the high tide in a couple of hours.'

Patrick brightened up considerably, but then furrowed his brow. 'Are you not coming Dan?'

'No lad. I'll not be going with you. Someone has to be here to look after Mammie. Anyway, you'll need my Passport. I will go to the docks and just take your place. Hopefully, the bosses will not notice which O'Hara boy is there as long as the work gets done. Just leave me your Wharf pass and your pay book. I'm sure your mates down there will cover for you.'

'What about when the police come looking for me?'

'We won't know where you are. Mammie only knows that I'm getting you out of the country. She doesn't need to know where you are going. It'll be fine, you'll see. Trust me.'

At that moment their mother returned with a small satchel. She also handed him his fiddle.

'Now then Patrick, there are a few clothes and some food to tide you over 'til the morrow. There's also a little money. Not much, mind you, but it will give you a start.' she started to cry again. 'Oh my darlin' boy, 'What will become of you? You'd best be going now before the police come looking.' She threw her arms around his neck and hugged him tightly. 'I love you boy, always remember that, and don't forget to say your prayers!'

It was just after midnight, when the brothers made their way down the river and onto the wharf, where the 'Irish Rose' lay alongside. They went aboard and Daniel introduced Pat to Captain Fitzharding, who gave him the necessary papers to sign and then directed one of the sailors to show him where to stow his belongings and where he would sleep. 'You stick with Mr Simmons for a week or so,' he said gruffly. 'He'll show you what to do.'

Pat accompanied Daniel back to the gangway, where the brothers embraced and hastily shook hands. 'You'll be fine, Pat. Captain Fitzharding is a good man. Just control that temper of yours and don't go getting into any fights now!'

His voice broke as tears threatened. He drew Patrick to him in one last hug. 'Take care little brother. I'm going to miss you.' He thrust his hand into his pocket and drew out a small bundle of notes, 'This is all I have at present Pat, but you'll be needing it in Australia.'

Before Patrick could say anything, Daniel turned and disappeared into the night. From the darkness of the wharf. Daniel breathed a sigh of relief as the 'Irish Rose' quietly slipped her moorings and slid out to sea.

When all the first frantic workings of preparing the ship to sail, and the clearing away and tidying of ropes was completed, Patrick took a break. He leant on the rail and looked back at the twinkling lights of Dublin, as the enormity of the last few hours began to sink in. He felt tears pricking. For a boy of sixteen who had never spent a night away from home in his life, the future looked a frightening prospect. He wondered if he would ever again see his family, or Dublin.

This place called Australia was a wild unknown to him. Somewhere out there it beckoned him. He stood on deck until he could no longer see the lights. A weak streak of moonlight shone through a break in the clouds and glistened on the black water. As the ship increased speed, the breeze stiffened. He took a deep breath and the salt burned in his nostrils and he was aware of the motion of the sea beneath him.

'Ever been away from home before lad?' the voice cut through the darkness and his thoughts. He turned to see the stocky bearded figure of Jake Simmons strolling toward him. 'No sir. I have not.'7.

'No need to call me sir, I'm a seaman like yourself. Call me Jake. Keep the 'Sir' for the Captain and his officers.' He held out a packet of cigarettes. Patrick politely declined. 'That's a nasty cut you have there on your face lad.'

Patrick thought quickly. 'Yes, I was larking around with my brother and I tripped and fell.'

He quickly changed the subject. 'Tell me about Australia. Jake. I don't know anything about it at all.' Jake leaned back against the rail. 'Well, she's a big country, hot and dry. Miles of nothing they tell me. Funny animals, lots of sheep and cattle, and black men. There is many an Irishmen like you are out there; trying to make their fortunes, I guess.'

'Doing?'

'Prospecting for gold lad! There's some of them made a new life out there, better than any they ever could have in Ireland. They say that in some parts, men find gold nuggets in the street.'

'How come you never were tempted Jake?'

'I'm no miner, lad. I have been a sailor for nigh on 30 years. I think there is seawater in my veins. No, I couldn't live away from the sea. Besides, I have a wife and family in Ireland. I see them when I can and I make a reasonable living doing something I like. Your brother would understand. Anyway, what brings you to join the 'Irish Rose?'

He was tempted for a moment to tell the truth, but then he remembered what Dan had told the captain.

'Well, as the youngest in the family, I need to earn a living and someone is needed at home to help my Mam. My father is not well and he has no job. He is not an easy man but Dan can manage him. I'm sure it will work out fine and Dan will be back on board in no time at all.'

Jake patted him on the shoulder. 'Time to turn in, young Pat. Some busy days ahead. You'll be just fine if you just stick with me and do as you're told.'

Later, as Patrick lay in his narrow bunk, he thought of what Jake had said about the gold. It sounded like a good thing. He would be able to send money back to help the family. The fact that he knew less about mining than he did about seamanship worried him not a scrap. With the enthusiasm of the young, he fell asleep dreaming of mountains of gold.

The next few weeks flew by as Patrick settled into his new life. His pleasant persona soon made him a favourite with the other crewmen. He was a strong young man, a hard worker and learned his tasks quickly, never needing to be told twice. Often in the evening, he would play Irish melodies on his fiddle and sometimes the crew sang along.

In the Bay of Biscay, the ship sailed into a storm and Patrick suffered his first bout of seasickness. He felt so terrible and so desperately homesick, that the thought of hanging seemed momentarily, less traumatic. Jake assured him it would pass, and at last it did.

As the ship sailed south, he saw huge jellyfish, stingrays, dolphins, flying fish, schools of unknown fish and sharks, large Atlantic Gulls, and once, an albatross, its huge wingspan dwarfing any other birds.

The foreign ports fascinated him. He went ashore with some of the other sailors and found interesting people, smells, sights, food and languages, so alien to his own. The ship docked in Le Havre, in France, Bilbao in Spain, Lisbon in Portugal then off to North Africa.

In the Canary Islands he saw his first tropical island, with exotic plants and birds. The colourful locals and their music was a revelation to him. For the first time, his homesickness began to abate. The fresh air and the sunshine did him good. His muscular frame filled out, and as he tanned, the red scar on his face began to fade, seeming to enhance, rather than detract from, his good looks.

He enjoyed the physical work of his new job. He painted and he scrubbed and learned to do amazing knots. In port, he helped load and unload cargo, a job with which he was very familiar. At night, he became accustomed to the rocking of the ship and slept soundly. When the weather was rough, he learned to balance himself against the slow rolling and pitching, and to read the weather from the skies and the colour of the sea. It was a good life.

He often thought of home and of his family, but gradually the memories became less raw; the separation less painful, as Patrick O'Hara began to grow up.

Down the west coast of Africa the 'Irish Rose' ploughed on. At length she docked in Cape Town, where the town seemed dwarfed by the mighty Table Mountain. Patrick was becoming accustomed to the heat and looked forward to short trips ashore. South Africa was no exception, although not for the first time, he was struck by the inequality between the black labourers and their white colonial bosses. He saw no white men working on the wharves, only those shouting out orders. He spoke about this to Jake who seemed more accepting of the situation.

'That's the way of the world lad.' He said sadly. 'Everywhere the Europeans have gone, it is the same old story. India, Ceylon, South Africa, China. You see it back in Ireland too. The English took all the land there for themselves.'

'That doesn't make it right!' Retorted Patrick heatedly.

'No lad, not right, but that's the way it is. They have done the same in Australia too. They took it over to develop penal colonies to transport all their prisoners. Fair few Irish went there as convicts too, mostly political. Although of recent years many of our people have gone out there looking for a better life, just like you.'

Patrick fell silent. He had not shared the real purpose of his journey with anyone, not even Jake He turned his attention back to the town, where a huge white cloud spilled over the flat top of Table Mountain like a giant tablecloth. He walked the short distance from the dock to the town. It throbbed with a heaving mass of humanity, all moving but seeming to go nowhere. On one side, he saw poor slum like dwellings, housing large families, many cooking outside over small fires. On the other, the affluent homes of some of the Colonists. Large lush gardens stretching back into the hillside. He noted too, the black labourers attending those gardens. Despite everything, they seemed happy and many sang as they worked.

Durban was a similar story, although the natives he saw there seemed more independent and stronger than the ones he has seen in Cape Town.

'They are Zulus', explained Jake. 'They were the bravest and fiercest warriors in Africa. The Zulu wars are legend. Did you never hear about Rorke's Drift?'

He had to admit he had not.

'Well, about 50 years ago, Rorke's Drift was an outpost garrison, actually a small hospital and supply base. A party of about 150 British soldiers and civilians held out against an attack by 4000 Zulu warriors in a battle lasting over 12 hours. The Zulus so admired the bravery of their enemy, that just when all seemed lost, they retreated, saluting the British as they left. It was a most amazing feat. There were eleven Victoria Crosses awarded following it, also five Distinguished Conduct Medals. Eventually the Zulus were defeated, but they have remained to this day, a very proud people.'

Patrick reflected on all this as he went about his work. He marvelled at how much he had already learned in the few weeks since he left Ireland and yet how much there was still to learn. The 'Irish Rose' continued her voyage east from the coast of Africa out into the Indian Ocean on her way to Fremantle, on the west coast of Australia.

He was excited to be landing in his new country. As the ship approached the coast, he stood at the railing, enjoying the sunshine and an unfamiliar odour which filled his nostrils. Captain Fitzharding joined him. 'Smell that? The smell of Eucalyptus trees, it gets me every time. The air here is so fresh and clean.' He closed his eyes and took a deep breath. 'Well lad, you've done well. Are you sure you wouldn't like to change your mind and stay on board. I can always use a strong young sailor.'

'Thank you sir, but I don't think I'm cut out for life at sea. When you get back to Dublin, will you tell my brother that I was fine. I'd like to think he would be proud of me.'

The older man patted him on the shoulder. 'Indeed I will. By the way, do you have friends, or somewhere to stay here in Fremantle?'

'No sir. Indeed I don't.'

'Well, there's a Mission for Seamen here 'The flying Angel Club'. The manager, John Mills, is a friend of mine. Tell him you're from the 'Irish Rose' and he'll take care of you for a night or two and steer you in the right direction' He held out his hand. 'Good luck young feller. It's been a pleasure having you on board.'

As the ship drew alongside , Patrick could see the frenzied activity on the wharf as preparations began for unloading cargo. With his pay in his pocket, he went to say goodbye to Jake and some of his shipmates. The parting from Jake was hard and he suddenly felt very alone and for a moment or two, felt his throat tighten as Jake shook his hand and wished him luck. Soon it was over, and he was walking along the wharf towards his new life.

CHAPTER TWO

AUSTRALIA BECKONS

Fremantle was a pleasant port city. The streets lined with sandstone buildings were broad and sunny with seemingly a pub of every corner. At one end of the main street was a round building, appropriately called 'The Round House' which had been an early prison and supply depot. Underneath the building there was a tunnel going to the docks to aid with the unloading and storage of supplies. On the hill behind the town was the imposing Fremantle Prison, its grim stone edifice glaring out over the port. Built by the early convicts, it served to remind Patrick of the reason for his presence here and sent a shiver up his spine. *You wouldn't want to be incarcerated in that forbidding place!*

He asked a passer- by for directions and soon found the Flying Angel Club. John Mills was welcoming when he introduced himself as one of Captain Fitzharding's crew, and after a hot meal and a bath, he asked about work on the goldfields.

'Have you any mining experience?'

Patrick had to admit that he had not.

'In that case it isn't much good going to the big mining companies.' said John kindly.

'Tell you what, I have a friend in Coolgardie who is really in the know about mining. He would probably be the person to teach you the ropes. I'll give you a letter for him.' John Mills sat down at his desk and took out pen and paper.

'How do I get to this place, Coolgardie?'

'Get a train up to Perth city, not a long trip, and catch the 'Prospector' going to Kalgoorlie. It's a long journey but you'll be fine. Get off in Coolgardie, just this side of Kalgoorlie, and ask the Station Master for directions to find Jim Sanderson. Everybody knows him up that way. He finished writing, folded the paper into an envelope, and handing it to him, shook his hand. 'There you are young fellow, and good luck to you.'

Later that morning, Patrick walked down to the railway station, not far from where the 'Irish Rose' lay alongside. He bought a ticket and climbed aboard the train. Some of the journey was along the coastline and he had a chance to admire the pristine beaches and blue water. As the train moved inland, he passed areas of comfortable one storey homes and pretty gardens before eventually arriving at the central station in Perth city. The Kalgoorlie train was not due to depart for some hours, so Paddy wandered off to have a look around. Although not a big city, compared with Dublin, it was a pretty place built on the banks of the Swan River, a broad sweeping expanse of water. There were a few imposing buildings, the town hall, like Fremantle Prison, built by convicts, as evidenced by its narrow arrow like window; the government printing office, two beautiful cathedrals, a large hospital. At the top of the main street, was an imposing barracks building and arch. Overlooking the city was the magnificent King's Park, a natural bush land, which was to be preserved for generations to come, with imposing views all the way to the distant hills.

Patrick bought himself lunch at a small café, then made his way back to the station. where people were beginning to congregate on the platform. Executive types in suits, with Gladstone bags, alongside families with small children who hopped excitedly up and down, and many young men like himself. Perhaps they too were off to make their fortunes! He bought himself a ticket and found a seat at a window and settled down for the adventure ahead. Sitting opposite, a young man, not much older than himself, was reading a newspaper.

He nodded briefly to Patrick. 'Good morning. Going far?'

'To Coolgardie.'

'Hope you're not in a hurry' his companion said wryly. 'This train has a habit of running very late. Some people reckon you can get off the front of the train, stretch your legs and hop back on the end of it. It's that bloody slow!"

Patrick laughed. 'No hurry. My time's my own,' His companion grunted and settled back to his reading.

At last the whistle blew, the doors of the carriages slammed shut, and the train started to move slowly away from the platform through a cloud of steam, quickly gathering speed. About half an hour later, they stopped at a large station to pick up and set down passengers. *Midland Junction*, said the sign on the platform. From there, the train climbed steadily up the escarpment. The views back to the city were breath taking, and Patrick felt his excitement rising.

They travelled on, through rolling hills with magnificent trees and beautiful wildflowers alongside the track. He found the colours so vivid and so different from Ireland; even the green was unfamiliar. Not the shamrock green of the fields around Dublin, but a silvery grey green. He saw strange looking animals, kangaroos, sitting by the track, and farther on, a camel grazed unconcerned as the train sped past. He found it all fascinating and the time just flew by.

They stopped at other small stations before pulling into *Northam*. By this time, his companion had finished reading and was rolling his newspaper, beginning to take more interest in his fellow traveller. 'Been here before, have you?' he asked.

'No, I have not. Just got off a ship in Fremantle. Hoping to get work in Coolgardie.'

'Got contacts there have you?'

'I have an introduction to a Mr Jim Sanderson.'

This information seemed to please the stranger, and he continued. 'I know Jim. Good bloke. He'll see you right. Been mining before have you?'

'No, but I am a quick learner.'

The man leaned across and offered a hand. 'Sam Kingsley. My wife and I, with my brother, help my dad run a cattle spread, *Brolga Hills*, up north with my dad, near a place called Walkabout Creek, about a twelve hour drive from Kalgoorlie as the crow flies.'

Pat took the offered hand and shook it warmly. 'Patrick O'Hara. I'm pleased to meet you. I'm recently from Dublin. Worked my passage out and arrived yesterday.'

The train started to slow down as it approached another station. *Meckering.*

'Well Pat, I suggest we get out here and stretch our legs. There is still a long way to go.'

The two men stepped down onto the platform, chatting companionably. They strolled up and down the platform before wandering into the cafeteria for a coffee and meat pie. Back on the train, they continued to chat and Patrick was fascinated by Sam's stories of the outback.

'You should come up and see us sometime Pat. I'm sure we could find some work for you at home. Can you ride a horse?'

'No. Guess I don't know much except loading and unloading cargo and how to be a sailor! But I'm always willing to try something new!'

'Not to worry. You're a strong young man and the world is there for the taking. That's what my old man always tells me. There's nothing you can't do if you really put your mind to it!'

The train sped on and as night fell, Patrick noticed a red glow on the western horizon.

'Fire.' Observed Sam. 'Not unusual out here. Fire is often caused by lightning strikes. It is all as dry as a bone most of the time.'

'Are we in any danger?' Patrick asked anxiously.

'No. I shouldn't think so. I've been through here with fire on both sides of the track. A bit scary, but it's quite spectacular.'

Over the next few hours Patrick watched as the fire drew closer. He could see flames leaping high into the air as the scrub exploded ahead of it. There were few trees, but those there were, were quickly consumed by the raging fire. At last, they left it all far behind, and by the time they pulled into Coolgardie station, next day, the sky was clear and sunny.

He said goodbye to his new found friend, and Sam gave him his address on the back of an envelope. 'If the mining doesn't work out, you know where to find me. Just ask. Everybody knows the Kingsley's at Walkabout Creek.'

Patrick carried his bag and his beloved fiddle along the platform to the ticket office. 'Good morning. I wonder if you might be able to help me,' he said, as the Station Master slid up the window of his small cubicle. 'I'm looking for a Jim Sanderson.'

The Station Master nodded. 'Go out the main entrance, turn left. You'll see a hotel on the next corner, same side of the street. *The Denver*, if you go in there you'll probably find him, or someone who can tell you where he is.'

'Thanks,' said Patrick, as he stepped out into the dusty street. He was immediately hit by a wall of heat, and dazzled by the brightness of the sunshine, and his lungs burned with the hot dusty air.

He followed the given directions and gratefully walked into the comparative coolness of the bar of the *Denver Hotel*. He ordered a drink and asked the barman about Jim Sanderson. The barman nodded. 'That's him down the bar, with the slouch hat and brown shirt'.

He looked along and saw a large man with a weathered face and a ready smile, and he heard a rich laugh in response to some comment. He walked over and held out his hand. 'Jim Sanderson? My name is Patrick O'Hara. John Mills suggested that I look you up with regards to finding some work.'

The man shook his hand. 'G'day! Pleased to meet you. How is my mate John?'

'He's well, and he sent you his regards.'

The two exchanged pleasantries as Patrick explained his situation. Jim listened and then said. 'Well I don't have much at the moment, but I know someone who might be able to help. Got any money?'

'A little' he acknowledged.

'Well there's old Bernie O'Farrell doing a bit of mining about five miles out of town. He could use some help from a strong young fellow, I guess. Especially a fellow country man! Tell you what. Get yourself a bed here for the night. We will pick up some supplies for him and I'll drive you out there tomorrow to meet him. Can't promise, but we'll give it a go.'

With a couple of beers under his belt and a good meal, Patrick retired to his small hotel room, feeling optimistic about the morrow.

The day dawned like the one before it, hot and dusty, even in the early morning. Patrick met Jim Sanderson in the lounge and together they went down to the General Store. At Jim's suggestion, Patrick bought himself a wide brimmed hat and a good pair of boots. They stocked up on some food supplies and a few bottles of beer. Five large drums of water were also added to the load on Jim's battered utility and they took off along a bush track to meet Bernie O'Farrell, planning to get there before the full heat of the day devoured them.

'Why does he need all that water?' asked Patrick.

'For washing the rock out of the pit; for drinking; washing; cooking. There's very little water here, except when it rains and then there is too much of the damned stuff.' He laughed. 'It is either a flood or a famine out here!'

As they drove along Jim asked Patrick a few questions about his home and his family. He had noted the scar on his cheek, and asked about it. By now Patrick had developed several stories. 'I was hit by a piece of timber when I was unloading a ship in Dublin', he said. 'Lucky I wasn't hurt more seriously!'

The bumpy track took them past mounds of dirt and wooden structures. Jim explained to him that these were the small mines prospectors dug looking for gold. It was hard work and every bucket of dirt had to be dug out and lifted by bucket to the surface for crushing and rinsing. 'A lot of work for often small returns', remarked Jim. 'I've been fortunate and had some really good strikes. Many aren't so lucky. Listen well to what old Bernie tells you. He has been doing this for a long time. He has forgotten more than most of us will ever know.'

'If he's been so successful, why doesn't he go enjoy some of his wealth?' Patrick asked.

'Gold fever, lad.' Jim laughed. 'Once you catch it, you are hooked for life! Anyway, old Bernie isn't what you'd call a city type!'

They finally pulled up next to yet another large mound of earth and a tattered tent dwelling, from which emerged a wizened old man with a long beard and whiskers.

'Hi there Bernie!' called out Jim. 'I've brought you out some supplies and a strong young man from Dublin to help you.'

Bernie O'Farrell approached cautiously, looking Patrick up and down as he grew closer. 'Hullo young feller.' He said holding out a grubby hand. 'From Dublin, eh?'

'Yes, Sir. I been working on the docks there since I left school, but. I was hoping maybe you could teach me a bit about mining. I'm a hard worker and I'm pretty strong.'

'You'll need to be prepared to rough it out here', said Bernie doubtfully.

'Happy to do that, Sir, honestly I am.'

'Well in that case, you had best be calling me Bernie like everyone else. No more of this 'Sir' business!'

Jim grinned. 'Does that mean I can leave him in your tender care Bernie?'

'Guess it does and all.' The old man laughed.' We'll give it a go, hey lad?' he said, as he slapped Patrick playfully on the arm. Jim took his leave. 'I'll pop out again in a couple of weeks Bernie. Anything you need?'

'Just another case of that beer and a bottle of whisky if you can manage it,' he said, as Jim backed up the utility in a cloud of red dust and took off with a cheery wave.

Over the following weeks Patrick worked harder than he had ever worked in his life. Bernie was relentless, pushing him from dawn to dusk, seven days a week. It was either so hot he felt he would almost certainly expire, or on some nights, so cold and wet he thought he might freeze to death. Life was hard at the workings but he learned much from the old man. What kind of rock to look for, how to follow a seam when, and if, you found one. Stripped from the waist up, he worked underground, with a pick and shovel, loading the rock into buckets to be hauled to the surface, crushed under the roller, washed and examined for any minute signs of the elusive metal. He and Bernie mostly worked in companionable silence, except for barked instructions from Bernie and muttered swearing from Patrick. In the evening, as they sat over their meagre meals and billy tea, they swapped stories about home, and sometimes Paddy played old Irish melodies on his fiddle and the old man became sentimental and lost in his memories. On Saturday night they indulged in a couple of beers.

'Only on Saturday night, mind you.' Bernie would say. 'Too many miners drink themselves to death!'

Once a month, they went into town to deposit their findings at the local bank for safe keeping. Bernie warned him that there were always people looking to make a quick quid by stealing someone else's find.

'They're not above hitting us over the head neither,' he reminded him on a regular basis.

Bernie's old truck managed to keep going although Patrick was sure it was only held together with string and wire! Occasionally they made the train journey into Kalgoorlie to the Assayer's office to sell their gold and Bernie gave Patrick a generous share of their profits as well as a half share in the mine.

'You deserve it lad. You work damned hard.' He said gruffly in response to Patrick's protests.

In return, Patrick bought and paid for supplies and equipment. He also bought a miner's licence so that he could work the claim officially, without Bernie, if necessary.

CHAPTER THREE

THE JOURNEY NORTH BEGINS

It was on one of these rare Kalgoorlie visits, that Patrick first set eyes on Clara, the daughter of the Assayer, John Ferguson, as she helped her father out in the office. With her golden hair, blue eyes and wonderful smile, Patrick fell completely under her spell. She was equally enchanted by the handsome young Irishman. The two young people hardly ever had the opportunity to speak to one another, but it was certainly a case of love at first sight. As he later said to Bernie, 'I have nothing to offer such a beautiful girl, so we had best find a whole lot more gold!'

Over the next year, he saw Clara two or three times and each time fell more in love with her than ever. Until one day he was bold enough to say to her. 'When I strike it rich, Miss Ferguson, I will come and marry you and carry you off!'

She, in turn, laughed prettily and suggested that she might just wait for him.

The day of the big strike, Patrick was above ground, boiling the billy, when Bernie began yelling from down the mine. He came to the surface waving his arms and jumping up and down.

'My God laddie, we've done it!' he cried. We've struck a seam and it looks really good! We're rich! We're rich!' Further examination showed that it was indeed a good find and over the next few weeks they brought more than a few ounces to the surface. The Assayer was happy to tell them that their strike was of good quality, and they would indeed be quite rich. Bernie's only concession to his new-found wealth was to buy a new utility, a bright blue one, complete with a heavy duty cover for the back, and two new wool blankets for them both. They also had a whisky on a week night!

One evening, Patrick went into the tent to give Bernie his evening meal, but found the old man tossing and turning on his camp bed, coughing and racked with fever. Alarmed, Patrick prepared to take him into the small hospital in Coolgardie. Bernie was unable to stand unaided and Patrick carried him out to the truck and propped him up between pillows and blankets. By then, he was mumbling incoherently, and he seemed not to know where he was. By the time Patrick reached Coolgardie, the old man was in a bad way. The nurse who received him at the hospital looked most concerned. 'I think it is pneumonia', she said shaking her head as she felt his rapid pulse and noted his flushed demeanour. The doctor will be along shortly. If you would just wait outside, please.'

As the hours dragged by, Bernie's condition deteriorated. Eventually the doctor came out into the waiting room to see Patrick. 'Has the old man any family?' he asked gently. 'If so, you had better call them. I am afraid he may not make through the night. His chest is very bad.'

'No, I don't know of any family. There is nobody, only me. May I see him please?'

The doctor nodded, and Patrick hurried to Bernie's bedside. He old man lay pale against the white pillow, his breathing laboured, his eyes closed, but when Patrick took his hand and squeezed it gently, Bernie opened his eyes briefly. 'Hullo .. there… Lad,' he said, struggling for breath. He closed his eyes again, and Patrick felt his throat tighten. He had grown very fond of Bernie over the months they had been together, and he had been like a father to him. 'Come on, old man, you need to get yourself out of here. We've gold to mine.' he said softly.

'Sorry.. lad,.. you'll.. have.. to do.. for both of us… I think.. this is.. the end ..of the line… for me." He took a deep painful breath. as he struggled to speak again. 'In my.. tin, under… my bed, you… will.. find my.. Will… All.. for you… now.. Pat lad.'

Patrick dropped his head over the old man's hand, until he suddenly became aware of the silence. He looked up at the wizened face, but Bernie O'Farrell had gone to meet his maker.

Patrick stumbled from the hospital and made his way up the street to the *Denver*, to look for Jim Sanderson. Jim was in his usual evening spot at the bar, and looked concerned as he saw the young man's face. 'What's up lad?'

'It's Bernie, he's just died in the hospital,' he blurted.

Jim sat him down and ordered a whisky. 'Here, drink this down and tell me what happened.'

In halting words, Patrick relayed his sad news. 'What will you do now, lad?' Jim asked gently 'Well first, I have to arrange a funeral for Bernie, then I guess I will try to sell the claim. Got no heart for it without Bernie. Don't suppose you would be interested in buying it?'

'Might be, for a fair price.'

A week later, Bernie was buried in the local cemetery in Coolgardie. Over a few drinks in the *'Denver'*, the sale of the mine had been negotiated with Jim, and Patrick returned to camp to collect his few belongings, with a generous cheque in his pocket Within the hour he was gone. On his way to Kalgoorlie..

He was soon settled in town, at a smart boarding house run by one Mrs Johnson . He began to court Clara Ferguson in earnest. Clara was everything he had ever imagined a woman could be. Apart from being extremely pretty, she was highly intelligent, with more than a small dose of common sense. They never seemed to run out of things to talk about, and eventually, with great trepidation, he told her how he happened to be in Australia, and of his catastrophic act in Dublin. He knew he was taking a risk that she might turn away from him, but he felt that he could not ask her to marry him unless she knew everything there was to know about him.

Clara listened solemnly, until he had finished his story. She then leaned forward and hugged him tightly. 'Patrick darling, I know that you would never deliberately hurt anyone. I am sure it was a terrible accident, but it in no way changes what I think of you, or how much I care. Let us agree, never to mention this again.'

Patrick was overcome with her acceptance of him, and immediately asked her to be his wife. He went to see her father, who gave his tacit permission for the couple to marry within the year, providing Patrick could satisfy him that he could keep his daughter in an appropriate manner.

'What are you going to do for a job now you've given up mining?' he asked Patrick, as they sat companionably over a beer in the *Palace Hotel*.

I haven't quite decided yet. Thought I might buy a business or invest some of the money. I'd like to buy a pub, or some land. Firstly, I have a friend up bush I would like to catch up with, Sam Kingsley.'

'Would that would be the Kingsley family from Walkabout Creek?' he asked.

'That's right. Do you know them?'

'No, not personally, but you have some powerful friends. They are a very well- known pastoralist family. Three or four generations up there, I believe.'

'Well, I thought I might take him up on his offer and take some time out to catch up with him. I have never been farther north than here. I would like to see the country and arrange some sort of security, before I settle down to married life!'

'Good idea, I am sure Clara would have no objections.' nodded his companion.

After talking to Clara, and feeling sure that she supported him, Patrick wrote to Sam Kingsley, expressing a wish to visit, and two weeks later received a warm letter in reply.

'Come for as long as you like.' Sam wrote. *'You are very welcome. We can have a look around to help you decide on a future investment.'*

A few days later, after a fond farewell to Clara, Patrick set off for Walkabout Creek, stopping only to buy a carton of beer and some chocolates for his hosts. Before he left, Patrick decided to write to his mother to tell her of her that he was alright and contemplating marriage. As a precaution, he did not give his address. He felt, that other than knowing he was in Australia, it was best that the family did not know exactly where he was. That way, nobody could alert the Irish police of his whereabouts, even inadvertently. He carefully folded four five pound notes between the pages, addressed the envelope, bought a stamp, and gave it to a friendly engine driver to post when next he was in Perth. If the man thought it strange that Patrick did not post it locally, he said nothing. There were many men with secrets on the goldfields.

The long journey to Walkabout Creek was revelation for the boy from Dublin. He fell in love with the wide open spaces, the ringing quiet and velvet star studded nights; the red earth, and the red barked gum trees. He drove carefully on the dirt road, little more than a track, and he gazed in awe, at the misty sunrise and the glorious scarlet sunsets, and was fascinated by the myriad of coloured birds and their morning and evening song. The mournful cry of the Mopoke at night, woke him from a restless sleep, and the frogs and cicadas chorused him until morning. He loved the purple shadows of the long evenings, and the staggering range of colours in the profusion of wild flowers along the way. He stood in wonder in a sea of Sturt Desert Peas, their red and black flowers covering the bush as far as he could see.

He watched the kangaroos and emus going down to drink at a water hole. They were unused to human contact and eyed him with interest. A curious rabbit sat observing him as he sipped his water from his water bag. A cheeky Willy Wagtail sat on the bonnet of his car when he stopped for a rest, and a sleepy lizard idly flicked a long tongue. It was indeed God's own country. Patrick felt a peace he had never known, and he blessed old Bernie for giving him this opportunity.

He noted the changing countryside as he travelled north; the trees changing to scrub, with rocky outcrops of the same stunning red. By the time he reached the turn off to *Brolga Hills* Station, he had almost decided that this part of the world would be his new home. He felt confident that Clara would love it too. He stopped at the end of the long dusty track up to the homestead, where he was welcomed by several barking dogs, a dark skinned stockman, Sam Kingsley, a young woman and an older man and woman. Sam stepped forward with an outstretched hand.

'G'day! Found us okay? Good to see you again. Pat O'Hara, I'd like you to meet my wife, Jill, my mum and dad, Marian and Rob. Dad, this is the bloke I told you about from Ireland!'

Handshakes all around, and after Patrick had handed over his gifts of beer and chocolates, the party moved through the beautiful manicured gardens into the comfortable stone homestead. 'Lovely place you have here,' he remarked to Marian, as he looked around the spacious room.

'Thank you,' she said, obviously pleased. 'Jill and I have tried to keep it homely. Rob's great grandfather established it here over 100 years ago. We don't have all the comforts of the big city, especially shops and hospitals, but it is a beautiful spot.'

'We've time for a quick look around before tea, haven't we mum?' Sam interrupted enthusiastically.

Marian nodded and the two young men stepped outside into the approaching evening. For Patrick, his first look at station life was an amazing experience. The property was very large, ¾ of a million acres, where they ran mostly beef cattle. They ran mostly Brangus cattle, a cross between the hardy Brahman and the good meat providing Angus. They had also horses. 'A passion of my brother's,' explained Sam.

'Steve is a top rider around here and he has ridden in other states, endurance, track racing, polo. You name it, he's done it. He's away in Melbourne at present. He's a great guy. You'll probably meet him later. He is due home this week.'

Patrick noted a large blue swimming pool in the green lawn at the front of the house, and a tennis court around the side. 'You really have everything you could want here, Sam!' he said enthusiastically. 'That's the way we like it.' Laughed Sam.

A wide creek wound its lazy way through the gully at the lower end of the property, and Patrick noted a number of small tin huts along the bank. 'That's where our stockmen and their families live,' explained Sam. 'Mum and Jill look after the babies and other kids, treats everyone's illnesses and injuries, and in return the women do the cooking and the laundry and cleaning for them.'

After a hot bath and a good dinner, Patrick sat on the wide veranda with Rob and Sam, enjoying a cold beer, listening to the cicadas and frogs near the pool, and the happy laughter from the river bank. Later he fell into the best sleep he had had for weeks.

Over the next week or so, Patrick, or Paddy, as the Kingsleys chose to call him, had many opportunities to hear about anything that might be of use to him, in the district. Once he had expressed a wish to stay in the area, Rob and Sam made every effort to find something to suit him. They drove him into the small township, some twenty minutes away, and introduced him to as many locals as they could. Eventually, he heard of the sale of the old pub, *The Imperial Arms*.

'She's seen better days, but there is a load of potential for a hardworking man like yourself, and the price is pretty reasonable too,' insisted Rob.

Patrick went in for a closer inspection. Rob was right. The old building had been sadly neglected in recent years, but was of a sound structure. 'There is a warm feeling in the old place. Just needs some love.' He told Jill

'From what you tell me about your Clara, you two are just the people to do that,' she said smiling.

CHAPTER FOUR

THE IMPERIAL ARMS HOTEL

He wrote a letter to Clara, for her opinion. Her positive answer, and a few more days of contemplation, and he made a decision. Patrick O'Hara became the proud owner of *The Imperial Arms*.

A couple of weeks later, Paddy drove back to Kalgoorlie; a great deal faster than he had driven up. He could hardly wait to see Clara to tell her all about his ideas for the old hotel. She was as excited as he had been, so Patrick went to see her father, to bring him up to date with his investment. and to request that he allow the young couple to marry sooner, rather than later, in order to take up their new enterprise. Thankfully, Mr Ferguson agreed, and on a sunny day in September, the two young people celebrated their marriage in St Joseph's church in Boulder. It was quite a social event in the town and many turned out to see the pretty bride and her handsome husband, and to share a drink later at the *Palace Hotel*.

The couple were very much in love. Patrick was delighted with his new wife. She was pretty, hardworking, adventurous and supportive. Her happy laughter rang out every day , and he felt very happy that he now had someone so lovely to help him start his new life. There was a nagging sadness that his family were not able to share his happiness, but promised himself that one day he would be able to take Clara to meet them. He continued to send them money when he could, often giving his mail to passing truckies to post from somewhere else. The last thing he needed was a policeman on the doorstep, to separate him from his new wife!

After a short honeymoon in Geraldton, Paddy and his new bride, made the long drive up country to Walkabout Creek, and took possession of *The Imperial Arms*.

The old hotel sat on a small patch of red earth on the corner of what passed as the main street in the centre of town. The paint was peeling away, and parts of the veranda railing leaned dangerously outward over the street. There were gaps between the floor planks , the front steps were cracked and uneven, and two large pots of dead plants stood guard at the front door. Under the veranda, a family of rats had taken up residence.

Paddy with some help from Sam set about cleaning, painting and repairing his new enterprise. Together, Jill and Clara attacked the small garden with enthusiasm, and soon the locals were gathering in admiration in front of their old hotel. The only store in town donated a length of red carpet for the front foyer and a young man from a nearby station, made them a new sign to put up. 'The Imperial Arms Hotel'.

After the necessary licences were issued, supplies of food and alcohol were ordered and delivered. Staff employed; Sally and Kevin Gregson, who had formerly run the old caravan park, stepped into the positions of housekeeper and cook, and Jim Malloy took over the bar. A couple of local girls became cleaners/laundry hands, and the hotel was finally ready for business.

At the opening, the bar rang once more with the clink of glasses and the laughter of hardworking stockmen and locals. The lounge was graced by smartly dressed ladies as they sipped their sherries, and swapped family news. The dining room buzzed, as well-cooked meals filled the tables, on the new check tablecloths and serviettes. The piano once again sprang to life, as Clara played some popular tunes for her new patrons. The old *'Imperial'* was back in business. The young couple quickly became very popular in the small town. Very soon, the hotel became once more, the social hub. Patrick's hardworking, and friendly nature was appreciated, and his pretty wife, much admired.

The few guests seeking accommodation, were treated to clean comfortable rooms, with soft beds, pretty curtains, and good tasty meals. Soon there were organised card nights, darts competitions and weekly musical evenings, and everyone appreciated the special function evenings, for birthdays, weddings, anniversaries and even wakes. The 'Regulars' soon took possession of their favourite stools in the bar, where they could be spotted at certain times.

The friendship between themselves and Sam and Jill quickly developed and they soon became almost inseparable and were often found enjoying a cold drink in the evenings. Patrick O'Hara never regretted his purchase of the *Imperial Arms*. He had never been happier, and he and Clara developed other friendships to last a lifetime. Their day to day existence was idyllic, and only enhanced by the birth of their son, Daniel, a miniature version of his father, in the same year that Sam and Jill welcomed their son, Jack.

With the added responsibility of motherhood, Clara relinquished some of her duties, and employed a new pianist, and a waitress. Daniel took to his role of husband and father with enthusiasm. His little family was the centre of his universe, and as his small son grew, he set about teaching the boy some skills, which he hoped would enhance his future life. He often took him camping overnight in the bush and taught him to play the Irish airs he loved so much on his fiddle.

Young Danny was an apt pupil, who, in turn, adored his fun-loving father. One night, as they camped out under the stars, they sat together around the camp fire. The flames crackled and curled to disappear as smoke spirals into the night. Paddy put his arm around the shoulders of his small son huddled next to him. 'Tell me, Danny, what do you see there?'

The boy laughed. 'Just flames Dad. They're very pretty, but they're just flames.'

'Nonsense lad! Look closely; you can see faces, places and when you try hard, you can sometimes see your dreams. Look! Do you see that lady sitting with her knitting? Well, I'm sure that is your Grandma O'Hara in Dublin town! And a magnificent horse rearing up! Can you see him?'

Danny soon took up the game. 'Dad! I can see a cave, and a dragon!'

Paddy laughed gently. 'You know son, I believe you will never feel more at peace than when you gaze into the flames of your camp fire. Come on now. Time to get some sleep.'

Danny fell asleep smiling. His small hand clutched in the comforting fist of his father. How he loved this man, his protector, his best friend, his world. Sometimes they took young Jack Kingsley with them, and the three of them explored the universe, and dreamed up impossible schemes.

As the orange of an outback sunset burned to its glorious end, Paddy enjoyed a beer, as he sat on the veranda with his wife. They both watched in amusement, as Danny, jumped from one patch of red earth to the next, between the spinifex. A dog, of indeterminate breed, barked playfully, jumping in unison beside him.

Patrick O'Hara was the epitome of a man who had it all. An imposing figure, he was strong and muscular, a legacy of his years in the outback. His friends would have described him as kind, amiable. A 'mate', always ready to lend a hand when needed. A gentle soul, who loved to play his fiddle, to sing and dance, quick witted, charming, and always a great favourite amongst the ladies.

Up until the disaster in Dublin, when he had killed that man in a fight, he had always been lucky. His father always said the devil was looking the other way the day when he was born! Paddy enjoyed all life had to offer. However he considered himself to be the luckiest man in the world when he married Clara. His devotion to Clara made it hard for anyone to imagine Patrick as the hard drinking, gypsy of his youth. He was a model husband, and in due course, loving father to Daniel. Clara often watched with pleasure, as father and son set off together on their adventures. Life was good for them all, and while Clara thanked God every day for her good fortune, she sometimes felt afraid. Was it all too good to last?

CHAPTER FIVE

THE SHADOW OF WAR

Danny was seven years of age, when the threatening clouds of war blew across Europe in 1939, and eventually darkened the sunny skies over Walkabout Hills. Talk in the bar was of little else but the war in Europe. Several local boys enlisted, including Steve Kingsley. The news from the front was worrying. Casualties were high. 'It will all be over soon enough.' Paddy told his anxious wife, as he kissed her gently. 'There'll be no need for me to be signing up, that's for sure. Australia is in no peril and Ireland is neutral! I have no great desire, at this time, to fight for England!'

When the news came of the loss of Steve Kingsley, Sam's elder brother from *Brolga Hills*, the entire community was shocked and saddened. Steve died in North Africa, in an unknown place with an unpronounceable name. His parents were devastated, and his brother, Sam, in anger and disbelief declared, 'Why did he have to die fighting in Africa? I never wanted him to enlist.

'This isn't our war! What does it have to do with Australia?'

In 1941, the Japanese offensive had caught the Allies unprepared. With so many Australians fighting the war in Europe, North Africa and the Middle East, Prime Minister Curtin had grave concerns about the possible defence of Australia. In Britain, Winston Churchill was unwavering in his determination not to allow any of the Australian troops to return home; at the same time, unwilling, or unable to offer any assistance. He was adamant that Australia was safe from any invasion. John Curtin was not so confident. Heated discussions followed between the two Prime Ministers, finally resulting in the return of some troops from Europe and the middle east.

The intention being, that these troops would be ready to defend the east coast of Australia or perhaps to go to Papua New Guinea, still an Australian territory, to repel a possible attack on Port Moresby.

America had been an interested observer, reluctant to commit to a war in Europe, until the bombing of Pearl Harbour, in December 1941. For the first time there was a very real possibility that Australia would be invaded, and after the attacks on Guam and Guadalcanal, later to be followed by the disastrous fall of Singapore. With the tragic bombing of Pearl Harbour, war became a stark reality to both America and more particularly, Australia.

Sam Kingsley, despite the pleading of his parents, announced his intention to enlist in the army. 'I want to fight the Japs in the Pacific, not Germans in Europe,' he insisted. 'So I'm off to Melbourne to join the Militia. They will not be going overseas but will be defending Australia if the Japs decide to invade the east coast of Australia. Are you with me Paddy?'

This ended Patrick's indecision, and he and Sam said farewell to their families and went by train to Melbourne, with many like-minded men, to enlist to fight a war they little understood.

They joined up and began two months of hard training in Bacchus Marsh, under the guidance of hard bitten veterans who had already seen war first- hand overseas, and who were singularly unimpressed with their new recruits. They became part of the 39th Battalion, B Company, and the two young men were taught basic skills in warfare, some first aid, and how to use and maintain their

.303 rifles. They learned to march; to obey orders without question. Most importantly, they learned how to kill. Their training was hard and not without its dramas. Sam, still mourning his brother, was an angry young man, easily provoked into fights. It usually fell to Patrick to keep him out of trouble. 'Keep your anger for the Japs!' he used to tell him.

As for Patrick, once he had made up his mind to go to war, he tackled it with his usual good humour and optimism. He was popular with his new mates and in truth, he began to enjoy many aspects of his new life. He had always enjoyed the company of like-minded men. However, the thought of what might lie ahead were never far from his mind. The casualties had been high overseas, and as the Japanese advanced through the Pacific Islands , it became necessary for the Americans to defend their interests there, together with the Australians. Especially when reports came through that the Japanese had landed in Buna, on the north east coast of New Guinea. (Still an Australian Territory).

Port Moresby was, at that time, protected by the Militia, and the New Guinea Volunteer Rifle {NGVR} made up of local police, plantation owners and their native workers, and a small number of troops. In 1942 there were approximately 400 Australian troops in New Guinea. The Japanese outnumbered them 10-1. In the beginning, the Japanese army was vastly underestimated by the top Australian advisors, and it was felt that they would easily be defeated. Contrary to what had been previously thought, the Japanese were a highly trained disciplined force, full of confidence after their bombing of Pearl Harbour and Guam. The latest Intelligence available, concluded that the Japanese were about to launch an attack on Port Moresby, from the land, and not from the sea, which was what was expected, and then to use Port Moresby as a jumping off point for a possible invasion of Australia. So it was that the 39th Battalion, (B. Company), together with remnants from other units found themselves on a ship from Sydney, heading north, bound for Port Moresby. Most of the men had never heard of the place, and those that had, could recall little that was useful. All of the young men had uniforms and guns, but most of them had little or no training. None of them had considered that they would be serving anywhere else, but in Australia.

Sam and Patrick had no practical experience of army life, apart from the few weeks training at Bacchus Marsh, but fortunately, they did have some knowledge of firearms and the bush, but the hardened troops on board gave them a hard time, calling them 'Chocos', suggesting that they would melt like chocolate when faced with an enemy. All this was going on whilst their officers attempted to make soldiers of them in the few short days of their journey.

Their arrival in Port Moresby was greatly welcomed by the local militia, but little or no preparation had been made for their arrival, and conditions were harsh. With no proper camps, kitchens or toilet facilities available, the troops quickly set about building them. The humidity was high, mosquitos plentiful, and flies in mammoth proportions. Within days, many fell victim to dysentery and malaria, long before they ever set eyes on the Japanese army. (Peter Fitzsimon – KAKODA)

It became clear over subsequent days, that it would be necessary to repel the Japanese advancement on Port Moresby, down a muddy, difficult track through the mountains. Most of it in a rough, largely unknown, except to the local natives, area, between Buna and Port Moresby, by way of a village called Kakoda, a few miles away. In Kakoda, there was a small hospital, various other outbuildings, and an airstrip, all of great strategic value to both sides.

This track was vital to the Japanese as a supply route to and from Port Moresby. It was also imperative for them to control the Western Pacific area, to stop access by the Americans. The Japanese plan was that Port Moresby would eventually be used as a strategic move toward the invasion of the east coast of Australia. From there, the Americans could easily be shut out of the western pacific region, and there would be plenty of room for airports and harbours, so essential for their ultimate victory.

Patrick and Sam knew little of this. They were simply told that their job was to prevent any Japanese soldiers getting down to Port Moresby by way of the Kakoda track.

There were rumours that the Australians were grossly outnumbered; some said by 10 to1. News had already filtered through of the efficiency and discipline of the enemy. There were also stories of their extreme cruelty and of a 'no prisoners' policy. The Australians were not foolhardy; there were those in their ranks who were hardened troops, who had fought many battles on the other side of the world; now together, they fought for their own land, their own homes, their own families, and there was an air of determination about them, which their leaders noted with pride. However, they were greatly under resourced, short on numbers, and many were already ill. For those soldiers who had not succumbed to illness, it came as quite a relief to be told that they would finally have a chance to actually fight their enemy.

Patrick and Sam sat near a camp fire, the evening before they were to move out.

'Are you scared Paddy?' asked Sam softly.

'Yes, of course. Only a fool would not be afraid, but courage isn't about not being scared, Sam; it's about doing what has to be done anyway! Yes. I'm a bit nervous, but just about as worried about being taken prisoner. Don't tell anyone. You?'

'Yes. I can't stop thinking about my brother Steve. I wonder if he ever thought much about dying. He was always such an 'alive' kind of man, if that makes any sense. He had so many plans for the future. He wanted to get married one day, and have a family. By the way, did you know that Jill and I are expecting another child in a few months. Got to be home for that!'

'That's great Sam! Congratulations! Did you know about the kid when you enlisted?'

'No. Jill wrote when I was at Bacchus Marsh. I wouldn't have signed up if I had known.'

He paused. 'Well, that's not strictly speaking true. No child of mine is going to grow up in a country over- run by little yellow men!'

Patrick patted him on the shoulder. 'That's the spirit! Look, I guess everyone thinks about those bad things when they go to war, but don't death become an over-riding thought! We just have to concentrate on teaching these Japs that we mean business! You and I are going to get through this. I promised your wife to take you home, so let's get out there and get those Japs on the run! We will make our youngsters proud of their dads!'

The fact that they had been instructed to write a Will, and a letter home to their loved ones, in case they did not return, had been a sobering experience for them both, together with instructions about who would be responsible for dealing with their pay whilst they were in action.

Early in the morning, the first group of the 'B' Company of 39th Battalion of about 100 Diggers set off up the track from Port Moresby, accompanied by their native porters.

CHAPTER SIX

THE KAKODA TRACK

The jungle was quite beautiful at the beginning of the track, and the going, relatively easy. There were large colourful butterflies and exotic birds, which flitted through the green canopy above. So thick was it, that in places it was almost dark and the sun barely filtered through. There were patches of bright moss, and bushes with coloured leaves. Nothing like the men had ever seen before, but the humidity was stifling, and they soon felt drained and exhausted.

As they began the climb towards the Owen Stanley Ranges, conditions became tougher. These young soldiers were new to battle, as yet untried. They struggled up the slopes with 65lb packs on their backs carrying their .303 rifles. Their uniforms soaked with sweat, their new boots rubbing their feet and ankles raw. At the end of the first day, when they had camped for the night, there had been so many blisters and twisted knees and ankles to be dealt with by the medics, and some so badly affected, that a number of the men had to be sent back to Port Moresby.

As the days passed, conditions worsened. They had not counted on the rain, which fell every afternoon, turning the already difficult track into a torrent of raging, stinking mud, increasing the ever present oppressive humidity, making progress almost impossible. Every step became a mud slide, every upward climb, a cliff, as the quagmire grabbed their weary shaking legs, and threatened to envelop them. There was little relief to be had in the valleys, where the men often had to wade through waist high freezing streams and torrents of water from the mountain tops.No relief on the slopes either, where they slipped and sloshed through the detritus of dead vegetation and deep sludge.39

They had only their ground sheets to shelter them from the interminable rain, through the mud and filth.Their boots stayed on, wet and muddy for days, until eventually their socks grew into the skin on their feet, joining bloody blisters. More men went down with dysentery and malaria. With limited food and no sleep, they were exhausted and sick. Insects were out in force, biting and stinging, and there was the ever present danger of snakes. More than once, Patrick asked himself what the hell he was doing there!

On a day such as this, Patrick and Sam were sent ahead to scout for the often elusive Japanese army. They were a few yards off the main track, moving quietly through the thick scrub, when Patrick suddenly stopped. 'Listen! Get down!' he whispered urgently, as he crouched low, near to the jungle floor.

'I don't hear anything except the rain.' Sam answered softly. 'Exactly. Too damned quiet; the jungle is never this quiet. No birds, frogs, nothing. Wait here!' Patrick carefully crawled forward to look over the mossy bank to the track below. He was shocked to see five Japanese soldiers walking down the track toward him. He felt a cold stab of fear as they drew closer and he could hear them talking softly, obviously totally unaware of the presence of the Australians. He scrambled back to where Sam crouched next to an overhanging vine. 'We need to get to hell out of here, back to warn the others! Let's go!'

They moved quietly, but had only covered a short distance when they again heard movement, this time ahead of them, between them and the rest of their company. More Japanese soldiers, a larger group this time, heavily armed and pulling a gun carriage with a machine gun through the mud. The men froze and then melted back into the jungle.

On their present route, the Japanese would be within striking distance of their mates in minutes.

Perhaps the lack of gun fire indicated that neither side had, as yet, seen the other.

No sooner had this thought crossed Patrick's mind than all hell broke loose. The jungle became alive with a cacophony of gun fire; the cries of wounded and dying men, the explosion of grenades, and the relentless 'ack- ack- ack' of the machine gun.

From their position behind the Japanese, Sam and Patrick managed to shoot the gunner. Then Patrick lobbed a hand grenade which took out the machine gun, but in doing so, alerted the enemy to their position, making themselves targets. Soon the gun fire was too close for comfort, and the two men moved back into the jungle, hoping to escape around the flank of the enemy.

Patrick felt himself spin around as he was hit in the left arm, a powerful push, rather than pain, which he knew would soon follow. Moments later, Sam gave an agonised cry, as a bullet found its mark in his stomach, and he fell bleeding to the muddy forest floor. Patrick sank down beside him, disregarding the mud. 'Oh God, Sam! How bad is it mate?'

Sam smiled weakly. 'I'm okay Paddy. Just don't let me die! I don't want to die out here.. please!'

Patrick tried to smile reassuringly, as he put his arms around him and lifted him from the mud.

'It's ok mate. We just need to get you out of here and down to the hospital!' but even as he spoke, he knew that Sam was badly wounded. His hands across his stomach were already heavily blood

41

stained, pieces of torn flesh and innards were seeping through. Patrick grabbed a wad of cotton bandaging from his pack and pushed it into the wound, then with his one good arm, he attempted to pick up Sam to carry him to safety.

As he did so, he heard the noise of approaching feet through the jungle, and was forced to lie down next to Sam, to avoid detection. As he peeped through the undergrowth, he saw two legs, literally two yards away, and then he saw the green uniform of a Japanese soldier. Sam began to groan, but Patrick quickly put his hand over his mouth, so that he stopped the sound before it began. With his heart in his mouth, Patrick watched his enemy; he seemed to be listening. Sam began to move about, to try to speak. Patrick pushed him down into the ground, and turned his head away from the direction of the soldier, who, satisfied he heard nothing, turned and walked back the way he had come.

Patrick realised he had been holding his breath. He let out a slow deep sigh, as he released his grip on his friend and gently turned him over. Sam was almost completely covered in mud, but his eyes were open wide. Patrick wiped the dirt from his nose and mouth.

'That was close, mate. Now to get you back to the medic.' But even as he spoke, he realised that Sam was dead. With horror, he stared at him. *'Oh God! He couldn't breathe with all that mud in his mouth and nose – I've killed him!'* Cradling Sam in his arms, he wept as he had never wept in his life.

How long he sat there in the mud he knew not, finally struggling to his feet, now painfully aware of his own injury, he wrapped a strip of his torn shirt around his arm Night was approaching, a moonless, black night. Patrick managed to get Sam across his shoulders, and he slowly made his way down the track, back toward his base camp.

It took him several hours to cover the relatively short distance, stopping frequently as the waves of dizziness swept over him, from the loss of blood from his shattered arm.

When he finally staggered into the clearing, his mates were quick to relieve him of his burden and to get him to the army medic.

After he had recounted the events of the day to his commanding officer, the Captain looked at him sadly. 'Sorry about Private Kingsley, but by knocking out that machine gun, you two probably saved many more Aussies today. Thank you O'Hara. Now, we'd better get some more treatment for that arm. The medic says you will have to go back to Moresby, possibly Australia. Looks like your war might be over, soldier.'

Patrick could not shake off his terrible feelings of guilt over his childhood friend. Had he sacrificed him to avoid detection by the Japanese? The other voice in his head said that, had they been captured, they would probably both be dead by now. But, what if the Japanese soldier had not heard Sam's groans? Would he be alive still? The army medic assured him that Sam could not have survived his injuries, but, what if..? The thoughts went around in his head. He had difficulty sleeping, and when he did, he woke in a cold sweat, Sam's plea ringing in his head. 'Don't let me die. I don't want to die- please!'

Within a few days, Patrick was back in Port Moresby, ready to be flown out to Australia for specialist treatment on his arm. The damage was extensive, with widespread damage to nerves, ligaments, as well as shattered bones. The army doctors told him he was lucky, so far, not to have lost his arm, but he had very little use of it. He felt that his arm might improve, but his heart was irrevocably broken.

CHAPTER SEVEN

BACK AT WALKABOUT CREEK

The first few months after Patrick had enlisted were hard for Clara, as they were for most of the women in Australia. She had to use inner resources she hardly knew she had. She often worked anything up to sixteen hours a day, and with the help of Jill Kingsley, and Sally and Kevin Gregson, she kept the hotel running. The thought that the war could not last forever, and her overwhelming love for Patrick, kept her going, when another might have given up.

Kevin had been turned down when he had attempted to enlist, 'flat feet' he was told, so together with the three women, he took on the task of running the *Imperial Arms*.

As often as he could, young Danny escaped the hotel and fled into the bush. He missed Patrick so much. He often felt his world was breaking up around him, and it seemed like the war would never end. He was afraid that he might never see his father again. He and Jack often sat near the creek, fishing, and dreaming of the things they had shared with their fathers in earlier times, and, hopefully, would again.

One afternoon, as the afternoon shadows lengthened, Danny was alone as he gathered some wood and built a fire. As darkness fell, he sat gazing into the flames. He remembered what his dad had said about seeing faces and places and dreams, but try as he might, he could not conjure up the one beloved face for which he longed. He tried to make sense of what he heard about the war, and what it actually meant, and he wondered whether his father was as frightened of it all, as he was. In his child's way, he tried to support his mother, but it was a big ask for a boy of his age The family were very distressed to hear of Sam's death and worried about Patrick's injuries.

The only good news was that he would be brought back to Australia for treatment, and might possibly be coming home. This proved to be the case, and following three or four operations on his arm and hand, and weeks of rehabilitation, Patrick O'Hara finally went home to Walkabout Creek. The red dust swirled lazily across the spinifex plains on that day. Clara and Danny were beside themselves with joy, and laughed and cried as they hugged him and each other.

Rob Kingsley and Marian mourned the loss of another son; Jill, a husband, and Jack, his father. Patrick went to see the family as soon as he got home. He didn't tell them very much about Sam's last few hours, only that he had not been alone and that he had been very brave. He stressed what a fine soldier Sam had been, and how proud his family should be.

Clara tried to comfort Marian, Sam's mother, and Jill his widow, by now heavily pregnant, Both were deeply shocked by Sam's death. Jill turned on Patrick, 'You said you would bring my husband home! What went wrong?' She sank into a deep depression, and no matter what he told her, she remained hostile, which only added to his already enormous sense of guilt. Sam's mother was inconsolable and within six months, Marion followed her son to the grave following a heart attack.

Clara was upset by the appearance of her once handsome husband. He had lost an alarming amount of weight, so that his clothes hung off his skeletal frame; his thick curly hair was thinning; his once twinkling eyes were dark and haunted; his left arm, twisted and useless. His state of mind was of greater concern. He spent much of his time walking through the red countryside, or sitting on the veranda of the hotel. He drank, more or less constantly, as he withdrew from his loved ones and friends. He slept little and spent most nights pacing the floor or sitting outside, gazing up at the night sky. When he did sleep, he woke from terrifying nightmares, in a cold sweat, as he imagined that he heard Sam calling out to him, 'Please, don't let me die!' In his dreams, the faces of Sam and of his adversary in Dublin, often blurred. He blamed himself for both of them and was constantly haunted by them.

With her usual optimism, his devoted wife felt sure that love and time would restore him to his former self, but this was not to be. Neither the love of his family, nor his return home, could give back what war, and his sense of guilt about Sam Kingsley, had taken from him.

Danny, tried in vain to recreate the relationship he and his father had shared before the war, but Patrick wanted none of it. He began to curse at the boy, once resorting to beating him with a stick for some imaginary misdemeanour. Despite Clara's protests, he continued to berate them both, as he slipped farther into his own private hell. His moods and violent behaviour became worse as the memories, sounds and smells of war threatened to overpower him.

The dreadful finality of all this came one sunny spring morning. Clara had risen early to cook breakfast for her few guests. Danny was up too, collecting eggs from the chicken coop. Patrick was nowhere around – not unusual given his behaviour of late. Clara called to Danny to go find his father for breakfast. The boy went out, as ever accompanied by his dog, bouncing excitedly ahead of him, then the barking became more persistent as Daniel followed him into a storage building behind the hotel. As his eyes became accustomed to the darkness, he saw his father sitting slumped again a wooden post. His first thought was that he was asleep, but as he drew closer, he recoiled in horror. A bullet had taken off part of his father's head and face, and there was blood everywhere.

A pistol lay discarded on the floor. Paddy O'Hara had found his peace, in a violent act of self-destruction.

Clara changed almost overnight. Her laughter and sparkling eyes were replaced by tears and sadness. Her sorrow alternating with anger. *How could Patrick do this?!'* She was unable to comfort her son, nor he his mother. There seemed to be a curtain of grief between them as impenetrable as a solid door. She knew he often wept privately for Patrick, but he did not confide in her, nor indeed in anyone, except for Jack Kingsley, who had already experienced the grief of losing a beloved father and his grandmother.

She sat through quietly through the inquest and the funeral that followed. Those, who just a few months before had welcomed him as a hero, now followed his coffin in silence, to the tiny churchyard, not far from the 'Imperial' hotel. After the funeral, everyone expected Clara to take her son and return to her parents in Kalgoorlie, but she insisted that she wanted to stay near Patrick. With the help of the Gregsons, she was more than capable of running the pub. After all, she had done a fine job during the time her husband had been away. Of course she would stay.

The locals banded together to ensure that Clara had all the help they could offer. They admired the tenacious young woman and wanted to keep her at Walkabout Hill.

With his father's death, Danny had to grow up very quickly. Increasingly growing tall and strong, he took over more and more of the work around the hotel as he tried hard to care for his mother, as he knew his father would have wished. She in turn, watched him sadly. The joy which had always shone from him, was no more. He spent much of his time, when not with Jack Kingsley, alone in the bush. From which he returned with a modicum of peace.

Jack, with the support of his grandfather, slowly came to terms with his losses.

Perhaps, because he had not seen his father after death, or perhaps because he was a less emotional boy than Patrick, his life returned to relative normality far sooner than Patrick's ever would. Although Jack's mother seemed less concerned with him than she had been, and with the birth of her baby daughter, announced she was returning to her native New Zealand with her baby daughter. After long discussions with her in-laws, she finally agreed to leave Jack with them, at least temporarily. That was the last the family heard of her for many years.

About that time, a letter addressed to Patrick, in Coolgardie, arrived at the hotel. The envelope was dirty and crumpled, and had obviously been in transit for a long time. Two or three addresses had been crossed out, and someone had written in red, 'Try Walkabout Creek'.

Filled with curiosity, Clara tore open the envelope and began to read.

> *Dear Patrick,*
>
> *Having no address for you, I am taking a chance and sending this to the Mission for Seaman in Fremantle, hoping they may have some idea where you are. I can't remember where Captain Fitzharding said he thought you might go ,and I have lost touch with him in recent years.*
>
> *We have all missed you very much, especially Mam. For a long time she used to cry about you every night; more so when she received the money you sent from time to time. Thanks.*

I am writing to give you the best possible news! The boy that we beat up in the pub in Dublin, turned up out of the blue on Saturday night! A bit scarred and looking the worse for wear, but ALIVE! You didn't kill him Patrick. This explains why we have had no police around.

The main thing is, if you want to, you can now bring your new wife home to meet us all. She would be very welcome.

I pray that you will get this news.
Your Affectionate brother, Daniel

Clara started to cry. If only Patrick could have known this. He might still be alive! She looked at the date. It had been written before the War! It had obviously been around, and probably sat in many post boxes. She looked at the address on the back of the dirty envelope, almost illegible now. She would have to write and tell the family the sad news of his death.

One morning, a few months after Patrick's death, Sally came to tell Clara, that she had a visitor. Rob Kingsley had come in from *Brolga Hills*. Rob had tried to offer friendship and practical help to Patrick, despite the loss of his two sons and his wife, but Paddy's guilt would allow him to accept nothing, blaming himself for the loss of Sam. Sadly, nobody had been able to reach Patrick. They never knew of his personal torment about Sam.

Rob stood awkwardly as Clara entered the room, and embraced her warmly. 'Clara, my dear, looking beautiful as ever! How are you?'

She was sad to see how much Rob had aged since Marion's death, but she returned his hug. 'I'm well Rob. How are you?'

The formalities over, they both sat down. Rob cleared his throat. 'Clara, I want to talk to you about young Danny. We both know that Patrick wanted Danny to have a good education. Had it not been for the war, he would have been sent away to school', He put up his hand as Clara began to protest. 'No, please wait until I have finished. I cannot really be both parents to my grandson Jack, and so I have decided to send him to Perth early next year to school, as Sam intended48.

I would like to see Danny go with him. What do you say?'

'Oh Rob! I have no money for a fancy education. There is barely enough to keep body and soul together these days.'

'You misunderstand my dear, I would like to pay for him to go with Jack. Before you say no, I think it would be good for the lads to go together. I think they need each other and I am sure Patrick would have liked that too.'

Clara felt tears welling. 'I know Patrick wanted him to go away to school, but this would cost far too much!'

'Nonsense Clara! I've more money than we can use in a lifetime. I would like to do this for the boy. God knows they have both lost enough! This would give them a new start.' So it was decided, and the two boys left for Perth and boarding school at the beginning of the next scholastic year.

CHAPTER EIGHT

TWO YOUNG MEN

To begin with, Danny hated his new school. He hated the crowds, the noise, the loss of the bush, and of course, his mother. Without Jack he probably would not have survived, or at least been very unhappy for longer. Jack's positivity and exuberant good nature, finally convinced him that there was a good side to all this education. He discovered that he was very good at sport, cricket in particular, and as he settled down, his school work began to improve. He still lived for his holidays in Walkabout Creek, but his horizons broadened, and he looked forward to his future.

The next few years passed quickly for Jack and Danny, and their friendship grew stronger, more like that of brothers. They were both bright students, excelling in most subjects. Danny represented his school in cricket and football. As his school years ended, he surprised everyone by announcing that rather than going on to university, he was going back to Walkabout Creek to help his mother run the hotel.

Jack, of course, planned on going back to the station eventually, which he would one day inherit from his grandfather, but he chose to go onto higher education, studying accountancy and animal husbandry. He became involved in a research program into cattle breeding, which took him all over the world.

Life in Walkabout Hills flowed on as always. Any concerns Clara may have had about Danny's ability to settle in a small town, after the big city, were quickly dispelled, as he set about his work with a cheeriness and diligence that reminded her of his father, before the war.

Welcomed back by the towns folks, he quickly consolidated his place at the pub. Clara was happy to see that Danny had regained his former sparkle, and whilst she knew he would never forget the horror of his father's death, he had reached a stage of acceptance and the ability to move forward.

When Jack Kingsley finally returned to Walkabout Hills, on the death of his beloved grandfather a few years later, it was as the owner of *Brolga Hills*. He brought with him a charming wife, Diana, an air hostess, he had met on a flight from Rome to Sydney, and had married six weeks later. Diana fitted into life at the station as if she had been there for ever. Life at *Brolga Hills* was good again.

Back in town, it was not unusual for Clara to employ temporary staff at the hotel, usually young back packers, trying to earn a bit of money to continue their journey. One such young woman was Suzanne Tremaine, a pretty red headed nurse from Cornwall in England. She was intent on seeing the world before settling down to marriage and children.

Clara liked the young fresh faced girl, who worked diligently behind the bar, in the kitchen, or washing linen – whatever was required. She also noted that Danny liked her too, and was amused to see him at a loss for words whenever Suzanne spoke to him. She encouraged her son's interest and was happy to note that Suzanne seemed in no hurry to move on. Especially when Danny found the courage to tell her how he felt, which she reciprocated.

Twelve months after her arrival, Suzanne and Danny announced their engagement, planning to marry in the spring, when her parents could make the trip to Australia from their home in England. The two young people drove down to Perth airport to pick up the Tremaines, and they quickly became part of the extended family in Walkabout Hills, staying for six weeks after the couple were married in the small Catholic church.

Clara loved her new daughter-in-law and was as delighted, as her parents were disappointed, when they decided to stay on and work with her at the hotel.

Their marriage was a happy one, enhanced, over the next three years, by the birth of their two children. Sam, the image of his father, and Marigold, a replica of her mother. Jack and Diana had also started a family and the young couples looked forward to an interesting future. Suzanne loved her life in the bush, and would have been content to stay forever, however, when the children still pre-schoolers, Suzanne's father died suddenly in England. Heartbroken, and under constant pressure from her mother, she begged Danny to take her back to England. Reluctantly, after consultation with his mother, Danny agreed, so they packed up their two children and left for a new life on the other side of the world.

With Danny's savings and some of Suzanne's inheritance, they bought the little pub, *The Pirates' Retreat,* in the Cornish village near her home. They both worked hard in their new venture, to make it one of the most popular watering holes for miles around. The villagers immediately accepted her husband, with his easy, relaxed open manner, and business boomed. Life was good for the young family.

Although there were times when Danny felt homesick for Australia, the parting from Walkabout Creek seemed a small price to pay for what he had now. Suzanne was not only his wife, his lover, but his best friend too. Together they often walked on the cliffs, as they talked, he began to see, through her eyes, the wild beauty of the Cornish coast. They shared everything, including a wonderful sense of humour. Danny often wondered how he ever existed before he met her. She in turn, adored him. He was the husband of whom she had always dreamed. She admired his qualities of fairness, justice, loyalty, his sense of humour, his common sense. He treated her with love and respect, and as such, was such a great role model for their children.

Once they were well established, Suzanne went back to nursing, just two nights a week in the nearby cottage Hospital, because she had wanted to, not because they needed the money. She knew that Danny's heart lay in the red outback of Australia, and she believed that one day they would return to Walkabout Creek. Perhaps when the children finished school. Her little nest egg would help, when that day came.

It was a morning like so many before it. Grey clouds, pregnant with rain, scurried across the winter sky, just as they had for a thousand winter days; but today was different; so different. Today, life would change forever for the O'Hara family. Suzanne was driving home after her night shift at the local hospital, looking forward to breakfast with Danny. Funny how breakfast with a loved one could be so intimate, so special. Even after sixteen years of marriage, Danny still had the power to excite her. His warmth, his sensual lean body, his slow drawl, only slightly modified by his years in England. She loved his contagious laugh, and his playing of practical jokes on her and the children.

The threatened rain began to fall. She smiled, almost home, and then as she rounded the bend between the high hedges, there in front of her, was a tractor, stalled across the lane. Everything happened so quickly. She jammed her foot hard on the brake - too late. A squeal and the car began to slide; a crash; a ripping of metal, then, nothing.

As she regained consciousness, her shoulder, was somehow pinned to the seat. Her head hurt, when she touched her face, her hand came away covered in blood. She tried to move her legs, but they were strangely disconnected . Suzanne knew instinctively that she was dying. There was no pain, no fear, just an eerie feeling of weightlessness, a sense of calm. Was this all there was to death? This clarity of thought, the clear pictures in her mind of her handsome husband Danny,with his soft gentle smile. Her sweet daughter Marigold, named after the russet marigolds she had planted the year of the child's birth and which matched exactly, the colour of her curls. Her son Sam, a replica of his dad with his long lanky limbs and engaging smile. 'God, I love you all so much' she said in a whisper. 'I don't want to leave you . I'm so sorry. Oh Danny. If only I could hold you all just one more time,'

Thoughts of her mother crossed her mind. Anne Tremaine, the kind soft Cornishwoman, 'Mum, please look after my darlings. I will be fine with Dad. He will take care of me.' Suzanne began to feel cold. It was becoming difficult to organise her thoughts. She thought she heard, Danny's voice, calling her name, but she couldn't be sure. Around her, everything began to fade. In the distance, a bright distant light beckoned. Her life was ebbing with every beat of her heart. Her last thought was of Danny, then oblivion. Suzanne O'Hara was dead.

oooOooo

Danny O'Hara was setting out the glasses behind the bar for the day's trading at *The Pirates' Retreat* as he waited for his wife. Always so punctual, it was unusual for her to be late. He glanced at his watch.'Where are_you, my darling?' He muttered, looking through the window. As he did so, he felt a cold shiver pass across his shoulders.

'Someone just walked across your grave', his mother used to say.

Half an hour later, Suzanne had still not arrived. He felt uneasy, as he walked down to the corner of the car park, from where he could see down down the lane.Perhaps the little mini had let her down again. *'Time we thought about a new car,'* he said to himself, as he turned back up the drive.

Danny was just about to go back inside, when a police car pulled up in the car park and the local sergeant and a young constable slowly climbed out. He looked at their grim faces and a cold dread passed over him. *Please God, No!*

Their words cut through to his soul and he heard a distant voice crying in anguish, 'No! No! No! Not my Suzanne! Please God, no!'

The men led him inside and sat with him, as they told the sad story. They said Suzanne appeared to have died almost instantly, with no time to reflect on the meeting with her maker, or the parting from her loved ones.

He went to the morgue, where, with a sense of unreality, he went through the motions of identifying the body of his wife. Despite her terrible injuries, her face was untouched, and he wept as he kissed her goodbye, and gently pushed her russet curls back from her empty green eyes.

On the way home Danny parked on the cliffs where he and Suzanne loved to walk. He sat on a small grassy knoll, staring down into the black Atlantic Ocean, and at the white spray as it threw itself at the rocks far below.

Life without his Suzanne was unimaginable. He thought for a moment that all that stood between them and an eternity together, was a short plunge from the cliff top. Then he remembered his children. They did yet know that their mother was gone. There was Suzanne's mother too. How great would be their grief. A few salty tears mingled with the spray and the wind. His curses joined the cries of the Atlantic Gulls wheeling overhead. As he continued to sit, he wondered how everything could look so much the same; while his life had changed forever. Slowly he pulled himself together, and went to collect his daughter, thirteen-year-old Goldy, from the village school, and finally around to see Suzanne's mother, and to contact his son, fifteen year old Sam, at his boarding school. One of the masters kindly offered to drive the shocked boy home.

The grandfather clock on the landing ticked away the hours relentlessly. In her bedroom, the young girl lay on her bed in the lengthening afternoon shadows. Hot tears staining her cheeks, sobs shaking her thin shoulders Downstairs, her father sat motionless. He had no tears, nor did he give any thought to comforting the child upstairs.

When the family finally came together, the shock was painfully evident. White faced and red eyed, Suzanne's sorrowing mother, Anne Tremaine, tried to comfort the youngsters, whilst her son-in-law sat staring unseeing into the fireplace, where a small coal fire spluttered half- heartedly.

'I'll take the children home with me for tonight, Danny,' she said quietly. 'Do you want to come?'

He did not answer, but gently shook his head. With a sigh, she gathered up her charges and mutely they climbed into the car and disappeared into the night.

The afternoon sun dipped into an inky ocean and as darkness fell, a pale moon shone weakly through the window. He continued to sit motionless in the gloom of the room, unaware of the now cold fireplace. He felt almost dead himself. Suzanne had been his world for so long; her loss was a huge cold lump in his chest, where once there was warmth. Finally, he wept as he had not done since his father's death and the tears felt as if they would never stop.

Following the coronial inquiry, Suzanne O'Hara was buried in the tiny churchyard, not half a mile from where she was born, just short of forty years before, and where her parents had been married. She was laid to rest, peacefully, enveloped by flowers, in a family plot with her father, grandparents and great grandparents, under a spreading oak tree, overlooking the sea. Rain threatened in an overcast sky, as Danny, with his children and their grandmother, stood shrouded in misery and disbelief.

The following days were grim. Whilst the young people and their grandmother clung together, their father removed himself still farther from them all. The locals closed ranks around the family attempting to support and comfort them, but as Danny continued to withdraw into himself, many felt concern for his safety and his sanity.

In the care of their loving grandmother, the two children slowly began to come to terms with the loss of their mother, and to a lesser degree, the distancing of their father. Eventually they returned to their studies. Sam to his boarding school in Sussex, and Marigold to the local school.

Goldy often walked along the cliff top. She felt very close to her mother in the place she had loved so much. Sometimes she scrambled down the steep rocky cliff, to the sandy cove below. Here she could relive the happy times they had played together on the sand. If she closed her eyes, she could see her mother's pretty face and hear her lilting laugh, as they ran, hand in hand up the beach, away from the chasing waves. Her loss was a physical pain.

Danny never mentioned Suzanne's name after her death and he quickly shut down any attempt on Goldy's part to discuss her. Her grandmother was her only source of comfort, once Sam had gone back to school.

Anne Tremaine was happy to talk about the lovely Suzanne and together they poured over photographs of her as a laughing child, the pretty debutante, the glowing bride and the proud mother.

Danny's devastation at his wife's loss was frightening to see. He seemed unable to relate to his children, or to Suzanne's sorrowing mother. He neither ate nor slept, spending much of his day in the tiny cemetery. He refused the comfort of the parish priest; his faith deserted him. He wished only to die, to be with his beloved wife.

Anne Tremaine viewed her son-in-law with concern. Several times he had mentioned suicide, and recalling what he had told her about his father's death, she felt that his only salvation might be to go back home. She encouraged him to talk about some of the happy times he and Suzanne had enjoyed together, especially in Australia, and she began to push the idea that perhaps he would be happier in his own country.

CHAPTER NINE

BACK TO OZ

The decision was made for him when he received a letter from Jack Kingsley, telling him of his mother's recent illness and of her difficulty running the *Imperial Arms* hotel. It was time to go home. He would put *The Pirates' Retreat* up for sale and to back to Australia, back to Walkabout Creek, where he had first met his lovely wife. Yes, he would go. Anne Tremaine hugged him tightly.

'My darling, you must do what is right for you. Leave the children here with me for the moment. Go find yourself again.'

When next Sam came home for a long weekend, Danny sat with his young family and tried to explain it all to them.

'I'm sorry kids, I just have to get away. I can't stand it here another day without your mum. I am no good to myself or to you until I can come to terms with all that has happened. I have already spoken to your grandmother and we've decided that you two should stay here for the present with her and continue your education. Once I have sorted myself out, I'll send for you.'

The children were devastated and begged him not to go. Goldy cried but Sam, trying to be grown up, put an arm around her shoulders.

'We'll be okay, Sis, I'll be here for you and it won't be for ever. We'll be fine Dad'!

Danny hugged them both and promised that there would be better days ahead for them all, but he felt that this would be best for them, and for him. The question was 'when?'

The time was decided for him, he received a cable from Jack Kingsley. His mother's health had deteriorated suddenly. She had now suffered a stroke and was seriously ill in hospital in Perth. He rushed up to London to get the first flight to Australia. Two days later, he arrived back in Perth and went straight to the Royal Perth Hospital to see his mother. Clara was weak, but recognised him straight away and smiled as she clasped his hand. 'Thank God, my prayers have been answered. My boy, I knew you would come.'

From the time of his arrival, Clara improved in leaps and bounds. Soon she was well enough to go home and the Flying Doctor was called on to fly her back to Walkabout Creek. Danny was glad to be back in the bush. There were so many happy memories there of his Suzanne, and of his dad. The locals were pleased to see him, and he quickly fell back into the routines of bush life. He went out to *Brolga Hills* to see his old friend Jack. He began to find some remnant of peace and happiness in his life, to talk again of his beloved. He took over the running of the pub and was happy to see his mother in her lounge chair on the veranda, gaily chatting with her many friends.

For the first few weeks, apart from a few hastily scrawled post cards, the family in England heard nothing, from him. Then the letters began to trickle in. Apparently, Danny had settled back in, and was now happy at the old pub.

'*My mother worked very hard whilst I was in England*' he wrote, '*but the pub still needs a bit of work, but it's a really nice to be home.*

He told them about the countryside, the people, his daily activites. He missed them, he said, but did not mention when they might be able to join him. A year later, he wrote:

'There is only one very small primary school here, and as that means you would both have to go to boarding schools over 1,000 miles from here, I think it best that you finish your education in England. You will need to have every opportunity in life, and I think your mum would have wanted you to stay with your grandmother for the time being'.

They were disappointed, but Dad usually knew what was best, so they settled down to their studies. In England the seasons came and went. The soft warm summer, the orange autumn, the cold dreary winter and the promise of Spring, but still Danny did not send for Sam and Marigold.

Whenever his mother raised the subject of his children, he quickly shut down the conversation. It was not until Jack Kingsley said casually one evening, over a beer, 'Danny, why don't you want to bring your children here?' that he finally was forced to verbalise his fears.

'I guess I'm just afraid Jack, afraid that something will happen to them here. Sometimes I think Walkabout Creek is cursed for the O'Hara family. First my Dad, then Suzanne. I would die if anything happened to the kids!'

Jack leaned across and put his hand on his friend's shoulder. 'That's nonsense,' he said gently. 'It's just life Danny. It doesn't matter where you are, mate. If it's going to happen, nothing can stop it. Look at my mum and dad! Go on, you need your kids and they need you. It would be great if our children could get to know each other properly.'

It had been two long years when finally, Danny flew back to England. He found his children much grown and very much more mature than he had expected. He and Sam found they had a great deal still in common, and he was impressed by his son's excellent academic achievements. Goldy was a replica of his Suzanne, and he laughed at her quirky sense of humour and her common sense attitude to life.

When it came time for Danny to return to Australia, Sam begged to be allowed to go back with him, and continue his education there. He had decided he wanted to do medicine at university, now that he had finished school. Danny was thrilled and he and Sam made enquiries about the likelihood of enrolling at the University of Western Australia. Goldy, still at school was very torn between going with her father, or staying on at school in England, and then going to Guy's Hospital to train as a nurse, as her mother had done. Family conferencing decided the issue, and she decided she would not go to Australia until her nursing training was completed.

With the future decided, Sam and Danny flew back to Western Australia, and Goldy and her grandmother continued their idyllic life in Cornwall.

The next three or four years sped by. Goldy completed her schooling and gained her entrance to Guy's Hospital. In London. She loved her nursing training, hard and arduous as it was at times. The work was interesting and varied. She studied hard and excelled in all areas, as had her mother. She learned a great deal during her time at the hospital – not just about anatomy, physiology, illness and healing, but also about birth, death, and more than anything, she learned about herself and life. By the time she finally graduated, Goldy O'Hara had grown up into a beautiful, confident, clear thinking young woman.

Sad to be leaving her beloved grandmother, but excited to start her new life in Australia. Goldy was encouraged by Anne Tremaine to follow her dreams of adventure, to embrace life, and to reconnect with her father. She sought registration to practice nursing in Western Australia, renewed her Australian passport, and booked her flight to Perth.

CHAPTER TEN

GOLDY O'HARA

Goldy strained to see out of the aircraft window, as the Boeing dipped and turned over the city of Perth, in Western Australia. The beautiful Swan river snaked gold in the early morning light, and the hills, to the east of the city, were dark ahead of the rising sun. It had been a long journey from London's Heathrow airport and there were still a few hours to go before she reached Walkabout Creek.The plane bumped onto the runway and taxied to a stop in front of the International terminal. She reached up to the overhead locker for her hand luggage, and slowly moved toward the exit.

It was already warm as she strolled through to immigration, collected her case, walked on to the customs' hall. She glanced around anxiously for her father. He had promised that either he, or a friend would be there to meet her, prior to the last step of her journey. She hoped, if not her father, maybe her brother Sam, but there was no sign of him. Finally she saw a young woman holding up a white card saying 'GOLDY O'HARA', and the attractive blonde stepped forward with a smile, as Goldy acknowledged her.

'Hi Goldy? I'm Caroline Brearley, a nurse from the Royal Flying Doctor Service. Your Dad asked if we could drop you off in Walkabout Creek on our way up North this morning. I'm here to drive you to the base at Jandakot, our small airport. We'll just chuck your luggage in the boot and we'll be off.'

Goldy liked Caroline straightaway. She was open and friendly. She looked capable and decisive and would inspire confidence in any patient.

'Your Dad says you have just finished your nursing training in London,' said Caroline, as they made their way across the crowded car park.

'Yes, at Guy's Hospital, actually.'

'Really?' Caroline looked impressed. 'If your Australian registration is in order, you should contact Community Health. They've been looking for a nurse for the Walkabout Creek clinic for over two years now. It can be hard to get good nurses to go to the more remote areas; I guess there are so many options for them nowadays, and Walkabout Creek is a bit off the beaten track.'

'But I don't know anything about the Australian outback, or the people!' Goldy protested.

Caroline laughed. 'You'll soon learn, believe you me. Nothing like learning on the job! At the end of the day we are all people, and we all have hopes and fears, and we all bleed the same colour blood! Hop in, I'll drive you the long way round, show you some of the sights on the way.'

Goldy remembered little, if anything of Perth. She was only three years old when she had left, but looking at it now, she was impressed with the lovely city, as it sat basking in the sun on the banks of the Swan River. There were long stretches of green reserves on either side of the wide water and there were already small boats and water skiers out and about. A busy little ferry was criss -crossing the river with early morning comuters. They drove away from the city and on to the Stirling Highway, down the coast to Fremantle, the port city. Fremantle had changed little from its early days as the main port. The Swan river was not deep enough to accomodate large ships, and Perth lay some miles upsteam.

There were no high rise buildings in Fremantle, but many imposing historical sites, dominated by the large prison, surrounded by a high stone wall.

'It was built by convicts when there was a penal colony here, and it is still in use today,' Caroline said. 'Pretty grim place isn't it? Mainly used for high security prisoners. Pretty rough, I should think.'

Goldy gave a shiver. 'I remember reading something about its early days. Apparently, people were transported out here for small misdemeanours, like stealing a loaf of bread! It seems pretty crazy to us today!'

They left the beautiful golden beaches to head inland, driving through sprawling suburbs and pretty gardens. Goldy noticed that most of the houses were single storey bungalows, so different from England. When they arrived at the airstrip at Jandakot, Caroline parked the car and the two young women strolled across to a large hangar. Goldy saw a pleasant looking young man in a khaki uniform, drinking coffee and chatting to an older man in shorts and a white shirt. Caroline gave them a quick wave. 'Hi guys. Come and meet Goldy O'Hara. Danny's daughter from England.'

The younger of the two men smiled as he shook her hand.

'G'day Goldy. I'm Caroline's husband, Matt. I'm your pilot for today, and this is our doctor, Ben Morris.'

The doctor stepped forward. His accent giving away his Canadian nationality, as he greeted her warmly. 'Welcome to the West, Miss O'Hara, a real pleasure. I know your Dad well. He's a real nice guy.'

'Grab a coffee if you like,' said Matt. 'Take off is in about thirty minutes. We are just waiting for an ambulance from the Children's hospital We are taking a little girl home after her surgery.'

With apprehension, Goldy eyed, the small Beechcraft Baron arcraft standing on the runway.

'It looks very small,' she said shyly to Caroline, who laughed heartily.

'You should have seen the ones we flew before this! She's a beaut little bird this one, and Matt here, can fly her in and out of anywhere. You'll be right!'

Half an hour later they were all onboard and very soon airborne. Caroline pointed out points of interest as they flew up the coast, over endless white beaches and a turquoise sea, before turning inland. The pattern of scrubby patches of bush amid the tangled web of mainly dry creek beds, was fascinating, and Goldy really began to enjoy her new adventure. 'Not too many landmarks,' she remarked to Matt. 'Do you ever have difficulty finding the landing strips?'

He laughed, 'You get used to it Goldy. My predecessor reckoned he would just look out for some vehicles waiting for him, and land there! Actually it's a bit more technical than that! The only real problem we have is when the airstrips get washed out in the wet. Can't land a dicky bird then.'

'The 'wet'?' queried Goldy.

Matt laughed. 'Sorry. The 'wet' is the season here when the monsoon type rains come in, between November and April.

The huge amounts of rain in a very short time, causes massive flooding.; everything floods. All that red dust down there becomes red mud, under meters of water. It happens so quickly you can hardly believe it'

As they flew on, Caroline gave Goldy a quick rundown on the Royal Flying Doctor Service, the 'RFDS'. She explained how it was established by the famous 'Flynn of the Outback', Pastor John Flynn, to provide medical assistance to those in the bush, isolated by time and distance. . She told her of the enormous benefits and comfort the RFDS brought to those outback people and how heavily they relied on the service. 'It makes me so mad that we still have to rely quite heavily on donations and fund raising' she said. 'We do get some government funding, but it is an expensive service to run, as you can imagine. Just keeping up with the supplies of Avgas needed to fly our planes can be difficult at times.'

Goldy found the distances between settlements astounding. They seemed to fly for ages with no sign of human habitation. They made a couple of scheduled stops on lonely properties At the first, they were cordially welcomed, as they delivered their small patient to her grateful parents. On another, where they provided some urgent medical supplies, they were given a very nice lunch, before continuing their journey.

'How do people contact you, when they need help?' asked Goldy.

'On the radio,' Matt told her. 'They call into their nearest base and we either give them advice over the air, or arrange to go out in an emergency and fly them back to hospital.'

'Radio advice must be difficult.' she said, thinking of her recent nursing experience.

Ben Morris joined the conversation. 'Can be challenging at times, Goldy, but all the doctors involved are very experienced, and we ask the right questions. It's usually pretty straightforward.

Every property has an RFDS Medical kit. All the medications are numbered in separate compartments, so it's often a case of "take two of number whatever." The real challenges are the emergencies, car accidents, machinery mishaps, pregnant mothers, snake bites, riding accidents and severe illnesses. A delay in getting help can be fatal!'

Goldy thought back to her training hospital, where they had complained if a doctor took more than five minutes to answer a call about a patient! 'What an amazing service you provide.' she said in admiration.

'We do our best.' said the doctor modestly.

By the time they approached Walkabout Creek, the sky was turning crimson as the sun started to drop in the west.

'There she is!' said Matt, indicating below, as they circled the town to announce their arrival.

Looking down, Goldy saw a small settlement of mostly wood and tin buildings. She noticed a fading sign on a large flat roof, '*The Emporium*'. 'What's the *Emporium*?' she asked, puzzled.In answer to her question, Matt laughed, 'That's the General Store, the only shop in town! It's the most amazing place! You can buy anything there from a bike tyre to a meat pie, or a pair of jeans, a pork chop or a transistor radio! Worth a look. You must check it out!'

The little plane touched down gently and taxied to a stop in front of a small rusty tin shed, A group of locals waited to greet them, and a tired sign, hanging by one nail, announced '*Welcome to Walkabout Creek Airport*'.

A solid wall of heat hit Goldy as she scrambled down from the plane.

She caught her breath and screwed up her eyes against the fierce glare of the late afternoon sun.

For a moment or two she saw nothing, and then out of the swirling dust, she saw a lanky figure, and heard the voice, she loved so well.

'Goldy!'

'Dad!'

The two ran across the dirt strip and met in a bear hug. Danny looked well. He was burned bronze by the sun, and his light brown hair bleached almost blonde. He looked taller than she remembered. He was still a very handsome man.

'Let's get you out of this heat sweetheart,' he said, putting his arm around her shoulders as he picked up her suitcase from the ground. He shook hands with each of the RFDS crew. 'Many thanks for flying this young lady up from the city,' he said. 'With no commercial flights, it means one hell of a drive up here from Perth, and it's all a bit much on top of that long trip from London. Thanks again.' He paused, 'If you guys can get back here on your way home, there's a bit of a shindig on tomorrow night to welcome young Goldy,'

Ben Morris gave a laugh, 'Well perhaps if we can remember something you forgot to order for your medical kit, we might just make it back. Poor old Matt won't be able to drink, as he's flying but he'll have to live with that!'

'Thanks so much for the ride.' said Goldy, as they walked away. 'It was really appreciated. Do try to get back tomorrow!'

'Sure thing,' called back Caroline as she climbed back onto the aircraft. They were anxious to be gone before nightfall, as there was no electric lighting on the airstrip.

Dan and Goldy watched the plane taxi down the runway, take off, and very soon it was just a speck in the crimson sky.

As they climbed into his dusty utility, Danny gave his daughter a long appraising look, and another hug. 'It's so good to see you my beautiful girl! You looked so like your mum, when you got out of that plane, it made my heart turn over. I can't believe how much you have grown up, but I guess it's been a while.'

'Well, five years, to be exact.' Goldy reminded him.

'God is it that long? I guess it must be, but at least you're here now!'

On the drive into town, Goldy had a chance to look around. There was low dense grey/green scrub, stretching to the far horizon, interspersed with deep red rocky outcrops. A few white trunked eucalypt trees were scattered through the low vegetation. In the distance, was a smudge of purple hills, and closer to town, a patch of shining silver water, shimmering in the late afternoon sun. 'That's the nearest thing we have to a swimming pool I'm afraid,' laughed her father, 'rather optimistically called *Lake Walkabout'*

They drove on past a collection of run down looking buildings from another era. Danny pointed out the police station, the little school, the 'Emporium', a garage, and tiny post office. A couple of places were boarded up, including the old nursing post. The old town hall leaned tentatively on a corner. Nearby, a church, a large white weatherboard structure, with a cemetery attached, stood imposingly on a slight rise.

'That's the local Catholic Church, St Augustine's. Interesting cemetery, mostly old miners and their families buried there. Lots of kids too; they died like flies out here in the early days from Typhoid and other diseases and dehydration.

Well worth a visit. It's the domain of old Father John. Now there's a character for you!' he laughed. 'Father John and the local Anglican minister, Reverend Franklin, have had a feud running for years. I guess they think they are competing for souls! There's the Reverend's church just up the road on the left.'

Goldy saw a modern, if more modest church, built from stone, with a neat wall around its smaller cemetery.

'I read that the local aborigines here are very traditional. How do they cope with mainstream religion?'

Danny looked thoughtful. 'With difficulty sometimes, I suspect. I think they take the bits that suit them and reject the rest! You must to talk to Father John. He's a really interesting old man; been here for forty years, they tell me. He loves to have someone new to tell his stories to.'

In a cloud of dust, they pulled up outside the hotel. At nearly a hundred years old, its soft white stone had long since been rendered pink by the swirling red dust. Her days of grandeur were well and truly over, but the old lady sat comfortably on the edge of town, amongst the peppercorn trees, red dust, and a small square of struggling lawn. Surrounded on three sides by wooden verandas, the upper floor had a wide balcony overlooking the street. Two broad stone steps led up to the front door. A rusty iron sign, almost illegible, announced, *'The Grand Imperial Hotel'*.

As Goldy contemplated her new home, a younger version of her father bounded down the steps, two at a time, to greet her warmly. 'Hi Sis. Long time no see!' Goldy hugged her brother enthusiastically.

'Sam! I was disappointed not to see you at Perth airport. I had no idea you would be here. What a lovely surprise!'

'Even university students get holidays sometimes,' he said. 'I thought I could help dad out for the summer, suprise you, and maybe make some pocket money at the same time!'

'How *are* your medical studies going?'

'Only two years left to go, thank god. Then I can be turned loose on an unsuspecting public! Scary thought, don't you think? Look at you, a beautiful young lady, and a fully qualified nurse to boot! Clever girl! Grandma O'Hara is so excited about your coming! Let's go and see her first!'

Arm in arm, the three of them went up the steps and into the hotel. The cool interior of the building was a welcome relief from the scorching heat. Clara O'Hara was waiting in the hall.

With her now silver hair piled on her head, she was the picture of a Victorian lady. Her warmth and dignity enveloped Goldy in an enthusiastic hug. 'My darling girl. You finally made it back to Walkabout Creek. Welcome home!'

To the right of the front entrance, there were two wooden doors marked *'Public Bar'*. This covered almost half of the ground floor across the front of the building. It was a large area with a concrete floor, fairly bare, with a few wooden stools and a long bar across one end. In the bar there were shelves sporting memorabilia, old photographs, and a stuffed python, all jostling for space with a myriad of coloured bottles and glasses. Danny called out as they passed the door.

'Hey Jim! Come and meet my daughter.'

A small wiry man emerged from the bar. His smiled broadly, revealing gaps, where once there were teeth.

'Goldy, you won't remember him, but this is Jim O'Malley, he runs the bar.'

He greeted her warmly with an Irish brogue straight from Dublin, 'It's very glad I am to see you again, Miss Goldy, indeed I am.' He shook her hand energetically.

'She smiled happily, 'I am very pleased to meet you, Mr O'Malley.

Her father laughed, 'Oh just call him Jim. Everyone else does! Too much of the 'Mr' and he'll be getting airs and graces and asking for a raise next! Anyway Jim, do you know where Kevin and Sally might be?'

'Fer sure boss. Sally be in the office and Kev's in the kitchen. Be seein' you later Miss Goldy.'

Behind the main bar, separated by a wide thin hatchway, was a smaller bar with 'Lounge' etched into the glass over the door. There were some old comfortable chairs around heavy wooden tables with thick glass tops. A large leather sofa sat in one corner, next to a tired looking artificial palm tree, On the floor was a red faded carpet, with a nondescript floral pattern, which might once have been roses. On the other side of the hall was a large dining room. There were about twenty tables, with the obligatory chairs. On the tables, were white cloths, each adorned with a small vase containing a plastic rosebud and some local greenery. There was the same faded red capet as in the lounge. Fringed light shades hung from the ceiling. At the windows there were dusty, once red, velvet curtains, which might well have been there when the pub first opened! An old upright piano stood in the corner and a musky smell of beer and cigarettes permeated the air. Danny was apologetic. 'Keep meaning to update but what with bills and Sam's uni fees, there hasn't been much spare cash.' he said ruefully.

'Well I think it's charming, Dad.' said Goldy, and meant it.

'Where do those doors go to?' she said, indicating two padlocked doors off the dining room.

'That's the old ballroom, complete with chandeliers and a stage. You'll have to ask Sally, if you want to see inside. She has the keys. In the early days, when the town was bigger and more prosperous, they used to hold fancy balls here, with a proper orchestra. Folk used to get all dressed up too. I believe the Governor and his wife actually came up on the train once!'

'I didn't know there was a train.'

'Well there isn't any more. When the gold rush was on, this old town fairly rocked, but then the miners moved on to richer pickings. There used to be ten pubs here once. Now my old *Imperial Arms* stands alone'.

Along the passage, in front of a small office, there was a dark wooden reception desk. A tired dried flower arrangement graced the counter.

'Sally! Are you in there?'

A short, plump, tired looking woman came out to greet them. When she smiled, her whole face was transformed and she was almost pretty. 'Well hullo love,' she said, extending her hand, 'You must be Goldy. Your dad's talked of nothin' else for weeks. Welcome home to Walkabout Creek! You probably don't remember me, but call me Sally. Me and my hubby have been workin' for your family for years. Kev does the cookin', and I do the housekeepin.'

'And the bookkeeping, *and* the ordering, *and* she pays the wages.' said Danny. 'I'd be absolutely lost without these two! Is Kevin in the kitchen Sally?'

'Yes he is. Cookin' up somethin' special, no doubt.' She turned back to Goldy. 'When yer ready love, I'll take you up and show you yer room. you'll probably more than ready for a wash. Men never think of these things!'

Kevin Simpson was a plump man, with a round jolly face. 'G'day love!' he beamed, wiping his hands on his apron before shaking hers. 'Nice to meet ya. Sal and me feel as if we know ya already, as we did when you was just a little nipper, but it's good to see ya home at last!'

The big kitchen was spotlessly clean, with a large scrubbed wooden table in the middle of the room, and a stove and range along one wall. 'Your Dad has made a big difference to this place since he came back,' he said proudly. 'Recently had this lot converted to gas.' he indicated to the huge ovens. 'What a difference that makes, I can tell you! It used to be so hot in here with the wood stove burnin', you'd think a fellar could melt!

There was a deep porcelain sink, and above it a wooden slatted plate drainer. Dozens of cups swung from hooks under the top cupboards and gleaming saucepans and cooking utensils, hung from an iron frame suspended over the table. A pantry with marble shelves ran off to one side.

'That's me cool room,' he told her proudly. 'Gets so cold it'd freeze the bum off an eskimo! Now of course, I've got these beaut fridges as well!'

Goldy smiled. There was something very lovable about the rugged Aussie, and she warmed to him immediately. She finally got back to Sally, who led her up a narrow staircase to a landing, from which three corridors ran in different directions.'We've twenty rooms and I've put you in the one at the far end, away from the bar,' she said kindly, 'Gits a bit rowdy down there on a weekend when the young fellars come in from the stations.'

'Stations?' queried Goldy.

'Cattle stations, love. The young guys are cowboys, we call 'em stockmen, station hands, or jackeroos!

They're mostly nice lads and they work bloody hard through the week, in all weathers, so they like to have a few beers and let their hair down when they get paid, and hit town.' She paused, and jangling a bunch of keys, pushed open a door, 'Here you are, love. Bathroom and loo straight across the passage. Just a tip,' she said, lowering her voice, 'Let the shower run for a couple of minutes before yer hop in. In the summer the water is boilin', and it's freezin' in the winter. Also gets rid of the rust in the pipes, so yer don't come out dirtier than when yer got in!

The loo chain needs one quick pull and one slow. Yer just hang on 'til the water starts to run. I'll leave yer now, love. Just come down when you're ready. Tea's at 6.30.' She handed her the room key on a worn brass tag, and left. Her rubber thongs flip- flopped down the passage, and then all was quiet.

CHAPTER ELEVEN

A MEETING IN TOWN

Goldy sat down on the bed and gazed around the room. It was sparsely furnished but clean and the bed, soft and comfortable. The furniture was all in the heavy dark wood she had seen downstairs. There was lino of an indeterminate colour, possibly blue, on the floor, and a brightly striped mat near the bed. The dressing table had an old tarnished mirror. The wardrobe so small that Goldy fleetingly wondered if it had come out of an old hospital, it was so like the ones she had struggled with during her training days! On one wall was a print of a drover with cattle and a red coloured dog. On another, a fly spotted calendar, two years out of date. There was an air of agelessness about it all. Rather like an elderly lady, left behind by the years. She threw open the glass doors and walked out onto the balcony, overlooking the street. She watched as the last rays of the sun finally dipped below the horizon. A mangy dog dozed on the warm concrete of the pub steps, and a group of small dusky boys played football in the middle of the red dusty road.

Goldy felt at peace and appreciated the tranquility. After she unpacked some of her things, she washed, changed, and went downstairs in search of her father and brother. She pushed open a glass door in the hall marked 'Bar'. A dozen pairs of startled eyes swivelled in her direction, as Jim rushed from behind the the bar, grabbing her by the arm, as he propelled her out of the room. 'You can't be going in dere, Miss Goldy,' he admonished her. 'No ladies allowed in the front bar. If you be wantin' a drink, you'll be needin' to go into the lounge, or onto the veranda. Niver, niver in the front bar, Miss. Niver!'

'What's all the fuss about?' asked Danny, emerging from the nearby office.

'I think I just had my first lesson in Australian bar etiquette.' she said laughing. 'Honestly Dad, you'd have thought I was stark naked, the look of horror when I walked into the front bar!'

He chuckled, 'A bit different from an English pub, I'm afraid! If you feel like a drink, Sam and I are going to have a beer on the front veranda with Grandma. What's yours?'

'A brandy and dry, thanks Dad,' she said, stepping out into the cool evening.

As the four of them sat in the fading light, Danny smiled broadly. 'How wonderful to have you both here at last. It's been far too long. I'm afraid I haven't been much of a father to either of you over the past few years' He lapsed into silence for a minute or so. 'Hope I can make it up to you now. Your mum was my world, you know, and I still miss her every day, even after all this time. I just had to get away and I knew you were safe with your Grandma Tremaine. She wrote regularly and kept me up to date. I'm not much of a correspondent, as you both know only too well. You're pretty good Goldy but I don't think your brother ever learned how to write!'

'Not fair!' protested Sam. 'I never forget birthday's or Christmas!'

His father gave a laugh and punched him playfully on the shoulder. 'That's true, son, very true! By the way,' he continued, 'how is your Grandma Tremaine? I guess she will really miss you Goldy.'

'Yes Dad, she will, but she says it is high time we were a family again. She's getting older, of course, but she's pretty spritely for her age. That reminds me, she sent out some gifts for you. I'll go up and get them.' She ran upstairs returning quickly with three parcels. A book of photographs of English rural scenes and a box of Cuban Cigars for Danny and a hand knitted scarf and glove set for Sam. For her Grandmother, a pretty boxed set of lavender soap and powder.

'Not much good to you up here, I'm afraid,' she said ruefully to her brother, as he unpacked his woollen gloves.

'No, Sis, but great for Perth winters! It can get pretty wet and cold down south. Good old Gran!'

Their grandma Clara was delighted. 'Trust Annie to remember how I love this soap and I just can never get it up here!'

Dan looked thoughtfully at his gifts. 'Dear Anne, she never forgets me, or my favourite brand of cigars. Haven't been able to get them out here for love nor money. I really must make an effort to go back to see her in the next year or so.'

As they chatted, an expensive sports car came to a halt in front of the pub. A pretty, slim girl well dressed in fashionable cream trousers, a blue silk shirt, high heeled boots and a wide brimmed Akubra hat, stepped out. She jumped up the front steps with a broad smile, as Sam stood up quickly to welcome her with a warm hug.

'Jo! Jo Kingsley. How are you sweetheart?'

'I'm fine.' she replied, in a warm rich voice. 'Hullo Mrs O'Hara. Hi Danny'.

She turned to face Goldy. 'You must be Sam's sister,he's been telling me about you for years. How do you do, Miss O'Hara.'

Goldy looked into two sparkling blue eyes and noted the warm smile. 'Oh call me Goldy, please! I'm fine thanks, and it's so good to meet you.'

Danny looked up at the young woman. 'Would you care to join us for dinner Joanne?'

'I'd love to Danny, but I'm supposed to be meeting up with my brother in the lounge in fifteen minutes.'

'No problem, bring him along too. I'm sure Goldy would like to meet him'.

'Thanks Danny, I'll have to clear it with him, but I'm sure it will be fine.'

'By the way, how are your Mum and Dad, Joanne? I have been meaning to catch up with them.'

'Actually, that's the other reason I am in town tonight. Mum wants to give a dinner party to welcome Goldy, next Saturday night, out at our place'.

'That sounds great. Please tell your mother we accept with pleasure.'

Jo smiled. 'Great! Shall we say about 6pm. Then there will be time to show you around, Goldy.'

'*Brolga Hills* is the biggest and best catttle station out here', interrupted Sam, enthusiastically.

As they spoke, Goldy noticed a young man, about Sam's age, walking up the front steps and across the veranda towards them. Half hidden behind dark glasses, he was handsome by any standards, tall, suntanned, with dark curly hair and an air of confidence that was hard to miss. He stopped by Jo's chair and Sam jumped up to greet him. 'Well hello Guy, I'd like you to meet my sister Goldy. Goldy this is Jo's brother, Guy Kingsley.'

He flashed a smile of impossibly white teeth and clasped Goldy's hand.'I'm very pleased to meet you. Sam has told me so much about you I feel as if I know you already! You're very welcome, Goldy?.... short for..?

'Marigold,' she said colouring slightly. 'Blame my mother. When I was born, she thought my hair was the colour of the marigolds in her garden!'

'Lovely,' he murmured. 'Red hair and green eyes. Sam, you never told me just how beautiful your sister is! You'll have to keep this one under lock and key, Danny.'

'Oh go on! You're full of it Guy.' laughed Sam. 'Sorry Goldy, he can't help himself!'

They drained their glasses and moved inside to the dining room. As they talked, Guy was charming, and as he ran his hand through his black shiny curls and removed his sunglasses, Goldy was again struck by his extreme good looks. *'One very handsome young man,and those dark eyes!'* she thought, *'very handsome!'*

During dinner she learned that Guy and her brother, had been at university together and they had shared a flat, before Guy graduated in Business Management. As the young men reminisced, Jo chatted to Goldy. A vivacious brunette, she bubbled with enthusiasm about her life on the station, and her interest in horses. Although she herself was not an expert, Goldy rode moderately well; she liked horses and was always interested to learn more. She enjoyed the young woman's company and was content to listen. Eventually, overcome by tiredness, she excused herself, kissed her father, brother and grandmother goodnight, said her goodbyes to Guy and his sister, and wearily climbed the stairs up to bed.

Looking for another pillow, Goldy went downstairs to find Sally Simpson. Sally was not in the office, but a pretty Aboriginal girl, with huge brown eyes and a wide shy smile quickly produced a spare pillow for her.

'Thank you...?'

'Suzi, Miss. My name is Suzi Quentin.'

'Thanks Suzi. My name is Goldy. I look forward to seeing you around. Good night.'

'Good night Miss.'

Despite her weariness, Goldy did not fall asleep immediately, but lay looking out through the windows at the dark velvet sky; at stars that seemed bigger and brighter than any she had ever seen before. They appeared to be so close she could almost believe that if she reached out she could touch them. The warm night was quiet, just the distant hoot of an owl, and the hum of cicadas. Apart from the sounds of nature, the silence rang around her. It was like nothing she had ever experienced before. There was an occasional distant murmur from the bar downstairs, but even that was almost lost in the vast darkness. Thinking of the miles she had travelled and the varied sights she had seen in the past few days, she sighed and snuggled down deeper. She thought about her mother. She wondered if she had felt like this when she first came. She sighed.

'I miss you Mum.'

Then her thoughts turned to the handsome Guy Kingsley, and his charming sister. She happily anticipated seeing them both again, and to visiting *Brolga Hills*. She was still thinking about all this as she finally fell asleep.

Goldy awoke next morning to the caroling of magpies. She didn't yet recognise them, but was enchanted by their melodious discourse. She heard the harsh 'caw' of the crows, but even enjoyed them. When she heard loud laughter from the Peppercorn tree, she jumped up in time to see a Kookaburra sitting preening himself, as he called out to another in a distant tree. She sank back onto the bed, savouring the luxury of a lazy Saturday morning! Finally dragging herself out of bed, she tackled the temperamental shower, tamed the loo chain, dressed and went downstairs to find something to eat.

The smell of freshly baked bread led her to the kitchen, where Kevin was turning out hot loaves onto wire racks. He glanced up as she appeared in the doorway,

' G'day love. Ready for some brekky? Bacon and eggs, toast and coffee do ya?'

'Sounds perfect thanks.' She was on her second cup of coffee when Sam arrived.

'Good morning Sis. Did you have a good sleep? You must have been exhausted from all that travelling. Any more coffee, Kev?

As he gulped the steaming brew, he said lightly, 'It was a good night with Jo and Guy wasn't it? By the way, what's your opinion of

Guy Kingsley? Are you going to join the legions of young women all over Western Australia, who lust after him?'

'They are both very nice, but no, I will *not* be joining the Guy Kingsley fan club. I make a concerted effort to avoid local heart throbs. If he's that popular, he will be far too full of himself for my taste. He is charming, and very good looking, but he must have *some* faults!'

'You'd think so,' he said thoughtfully, 'but I haven't found them yet. All that charm and those good looks and he's rich too. The only son of a very old pastoralist family. Wait until you see *Brolga Hills*, it is just the most magnificent place! I'm very disappointed in you Goldy. What could be better than my beautiful sister falling for my best friend? You might even put in a good word for me with Jo. She's a really great girl.'

'As if!' she laughed, poking her brother in the ribs.

Sam feigned a hurt expression, 'Is this to be all the thanks I get for trying to line you up with the most eligible bachelor within five hundred miles?'

'Oh, go do some work Sam! I'll see you later.'

Goldy remembered Matt's comments about the Emporium, so she took herself off to have a look around. She found it to be exactly as the young pilot had described. The variety of goods was astounding! She picked up a small sewing kit, sandwiched between the riding boots and the baked beans, and there were rubber thongs between the flyspray, and the tinned Fray Bentos Steak pies. She must have spent a good hour in there. She was trying on a variety of wide brimmed cowboy' hats, when she felt someone looking at her. She turned around, and looked into the bluest eyes she had ever seen.

'The white one suits you best,' said the owner of the blue eyes, a tall, tanned, well built young man, with a cheeky grin and unruly blonde hair. 'Definitely the white one!'

'I don't recall asking your opinion,' said Goldy archly, to cover her confusion.

'Well, you seemed to be having a problem making up your mind. I was only trying to help. Sorry. Say, aren't you the girl who caused the stir in the bar last night?'

She groaned. 'Afraid so. Sorry about that.'

'You're a Pom, aren't you?'

'A Pom?' 'English.'

'Yes, well half Aussie, half English anyway. I only arrived yesterday. Is it that obvious?'

'Well, apart from the accent, I haven't seen skin that white since my mum found a snake in the washing basket!' He laughed, a warm infectious laugh, and Goldy found herself laughing with him.

'Charlie Wentworth.'

'Goldy O'Hara, she answered taking his extended hand.'

'And this,' he said, indicating a pup sittting six inches from his heels, is *Rufus*', he's a red cloud kelpie'.

'Hullo Charlie, and hullo *Rufus*.' The dog wagged his tail at the sound of his name and licked her hand.

'You must be Danny O'Hara's girl? I heard you were coming,'

She nodded. 'Seems like everyone out here knows everything!'

He laughed. 'Not much goes unnoticed I'm afraid. One of the perils of small country towns!'

He looked at her appreciatively, 'My dear old dad always told me to marry a girl whose dad owned a pub! Don't think I ever met one before. Certainly not one so pretty!'

She liked the young man. His easy charm put her at ease, and in answer to his questions, she found herself telling him how she had ended up in Walkabout Creek. 'My mum was killed in a car accident a few years ago. Dad couldn't cope at all, and he decided to leave England and come back out here – he's Australian, you see, and they actually met here in the pub when Mum was on a working holiday. My brother and I were still at school when Mum died, so we stayed with my grandma in England, I stayed until I finished my studies, but my brother came out to be with dad. You probably know my brother, Sam?' He nodded.

'Well,' she continued, 'he finished his schooling in Perth and then went to university here, but I stayed in London to do my nursing training. Now I'm here and that's really all there is to know.

What about you? How did you get here?'

He leaned casually against the counter. 'My brother David and I came across from Far North Queensland three years ago, and just never left. My old man has a spread over there, but successive droughts all but wiped us out. There was hardly enough to support Mum and Dad, let alone three sons. Dad originally came from the West, so we two came over here to work out at *Brolga Hills*, for the Kingsleys. My eldest brother Andrew, is still at home. He's married and manages the property with Dad.'

'Do you like it over here?'

'Yes, it's good.The boss, Jack, and his wife Diana, are okay. Jack and Diana Kingsley are really nice people. Their son's a bit of an arrogant bastard, the daughter's a good sort though, or so my brother reckons!

'So does mine!' she laughed. 'Have you been home since you left?'

'No. Just haven't got around to it yet. My brother has been back a couple of times, but I never quite seem to get myself organised. I will eventually. It's beautiful country where I come from.

You should go see it one day.'

He seemed to hesitate for a few moments, then he said. 'Does Goldy O'Hara like to dance?'

'Yes, I do actually, why do you ask?'

'Well, every so often we have a dance in the old town hall. In fact there's one coming up soon. Good fun for everyone. There's a little three piece band that comes in, the ladies put on a good supper, and the pub provides the drinks. You should come along. If you do, you might just save me a couple of dances will you? Gotta go! Remember, buy the white one!'

He blew her a quick kiss and was gone.

After fumbling with the strange money, Goldy dutifully bought the white hat and humming cheerfully to herself, sauntered back to the pub. *This place improved by the day. Two handsome men in two days!*

The object of her interest was, at that moment, thinking about the young lady with the lovely red hair. He was surprised that he had found her so interesting. Pretty? Yes she was, but he knew many pretty girls. There was just something about this one that intrigued him. He looked forward to seeing her again.

CHAPTER TWELVE

SETTLING IN

Her dad and Sam were in earnest conversation in the office when she arrived . She noted they quickly changed the subject when they saw her. Her dad looked up. 'Hi darling. Don't forget the party tonight. Your chance to meet the population of Walkabout Creek.'

The evening turned out to be a great success. She met the local police sergeant and his wife, Bob and Betty Paterson. There was a very young constable, Brian Wilcox and his equally young girlfriend. The post master John Jenkins and his wife Mollie. Their son was on a working holiday in Britain, so they had lots of questions. A couple of station managers and their wives were also very welcoming.The schoolteachers, Anne and Jill, were two level- headed young women, whose stories, she found very entertaining. Neither had ever been out of the city before, and easily related to Goldy's concerns.

'Don't worry at all. It's amazing how quickly you settle in.' Anne told her. 'You'll feel like a local in no time.'

'We live across from the police station.'added Jill. 'Drop in any time after school, if you need some company.' She added a whispered aside, 'Don't tell Mollie Jenkins anything you don't want the whole town to know! She's a very kind woman, but she just can't help herself!'

Guy and Jo arrived with their parents, Jack and Diana Kingsley. It was easy to see where the young Kingsleys had inherited their good looks! A handsome couple, Diana, an ex airhostess, was a stunning blonde, tall and slim.

Her husband was tall and rugged, with thick dark hair, shot with silver, and a beguiling smile.

Goldy and Jo had hit it off straight away, and now she discovered she had as much in common with Jo's mum, Diana. They had similar tastes in music, theatre and books, and Diana had travelled extensively and knew England well. Goldy noticed that Jack Kingsley had a notable limp and walked with a stick; later she asked Sam about it.

'Apparently, he had an accident some years back,' he told her. 'got smashed up really badly by a rogue bull. Guy said he was lucky not to lose his leg! Unfortunately he doesn't ride any more, much to his sorrow. I am told that in his youth, he was a noted horseman around these parts. Nowadays, he leaves it to Guy and Jo. She's quite a legend out here - as good as her Dad, and better than Guy, much to his annoyance!'

Just then, the RFDS crew arrived. 'We forgot to leave you any adrenalin in your emergency kit,' said a laughing Ben Morris to Danny O'Hara, as he walked in.

'Slack, very slack, Doctor Morris.' laughed Danny, pouring him a drink.

Goldy was happy to see Caroline and Matt again, and shared her first impressions of Walkabout Creek with them both. During the evening, Goldy had ample opporunity to observe the handsome Guy Kingsley. Her first impression had been spot on. Guy was extremely confident, bordering on arrogance. She could understand why the girls were so fascinated by him. She doubted anyone had ever refused him anything in his life. Sam was right. Guy had the lot, money, brains, charm, good looks and sex appeal. She tried not to think too hard about that last one!

He spent much of the evening hovering around her, paying her compliments and dropping the occasional hints about her charms, good looks and beautiful body!

Her brother Sam, enchanted with Jo, spent as much of the evening around her as he could. –

As did most of the young men in the room! At one stage, Guy followed Goldy out into the veranda. 'How do you like it here in our little town?' Without waiting for an answer, he went on. 'Bit hard having to meet us all, en masse, so to speak, but a new face is always cause for a party, especially such a pretty one,' He leant forward, attempting to steal a kiss behind the potted palms. She jumped back. 'Please Guy, don't do that! People are very kind and I really appreciate the effort you have all put in tonight, honestly I do, but I don't like people to take liberties.'

'That was not my intention, I'm sorry if that is how it came across. I just think you are one of the most enchanting girls I have ever met and I hope we can get to know each other better, without the crowd,' he said silkily. 'Tell me Goldy, do you ride?'

'I do, but nowhere as well as your sister, from what I hear. 'she admitted.

'Yes, Jo's pretty good. Tell you what; you had better come out to the station one day. We've some good horses out there. I know Jo would love to show you around. You can bring Sam too, if you like. Just to show you, I have no ulterior motives!'

Goldy blushed. 'Thanks for that, Guy, I'll talk to Sam.' She turned away and hurried back inside.

As she passed the open door to the bar, she saw Charlie Wentworth, sitting on a bar stool, glass in hand. He gave her a cheeky grin and a mock salute. She smiled back warmly.

When she commented later to Sam that she found Guy Kingsley's attentions rather confronting, he merely laughed. 'He finds you attractive Sis! I know girls who would die for some attention like that from Guy Kingsley! Just enjoy it!'

Later, when the goodbyes had all been said and the last guest had gone, Goldy and her father were together on the balcony. Danny said, 'Well, darling, what do you think of the residents of the Walkabout Creek district?'

'They all seem very nice, Dad. Very friendly.'

'Well, you were certainly the hit of the evening! Time to turn in sweetheart.' He hugged her tightly, kissed her on the top of her head and walked inside.

A few days later, Goldy was sitting on the veranda of the hotel, writing to her grandmother in England. She watched with interest as Sergeant Paterson drove up to the door in a cloud of red dust. He jumped out and hurried up the front steps.

'Glad you're here Goldy! I wondered if you could come out and give me a hand. There's been an accident just outside town. A truck has turned over and the driver is trapped inside. I have called the Flying Doctor, but it will probably be about an hour before they can get here. I could do with your nursing expertise. He seems to be bleeding a fair bit! Will you come?'

The truck was lying on its roof, balanced precariously on a bridge, over a deep dry creek bed.

'Looks like he took that bend too fast and just couldn't make the bridge squarely. There have been several accidents like this since in recent years,' remarked the policeman. 'Have suggested to the shire that they straighten out the bend a bit, but things move slowly up here!'

A small crowd of spectators had gathered, and Constable Wilcox was effectively keeping them away from the wrecked vehicle.

'Where do people come from?' asked Goldy in amazement.

'Dunno, but they always appear.'

Goldy hurried across to the wreck and climbed up to the driver's door, which was hanging open.

Inside, she could see the driver. He was lying face down, a large gash in the back of his head bleeding profusely. His body draped over the upturned front seats, his lower body underneath the crushed cab of the truck. He was moaning and appeared to be unable to move. Goldy quickly jumped in beside him. 'Hello, my name is Goldy; I'm a nurse, and I am here to help you until the doctor gets here. What's your name?'

He lifted his head slightly, 'Doug, Doug Watson. Can you get me out of here love?'

'We're going to give it a go Doug. She grabbed a towel that had fallen off the seat in the crash, 'firstly, I need to put some pressure on that cut. Tell me, have you any pain? Can you feel your legs?'

The young man affirmed both. He was able to move his toes, and had pain in his right shoulder and arm. Her first assessment was that he seemed to have no neck or spine injury, his pain came from his arm and shoulder, doubled under him.

'I don't have anything to give you for the pain I'm afraid, but I will stay with you.' Goldy gently squeezed his free hand.

' We need to get him out.' She called to the policeman.

'Sorry Goldy, but you need to get out of there, NOW! Smell all that fuel? This is too dangerous for you. One spark and this whole thing could go up in flames!'

As Goldy started to climb out of the cabin, Doug grabbed her hand. 'For God's sake don't leave me here! I don't want to die!!'

Goldy hesitated for just a moment, before climbing back in and taking Doug's hand firmly in hers. 'It's okay. You and I are in this together, and we are not going to burn to death, trust me!'

By now, the police had moved the small crowd back some distance from them, and Goldy felt a cold finger of fear. Burning was not something she wished to contemplate. Twenty minutes later, she was still crouched in the crushed cabin, holding Doug's hand, trying to be cheerful whilst she really felt like crying.

'You look like you need a hand young lady.' A familiar voice broke through her fear.

She looked up into the blue eyes of ....Charlie Wentworth. 'Thank Goodness! Can you help me get this man out of here? I am not strong enough to move these seats and I need to get him out as soon as possible. The police can't help, they just want me out of here!'

Charlie immediately started to pull at the twisted seats and gradually they started to move. 'Just relax Doug, I will have you out of here in no time.' He turned to Goldy. 'You support his chest while I move this seat out of the way, then I'll try to kick this windscreen out. We need to keep him straight when we lift him clear, just in case there is any damage to his spine.'

'How come you know what to do?' asked Goldy.

'Well, I suppose when you grow up in the bush, you are often a long way from medical help, you pick up things along the way. Don't have your skills, but I know a little bit.' By now, he had thrown the twisted front seat out of the cab and crawled out onto the bonnet.

With one mighty kick, the windscreen disintegrated into a thousand pieces. Together, he and Goldie carefully pulled the man through the front of the cab and gently lowered him on the ground. The police then hastily moved him away from the vehicle, onto a stretcher, keeping pressure on his cut head and into the back of the police wagon, which took off for the airstrip.

Goldy breathed a sigh of relief. 'Thank you so much for your help. I have to admit I was so scared! I didn't want to burn to death!'

Charlie laughed. 'Not much chance of that. That truck was full of diesel. Doesn't go up like petrol, certainly not with a spark. Nevertheless, you were very brave Miss O'Hara.'

'How did you know his name, Charlie?'

'Who? Doug? He works out at Brolga Hills for Jack Kingsley. He was supposed to be bringing in some parts for a new windmill. Guess they won't be much use, looking at the state of the truck!'

CHAPTER THIRTEEN

BROLGA HILLS

Next weekend was the dinner at *Brolga Hills* with the Kingsleys. How Goldy wished she could find an excuse not to go. She did not feel at all comfortable with Guy. He had a certain animal magnetism about him, but she was uneasy with his attention. However, she was really looking forward to meeting up again with Jo.

Brolga Hills was a magnificent colonial homestead, of stone construction with wide verandas on all sides. Built on a rise, it had sweeping views of the country, all the way to the distant purple hills. The property was surrounded by a white post and rail fence. An imposing ornate iron gate stood at the entrance to the wide sweeping drive. It was all very grand.

It was just as imposing inside as out. All the rooms were beautifully proportioned and tastefully furnished and decorated and all had high ceilings. There were some magnificent antiques, including a french china cabinet which Goldy thought must have been at least two hundred years old. There were some beautiful Monet and Renoir prints on the walls, and a white grand piano in the main sitting room.

A large open stone fireplace dominated the smaller of the two sitting rooms. 'Wonderful on cold nights,' enthused Diana Kingsley.'Cold nights?' queried Goldy.

'Well, we really are on the edge of the desert out here. It can go from 45 degrees Celsius in the daytime to minus 4 at night! We really appreciate the fire then, I can tell you! Anyway, do come out and see my garden before it gets dark!'

The gardens were beautifully landscaped, lush and green, with huge jacaranda trees around a stylish swimming pool. Down one side of the house was a magnificent rose garden.

'My pride and joy,' beamed Diana. 'At last count I had over a hundred!'

'It's beautiful.' Said Goldy, sincerely. 'How do you keep it all looking so green?'

'Bore water.' said Jack Kingsley. 'If you look out to the south paddock, you can see the big windmill. That's one of two that serve the homestead.'

Guy and Jo led ther down to see the stables. Like the rest of the property, they were beautifully appointed and maintained.They proudly discussed their horses, as Jo enthused, 'This is our pet project, we're trying to improve the strain of stock horses we have here, aren't we Guy?'

Her brother nodded. 'Yes. Four of these lovely mares were in foal when Jo and I bought them in Adelaide last year, and now we're on the lookout for a top stallion.'

'More bloody money,' muttered Jack to Dan.'They just eat the stuff!'

'Go on! ribbed Danny, 'You can afford it!'

'And they are very beautiful,' whispered Goldy.

Jack laughed and shrugged. 'I can see I will get no support from you two!'

Behind the stable was a tennis court. 'Do you play, Goldy?' asked Diana.

'Yes, but not very well. I used to play a lot at school, but I haven't played for ages,' she replied.

'You must come out for one of our tennis days. It's so hard to get up the numbers; Jo is always too busy with the horses to play, and I certainly need the exercise!'

Looking at her slender form, Goldy rather doubted that. Diana Kingsley was a charming woman, sophisticated and vibrant.

In her company, Goldy almost forgot her reservations about her son. Guy, on his best behaviour, was charming, until she began to think she might have been a bit hasty in her earlier misgivings about him. As the evening progressed, Goldy liked the family more and more. She and Jo had hit it off straight away when they first met and she now felt that she had really made a friend of Diana as well. She found his father, Jack, to be a quiet, charming man,with a very dry sense of humour. She liked him enormously.

Dinner was an extravagent affair of roast beef with all the trimmings, and a homemade apple pie and icecream. Goldy noted that all the tablecloths and napkins were of fine linen, beautifully embroidered. The wine glasses were finest crystal, and the coffee freshly brewed. After the meal, the men retired to another room to play billiards and drink port, while the women drank coffee in the lounge, laughing and swapping stories, as the domestic staff cleared away the dishes.

Later, on the way back into town, Goldy dozed on the back seat. She was half asleep when she heard Sam say, 'What did he actually say, Dad? Does he really think you would do anything to damage the place? What the hell do you do now?'

She heard her father sigh, before replying. 'Nothing I can do for the moment, son. Just give me time, I think I can talk Jack around, if you can shut Guy up!'

Sam snorted. 'Right now I think Guy's more interested in my sister, than he is about pursuing legal arguments!'

'Perhaps we should encourage her to be a bit more receptive!' Dan said thoughtfully, ' She could do a lot worse you know.'

Goldy resolved to wait until morning and then ask about their strange conversation.By morning she had forgotten the exchange in the car. Her mind was on other things.

She had decided to follow up on Caroline's suggestion of enquiring at Community Health about reopening the boarded up clinic, near the post office. She had peeped inside between the wooden slats. There was a heap of red dust, but nothing a good scrub couldn't fix. Some basic stuff; a desk and chairs, a fridge, a filing cabinet, and some old fashioned scales. A good clean, a few medical supplies and some paperwork would make a world of difference.

She went back to the pub and penned her letter to Perth, to apply for the position, explaining her circumstances and enclosing her qualifications and resume.

A few days later, Goldy noticed two men, whom she had not seen previously, in earnest conversation with her father in the lounge bar. One of them, a large fleshy individual, was leaning across the table in an almost threatening manner. 'Now listen here O'Hara, all you have to do is to get Jack Kingsley to sign the bloody papers and we will all be happy.

We'll pay you well, don't worry.'

She heard her father reply quietly, 'I've already told you I am not interested. You guys think that just because you're part of a big company, you can buy anything, and everyone has to do what you say. Well you're wrong! Neither Jack Kingsley nor I are signing anything!' '

The second man leaned forward and said something Goldy could not hear. Pushing back his chair, Danny stood up. 'I've had enough of your bully boy tactics! Go to hell! 'I've nothing further to say to either of you. Good morning gentlemen!'

The men rose abruptly and strode angrily out of the pub, to a waiting car.' We usually get what we want eventually and you will live to regret that decision, I promise you!' growled one of them, as he climbed into the driver's seat and slammed the door. As the car reversed out of the car park, Goldy saw a logo on the door. *Yellow Metals. Melbourne.*

'Who were they, Dad?' she queried, joining him at the table.

'Nobody to worry your pretty head about.' he said smiling. 'Just couple of mining bosses, intent on getting their own way.'

'Over what? They seemed pretty angry.'

'Full of hot air! Anyway, have you heard from Community Health yet, about that job?'

'Not yet, but Dr Morris promised to put in a good word for me, and Caroline seemed to think it would be fine.'

'Well, I have to go out to *Brolga Hills* see Jack. Do you want to come?'

She thought of Guy and hesitated. 'No thanks Dad, I have some washing I want to do.'

'Guy will be disappointed,' he teased, smiling.

'What is it with you and Sam? You both seem to think I should fall madly in love with him! To be perfectly honest, I am not sure I particularly like him.'

'Well he's certainly most eligible. You could do a lot worse, and he's obviously very taken with you.'

'Spoilt little rich boy!' she declared

Goldy went across the back courtyard to the laundry, and as she rinsed her clothes, she idly thought back to the two mining bosses. She saw her brother sweeping down the yard and called out to him, 'Sam! May I have a word please?'

He put aside his broom and walking over, leaned on the door frame. 'What's up Sis? Want to know how to catch Guy Kingsley?' He ducked as she threw a wet flannel at him.

'Not that again! No, I want to know what those mining people want with Dad, and what were they so angry about?'

Sam looked thoughtful. 'I don't suppose there's any reason you shouldn't know.You see, Dad took out a claim on some land, where we know there is gold; maybe quite a lot of gold. This mining company wants Dad to sell them the lease, because it adjoins one of theirs, and it would allow them to expand at far less cost than further exploration in another area. They are prepared to pay a lot of money for it.'

'Why won't Dad sell?' she asked.

'Well the claim is on *Brolga Hills* land, the Kingsley's place, and Jack would have to sign permission for it to be mined. Whilst Dad wants to mine there in a small controlled way, with a view to minimal environmental impact, there's no guarantee that a big company would be so concerned. Dad has almost talked Jack Kingsley around to his way of thinking, but Guy is still pretty anti, he's a real greenie, that one!'

'It's so beautiful out there, I could understand someone not wanting mine shafts on their land.' she said thoughtfully.

'Dad would never sell Jack out like that, but better Dad, than Yellow Metals.'

Sam went back to his sweeping, and Goldy thought about what he had told her. She remembered the conversation she had overheard in the car that night. So *that* was one of the reasons they wanted her to distract Guy Kingsley! They wanted his interest diverted so his avid opposition to any mining on *Brolga Hills* station would not interfere with Jack and Dan's negotiations.

Anxious to hear about her application, the next afternoon, she went in to the Post Office. Still no news. It was over a week later that Mollie Jenkins handed her an official looking envlope, with a Government stamp on it. 'Looks important.'she said, curiously. 'Hope it's good news!'

'Yes, I hope so too.' said Goldy as she ran back to the pub. She sat on the veranda and hastily tore open the envelope.

'Dear Miss Jensen', she read.

'We acknowledge your application for the position of Remote Area Nurse, stationed at Toolamulla.

We are pleased to advise that your application has been successful, subject to a satisfactory medical examination and completion of your Orientation Program. Attached is a list of Centres where these things may be undertaken. Enclosed also is a Job

Description and a list of uniform requirements.

Furthermore, it will be necessary to reopen, clean, re-equip and restock the Toolamulla Centre. We will arrange this in due course. If you contact this office, at the number shown below, you can make all the necessary arrangements.

Congratulations on your appointment. We trust you willl find it challenging and rewarding.

Yours etc'

Goldy ran inside waving her letter. 'Dad! Dad! Sally! Where's dad?'

'Upstairs love, but I think....'

Goldy didn't wait to hear the rest. She raced up the stairs two at a time and threw open his door. There was a frantic scurry as her father leapt up from the bed, grabbing for a towel, then she saw Suzi, trying to hide under the sheet.

'I'm so sorry Dad.' she stammered. 'I had no idea there was anyone with you. I'm really sorry! She backed out of the room, hastily closing the door, hot tears scalding her cheeks.

Sally came slowly up the stairs and took her in her arms. 'I'm sorry love. You didn't give me time to stop you.'

Goldy buried her face in Sally's ample bosom. 'I just never thought of Dad being with another woman, after my mum,' she sobbed. 'I should have! He's still a good looking man, and I understand he must have needs, but I just couldn't imagine it would ever happen.'

'Don't cry love,' said Sally softly. 'He's been with Suzi for a couple of years now. She's a nice enough girl and I suppose we've all got used to it now, but I can understand it's a bit of a shock for you.'

'Does Sam know?' Goldy asked tearfully.

'He does.' said Sally, handing her a clean white hankerchief. 'C'mon love. Let's go and get a cuppa and see what my Kev's been cookin' up.'

She took Goldy's arm and led her downstairs to the kitchen. 'Me little darlin' is a bit shaken up, Kev, and we need a cuppa, and a slice of your nice boiled fruit cake, don't we love?'

Goldy attempted a watery smile. 'That sounds lovely.' she said. 'And thank you Sally. I'm sorry I was such a drama queen!'

Later, Goldy sought out her brother. 'I think you could have warned me about Dad and Suzi!' she growled indignantly.

'Why? I didn't think it was anyone else's business, to be quite honest. He's not accountable to us, you know. He is a grown man!'

'I s'pose you're right, Was a bit of a shock, that's all.'

It was hard to face her father over the tea table that night. Eventually she said. 'I'm sorry I burst into your room today. I should have knocked. It was very remiss of me. I apologise'.

'No Goldy, I apologise. I should have explained to you before, how things are between Suzi and me. I'm very fond of Suzi, but she will never take your mum's place. Please believe me.'

'You don't owe me any explanations, Dad. I just got a surprise, but I'm okay now. We are both adults and we are entitled to do what we want, with whom, when we choose. Just one thing, will you please lock your door in future?!'

They both smiled, and he leaned over and kissed her gently,

'Thank you my darling. By the way, what did you want to see me about in such a hurry?'

In all the drama, Goldy had all but forgotten the crumpled letter in her pocket.

She pulled it out and handed it to him. He smoothed it out and began to read aloud. 'That's wonderful sweetheart. So you will stay here with me for a while now?'

'Absolutely dad. Just try and get rid of me! By the way, I'm going to need your help. I don't know where any of these places are that they are talking about. Kalgoorlie, Port Hedland, Geraldton. How will I know which one to choose for my orientation? They also say I can go to Perth.'

'If it's after Sam goes back to uni, you could go to Perth and stay with him while you do it. Let's check some dates.'

The incident over Suzi behind her, signalled a change in the relationship between Goldy and her grandmother. They grew closer and Clara was the confidente, that Goldy has missed since she left her grandmother in England. They began to talk about all kinds of things and Goldy even told her about her misgivings over Guy Kingsley. 'He makes me feel uncomfortable' she admitted.

'I believe half the girls in the district have got a crush on that young man,' said Clara 'Good family but I'm a bit inclined to agree with you, there is something a bit unsettling about him. Too good looking and too rich for his own good, I think! I say always go with your instincts, darling.'

With the passage of time, Goldy felt more able to talk more about her father and Suzi. 'How do her family feel about her being with a white man, like my Dad?' she said to Sally one day.

Looking up from her ironing, Sally was thoughtful. 'Not too happy, I'm afraid. 'The story is, that Suzi was promised to an old man, a tribal elder, and he wants her. That's why Suzi stays here at the pub. She wants to be with yer Dad, and he wants to be with her.'

'Would marrying her be a solution?'

'Not really, love. Y'see the family say she's already married. There'd be serious repercussions if yer dad tried to make it legal. I s'pose they all hope he'll get tired of her and send her packin', like lots of white fellars do, but that's not very likely, knowin' yer dad. I really don't know how it will end. I just hope nobody gets hurt in the process!'

Goldy often ran into Charlie Wentworth and *Rufus.* around the town. They always stopped to have a chat, and when one evening, he suggested they have a drink together in the lounge, she gladly agreed.

Jim Gregson eyed him speculatively, 'Goin' up in the world are we? The lounge, no less. What'll it be?'

'Beer for me, please Jim, and the young lady will have.. ?'

'A bacardi and Coke, thanks Charlie.' she replied, bending down to pat *Rufus*, who lay panting at her feet, rolling over to have his pink tummy scratched. He brought the drinks over from the bar and sat down. 'Now tell me, what have you been up to lately?'

Goldy told him about her new job, starting shortly.

Charlie felt his spirits rising. 'That's great news,! So you'll be staying in town? I'm really happy to hear that.'

'Yes, I'm looking forward to it too.' she replied warmly. *'and not just to the job,'* she thought, eyeing off his clean white shirt and cream moleskin trousers. 'Incidently, I was out at Brolga Hills long ago. I hoped I might have seen you there.'

'Sorry, I don't hobnob with the boss these days. Before Guy came home I was often invited up for meals, but things are different now. The staff quarters are quite a long way from the homestead.' He was a bit downcast, but brightened up as he said, 'The dance is coming up in two week's time. I hope I'll see you there? Remember, you promised to save me a couple. The Cha cha's my favourite. Don't forget!'

Later, as he stood up to leave, she smiled. 'See you soon? He waved and gave her a cheeky grin as he walked out into the corridor. He nodded to Sam as they passed in the doorway. Sam sauntered into the lounge and sat down next to his sister. 'I didn't know you knew Charlie Wentworth, Sis?'

'I don't know him well, but we've met a few times.'

'You know he works out at *Brolga Hills?* Guy says he's bad bastard! Perhaps you shouldn't get too friendly with him. Although, Jo says his brother David is a nice bloke.'

'I like him.' protested Goldy. He's always been very nice to me.'

'Just take care Sis,' Sam patted her on the shoulder. 'I'd hate to see you get hurt.'

CHAPTER FOURTEEN

THE DANCE

Two Saturdays later everyone descended on the town for the dance. Goldy wondered, as she put on a pretty dress and some strappy sandals, where all the people came from. She swept her hair up in a chignon and accompanied by her father and brother, strolled the few hundred yards to the town hall The music was already drifting into the street as they approached the hall They paid their admission money to the happy looking woman who sat at a small table just inside the door. At the far end of the hall a plump lady was pounding the keys of an old piano. A man in a cowboy outfit of jeans, checkered shirt and boots, strummed a guitar. Another played a clarinet, whilst a fourth plucked away at an instrument that looked very like an old tea chest with a broom handle attached, with just one string.

'That's a bush base', whispered Danny. 'Makes a mean sound!'

The old hall had been spruced up by the local ladies for the occasion, complete with balloons and streamers. In the side room, the brightly coloured trestles bowed under the piles of delicious food. There were kegs in the corner and a large tin bath of ice, filled with wine and soft drinks.

Guy Kingsley appeared at her side to lead her off in the Flirtation Barn Dance. At about the fourth change, her heart gave a lurch as she found herself face to face with Charlie Wentworth.

'Hi Goldy. You look very pretty tonight! Don't forget my Cha Cha.

Where are you sitting?'

She indicated a table in the corner.

'Good. See you soon' he called as they were swept apart. The evening had taken on a new excitement for him.

She had a dance with her dad, one with Sam, and a couple with Guy before the Cha Cha was announced.

'Sorry Guy', she said, as he went to stand up. 'This one's promised.'

On cue, Charlie appeared to lead her onto the dance floor. He was a good dancer and they moved well together. When she remarked on his skill, he laughed.

'You can thank the Christian Brothers in Brisbane for that! Ballroom dancing was compulsory for all boarders. Guess they didn't want us looking too much like country bumkins!'

They were both laughing as the bracket finished. They stood together on the floor talking and when the next bracket was announced, they automatically went into each other's arms. He smiled as he took in the heady scent of her clean hair and light perfume, she snuggled closer as she noted his white smile and sparkling blue eyes. He smelled of some unknown aftershave and she closed her eyes as she breathed it in.

'You are quite a girl, Goldy O'Hara' he murmured as the dance ended. 'Let's go and get some fresh air.' They went out through a side door. Charlie leaned on the old hitching rail, his arm loosely round her shoulders. Goldy looked up and murmured breathlessly, 'Would you look at that sky! Have you ever seen anything so beautiful?'

Charlie turned and looked down at her, the moonlight shining on her lovely hair.

'Yes.' he said softly. 'I think I have.' He bent over and kissed her gently on the cheek. It was a chaste kiss, but caught her unawares, she felt her colour rise, and she pulled back. 104

'I'm sorry Goldy, got a bit carried away. I promise it will not happen again. Sorry. Tell me, have you ever seen the bush at night, outside town?'

She shook her head. 'Only coming back from *Brolga Hills* in the car, or from the hotel balcony.'

'No, I mean the real bush. You must come out with me one evening and I'll show you just how beautiful it really is out there.'

She laughed. 'It's a date!' They were standing quite close together, his arm still around her shoulders. The next instant, the door was flung open and an angry Guy Kingsley pushed them apart. 'Take your filthy hands off her!' he shouted, as he hit Charlie so hard that he fell over the railing and into the dirt. Like a cat, he sprang lightly to his feet, swinging a punch at Guy. As the two men continued to brawl, his brother David, her brother Sam and her father, appeared at the open door and struggled to separate the two young men.

'What the hell is going on?' demanded Danny angrily.

'This bastard was mauling your daughter!' growled Guy sullenly.

'He was doing nothing of the sort!' Goldy gasped indignantly.

'Go back inside, Goldy.' said Dan. He turned to Charlie. 'I'll thank you to stay away from my daughter, young man. You're playing way out your league.'

'Yeah, stay away from Goldy or I'll punch your lights out! Hissed Guy, as Sam steered him back into the hall.

'Sorry Goldy,' muttered Charlie as she turned to leave. He wiped his bloody nose on his sleeve.

'No, it wasn't your fault, honestly. I'm the one who's sorry.' she touched him awkwardly on the arm.

'Come on Goldy.' said her father, as he led her back inside.

For her, the pleasure has gone from the evening, and after supper, she complained of a headache and said she was going back to the pub.

'I'll walk you back.' offered Sam.

'Nonsense! It's only a two minute walk. I'll be fine, honestly. You go dance with Jo. You've been giving her the eye all night. Find some courage, brother!

'I wish she'd been giving *me* the eye!' he smiled wryly. 'Are you sure you'll be okay?'

'Absolutely! Go to it.'

As she walked slowly back to the pub, her thoughts were all of Charlie. *What could her father possibly have against him?*

She was just stepping up onto the veranda steps when she saw a figure sitting half in shadow,

'Charlie? Is that you?'

The tall figure unfolded, stretched and stood up stiffly. 'Yes, it is. I have to wait for David to drive me home. I think he might be a while. He took two of the girls from *Dingo Hills* station home. One of them has been been a bit keen on him for ages, much good may it do her! So God knows when he'll be back. I told him to meet me here. I hope that's okay.'

'Of course it is. Come inside. I'll make us some coffee.'

He followed her reluctantly. 'I don't want to cause any more trouble for you with your father. I like him. He's a good bloke.'

'Well come into the upstairs lounge. He won't see you there, even if he does come home early.'

Goldy made some coffee and grabbed a few slices of Kev's fruit cake, which she put on a tray and carried up the stairs. 'Come on, don't be silly. There's nobody here. Everyone's gone to the dance.'

They moved into the small sitting room on the landing near Goldy's room, to drink their coffee, and as she put down the tray, she noted the cut on Charlie's face, still oozing blood.

'Let's have a look at that. Guy sure spoiled your good looks, and there is blood on your nice shirt! Come into the bathroom and I'll give it a wash. I'm sure I have some plasters in my luggage somewhere.' Goldy searched her suitcase, only partially unpacked, and emerged triumphantly with a small packaged dressing. He winced as she expertly cleaned and covered the wound.

'I'm sorry, Goldy. I didn't know you were Guy Kingsley's girl. If I had, I would never have presumed to.....'

'I am not Guy's girl!' she interupted vehemently. 'Actually, I don't even like him! It's just that he's my brother's best friend and we seem to get pushed together rather a lot. There is certainly nothing between us as far as I am concerned!'

'I'm so glad to hear that.' he said, smiling for the first time.

'Come here, Charlie Wentworth,' she laughed. 'Let me bind up my wounded hero!' She sat him in a chair and as she leaned over him, he slipped an arm around her waist with a mischievious smile. She moved gently away from him.

'What have people around here got against you?'

He sighed and took his arm away. 'I guess you'll hear about it soon enough. Best you hear it from me first. I did come across from Queensland three years ago, like I told you, but I'd been in a bit of trouble. My brother David and I were having a drink at our local pub, when David got into a fight with this guy from Longreach. Anyway, he pulled a knife on Dave and went at him. I grabbed him to take the knife away and God knows what happened next, but he got stabbed with his own knfe and subsequently died. I was arrested and charged with manslaughter and did some gaol time.' He continued. 'My dad and Jack Kingsley were pretty good mates from way back.They had been to school together with your dad, in

Perth. So when I came out of prison, dad thought it might be a good idea for me to get a fresh start somewhere else, so he contacted Jack, who offered David and me a job on Brolga Hills.My grandfather had a property near here in the west before he went to Queensland, so he knew I would like it here..

Everything was fine at first, until Guy came back from university and started throwing his weight around. He told anyone who would listen about my conviction and he wanted his dad to sack me. Guy never liked me much. I think he might have been a bit jealous. His old man treated me almost like a son. He made me head stockman, and even if I say it myself, I did a pretty good job. Guy has had it in for me ever since.'

She moved closer to him. 'Oh Charlie, that is so unfair! Just awful! but I don't understand, if it was an accident, how could anyone blame you?'

'Well, the judge said he didn't believe that I intended to kill the guy, but I needed to learn to be more responsible. So he sentenced me to three years, of which I served eighteen months.

Guy took it on himself to tell people that I deliberately killed the guy, and that it should have been a murder charge. He said I was lucky not to get life!

Honestly Goldy, it was a tragic accident. I swear not a day goes by when I don't relive that night. I was just protecting my brother. I never meant for anyone to get seriously hurt!'

She reached for his hand. 'I believe you Charlie. I just know that you would never hurt anyone intentionally.'

They sat for a long time talking, and it seemed to Goldy that she has known him all her life. The more time she spent with him, the more she liked him. It was after midnight when David arrived back into town.

'Think I'd better lie low for a week or two until this all blows over.' said Charlie quietly.

'Don't leave it too long,' she said, touching his arm gently.

As Charlie carefully negotiated the iron fire escape, she waved him goodbye, as he climbed into the truck. He certainly was different from most of the young men who had crossed her path so far. She looked forward to seeing him again.

CHAPTER FIFTEEN

JOANNE KINGSLEY

Joanne Kingsley looked on in quiet amusement at her brother's futile attempts to impress her new friend, Goldy O'Hara. 'A new experience for big brother,' she said laughing, as she and her father enjoyed a quiet stroll down to the stables.'

Jack chuckled. 'Yes, it won't do him any harm. He is much too used to getting his own way with the ladies. I must admit I am surprised none of them have trapped him into marriage yet!'

'He's too smart for that, Dad. Anyway, he always wants what he can't have, so I guess that goes for Goldy!'.

Her father looked thoughtful. 'Anyway, I have it on good authority that Goldy is much more taken with Charlie Wentworth than she is ever to be with Guy.'

Jo looked surprised. 'Is that a fact? Well she is a dark horse. She has kept that to herself! Oh well, Charlie is a nice man. She could do worse, and he will do alright for himself.

Probably make a good station manager one day.'

'What about you, young lady? Is there no nice young man who has caught your fancy yet?'

'You know me Dad, love 'em and leave 'em. No, there's nobody special. For a while, I rather fancied Sam O'Hara, but he's not really a country boy, and I don't really see myself as a city doctor's wife. You know how I hate the big city! The local guys are okay, I guess, but I always feel more like one of the gang when I am out with any of them. If not that, then they are falling over themselves to show me how good they are!'

Jack laughed again, 'What about young David Wentworth? He'd be a good catch. Not wealthy, I grant you, but Nice looking, hardworking and dead honest.'

Jo blushed, but said quickly, 'That's true Dad, but he's so shy. Anyway, he's more like a big brother really.'

'Plenty of time, sweetheart. The right one will come along, I'm quite sure.'

'Maybe. Anyway, I'm just going to feed up, so I'll see you at dinner.'Shealked into the stable and picked up a feed bucket, as her father turned to walk to the homestead. He looked back at her with a sigh. She worried him, this pretty, headstrong daughter. Quick tempered, but charming, a load of fun, but very uncompromising.

Things were very black and white to Joanne. Once let down, there were no second chances. She rode as well, if not better, than anyone he had ever known. Utterly fearless, competitive to a fault, she always had to win at everything. She lived and breathed for her horses, spending every spare minute training, riding, or reading about horses.

When she was at boarding school in the city, she was so miserable without a horse, that he and Diana found it necessary to bring her home, to finish her education by correspondence. She seemed to have no ambition that did not involve horses. Jack was thankful that he could afford to indulge her, but he worried about her future all the same. Unless she married well, life might be difficult for her once her parents were gone. Who knew if Guy would be prepared to give her that same freedom? At present she was very involved in a project to improve the stamina and breeding of their stock horses, but it all took time and money. He wondered where it all would end.

Jack himself had been a top equestrian before a near fatal accident had put an end to his ambitions. He had been the victim of a crazed bull, who had gored him and thrown him against a fence, crushing his leg and pelvis. His recuperation had been long and painful, and a leg unable to bend, put an end to any future riding. Fortunately, his father had insisted on a sound education, and had encouraged him with his studies on management and stock breeding.

He wasn't sure that his daughter had sufficient business skills, or that she could develop them. Guy certainly had. Jo had at one time, been keen on the idea of setting up a farm stay business for young people from the city, but her initial enthusiasm waned, and the project was abandoned. Her reason being, that she didn't like inexperienced riders 'ruining' her horses.

Since Goldy's arrival, the two young women had formed a genuine attachment to one another, and they were often seen closeted in some corner, laughing at their own private conversations. It was a novelty for Jo to have a girl of her own age to talk to. Observing Jo one day, Goldy said, 'So, when are you and the handsome David Wentworth going to get your act together? You obviously get on well together!'

Jo laughed, 'They do breed them pretty dishy in Queensland don't they? I'm afraid I don't think it is ever going to amount to anything. When he first arrived, I was quite keen, but he didn't seem to return the interest. Yes, I do like David, but he's so quiet, you would never really know what he was thinking, if anything! I could never marry a man who didn't adore me as much as my dad adores my mother. Anyway, I couldn't take any man too seriously if I can beat him in a horse race! I'm pretty sure I can beat him every time. Anyway, what's this you're not telling me about Charlie? You are a dark horse, Goldy!'

Goldy looked flustered. 'Don't change the subject Jo Kingsley! What on earth has a horse race to do with falling in love with a gorgeous man?'

'It's not quite like that, Goldy. It is just that I need to have respect for him in all areas. I can't help myself, I know I am competitive, but just ignore me…you're beginning to sound like my Dad. Anyway, I notice that my brother is paying you a lot of attention. How do you like him?'

Goldy hesitated, she did not wish to offend her new friend, but she couldn't lie either. 'Well,' she began slowly. 'Guy is very handsome, charming, attentive and everything, but he's really not for me. Sometimes he comes across as a bit…. Arrogant.'

'You might think so, but actually I think he has just been a bit spoilt. There aren't many girls who can, or do, resist him, but he's really quite sweet once you get to know him better. He is the best brother in the world to me. Don't write him off completely.'

Following his altercation with Guy Kingsley, Charlie wisely gave Walkabout Creek a wide berth for the next couple of weeks, as Goldy put her energies into cleaning out the neglected Clinic. It turned out to be quite an experience for the girl from Cornwall! She was confronted by spiders, lizards and multiple creepy crawlies, which were all totally unfamiliar to her. Especially alarming was the carpet python she found sleeping in the rafters! Jo thought it was very funny and gently removed the python and released him in the bush outside town. 'You will just have to get used to them all, Goldy. Just stay out of their way, they are not going to chase you!'

It was decided that Goldy would fly to Perth with her brother, when he went back to university. Goldy was to stay at the flat with him while she did her Orientation program, before starting work at the Clinic. Their father promised to drive them to the nearest commercial airport. Community Health were to provide a vehicle for her to drive back to Walkabout Creek. Danny agreed to fly down to help her drive back. 'It's a long way when you are not familiar with conditions here, especially the gravel roads and bush tracks.'

Goldy was only too happy with this arrangement. She had been very apprehensive about the long journey home. So much of the country looked so much the same to her, she was frightened of getting lost!

The day finally arrived and the three of them set off for the nearest domestic airport. The aircraft squatted on the strip, and a small group of people milled around, waiting to board.

'Thanks Dad,' said Sam, giving Danny a warm hug. 'It's been great being with you over the holidays, especially with Sis being here as well. I'll see you when you come down to drive her home. Okay?'

Goldy hugged her father tightly, as she kissed him goodbye. 'Wish me luck!', she called cheerily, as she walked across the tarmac. 'See you soon.'

After a long flight, they landed a Perth Airport, where Goldy had previously been just a few weeks before. Sam hailed a taxi and they were soon on their way. Goldy enjoyed the drive down Eastern Highway, across the Causeway leading into the city.

They did not go into the city centre, but took the leafy Riverside Drive, along palm fringed playing fields As they drove around the river under King's Park, the view across to Canning Bridge was magical, the twinkling lights of the Kwinana Freeway on the other side of the Narrows Bridge, reflected in the dark water. A few minutes later they arrived at Sam's flat near the University.

'Hope you don't mind sharing the spare rooms with all my books and junk,' he said apologetically, 'I wasn't expecting guests! I'm afraid the room needs airing, it has been shut up for weeks, but at least the bed is comfortable!' Sam walked through to the small kitchen to put on the kettle. 'Actually, Jack Kingsley owns the building and he prefers that I don't let anyone stay here when I am away. Guy and I used to share it, before he graduated. I was afraid

I might have to move out when he left, but Jack has been very good to me. He only charges me a very small rent. Once I qualify, I will ask him to draw up a proper lease agreement. Flats here, near the university, are at a premium, and I have been extremely lucky.'

Early next day, Goldy prepared to set off to find the Community Health office in West Perth.

'That's not far from here,' said Sam as he searched for his bus timetable. 'The bus goes almost straight past where you have to go. I'll see you get on the right one. You just need to ask the driver to let you off at the right stop. Okay? I will meet you when you finish about five.'

Goldy found the place without too much trouble. She hesitated nervously at the front door, before pushing it open. She was immediately put at ease by the friendly receptionist, who welcomed her warmly, pointing her in the direction of the coffee machine, on the way, introducing her to two other new recruits. Cherry McLeod was from Queensland and had been doing similar work, as a remote area nurse there. Recently engaged to a young man on a station in the state's north, she had applied for a position nearby. The other, Jean Murray, like Goldy, had just arrived from overseas, New Zealand. She too, was inexperienced and she and Goldy feel an immediate bond.

Jean was to be about 200 miles from her, so the two girls promised to keep in touch and to support each other as much as possible.

Following a medical examination, all their qualifications and eligibility to practise in Western Australia were examined and current driving licences sighted. Their police clearances were checked and they were measured for their uniforms, beige or teal blue, with cotton hats to match. 'Hats to be worn at all times outdoors,' they were reminded.

The first week of the orientation simply flew. There was so much new material to be absorbed. The actual nursing and emergency information were no problem for Goldy, but she listened avidly to

116

all the information on Aboriginal customs and taboos. 'Remember,' said the lecturer, 'that customs may well not be the same in different regions. Learn to listen to what your indigenous health workers tell you. Keep your eyes and ears open.Always be respectful. These people have survived for 50,000 years before we came along. They are not ignorant. Their ideas may be different, but they know, far better than we do, how to survive the harsh conditions out there in the bush. It is not our mission to turn them into Europeans, but to help them use our western knowledge to improve their own health and conditions.'

Week two was taken up with more practical issues. The girls teamed up with nurses working in the communty areas in, and around, the city. Goldy went to a primary school, to learn about testing the children for sight and hearing and how to conduct comprehension tests. She visited a high school and learned the requirements of the older children, including sex education. Then she went to an adult day centre, to observe the assessment process and the activity programs there. A day was spent in the immunisation clinic, followed by a written examination about the ages of children and varying doses for their immunisation schedules. There was half a day at the sexually transmitted disease clinic. 'Quite a problem in some of the communities' advised their instructor.

Another day found the nurses working alongside Infant Health nurses, checking and weighing babies. Back in the classroom, they had to learn about the various forms of documentation; they each had a procedure manual, and were told to learn it from cover to cover.They received given copious lists of whom to contact, for what. A time schedule for reporting in on their radio every day, and so it went on. The last day was devoted to a short course on vehicle maintenance, before they were allowed to take possession of their large four wheel drive landrovers. Taken to a sand patch, they were made to bog their vehicles, and then taught how to get out of the bog. Privately Goldy thought she would never have driven into the sand in the first place, but she wisely kept her opinion to herself, in front of the rather chauvinist demonstrator!

They were taught how to make an emergency fan belt; how to repair a tyre with spinifex grass, if you didn't have a spare. Told to stay on the track, even if there was water, rather than attempting to take to the bush to go around it, and most importantly, 'Stay with your vehicle if it breaks down, and always carry spare fuel and plenty of water at all times.'

Eventually, it was all over. They were given their identification badges, fuel cards; numerous books, requisition books, reporting books, records and contacts. Because Goldy's was a new post, or at least a re-opened one, she had to take charge of a new four wheel drive and her vehicle was tightly packed with supplies. She was told that further medical supplies would be delivered within a month. The girls exchanged addresses and radio call signs and had one final dinner together before going their separate ways.

Goldy went back to Sam's to wait for her father, due to arrive later in the evening. When she reached the flat she heard voices, and as she walked through the door, she was very surprised to see none other than Guy Kingsley, sitting drinking beer with her brother. Sam was the first to speak. 'Something came up and Dad couldn't make it Sis, so Guy kindly volunteered to fly down, to drive you back to Walkabout Creek. Isn't that great?' 'Great.' she echoed weakly.

CHAPTER SIXTEEN

THE LONG DRIVE HOME

Goldy was totally dismayed at the thought of spending all that time with Guy, but there was really no alternative.

'Yes,' said Guy, 'we'll need to get moving early tomorrow, we might get as far as Carnarvon,then an overnight stop should see us safely home on Sunday night,'.

Sam appeared totally oblivious to her discomfort, as he talked on. 'You'd better go pack Sis, when a bushman says 'early' he *means* early. Like about four or five am!'

True to his word, Guy drove out of the sleeping city before five am, and they were well out into the country by the time the sun rose. They took a break for breakfast at a roadhouse, before setting off again. Goldy drove the second leg on the bitumen road to get a feel for the big Landrover, and the morning passed uneventfully. Guy was pleasant, as he pointed out things of interest to her, and discussed some of the the conditions it was possible to run into on such a long drive, such as gravel roads, flash flooding, wash-aways, not to mention road trains, caravans and farm vehicles. He was being so nice, that Goldy wished she could shake off her misgivings.

She remembered what her Grandma had said, 'Always go with your instincts, love.'

They broke their journey for lunch. This time, in Geraldton, a large country town. Goldy liked the wide streets and the shops with their shady verandas.

She called into the local Community Health Office to meet the staff, and to drop off a box of Requisition books, she had been asked to deliver.

'Walkabout Creek? Gosh there hasn't been a nurse there for a few years!' said the senior nurse. 'How are you going to survive out there?'

Goldy explained about her dad and the pub, adding she had already spent a few weeks there.

'Well, best of luck.' said the nurse, as she walked Goldy back to the vehicle. 'By the way, who's the hunk you've got with you?' she nodded toward Guy, leaning nonchalently on the door.

'A mate of my brother's', answered Goldy quickly, 'He's helping out with the driving, so I don't get lost!'

The nurse sighed.' I wouldn't mind being lost with him for a day or two! Lucky you!'

Goldy clambered back into the seat as Guy reversed out of the car park and drove back onto the highway. *What was it with all these women? All crazy about Guy Kingsley!* Well she certainly wasn't!

It was evening when they drove into Carnarvon. As they parked on the water front, or the Facine, as Guy called it, the sun was setting, as they sat on the grassy foreshore to watch it slip into the sea, in a blur of gold and orange, leaving behind a sky of flamingo pink, with grey clouds. The palm trees along the walkway stood silouetted black against the pink sky. It was all very lovely.

'Come on, let's get some food into you,' said Guy indicating a small clean cafe near the waterfront, where they perused the menu and settled for fresh fish and chips. Goldy was beginning to relax. Guy was actually quite good company, and she found herself enjoying the journey. He had not put a foot wrong since they left Perth over 12 hours ago. He had made no personal remarks about her, and no snide comments either. Perhaps, after all, she *had* misjudged him. They booked into the rather ramshackle hotel, and were shown two dingy rooms. However, the beds were soft, the linen clean, and the service satisfactory.

'How about a drink before you turn in?' suggested Guy.

She agreed, and they made their way downstairs to the lounge.

'We will have to make another early start in the morning. Shall I give you a call?' he said pleasantly as they went upstairs to their respective rooms.

'Yes please! Then I won't have to worry about sleeping in. I am really tired tonight. Thanks Guy. See you in the morning.'

Goldy was not sure what woke her up, it was still dark. She leaned out of bed and turned on the bedside light. Guy was standing by her bed, clad only his pyjama pants.

'Oh, it's not time to get up yet is it?' she moaned wearily, sitting up and rubbing her eyes.

'No, it's only 3am' he laughed. 'I just thought you might be lonely in a strange place and might appreciate some company.' He moved across the room and sat on the side of her bed.

'Get out of here Guy' she said crossly. 'I'm not lonely and I don't need company. I just need some sleep!'

He didn't move; just sat looking at her. 'Goldy, you have been giving me the eye all day.

Bet you were just thinking about tonight. So what's with the games?' Here I am! He leaned over and kissed her firmly on the lips, as he put one hand boldly on her breast. 'You know you want to and there's nobody here who knows us, nobody to report to Daddy, so what's the problem?'

She struggled away from him. 'The problem is, Guy Kingsley, that I don't fancy you one little bit!

I don't want you in my bed, so will you please leave?'

'Playing hard to get? Just makes it that much more challenging. Come on. You might enjoy it, and I promise you will never think of Charlie Wentworth ever again!' He kissed her again, his tongue exploring her mouth. This time when she pushed him off, he sat back and lifted his hands in mock surrender.

'Okay, Goldy. You win this time. But I will have you eventually, and that's a promise.'

He exited as quietly as he arrived. Goldy lay in bed, her heart pounding. *The cheek of the man! Did he honestly believe he was so irresistible, that no girl could ever refuse him?* She rolled off the bed, padded across the room and locked the door.

Next morning she was awakened by a gentle tapping on her door. Guy called softly, 'Come on sleeping beauty. It's 5.30 and we need to get going. Meet you downstairs in fifteen minutes.'

The sun was rising over the green banana plantations to the east of the town, as Goldy threw her small bag into the back of the Landrover. Guy gallantly opened the car door for her and offered her a hand up. It was as if last night had never happened.

For the next couple of hours, until they pulled up for breakfast, he chatted companionably about his life on Brolga Hills, horses, his sister, Goldy's brother, anything, except what had happened the night before! Before they took off again, he bought some sandwiches and a few bottles of cool drink. 'No road houses where we are going, for a while,' he said lightly.

They shared the driving, and some hours later, when they turned off the main road onto the gravel, he went to great pains to teach her how to cope with the unstable surface; how to avoid skids, how to recognise potholes hidden under red dust, 'bull dust', and what to do if she needed to stop suddenly. Goldy was grateful for his help, and before long she was driving confidently through, the 'back country'. She was very excited to see a mob of kangaroos by the roadside, then a flock of emus ran alongside them for half a mile, before veering off into the bush. Guy pointed out a huge wedgetail eagle, with a wingspan of over five feet. He laughed at her enthusiasm. 'You won't be so happy if you hit a roo or an emu, or if you collect an eagle through the windscreen. They can make a hell of a mess of your car! Also, it's wise not to drive at night if you can avoid it. Kangaroos are an absolute menace, especially out near Walkabout Creek. Not to mention stray cattle!'

It was almost dark when they finally reached the *Grand Imperial*. Danny O'Hara was waiting on the steps to meet them. 'I was beginning to think you two had got lost!' he said jovially.

'Just trying to teach your daughter how to handle these gravel roads, Danny. If she's going to be out on them every day, we need to make sure she will be safe!'

'Thanks Guy, that's very decent of you. I appreciate it.'

Guy smiled wryly at Goldy. 'We wouldn't want anything to happen to you, would we? You have so much to look forward to!'

She felt the colour rush to her face. Her father shook Guy's hand. 'Thanks again. Will you have a drink, or something to eat?'

'No thanks, I need to get home. Are the keys to my car the office? Doug promised to leave them there for me when he got back from the airport.'

'Yes, he did. Hang on, 'I'll grab them for you.' He was back in a minute.

'Here you are!' He threw the keys to Guy, who caught them deftly. He gave Goldy a lingering kiss. 'Don't forget, I'll be waiting for you.' He said softly. Then he ran down the steps to where his car was parked spinning the wheels as he took off in a cloud of dust.

'You two seem to be getting along well.' remarked her father cheerily.

'Don't believe everything you see. I still think he is an arrogant bastard' growled Goldy crossly, as she fled upstairs, leaving her father gazing after her with a puzzled expression.

CHAPTER SEVENTEEN

THE CLINIC OPENS

The next few weeks were very busy, while Goldy established herself in the Health Clinic. She got in touch with a former Health Care worker in the community, as she had been advised. Sylvia Cooper, was an Aboriginal health worker, married to Russ Cooper, a bulldozer driver with the local shire, and she was delighted to be offered her old job back. Sylvia was a big asset. It was greatly to Goldy's advantage to have someone who knew the community so well, and who understood how the clinic was supposed to run. She took Goldy out to meet the leaders in the community; brought in the babies for their health checks and immunisations, and filled her in on who was who, their circumstances and history.

There was a small flat attached to the clinic, which Goldy had been told was hers. When she had told the Supervisor in Perth that she was living at the pub, she had been told quite firmly that the service was a 24 hour one and she was expected to be available at any time. At first she had been upset, wanting to spend as much time as possible with her Dad, but after discussion with the local police sergeant, a compromise was reached. Any night she wanted to stay at the pub, she would switch the call system through to the police station and they promised to alert her to any real emergencies. Actually, when she thought about it, it was quite pleasant to have a little corner of her own, literally a three minute stroll from the pub.

After she had been out to meet the community leaders, Goldy went down to the school, to visit Anne and Jill, and to review the health programs there.

She was impressed by the existing procedures. The 40 children were picked up by a community bus every morning and delivered to school. As they arrived, they were directed to the showers, their dirty clothes discarded for washing, clean ones provided as they emerged from the showers. Any obvious cuts or wounds were dressed, and all the children were checked for lice, scabies, impetigo, and treated before they went into the class room. At lunch time, they were given a hot meal of meat, usually kangaroo, and vegetables and after school, were are sent home in their clean clothes. All the washing and cooking was done by two indigenous women, recruited from the community. Goldy expressed her admiration for the systems they had in place. The teachers were pleased, and the foundations laid for a good combined effort in the future.

If a Specialist medical service visited, it was comparatively easy to bring the children in for appointments for medicals, or follow up from hospital.The clinic in town was open every morning early, until noon. The afternoons were mainly kept for visiting or trying to track down various clients or families. Sometimes it was to check on a dressing or a rash; to check a contact for a sexually transmitted disease, often a difficult procedure. People were reluctant to admit with whom they had sexual relationships, because of strict community codes about different 'skin' groups, which decided who can go with whom. There were harsh tribal punishments inflicted on those who transgressed. This was an area where Sylvia Cooper came into her own! She always knew about everything that was going on in the community, often saving Goldy many hours of futile work. Of course there were the routine duties; the baby weighing, the immunisations, daily dressings; S.T.D contacts and treatments; the school health checks, the interminable records and general reports to head office. Then there were the emergencies.

At first, the level of domestic violence shocked Goldy. So many women arrived at the clinic with large open wounds inflicted, often, by their partners, or sometimes by the other women. Sylvia told her that this was a much bigger problem now that her peope had drinking rights. Some pension days, Goldy was forced to close the clinic because of the threatening behaviour of a minority of her clients. She became very adept at stitching them up, after their frequent altercations!

Part of Goldy's role was to provide support to smaller communities out of town, and to some of the nearby camps, especially if there were children involved. Once a month, she and Sylvia packed up the Landrover, and spent a long day on the road. They set off early with a meticulously planned itinerary, which they gave to the local police, in case they didn't return on time, or had a breakdown.

The two women really enjoyed each other's company. Sylvia liked Goldy. She always found her ready to listen, always willing to learn. She was unlike many of the nurses she had been with in the past! Goldy appreciated Sylvia's knowledge and her good humour, and they worked well together, in a spirit of mutual respect and friendship.

On this particular trip, Goldy woke early at the pub, to the magpies carolling, and a gentle mist drifting over the town. In the quiet peace, she heard the distant barking of a dog. She dressed quickly and ran down to the kitchen for some breakfast. Kevin had already prepared a hamper for her to take and he carried it out to the land rover for her. 'What time will you be back love?' he enquired. 'Shall I save some dinner for you?'

'No thanks, Kev. I have no idea what time we'll be back, but it will be fairly late.'

'I'll leave a tray in the pantry for you then.' he said cheerfully.

After a quick goodbye to her father, Goldy drove around to pick up Sylvia from her small house on the edge of town, and they were soon on their way out, heading north. Their first port of call was *Rocky Glen* station, where the manager's wife had just arrived home from Perth a few days earlier, with twins. The babies were weighed and measured and their nutrition discussed with their anxious mother, and her condition assessed. All was well. From there, they headed east to *Wattle Rise* homestead, where Hector Jones had recently sustained a broken leg in a riding accident.

Goldy had been asked to check on his plaster cast before the RFDS's next clinic run. He also had sutures in his head needing to be removed. While they were there, they checked on some of the children from the camp near the river. A couple had scabies, and after treatment, Goldy left their mothers with some cream and instructions about washing their bed linen. 'Of course you know they won't do it.' said Sylvia. 'They don't understand the causes of infection and disease like we do. They think you get sick because someone wishes it on you. You know, a bit like pointing the bone! But, they will agree with anything you say, because they don't want to offend you.'

After they drove away from *Wattle Rise*, they parked in a shady spot and Goldy took out Kevin's hamper. As usual, he had done them proud. There were tasty pasties, sausage rolls, chicken, salad, fruit, and numerous cakes and biscuits, along with some flasks of tea and coffee.

After a leisurely lunch, the girls took off for *Brolga Hills*, where Goldy was to immunise some of the children many of whom missed the regular clinic.

She was hoping to see Charlie, whom she hadn't seen for a few weeks, but she was disappointed when she was told that he was some 20 miles away, mending a windmill and unlikely to be back before dark.

Guy was not around, which was a relief, but she was happy to have a quick cuppa with Diana and Jack Kingsley. Jack liked the pretty girl. He had been very distressed by the scene at the dance between Guy and Charlie. He was fond of Charlie and he believed that if he and Goldy had feelings for one another, they should be allowed to explore the relationship. Danny was extremely angry and had forbidden his daughter to see Charlie again. Jack wondered if he might feel differently if it were his daughter, Joanne, and he sighed. Danny could be a hard man, when he chose.

After the two women arrived back in town and Sylvia was dropped off at home, Goldy was surprised to hear loud voices emanating from the office at the hotel. She hurried inside and found the police sergeant, Bob Paterson, Sally, her father and Jim O'Malley, the barman, in a heated discussion. Shortly afterwards, Jim was unceremoniously handcuffed, and led across to the police station, swearing that Danny would be sorry for calling the police!

'What on earth....' she began.

'Bastard's been robbing the till!' said Danny, angrily. 'Just did an audit and I reckon he must have milked well over $1000 this year alone, based on average takings. No wonder I am finding it hard to make ends meet!'

CHAPTER EIGHTEEN

MILLY DOWNS

The next day was Saturday, and Goldy was looking forward to her customary lie-in. As she awoke, in her little flat, she was irritated to hear a knock on her door. She glanced at the clock, 6.30 am! *Who has hit whom. at this hour of the morning?* She crawled into her dressing gown and struggled to the door. She was delighted to find Charlie standing on the doorstep, his beloved *Rufus* panting happily at his side. 'Good morning. lovely lady.' he said with an exaggerated bow, as he produced a bunch of wildflowers from behind his back. 'Time to get up, sleepy head. You and I are going out!' He ignored her protests, as he went through to the kitchen to put the kettle on. 'Hurry up and get dressed. I'll make you a coffee!'

Soon they were climbing into his small truck, laughing like naughty children.

'Where are we going?' she asked.

'Wait and see. Its' a surprise!' he said, as he grinned mischieviously.

They drove about five s short distance out of town, before turning off down a little used bush track, by a rocky outcrop. They went on for another couple of kilometers, and topped the crest of a hill, went a short distance, crossing a shallow creek, when Charlie pulled up and turned off the engine.'This place is called *Milly Downs*. It belongs to an old man called Yuri Astanov, who migrated here from Europe many years ago. You might have seen him at the pub. He's a nice old man. He spends quite a bit of time time at the weekend, propped up in the corner with a glass of vodka. Funny old cove with a long white beard. He doesn't do much with the place these days,. He lost his wife and son a few years back, but he doesn't want to move off the station, so I help him out from time to time with a bit of fencing, a few odd jobs or branding. In return, he lets me come out here whenever I like'.

He turned the motor on, as he backed up and turned around. 'C'mon, we had best go and see him.' They turned off onto a narrow track. In front of them was a small, neat house, surrounded by a pretty garden. As they stepped out of the vehicle, an old man, in baggy clothes and a soft cloth cap, came slowly down the steps to meet them. Charlie went forward, his hand outstretched.

'Good morning, Yuri.' I have brought a special young lady to meet you today. Goldy O'Hara. Her father owns the hotel in town. Goldy this is my friend Yuri Astanov.'

Yuri took both her hands, his blue eyes twinkling in his weathered face. 'Hullo, Goldy. I can see you must indeed be special. Charlie has never before brought a lady to see me. You are very welcome.'

'Goldy has never been out in the bush before; she has just come from England, so I thought she should see *Milly Downs*.'

'Ah, you will find it so different from Europe. When my wife and I came from Russia, we never thought we would learn to love it here, but we did. Now I am, how you say? A dinkum Aussie!'

After they had shared a cup of coffee with Yuri, and admired his garden, Charlie was obviously wanting to move on. 'I will be out later in the week to do that fencing for you, but if it is ok with you, I'd like to take Goldy down to the creek for a picnic?'

'Of course, Charlie, of course. I hope, lovely lady, that you too, will come again to see me very soon?'

Goldy moved forward and gave the old man a hug. 'Of course. I will look forward to seeing you again very soon.'

'What a wonderful old man!' she as she climbed back into the truck. They drove a bit farther on, over a hill, until Charlie stopped again. Spread out before them in a shallow valley, was a crystal clear pool, with white sandy edges. A rainbow of multi coloured budgerigars, almost obscured the surface, and huge white ghost gums threw mosaic shadows over all.

'It's beautiful Charlie!' cried Goldy, as *Rufus* scrambled excitedly from the truck and bounced noisily into the water, scattering the birds in a frenzied exodus.

'Yes,' he said happily, 'it sure is. It's one of my favourite places! It is my dream one day to own *Milly Downs*. Not a large property by *Brolga Hills* standards, but I love it. I save almost all my pay so that one day, with a bit of luck, when, and if, Yuri is ready to sell, I might just be able to make an offer on it.. I reckon it would be a wonderful spot to live and raise a family and....' He broke off as *Rufus* rushed from the water and shook himself all over them! 'Damn dog!' he cried laughing. 'Oh well, I guess he's enjoying himself as much as I am!'!

'Me too!' agreed Goldy.

Already the morning sun held promise of the heat to come. Goldy gazed longingly at the cool water. 'I think *Rufus* has the right idea! Is it safe to swim here?' she said, remembering a conversation she had had with Caroline about crocodiles and leeches.

'Absolutely. You will see that creek we crossed on the way in, flows in and out of the pool and it's very clear. I'll beat you in!'

'I haven't any bathers!' she exclaimed. 'If I swim in my undies, is that okay?'

'I promise not to look.' he said, laughing as he stripped down to his.

Hand in hand, like two excited children, they ran laughing into the water, *Rufus* bouncing around them in cicles, barking happily. At first it was so cold it almost took their breath away, but as their bodies adjusted to the temperature, it was cool and refreshing. They swam for about an hour, laughing and splashing, whilst Charlie made a garland of water lilies and twisted it into her russet curls. He held her gently in his arms, as *Rufus* splashed happily. Eventually they left the water and threw themselves down on the white sand. Goldy laughed as Rufus shook himself dry all over them both. 'Get out, horrible creature! Charlie, I am ravenous! Some man I know, would not let me have any breakfast this morning!'

'Not to worry. That same man has a picnic hamper in the truck; courtesy of Mrs Kingsley. What would you like?' Together they explored the contents of the basket - Egg and bacon pie, sausages, hard boiled eggs, muffins, sandwiches, fruit cake and two large thermos flasks of tea and coffee.'God bless Diana!' she sighed, as she tucked into another blueberry muffin, and *Rufus* chewed happily on a cold sausage.

They had another couple of quick dips before spreading out a blanket under the trees, to sleep away the heat of the day. In the late afternoon Charlie started to gather wood to set up a camp fire. 'Gets cold quickly once the sun goes down. Better get your clothes back on, or you'll freeze.'

'Aren't we going back to town?'

'No, not yet. It's all part of the surprise.'

Once the fire was burning cheerily, Charlie fetched a billy can from the back of the truck.

'Absolutely nothing like fresh billy tea.' he enthused, as he filled it from the stream, dropping in a handful of tea, and positioning it over the fire. Soon they were lying back with a mug each of hot, sweet, tea. *Rufus* lolling sleepily with his head on Charlie's feet.

Goldy couldn't remember when she last enjoyed herself so much. She rolled over on her side to face Charlie.

'Thank you so much for sharing today with me. I think it is such a special place. I hope you *can* own it one day.'

He gazed thoughtfully across the darkening water. 'I hope so too, and I hope that maybe a lovely lady will want to share it with me,' He looked at her, smiling gently. 'You are a very special girl, Goldy O'Hara, very special, but hey take a look!' He broke off to direct her attention to the glorious sunset. The sky was now crimson and yellow, with splashes of bright pink, and the soft grey streaks of evening; it was magnificent. The air was thick with the noises of a thousand birds beginning to roost for the coming night. 'Going to be another hot day tomorrow,' he remarked, as the sun finally sank behind the purple hills and slipped from view. Within minutes, it seemed as if the night had thrown a dark star- studded velvet cloak over everything A million pin points of light shone above them, as the moon, huge and bright, appeared slowly above the horizon. It was a magical night.They lay there together on a rug and he pointed out various constellations. 'They are different from the ones you see in the northern hemisphere,' he told her. 'Look there? That's the Southern Cross. There's Orion.'

Goldy snuggled closer to Charlie as she gazed up into the night sky. 'When my mum died, my Gran used to tell me that if I looked up into the sky at night, I might just see a star that would be looking down on me, keeping me safe. Sometimes, when the sky was cloudy, you couldn't see any stars, then I was afraid. Afraid that my mum was gone forever. Do you believe that Charlie?'

'I don't believe our loved ones are in the stars, but I do believe they are somewhere, looking out for us. My Grandfather used to say he would be in the wind; in the dust, in the waterways, in the trees, and if I listened very hard, I would hear him. Sometimes I believe I still can.'

'That's a lovely thought, Charlie.'

'Well, he was a wise old bushman, so I guess that's where he would want to be. In answer to your question, I think your mother is in your heart. You can see her in your mind, and hear her too.'

'Do you believe in heaven Charlie?'

'What, a place where I sit on a cloud, in a long white robe, playing a harp for ever more? No fear! If there is a heaven, it would be a beautiful place with all the people and the animals I love. What about you?'

'I don't know really. I just think there must be something after this life, or there doesn't seem to be much point in being here. Everything has a reason for being, but if death is the end, then I am very confused.'

'Right now, Goldy O'Hara, this is the nearest to heaven I may ever get. If so, this will do me just fine,' He kissed her gently. Her heart gave a flutter, and this time she did not pull back. They lay there quietly for a long time, and then Charlie sighed, 'I can't imagine not being able to look up at that sky every night. I just think it is the most wonderful thing. Pity those poor city dwellers; even if they can see the sky, it is never as clear and beautiful as this.'

She nodded slowly in agreement. "I certainly is beautiful. Thank you for sharing this with me.' She leaned over and kissed him gently on the cheek. The ringing silence of the bush was even more awesome than it had been in town, and Goldy thought it to be one of the most beautiful nights she had ever seen. She wished she could stay there forever, but eventually Charlie held out his hand to her. 'Come on, beautiful lady, I need to take you home!'

Goldy packed up their belongings and the remains of the picnic basket, while Charlie doused the fire, scattering sand on the embers. 'You have to be incredibly careful with fire out here,' he told her. 'if it gets away in this bush, there's no stopping it. It can burn for weeks on a hundred mile front'

Goldy felt disappointment she did not quite understand. 'I wish we didn't have to go home so soon, Charlie.' she said sadly. 'I'd love to stay here with you.'

'I know. I must be mad, taking you home, but I only have a certain amount of will power, and even if you didn't really mind, you are not a one night stand, my Goldy. You're for the long haul, and I want to be there at the end of it! so let's go!'

They drove companionably back into town. Goldy with her head on his shoulder as he whistled happily. Rufus occasionally licking her arm. Charlie dropped her off at her flat, with a lingering kiss and a promise to see her again soon.

Later that night, Goldy called in at the pub to see her father. He was sitting on the veranda, with Grandma Clara, a beer in hand. 'Hullo darling.' he said warmly. 'Where have you been? I missed you.'

'Actually I went on a picnic, with a friend.', she said carefully.

'Am I allowed to know the name of this friend?'

She took a deep breath. 'Actually Dad, I was with Charlie Wentworth. And before you say anything, I think you ought to know that I really like him and I think I am actually falling in love with him'.

CHAPTER NINETEEN

TROUBLE

Danny looked grim. 'No daughter of mine is ever going to be wasted on a murderous swine like Charlie Wentworth! Do you hear me, Goldy? Never! I will see him dead first!'

Goldy began to cry. 'I like him dad, and I want to go on seeing him, with or without your blessing, but I wish you would reconsider please!'

Danny looked at her, her tear stained face gazing pleadingly up at him. She was so like her mother, his beloved Suzanne. His tone softened,

'I can't stop you from seeing him Goldy, but I will do everything in my power to prevent this becoming too serious. Please darling, can you not see that it will be doomed from the start? I have told you before, he has no career prospects, no money; nothing to offer you! What kind of a future will you have with a cowboy, for God's sake?! Why can't you choose someone like Guy Kingsley? He's a much more suitable match and he would marry you tomorrow if you'd have him!'

'Dad, I don't like Guy, and anyway, I'm really falling for Charlie!'

Danny stood up. 'I can't deal with this tonight; we will talk later. Good night.'

Her grandmother lent over and took her hand. 'He'll come around sweetheart. Just be patient'

Goldy sat on the veranda for a long time, finally she sighed, stood up, and walked back to her flat.

As Danny sat on his bed, he swore under his breath. 'You bastard, Charlie Wentworth. You are not having my Goldy, not if I have anything to do with it!' He said nothing more to his daughter, but next morning, he drove out to *Brolga Hills* to see Jack Kingsley. 'Keep young Charlie Wentworth out of town and out of my pub, or I swear I'll kill him. I don't want him anywhere near my daughter!' he raged.

Jack looked irritated. 'Come off it Danny! Don't you think you might be over – reacting just a bit? Charlie's not a bad lad. Sure he made a mistake in the past, but I believe he's paid for it, and I think he deserves to be able to live a normal life now, don't you?'

'Not if that includes my daughter!'

'Danny, I know Charlie's father well. Charlie and his brothers have been well brought up, well educated, and if Charlie and your daughter have a thing going, I don't think there is much you can do about it! She's over twenty one, and so is he.'

'So you think it's okay for him to be sneaking around, taking advantage of my Goldy?'

'I just think you should stop playing the outraged father. Back off a little. Maybe it will pass. If not, you'll just have to make the best of it, I'm afraid.'

Danny strode angrily out of the homestead. He went down to the staff quarters, and saw Charlie saddling up his horse. 'Hey, Wentworth! I want a word with you!'

Charlie stood back from the horse, observing the irate man idly. 'If this is about Goldy...' he began,

'You bet your sweet life it's about Goldy! Just keep away from her. Do you understand me?

'Stay away from my daughter!'

'With due respect, I think that decision is up to Goldy.'

On hearing raised voices, Charlie's friend Doug emerged from the stables. 'Is there a problem Charlie?'

'No mate. Mr OHara was just leaving.' Charlie sprang into the saddle and turned his horse's head to leave.

'You stay away from my Goldy or so help me, I'll kill you!'

'Not if I get to you first!' Charlie growled, as he tipped his hat. 'See you O'Hara.'

Still angry when he pulled up outside the pub, Danny strode inside and angrily confronting his daughter. 'I don't want you behaving like some love sick teenage! Stay away from that murdering bastard. He's no good Goldy!'

'Dad, I know the whole story about Charlie's problems in Queensland. It was all a terrible accident.'

'Accident be damned! You are not to see him again. I'll lock you in your room myself, if I have to!'

'For God's sake Dad! I'm not a child. I'm not a love sick teenager. I really like Charlie, and he cares for me and you can't stop us seeing each other, anymore than I have any say about you and Suzi. I thought we agreed that we were adults, and could make our own decisions?'

Danny stopped, and looked at his daughter before taking her in his arms, 'Darling, I love you and I just don't want to see you wasting yourself on someone like that. He's got nothing to offer you, no money, no real prospects and a dodgy past!'

'But that's for me to decide, Dad.' she replied gently. 'He is a good man; a kind man and he cares for me, as I do for him. Please try to understand.'

He shook his head sadly, as he held her close.

Next time she saw Charlie, she told him what her father had said. 'I can't do this to him,' she cried. 'I don't know what to do. You are two of the dearest things in the world to me, and it seems I can't have you both!'

Charlie was distressed to see her in such a state. He resolved to speak to her father again..Without saying anything to her, he went over to the pub. Kevin was walking out of the kitchen when he heard raised voices in the office. Charlie was angry and Danny was talking loudly over him, quite adamant that he is not going to listen to anything the young man might have to say. Kevin heard him shout.

'What do you mean, you want to marry Goldy? Let me be quite clear about this. You will marry my daughter over my dead body!'

Then he heard Charlie's heated reply. 'Whatever it takes, mate! I will marry Goldy, if she'll have me, and you are not going to stop me!' With that, the young man stormed out of the office and down the steps of the pub.

Goldy was writing up notes in her office when a shadow appeared in the doorway. She raised her head to see Guy standing there. 'Hullo Guy,' she said politely, 'What can I do for you?'

'Actually, it's what I can do for you.' he said with his usual slow smile.

'Oh? and what might that be?' *God he was attractive! Shame about the arrogance!*

She knew she sounded irritable but she didn't care. She had managed to avoid him for the past few weeks , and she was not particularly pleased to see him.

'Well, my mother's organising a fund raising evening for some local ladies on Saturday night, and she would like you to come.'

'Thanks Guy, but I am not driving to *Brolga Hills* at night. It's too far out. Far too many kangaroos on the road'.

'Mum's already got that covered,' he said, unruffled by her terse tone., 'If you drive out about six, she says you can stay the night and drive back in the morning. Please say you'll come. Mum's really counting on you.'

Goldy hesitated for just a moment, then agreed. After all, her quarrel is was not with his mother.

'That's great! See you around six.' With that, Guy was gone.

Her father settled down a little over the next few days, and at least they were able to talk to one another. He promised not to argue with Charlie again, and Goldy promised not to make any life changing decisons, until her brother returned for his mid year holidays.

'How about dinner with your old dad on Saturday?' he said, in reconcilitory tones.

'Sorry dad, I'm helping with a fund raising ladies' night for the RFDS. I'll be staying overnight at the Kingsley's. Let's make it next week.' She kissed him quickly on the cheek.

Saturday night, she dressed up a little to go to Brolga Hills. Diana Kingsley always looked so well groomed! She dabbed on a little perfume and climbed in the Land rover. She refuelled at the garage and started up the motor. She enjoyed the late afternoon drive out,especially if she didn't have to drive home in the dark. It was early evening, as she drew near the homestead. A chill was starting to settle over the bush, heralding a cold night. Initially, she had not been happy to stay out there, but now she was glad she did not have to face the cold, lonely drive back into town.

She parked the vehicle and walked up the front steps to the door, but before she had time to knock, it was opened by a beaming Guy. 'Hullo Goldy O'Hara! What a nice surprise. Come in. Here, let me take your things.'

A little bewildered by his welcome, she handed over her coat and overnight bag, as she walked inside.

'Tell me,' he continued, 'What are you doing here? Not that it isn't great to see you!'

'You asked me to come tonight,' said Goldy, irritably. 'For the RFDS Fund raising.'

'No Goldy, that is *next* Saturday!'

'I'm *sure* you said tonight Guy!'

'Well now you are here, you had best stay to dinner, anyway,' he said gallantly. The fire has just been lit.'

'Thank you, but perhaps I'd better clear that with your mother first,' she said, looking around for Diana. The place was eerily silent. She turned on him. 'Where is your mother?'

He did not meet her gaze, and looked a little embarrassed,

'Just what is going on here Guy?'

He closed the door and faced her. 'Nothing is going on, Goldy, but Mum's not here. She's gone to Perth for a few days; Dad and Jo too. At least you must have a drink and something to eat before you go.'

He poured two glasses of wine, handing her one as he walkd across to the fireplace and put a log on the burning embers, watching as it caught, and a spurt of yellow flame rose up the chimney. He made polite small talk, for which Goldy was grateful. She hadn't been alone with him since their journey back from Perth, which he appeared to have forgotten, much to her relief.

'I was about to have some dinner, Won't you join me?' he asked pleasantly. 'Cook left a nice casserole in the oven.'

She sat down reluctantly, admitting to herself that it did smell good, and she was hungry. He put the food on the table and poured them each another glass of wine. 'This isn't so bad is it? he said pleasantly. He suddenly reached across and took her hand. 'I'm sorry Goldy, I *did* deliberately tell you the wrong day! I just wanted to spend some time alone with you, so you and I could get to know each other better. I really like you a lot, more than a lot, actually, and I don't think you really appreciate what I can offer you. One day *Brolga Hills* and all this, will be mine and Jo's and I would like to share it with you. If marriage is what it takes to have you, then I'll marry you, but I want you, and I *will* have you.'

Goldy looked coldly at him, as she stood up. 'I think I would like to leave now. Could you get me my coat please?' She put the untouched glass on the mantlepiece He looked amused. 'And if I refuse?'

'Then I'll just be a bit cold!' She fumbled in her handbag for the car keys. Damn! They were in her coat pocket!' She turned back to face him, 'I want my coat, please.'

He looked amused. 'No, not yet.'

'Okay. I'll just have to walk!'

'Don't be ridiculous, Goldy. It's a forty minute drive. How could you possibly walk that distance in the dark? Apart from which, you'll freeze to death!'

'I'll go down and get one of the boys to drive me then!'

His smile faded and Guy narrowed his eyes, 'That's right. You've a soft spot for the Wentworth boys, haven't you? I remember now. Not so standoffish with young Charlie, I suspect. I think I might have to persuade Dad to get rid of him. I am sure I can find a good reason why we should sack him. Of course, if it is really important to you, I could possibly be persuaded to change my mind.'

Goldy was suddenly afraid. She made a move toward the door, but he was quicker.

'Oh no! You are not going anywhere, until you and I have a little talk. You know what I want, and I usually get what I want.' His tone was threatening. 'Just a couple of hours and then I'll give you your keys. Or,' he said silkily, 'you might just decide to stay after all.' He moved quickly to put his arms around her and began to kiss her. With all her strength, she pushed him backward and he almost fell to the floor. He straightened up slowly, his face dark with anger. 'You have played me for long enough!' he growled hoarsly. 'I told you I *will* have you and I will, so you may as well give in now.'

Goldy thought about screaming, but as if he could read her mind, he said. 'Don't even think about yelling for help. I doubt whether anyone would hear you. They wouldn't come even if they did. They'd probably think one of the camp girls was up here having a wild night. Of course Charlie Wentworth might come, but I'd have to tell him that you and I were having crazy sex, and just got a bit noisy! He might even take a punch at me, and then he *would* have to go.I mean, a charge of assault, with his record, would probably see him put away for another few years, what do you think?'

'If you force me Guy, I will go to the police,'

'I don't think you will, Goldy' he said confidently. 'Anyway, who's going to believe you? You come out here often; many people probably think we are already a couple, and of course, there is the matter of Charlie Wentworth's job. I think we understand one another.' He pushed her gently onto the sofa and stood looking at her.'You know Goldy, I didn't want it to be like this between us. I want you to come to me willingly. I really do care for you, but you just keep giving me the cold shoulder, and every time you do, I want you more. You are driving me insane. I just want you to like me, not fight me. Could you not try? I'll make it worth your while. I'll do anything you ask, if you'll only try.'

When he saw he was making no progress whatever, he changed tactics. 'Okay Goldy. Have it your way, but at least, stay for the evening! That's all I'm asking. I promise I won't touch you."

Goldy thought long and hard. Finally, against her better judgement, she said. 'I'll stay for a little while, if you promise to leave Charlie alone, stop bullying him? Promise you will not try to get him sacked, and stop telling everyone he is a murderer. If you agree to that, I will stay for an hour or so, and then you will give me my keys, okay?'

He seemed relieved. 'I promise. Just stay. Please!'

She thought, quite dispassionately, that as a male specimen, he was quite magnificent, and had she not been in love with someone else, she might have been tempted. He was certainly handsome, and could be very charming when he wanted to be. She decided that as a purely erotic experience, he would probably be quite fun. But her heart was already Charlie's.

The evening passed fairly easily, with Guy doing much of the talking. He told her the history of *Brolga Hills* of the struggles his great grandfather had to establish the property. He shared his hopes for what he wanted to do when he was finally in charge of the place. He talked again about the plans he and Jo had to improve their stock horses, and the cross breeding of cattle on the station. Although it was all new to Goldy, she found it interesting. Guy wanted to know about Goldy's life in England before her mother's death, and what hopes she had for her future.

When she finally stood up to leave, Goldy realised she had drunk quite a lot of wine during the evening, and she felt anxious about driving home. Guy saw her dilemma, and gallantly gave her the key to the spare room.

'It has an ensuite, so you will be quite self-contained in there,' he told her. 'I will see you in the morning. I'm sorry if I came on a bit strong, Goldy. I thought maybe you were just playing hard to get, but I was wrong, Please forgive me, I hope we can stay friends?'

Early next morning, Guy walked her outside to her car. As she started up the motor, he leaned in the window and kissed her on the cheek. 'Thank you Goldy, for staying. I did enjoy your company. I'm only sorry it started off so badly! But if you ever change your mind about Charlie, just remember, I'll always be here, and I can promise you a better life than he could ever hope to do.'

Goldy, drove back to town, to her flat. She went inside and sank down in the armchair. She had been in some strange predicaments in her life and done some strange things but this one really took the cake! She thought wryly of the nurse in Geraldton on the way up from Perth, who so desperately fancied Guy. *I guess he wouldn't have had any problems with her last night!*

CHAPTER TWENTY

THE RESCUE

That evening she was sitting on the veranda at the pub, waiting for her father, when she saw Charlie's car pull up. She jumped up to greet him, but her smile faded as he angrily jumped onto the veranda and grabbed her arm.

'How stupid do you think I am? Treating you as something so special!' He hissed. 'I saw you leaving the homestead this morning! Had a hot date with the boss's son did you?! How *could* you Goldy? *How* could you do that to us? Spend the night with *him!* Don't bother to deny it! I know Mr and Mrs Kingsley and Jo are away, and your car was there all night.You were there, alone with him! Anyway, he's already told me this morning what a hot little piece you are! Don't speak to me, do you hear me? I have absolutely nothing to say to you. We're through!' He shoved her away from him as he turned, jumped in his truck and was gone. The entire demolition of her world, took less than three minutes.

Her father, unseen, had witnessed the entire thing. He came over and put his arm around her.

'Did you spend the night with Guy?' he asked gently.

'Yes,' she sobbed, but it wasn't what you think!'

'You don't have to make excuses to me darling. I am just relieved you have at last come to your senses!'

She turned away from him in despair. How could she ever put things right with Charlie?!

A few nights later, she was sitting in her flat listening to some music, when there was a loud knock at the door. *Charlie*! She thought for a moment, as she ran to open it. It was not Charlie, but his distressed brother, David, who stood on the doorstep.

'David! Come in. What's wrong? Is Charlie all right?'

He looked anxious. 'Can you come Goldy? Charlie's in the pub drinking himself silly and he's talking about shooting Guy Kingsley and your Dad! Dan tried to talk to him, but he took a swing at him! I think they're about to call the police!'

'David, I am probably the last person in the world he wants to see right now, but I'll try.' She grabbed her keys and shut the door behind them. They ran the short distance to the pub, and she could hear raised voices as she went up the front steps. 'Get Charlie out of the front bar, *now!*' she instructed David. 'Tell him someone needs to see him urgently; tell him anything, but just get him out of there! Hurry!'

After what seemed like ages, David emerged from the bar, dragging a very inebriated Charlie by his shirt front. When he saw Goldy, Charlie crumpled up and would have fallen if they had not grabbed him. They lowered him into one of the big cane chairs on the veranda. Goldy put an arm around his shoulders. 'Hey, what do you think you're doing my handsome cowboy?'

He looked at her blearily.'Is that you, my Goldy? They are all trying to take you away from me!' he mumbled. 'Guy, your Dad. They' re all against me!'

'Nobody can take me away from you darling. It's all talk.'

'I feel awful, Goldy. I have been drinking for days and my head hurts! He sank his head into his hands, 'Oh, God, how my head hurts!'

She made a quick decision. 'Quick David, help me get him down to my flat. He can sleep it off there.' She was grateful that everyone assumed that his brother would take Charlie back to Brolga Hills, so they were able to get him to her place, unseen.Together, she and David removed his boots and socks, then his jeans and shirt. 'They smell as if they've been there since Sunday, too.' she said wrinkling her nose. 'I'll get a basin and we'll see if we can't clean him up a bit.'

They worked quickly, but before they had finished, Charlie was asleep. Goldy covered him with a blanket, before bending to kiss him lightly.

'Gosh, Goldy.' said David, 'I'm a bit confused. I thought you and Charlie were the real thing, but then he tells me you spent the night up at the homestead with Guy, when the boss and his wife and daughter were away. Charlie's real broken up about that!'

'David, it wasn't the way it looked, honestly. Yes, I was at *Brolga Hills* on Saturday night, Guy got me there on false pretences. He told me his mother wanted me out there to help organise something, but when I got there, she wasn't there', she paused. 'He told me that she had suggested I stay the night, because she knows I don't like to drive out there at night. Guy deliberately gave me the wrong date; I didn't know, until I arrived, that everyone was away, and I was there on my own with him. Anyway, to cut a long story short, he refused to give me my car keys, when I knocked him back, so I had to stay all night. I slept in the spare room with the door locked. End of story.'

'So you and Guy weren't, eh, having it off, so to speak?'

'I don't even like Guy Kingsley, so I would hardly be going out there for a secret rendez-vous, would I?'

'Why didn't you tell Charlie this?' he asked her.

'I tried, but he didn't give me a chance to say anything. He just abused me and drove off. I haven't set eyes on him all week."

'He's been hitting the bottle real hard,' said David. 'He thinks the world of you, you know.

I've never seen him like this over any girl before.'

'And I feel the same about him. Look he can stay here with me tonight. Just one other thing. Can we get him some clean clothes? These smell like something died in them!'

He laughed. 'We usually keep some clean gear in a box in the back of the truck, in case..' he hesitated and looked away, 'in case we get lucky!'

'Well I think he just got very lucky.' she laughed.'

'Also, can I bring *Rufus* inside? He's looking pretty sorry for himself."

By the time David had collected some clothes from the back of the truck, and returned with *Rufus* in tow, it was dark. Goldy shoved the dirty clothes a bag and gave them to him to take home.

'Would you like something to eat? I'm sure Charlie will be hungry when he wakes up. I don't suppose he's eaten much all week. Rufus neither, I bet! A bacon sandwich and a coffee do you?'

'Righto, that sounds great, thanks'.

Goldy busied herself in the kitchen 'Just give me a minute or two.' *Rufus* followed her hopefully. He sat looking at her with sad amber eyes, head one side, tongue lolling from his pink mouth. She found some minced meat in the fridge. 'Here you are old boy. Poor neglected creature!' In no time at all, she had organised a tray with bacon sandwiches, cake, fruit and a jug of coffee. When she got back to the bedroom, she heard David and Charlie talking together, very quietly.

'Brought you guys something to eat, and some coffee.' she said cheerfully,

'Thanks Goldy,' said David 'but I need to eat and run, to get back to Brolga Hills tonight, I can pick Charlie up tomorrow if you like. About nine in the morning if that's okay?'

After grabbing some food, and gulping down his coffee he made a move to leave, 'Can I leave the dog here with you too? He howls like a banshee when Charlie's not there.'

'That's fine, David See you in the morning, and, thanks.' She walked him to the door. Then she went back to Charlie, who was ravenously devouring a bacon sandwich.

He looked up sheepishly as she sat down next to him. 'Goldy', he said softly, 'David told me what happened on Saturday, with Guy. I feel such a bloody idiot. I should have known better. Can you ever forgive me for doubting you?'

'There's nothing to forgive. I would probably thought as you did, if I had been in your shoes,' she said, holding him close. 'Honestly, it is all okay. Just promise me you won't go after Guy!'

After some more food and strong coffee, Charlie fell asleep in her arms. *Rufus* curled up contentedly on the end of the bed. She set the alarm for 7.30 and snuggled down with Charlie. She felt warm and comfortable. It seemed the most natural thing in the world to have him here beside her. She awoke at first light, to find him looking at her. It felt completely normal to see him there. He kissed her tenderly.'I think it's time we sorted a few things out.' he said. 'Can't talk now. I have to get back to the station and get some work done, or I'll be looking for another job! How about I come in to town on Saturday night, you can cook me dinner, and we'll talk. What do you say?'

Goldy kissed him. 'I say that is a brilliant idea!' She cooked them both breakfast and David arrived soon after. After a quick goodbye, she stood in the doorway watching tenderly as he drove away with Charlie and *Rufus*. She felt a little confused. He obviously liked her, but had made no moves on her, apart from a few sweet kisses. Perhaps she felt more than he did? The time was fast approaching when she would have to find out for sure.

Goldy worked hard on Saturday, preparing dinner for Charlie. She had a roast leg of lamb with roast vegetables and a homemade gravy, and she baked an apple pie to serve with cream to follow. She picked up some wine and beer from the pub, and begged some cheese and crackers from Kevin, after swearing him to secrecy. She took special care with her makeup and hair and wore a pretty blue dress that she knew suited her. She intended that tonight,she would try to discover just how serious he really was. He had been very angry when he thought she had spent the night with Guy, but that could have been bruised ego. There was much about men she did not really understand.

He arrived promptly at 7.00, and she noted, with pleasure, that he too had made an effort. He wore a clean white shirt, cream moleskin trousers and his unruly curls were freshly washed, he smelt of some manly cologne she couldn't quite place. He greeted her warmly with a kiss, and again shyly produced a bunch of wildflowers from behind his back. 'Beautiful flowers for a beautiful lady' he said with an exaggerated bow.

Dinner was served and Charlie proved to be the perfect guest. He opened the wine and proposed a toast 'to the hostess with the mostest'. After he had finshed, he sat back contentedly. 'It was lovely thanks, Goldy, that's the best meal I've had since I left home!' As they cleared the table and she prepared to wash up, Charlie picked up a tea towel. 'See,' he laughed. 'I'm really quite domesticated!'

As they finished up, he slipped his arms around her waist and kissed her gently on the cheek. 'Come and sit down with me. I want to talk to you.'

They sat close together on the soft sofa in the lounge room. He held her close and kissed her gently. 'What is it about you Goldy O'Hara? I just don't seem to be able to get enough of you. You aren't like the other girls I've known. You just fascinate me!'

She smiled gently. 'I don't know Charlie, but I feel the same about you.'

'Let's put on some music and dance' he whispered, as he held out his hand to stand her up and lead her into the lounge room.

Goldy put on some music and they began to dance around the room. Charlie held her close and nuzzled his face into her sweet-smelling hair. 'You smell good enough to eat', he murmured, 'just a well we've eaten.or you might be in danger. Come to think of it, you might be in danger anyway, of having me fall in love with you!'

'That wouldn't be so bad would it?' she asked smiling up at him.'I was really beginning to think you were not that wrapped in me. You never made any great advances and I was wondering if you might have someone else tucked away somewhere!' She was unprepared for the shock on his face.

'Goldy! the only reason I haven't said much before, is because I didn't want to frighten you off, and I'm not sure I'm much of a catch for you. Your dad certainly doesn't think so! I didn't want you to think I was just a randy cowboy out for a bit of fun. You are so special. Don't you remember what I said to you at *Milly Downs*? You are not a girl for a one night stand, you're a girl for life. You are the loveliest girl I have ever met in my life, but I figured you could have anyone you wanted, so I didn't think I had much of a chance.'

'Oh Charlie, you are an idiot! You are a very special guy. Any girl would be lucky to have you care for her, and that includes me.' He looked so forlorn that she kissed him softly on the lips. The effect on them both was electric. Goldy felt light headed and her knees felt like jelly. Charlie kissed her back with a passion that threatened to overcome them both.

Suddenly gone was the laughing young man, as he wrapped his arms tightly around her and they moved gently to the music. He kissed her tenderly. I don't think I can fight this much longer,' he groaned.

'Then don't darling.' She said as she took his hand and stepped through to the bedroom, his lips hardly leaving hers. At this point, *Rufus* looked bored, and climbed onto the sofa and went to sleep

They stood quietly, with their arms around for what seemed like an eternity, until Charlie said quietly, 'Are you sure this is what you want Goldy?'

In answer she kissed him again, this time with more passion. 'I have never been more sure of anything in my life,' she whispered. He slowly undid the buttons on her dress, and as she stepped out of it, she reached out for him, He stopped suddenly and looked at her in wonder. 'You are quite the most beautiful creature I have ever seen.' he whispered hoarsely. 'I must be dreaming.'

He kissed her softly, moving from her face, down onto her neck and then to her bare shoulders with increasing urgency.

Goldy suddenly stiffened. 'Charlie, I want you too, but I am not on any form of birth control or anything'. She said anxiously.

He laughed softly.'Don't worry my darling. Would it upset you very much if I said I carried condoms in my wallet? Even lonely cowboys get lucky sometimes!

'Though never this lucky', he added hoarsely.

Goldy laughed as she raised her arms to embrace him. 'Charlie Wentworth, you're impossible, but I think you are amazing!'

There seemed to be no shyness between them and the night was glorious for them both. Neither one was inexperienced but it seemed to them both that this was a first time coupling of such joy and passion, that both of them were left exhausted but fulfilled. It was like nothing either had ever experienced before.

As they lay quietly in each other's arms, Charlie said gently, 'You know the French call this, *le petit mort*, 'the little death' I never understood why, until now. God I'm tired! But that was so wonderful, sweetheart. I love you so very much. By the way, do you love me?'

'Of course, my darling.' She kissed him but he was already asleep.

When Goldy awoke next morning, Charlie was already up and about, appearing at the end of the bed with a cup of tea and a plate of hot toast. 'Good morning darling girl!' he exclaimed. 'I thought you'd need some sustenance after that wonderful night.' He kissed he soundly as he sat down next to her on the bed. The kiss quickly erupted into passion as the tea and toast lay forgotten. The urgency overcoming them both. 'You are impossible, and I love you' she said breathlessly, as he lay down beside her and she opened her arms to receive him.

'Darling, I have to go,' he said finally. 'I'm supposed to be helping Doug repair some stock fences today, but I promise I'll try to get back as soon as I can. I love you.'

Goldy watched him dress, through sleepy eyes, then he gave her a final kiss, as he let himself out of the flat. She curled up in the warm bed and drifted back to sleep, thinking about him. 'My Charlie Wentworth. What a man!'

CHAPTER TWENTY ONE

TADAWALLA

Her new job kept Goldy very busy, she enjoyed her interaction with all her patients. She remembered an old Scottish tutor at Guy's, who always said, 'Every patient can teach us something, about them, and more about ourselves'. Every day, she planned out a well balanced program. See those ten childen; visit x number of contacts of the latest sexually transmitted disease; complete the immunisation schedule for baby so and so. It never seemed to go to plan! Those children were not at school today. No contacts could be identified! The baby for immunisation had gone to some far distant place to a funeral with its mother. She could waste an entire day driving from place to place, as she was frequently told, 'He was 'ere sister, but now he bin gone some udder place, mebee in town, mebee not.'

Every afternoon, she was alotted time to call in on the two-way radio to her nearest base. She was delighted to hear her friend Jean Murray, from her orientation course, calling in. They were able to talk briefly and share experiences which strengthened the already strong bond between the nurses. After she talked to Jean, she felt more confident and less professionally isolated. The Flying Doctor visited monthly, and although it was often Caroline Brearley and Dr Ben Morris, who attended, Matt was not always the pilot, and Goldy soon got to know all the crews and she liked them very much. Occasionally she had to call them in to deal with emergencies and that could be pretty stressful at times.

Late one afternoon, there was a great fuss going on outside the clinic.A crowded tray-top truck was parked outside and an angry crowd of Aboriginals was milling around it. As Goldy went to investigate, she saw an old man, barely conscious, with a bloodied rag wrapped around his head.

She recognised him as one of the most senior elders in the community. She quickly summoned Sylvia, 'What is going on here?!'

After a few hurried words, in a language still unknown, to Goldy, Sylvia reported back.'This man, Ningali, has been promised a young woman as a bride but one of the young men decided he wanted her too, so he took the girl and he hid her someplace. Then the old man, he got mad and threatened to punish this young man, so the boy hit Ningali over the head with an iron bar, and now it looks like Ningali is dying!'

'Well, we must bring him in and see what can be done,' said Goldy. 'He looks like he might need to see the doctor pretty quick.'

Sylvia took her by the arm, 'Goldy, if you treat him here and he dies, you might be in big trouble. The community might say it is your fault. Anyway, if he dies here, no people will come inside the clinic for one year. That is the rule here, when somebody dies.'

'Well, he can't just be left to die in the car park!' said Goldy indignantly. 'Bring him in here!'

When she examined the old man, Goldy felt a sinking feeling. He was barely conscious, his face contorted with pain and fear. His blood pressure was rising rapidly, his pupils were uneven, barely reacting to light. He showed the cardinal signs of intercranial pressure – bleeding inside his skull, which if not contained, could force his brain matter into his spinal cord cavity , called 'Cloning', it was invariably fatal.

She ran to the radio to call the RFDS. She explained the situation and ended, 'I need a plane as soon as possible to get this man out of here and to hospital! It an extreme emergency!'

Dr Ben came on line. 'Goldy? I'm sorry, but we don't have a plane that can get to you before at least seven o'clock tonight. All the pilots are out of hours, - basically flown more than seven and a half hours in 24 hours We will come as soon as we can! Can you keep him alive for a couple more hours?'

'God, I hope so, Ben.' she said, trying not to panic. 'Right now I have about two hundred agitated people outside. I don't know what will happen if he dies!'

'Just do your best, Goldy. You're a good nurse, so just do your best.' He gave her some instructions, which she faithfully recorded, before signing off.

'Call me every hour.' Ben had instructed. 'I'll try to talk you through. Good luck!'

Goldy checked her watch, 3.30. It would be at least four thirty or five o'clock before the RFDS would be there! At 4.30 she called in again. 'Patient still non responsive; blood pressure still going up. Pupils uneven; reacting sluggishly.'

At 5.30, 'Patient deteriorating; non responsive, blood pressure, stable but high.'

Goldy looked up as Sylvia ushered in an old man with a shock of long white hair. He was painted with red ochre and white clay. Half clad, with a kangaroo skin cloaked around his shoulders, and a necklace of animal teeth around his neck. Before Goldy had a chance to protest about this wild man in her clean clinic, Sylvia said urgently. 'This is Tadawalla, he is the medicine man from Ningali's community. He says he can help, if you will let him.'

'He couldn't do any worse than I am,' sighed Goldy. 'Yes, okay.'

'He says we must put the old man on the floor. He needs to be near his mother, the earth.' said Sylvia. Together, they lifted him gently from the bed and laid him flat on the ground. Tadawalla crouched over the old man, his hand in the middle of Ningali's chest, level with his heart. He began to stroke his own arm from shoulder to finger tip, all the time chanting in sing-song tones.

'What is he doing?' whispered Goldie.

'Passing strength from his body into Ningali's.' she answered quietly.

Then Tadawalla pressed his fingers firmly over the old man's eyelids and spoke sharply to him. Goldy drew a sharp breath, as the patient opened his eyes!

At 6.30 pm she called Dr Morris. 'Conscious state lighter, blood pressure high but remaining stable, and by the way, I have a local medicine man here with me now!'

Ben gave a laugh, 'Good for you Goldy! Share the blame around if it goes wrong! You're doing real fine, honey. We will be there in half an hour.'

Tadawalla sat looking at the old man for a few minutes; then he said something directly to Goldie, who shook her head as she enquired, 'What is he saying, Sylvia?

'He says, too much blood in the old man's head. He says he must remove it.'

'Tell him to go for it. We've nothing to lose.' *Except my Registration,* she thought desperately.

From under his kangaroo cloak, Tadawalla produced a short piece of thick fencing wire, and an empty corned beef tin. He ran his hand over Ningali's skull, coming to rest near the cut over the left ear. As Goldy watched in horror, he began to force the wire through the bone, twisting it wildly. When he was satisfied with its position, he pressed the skull near the wire and a slow stream of blood began to run into the tin. After a further ten minutes, he sat back, and directed Goldy to examine the patient. Ningali was now conscious and began to talk slowly. His blood pressure was slightly lower, and his pupil reaction was better. Goldy felt more optimism than she had all day.

Dr Ben radioed in 'On our way in, we'll on the ground in 15 minutes. When we get closer, the pilot will fly over the town, so you can get the flares lit to guide us in. Be there soon.'

Goldy called the police station. 'Flying doctor on his way. When the pilot flies over, can you please light the runway flares? Thanks a million. Sylvia will drive them here to stabilise my patient for transfer. Thanks.'

'Will do Goldy!' came the cheery reply from young constable, Brian Wilcox. 'I'll let Sergeant Paterson know!'

Shortly after that, they heard the noise of the Beechcraft Baron overhead, and Sylvia took off in the Landrover to meet them. Goldy tried to explain to Tadawalla that the plane would be takng the patient to a big hospital to make him better. He seemed to understand and nodded his approval.

A short time later, the Dr and Caroline appeared at the door, Goldy almost cried with relief. She told them what Tadawalla had done, but neither of them appeared at all phased.

'Strange things far beyond my comprehension go on out here. I've given up questioning', was the doctor's only comment. After checking the patient's vital signs, they strapped him to the RFDS stretcher, and put him in the back of the landrover.

'Are you coming down to the strip with us, Goldy?' asked Caroline.

'Yes, I'd better!' said a relieved Goldy. 'I'm suppposed to stay at the strip until you take off.'

'Good. Doc and I can ride in the back with the patient so there will be tons of room.'

'Perhaps Tadawalla would like to come,' said Goldy, but when she turned to ask him, she found he had gone.

Down at the strip, the plane was being refuelled as it waited for take off. As soon as the stretcher was loaded,the engines began to turn over. The police and other locals, added more oily rags to the 44 gallon drums lining the strip and as they flared brightly, the little plane began to taxi. Just when it seemed it might overshoot the runway, it rose sharply and soon disappeared, as a speck of light in the late evening sky.

Goldy felt exhausted. It had been a long day. She drove Sylvia home, and then returned to her flat, where she fell onto her bed, fully clothed, and was soon asleep.

The next day she received a relayed message from Royal Perth Hospital. Her patient had been to theatre where the surgeons had performed burr holes to relieve the pressure in his skull and he was expected to recover. Job well done!

That afternoon, Tadawalla appeared at the clinic, as mysteriously as he had disappeared the night before. Goldy explained, as simply as she could, what the surgeons had done in Perth. He listened intently, and then a beaming smile lit up his face. 'I understan' you Missus. They do same like me!' He mimed forcing his fence wire into his skull.

Goldy laughed. 'Yes Tadawalla, same like you! You saved Ningani you know.' she said seriously to him. 'You stop him from done finish.' He looked thoughtful for a moment, then he said,

'No Missus. Togeddar we save im!' 'Okay.' she said, laughing. She was still laughing, when she realised that once again, he had gone.

Next day was scheduled for immunisations. Goldy always dreaded this day. The children who were booked never turned up, and those who did were often months, if not years behind schedule. So it was with great amazement, she opened the clinic door to find more than twenty children patiently waiting for her. Next to them, now divested of his paint and jewellery, sat Tadawalla, smiling happily.

Sylvia spoke to him briefly, then she smiled. 'He says that you and he together, make very good medicine, so he has brought the children for your medicine, so they will not get sick!'

If head office wondered about the improved immunisation statistics from Walkabout Creek, they never said anything, and Goldy didn't either!

CHAPTER TWENTY TWO

THE PARTIES

It was Danny O'Hara's 55th birthday. There were cards and greetings and Kevin baked a special cake with 'Happy Birthday Boss', in blue icing. Goldy had bought him a silver case for his Cuban cigars when she had been in Perth. She had his initials 'DJ' engraved on the outside. Inside, was a small inscription *'To the best Dad in the world. Love Goldy'* Danny was thrilled with it. 'I will carry it always, it's lovely.Thank you darling.'

Even Sam excelled himself and sent a very grand fobwatch, on a gold chain. Suzi bought him a new Akubra hat, although he protested it would need at least twelve months of dust, sweat, and hard wearing, before it would be a genuine bushman's hat. They had a special dinner at the pub, to which everyone was invited. Except of course, for Charlie Wentworth. There was much laughter and raucous singing, and everyone had a good time.

All Goldy's concerns about Guy Kingsley were gone. It was apparent that he had kept his side of the bargain. Charlie seemed to be having an easier time on the station. Guy no longer bullied him or reminded everyone of his history. 'He must have decided I wasn't such a bad guy.' Charlie said to Goldy, one evening. She said nothing. She seldom saw Guy these days, although she saw Jo often. Jo was even giving her riding lessons.

'My God, that must be a first!' laughed Jack, when he heard.

Goldy hoped that Guy had given up on her, and that he would keep continue to keep his word! Now she had her own flat, life was much easier and she saw Charlie most nights.

He was still upset with her father. 'He just will not give me a chance to prove myself worthy of you.' he complained bitterly to her.

'Don't worry, my darling, Grandma and I are working on him and he is starting to come around.' she reassured him.

Jack Kingsley was still at odds with Dan over the mining lease, he had taken out over *Brolga Hills*. Whenever the two men tried to discuss it, tempers flared on both sides. 'You are an envionmental terrorist!' accused Jack

'And you, are a stubborn old traditionalist! Better me, than the big companies, Jack!'

So the arguments went back and forth. Guy always took his father's side, but it seemed nothing was ever resolved. Diana merely shrugged her shoulders. 'They can sort it out,' she said to Jo, 'They are supposed to be grown up men'

One afternoon, a battered old chevrolet pulled up outside the pub. It was the new barman, and he introduced himself as Troy Anderson. He had been working in a pub in Hall's Creek, and looking for a change, when he heard that Walkabout Creek had a vacancy at the hotel for a new barman.

'Your dad's got a good reputation around the traps.' he told Goldy. 'I heard he was a good boss, so here I am!'

Danny was equally pleased. 'He has excellent references and some of the regulars know him too. Seems he's been in Nullagine, Marble Bar and Fitzroy pubs over the last 20 years. Comes highly recommended.'

Troy was a mountain of a man, who proved to be a true gentle giant.

In no time, he was an integeral member of the staff, and as Sally remarked, it seemed like he had been there for ever.

Goldy felt sad about Jim O'Malley; she thought he must have had a good reason for stealing money from the bar, but what it might have been, she could not imagine. After a short jail term, he had disappeared from sight.

The Reverend Franklin did not frequent the pub, in keeping with his religious beliefs. However, Father John Flynn occasionally came in 'for a medicinal brandy'! Goldy saw a great deal of them both, as she managed some of the more complex social issues in town. Despite their differences on things to do with doctrine, they could both always be relied on to provide a blanket, food or clothes for a very disadvantaged persons, or family. She especially loved Father John. The old Irish priest was an absolute mine of information for Goldy. What he didn't know about the culture and customs of the local indigenous people just wasn't worth knowing. Many times he saved Goldy from what could have been embarrassing breaches on her part.

Goldy liked both ministers. Reverend Franklin was a charming man too, and he had a font of stories and information about the district. He and his gentle wife Rachel, lived their faith to the full, and were much respected by their small congregation. But it was Father John who accepted their flock's explanations that, 'Dis not God's business, dis Black fellers' business.' Thus ensuring that his church was always full to bursting on Sundays, when the hymns rang out in glorious discord.

However when news came through of Rev. Franklin's imminent transfer down south, there was genuine sorrow in Walkabout Creek. The ladies of the town decided to put on an afternoon tea, to say thank you and goodbye, to these good people. The reverend Franklin announced from the pulpit that there would be a small farewell party the following Saturday, and invited his followers, of about twenty five people, to attend. Father John did the same, to his larger congregation.

Everybody who could, did their bit for the party. Kevin cooked cakes, sausage rolls, chickens, sausages. He made trifles, half non-alcoholic, for the true believers, and the other half heavily laced with brandy. Large Pavlovas with cream and fruit graced the trestles, draped with white sheets from the nursing post. There were jugs of fresh fruit juice, lovingly squeezed by hand, and bottles of coca cola, all supplied by the pub. Diana Kingsley promised a large farewell cake, and the teachers made sandwiches.

'Enough to feed an army!' said Sally, Sylvia made some Emu rissoles, which she said, her husband adored!

Finally Saturday arrived. A sedate group of the town's people gathered on the grass under the trees, outside the Uniting Church. Each person had a dainty plate of food and a teacup of refreshment. When, as one of the oldest residents, John Jenkins, the Post Master, stood to pay tribute to the Reverend and his good wife, everyone gave him their full attention.

However, no sooner had he begun, when he became aware that his audience appeared to be distracted. Slowly, they all turned to look out across the lonely bush. In the far distance, there were large clouds of red dust, rapidly approaching the town fom various directions. There were small dark centres in these clouds, like a giant swarm of red and black bees, bearing down on the town, making a huge roar in the still afternoon.

As they drew nearer, they could be identified as vehicles. Vehicles of every shape and size, and from which, as they pulled up outside the church, literally dozens of people emerged, all laughing and waving, as they called out to the Reverend . 'We all bin comin' to say goodbye to you and Missus!'

Before anyone could say a word, or move a muscle, the crowd swarmed past the tables, grabbing food with both hands. Goldy looked around in time to see her piece of chicken disappear from her plate! Within ten minutes, the tables were bare. All the soft drink bottles had gone, and as quickly as they had arrived, the crowd disappeared!

The stunned party goers, gazed forlornly after the vanishing hordes, and the empty tables, until Sylva recovered enough to say, 'Anyone for an Emu Rissole?'

The two church men were to learn the hard way, that, 'Come one, come all' was part of the culture. One of the best examples of socialism in the world! It was a send off that was long remembered in Walkabout Creek.

oooOooo

Although her nursing training had been one of the best in the world, Goldy still found herself at a loss, on occasions. During one of her morning clinics, a small boy had appeared. 'Scuse me Sister. My dad, he say can you come and see my mum. She gotta sore eye.'

Goldy assured hm she would see her later that afternoon. The boy left, apparently satisfied, and she continued working. After lunch she went out to the camp where the family lived. She found the boy, but no sign of his mother.

'Where's your mum?' she asked him.

'She 'round the back.' he said, as if she was asking a really dumb question.

As she walked through sand and spinifex to the back door, she saw the poor woman. She did indeed have a sore eye! A long spear was embedded in her eye socket, pinning her to the ground! When her husband emerged from the shanty, Goldy asked him what happened. He looked at her for awhile, then he said casually. 'She wouldn't stop naggin', naggin', naggin'. So I jest shut her up.'

That was another case for the flying doctor! The woman lived, but of course lost her eye.

One of the old women at another camp, had had a crippling stroke a year before. She spent her days sitting on an old mattress, in a dry creek bed, with a tin of water and a tin of tobacco. She couldn't walk, but she was always cheerful, when Goldy called to see her. One day, she noticed the children were playing a game nearby, involving an apparently modern wheelchair.

'Why don't you use your wheelchair?' she asked the old woman.

'Wheels no good Missus.' she replied sadly. Closer inspection revealed the tyres had torn badly on the river stones. 'And,' the old woman continued, ' he can't go in der sand. Git stuck.' Goldy discovered that the expensive chair had been supplied by a city hospital, when the woman had been discharged and flown home, some weeks previously.

When Goldy returned to the clinic, she called the hospital. She asked to speak to the Occupational Therapist, who had supplied the chair. A pleasant voice advised her that she had the right person, so Goldy asked if some thorn proof solid tyres could be provided, and told her of the difficulties in the old woman's environment. The distant voice immediately lost its warmth. 'Honestly, you nurses need to use your initiative! All you have to do is put down a few slabs from her home to the main road!'

'Thank you,' said Goldy, politely.' I'll just need to work out how many slabs are needed for three hundred miles!' She put down the phone, shaking her head as she went back to work.

Another of her old women appeared frequently at the clinic, bleeding profusely from severe cuts around her head and face, inflicted by her husband. Goldy had seen them together in town and they had always seemed to get along well, in between these savage beatings. One day, as she stitched up yet another gash, she asked Tom 'Why do you keep bashing Mary up like this?'

He looked surprised at her question. 'Well, Missus, she keep on runnin' away!'

She turned back to her patient, 'And why *do* you keep running away, Mary?'

'Cos he keep on bashin' me, missus!'

Sadly, one day he hit her too hard; as he told Goldy.

'I sorry Missus, but dat Mary, she done finished'

There were times when Goldy wondered if she was making one scrap of difference to the lives of the people. She confided to Charlie, that it often seemed like nothing she did improved their situation. 'They just don't seem to get it sometimes.' she wailed. 'Last month, I gave out milk powder to the young mothers. I taught them how to mix the powder to the right strength, and when the tin finished in two weeks, they were to come and get more.'

Charlie nodded. 'and'?

'They never came back, so I went out looking for them. They told me that if they didn't use as much powder, it lasted a whole lot longer! Honestly Charlie, I feel like I'm fighting a losing battle!'

'Did any of them come back for more?' he asked.

'Only one.' she wailed

'Then you had some success, didn't you, darling? You have to learn to take little steps; to celebrate small victories. You can't change the world overnight, 'specially one that has been going quite well without us for fifty thousand years!'

On one of her frequent visits to Milly Downs, Goldy told Yuri of her concerns. To her surprise, he laughed. 'Do you know Miss Goldy, every nurse who has ever been out here in the last 30 years, has had the same problem. You know, you cannot expect these people to just accept what you tell them. They have been doing things their traditional ways for so many years. It is hard even for someone like me from a different culture to adapt to the way of life here, and yet I come from a European country. How much harder for someone from a culture 40,000 years old.?'

'You make me feel so much better, Yuri,' said Goldy. 'but how can I really help?'

Yuri puffed on his pipe for a minute or two, before he answered. 'I think you have to listen, to learn, and to respect what the people know and believe. Then you try to build on that, until they trust you enough to try it your way.'

'You're right you know, Yuri.' Goldy then told him of her experience with Tadawalla and the head injury. 'The principle of treatment was the same as modern doctors use, but he did it in a very primitive way, but the result was the same.' Goldy leant forward and hugged him. 'You are a very wise man Yuri!. Thank you. I feel so much better.'

On another day, as she and Yuri sat on the veranda of his small home, watching Charlie repair the garden fence, Yuri said, 'Are you going to marry my Charlie, Miss Goldy?'

Goldy laughed. 'Well he hasn't actually asked me, but I guess if he does, I will.'

'Don't leave it too long; life has a habit of making decisions for us if we don't get there first. When I first came here, my Natasha and I had so many dreams. We wanted to get everything here up and running, before we had some more children, but....' The old man put his hand to his head, and Goldy quickly leaned over and took his hand. 'Oh Yuri, do you want to tell me what happened?'

Yuri took a deep puff on his pipe, before he began. ' As you may, or may not know, my family were Russian Jews in St Petersburg. My father was an engineer in the service of Tsar Nicholas. When the Tsar was murdered, my parents and my sister Tatiana, escaped to Poland, where he set himself up as an engineer working for a company in Warsaw, where I was born. We were very happy there, but when the war looked as if it would darken Europe, he decided that the family should leave. My sister refused to leave my mother, who refused to leave my father, and I, as a schoolboy, was sent to a cousin of father's in France, and went to a little school, near Marseille.'

'Why did your father not leave?' Goldy asked gently.

'I really do not know,' he said sadly, 'maybe he felt he had to make a living for his family. Maybe he really didn't want to see what was coming, but I just don't know. What I do know is that when Hitler invaded Poland, my family were arrested by the Gestapo, sent to a prison camp, and we never heard anything from them ever again.'

Goldy felt tears pricking, but she swallowed hard. 'and you, Yuri, what happened to you?'

'Well, my relatives were killed in the war and I was pretty lucky not to be found or imprisoned, and the brothers at the school cared for me until I finished my education, and went to work. Then I met my darling Natasha. She worked for a local dressmaker. You know, she was the most beautiful thing I had ever seen!' Yuri smiled, and for a few moments seemed lost in memories.

Suddenly, as if he suddenly remembered his visitor, he continued. 'Ah Natasha. Like me, she had lost all her family. We married very soon after we met. So great was our love, you understand. She was everything to me. Then we had our son. Life was so wonderful for us.'

'Why did you come to Australia?' asked Goldy. 'It must have been so different from your life in Europe!'

'Well, there wasn't much work there at that time, so I decided I wanted a better life for my family, and to, how do you say? 'make a long story short', we ended up in Australia. The little money we had saved up, bought us this bit of land out here at Walkabout Creek. There was nothing here, no house, no fences, nothing.'

Goldy shook her head. 'I can't imagine how hard that must have been, Yuri!'

He shrugged. 'We were young, we were free, and we had each other and the boy. We were working for our future. This,' he waved an arm around, 'I built with these two hands. My Natasha, she worked so hard, and she make a lovely home for us here. She plant a garden and she grow vegetables so we can eat. She sell them in town so we can buy a generator for electricity, and old man Kingsley, he give me a pump for the water, send some nice young men to help me with fencing, and then he sell me some cattle. All this we do so our boy will have a good life one day. We hope to have more sons, but we decide to wait until we have a better place.'

Yuri stopped, he pulled a handkerchief from his jacket and wiped his eyes. 'It was my son's birthday, and Natasha, she wants to make for him a special day. She wants to go into town to get some ice cream and maybe candles for his cake. It has been raining, you know. Very much rain, and the creek is running very fast. I tell her to wait and we will go together, but she didn't want to wait, and she and the boy took off in the old car.

When she get to the crossing, the water was flowing fast. She should not have tried to cross, but she did. They were swept away. Both drowned. Their lives, and mine; all over, all gone.' Yuri began to weep quietly.

'But you stayed on here?'

'I had nothing anywhere else. Natasha and I had built memories here, so I stayed. People have been kind. Like your Charlie. He often does work for me. Will never take any money from me.

He is such a good man. Don't let him get away, Miss Goldy!'

They had another cup of tea together and then Goldy drove back into town. She felt sad for Yuri. With a bit of luck, maybe she and Charlie would share a love like that.

CHAPTER TWENTY THREE

DAVID WENTWORTH

Joanne Kingsley leaned idly on the white railing, watching with contrived disinterest as David Wentworth took the young filly through her paces. A three year old Quarter horse, *Misty*, was being retrained for the work for which she was bred; herding and cutting out cattle on the station. After a year at the hands of an relatively inexperienced new stockman, *Misty* had developed some bad habits, which David had been asked by Jim Kingsley to address, and to get her back up to scratch.

Much as she hated to admit it, Jo knew David was good with horses; very good. Earlier she had asked her father if she could work with *Misty*, but he had insisted that David take on the job. As she watched him, she appreciated her father's judgement. David handled the filly gently but firmly, talking quietly to her, as she watched him and whinnied appreciatively.

Never force a horse, lead her gently Jo reminded herself. *Get into her head; understand how she thinks; let her know what you want; work together.* David was doing that magnificently.

Jo had always been a top class horse woman. Riding since early childhood, she was fearless. There was not a horse that she could not, break, train, ride or handle. Her father claimed she was the best rider in Walkabout Creek.

She rode at every event, flat races, cross country, rodeos and had won every cup and ribbon available.

The boys on the station bragged about the boss's daughter although they were all in awe of her accomplishments.

She was a very pretty girl, who could be the belle of the ball, but was far more at home in jeans and a checked shirt. Charming and articulate, she could nevertheless swear with the best of them if the occasion demanded it. She herded cattle with the men, was involved in branding, vaccinations, castrating. She erected fences, built stables and carted water, feed and hay. Could mend a windmill and anything else the station boys could do; usually better.

Many of the young men who either worked or passed through Toolarook, had made a play for the feisty young woman, but apart from the occasional dalliance, Jo largely ignored them. As she confided to her father, 'Most of them just want to prove they can beat me at something, so they can brag to their mates!'

That was until the Wentworth boys, David and Charlie, arrived from an outback station in Queensland. Their father was a schoolmate of Jim Kingsley, and he had known them all their lives.

The two handsome young men were very different. David, the younger, was tall and dark, with a shy smile that belied his dry sense of humour. He spoke only when he had something to say, and made little small talk. He played a guitar, and she could often hear the melodic sounds drifting up from the staff quarters in the peaceful evenings. He was awkward around women and few were determined enough to stay around long enough to get to know him better.

His brother, Charlie, blonde with flashing blue eyes and a hearty laugh, had all the confidence that David lacked. He charmed and cajoled his way through life, every day.

Both men were superb horse men; a talent not lost on Joanne, whose initial reaction ranged between admiration and jealousy and a determination to beat them both at any cost. As she watched David working with *Misty*, she could not help but notice his broad shoulders, long legs and a fine muscular physique. A very nice looking man, she admitted to herself. He in turn, noted her interest and whilst pulling his hat down farther over his face, gave a cursory nod in her direction. 'Do you think *Misty* is coming along okay?' he asked

'She was always a good little filly, until some city slicker got hold of her. Not hard to get her back to form, she's a natural.' Feeling embarrassed at being caught showing interest, Jo turned away from the railing. 'I've got to go. Work to do in the stables. '

'I'll give you a hand. I have almost finished here for now.' He started to lead *Misty* to the gate.

'I'm fine thanks.' called Jo over her shoulder.

David followed her closely, and after giving *Misty* a drink and some feed, went into the stable, where Jo was repairing a shattered door, destroyed by a skittish horse the day before. David sat in companionable silence on a bale of hay, watching her work.

Finally, she could stand it no longer. 'Don't just sit there gawking! Make yourself useful!' She tossed him a screwdriver. 'I'll drill the holes – you put the screws in!'

He did as instructed, and soon the job was done.

'Want a cuppa?' she asked, wiping her hands on her jeans.

'Sounds good. Thanks.'

They walked up to the kitchen, Jo several paces ahead of him. She poured out two mugs and cut some fruit cake. David observed her furtively from behind his mug. *'What a fantastic woman she was,* He wished he could tell her how he felt about her, but he didn't have the words. Charlie would have known what to say, but David could only munch quietly on his fruit cake and dream of how nice it would be if he could only kiss this sweet girl and perhaps sweep her off her feet.

She finished her tea and stood up. 'I'm going into town this afternoon. Want to come?'

'Yeah. That'd be good.'

'Meet you at one o'clock at the car.'

'Thanks.'

'Like pulling teeth, trying to talk to David.' She said to herself as she walked away. *'Gorgeous man, but hard work. Possibly not worth the effort, but then again, maybe he was!'*

Meanwhile, the man in question was castigating himself for his lack of finesse and inability to talk to the pretty Miss Kingsley. He sought out Charlie, who was cleaning a saddle in the tack room.

'What's up bro.' Charlie asked, noting David's glum expression.

'Nothing really. I just wish I knew how to tell Jo how I feel about her. I really like her a lot, but I'm no good with words. Anyway, it probably wouldn't be any use. After all, I would hardly be in the running what with her being the boss's daughter.'

Charlie stopped polishing the leather. 'Have you said anything to her at all?'

'No, not really. You know what I'm like around women.'

'Then how the hell is she supposed to know how you feel, if you don't tell her?'

'I thought women just knew these things,' said David lamely.

Charlie looked skyward. 'Honestly Dave! At this rate you'll be a bachelor forever! Just talk to her will you! Just tell her you think she's great and take it from there.'

David looked doubtful, but said he would try. A few days later, he was watching Jo as she worked with her horse, a beautiful paint mare called *Justa*, down in the training yard. When she was finished, she started to walk up to the stables, and stopped to speak to him. 'Any tips?' she said cheekily.

'You don't need any from me.' He said falling into step beside her. 'Where did you learn to work so well with horses?'

Jo looked pleased, and she blushed prettily. 'Thanks for that. My Dad taught me everything I know. He was the finest horseman around the district before he had his accident. Sadly, he doesn't ride at all anymore, but he keeps an eye on me.'

'You've learned your lessons well. I don't know many people who do it better. You really love that horse of yours don't you?'

'Oh yes, more than anything else,' she said, 'but then I doubt you could understand.'

David smiled, his eyes dancing. 'try me.' 'Well,' she began slowly, 'when you love a person, you can never know what they are thinking, or even if they really love you in return.

You can never be sure if, or when, they will transfer their affections to someone else – but my *Justa* here, well she loves me as much as I love her; without reserve. I love her, trust her, care for her. She, in return, trusts me. She doesn't care if I am grubby, tired, sweaty; she still feels the same whether I am dressed up, or in my work clothes. She always gives me her best. She doesn't throw a tantrum if I talk to another horse! I understand when she's having an bad day, and she seems to know when I am too. She is never judgemental, she doesn't care if I'm pretty or not, fat or thin, she just accepts me the way I am.'

'Actually, I do understand Jo.' David nodded thoughtfully. 'I felt like that about my big bay, old *Fergus*. Absolutely broke my heart when I lost him. He was 29 years old, but he had a cancer which was causing him a lot of pain. I had to have him put down, but honestly, it was like losing one of my family. I don't think anyone else really appreciated how much it hurt. Some stupid guy told me to get over myself. He said 'It was only a bloody horse, for God's sake!'

Jo grimaced, and reached out to pat him on the arm. 'Oh David, that was so cruel! Did you tell him how it made you feel to ride?'

'I tried, but it's really hard to explain to someone who doesn't ride. When I'm on a horse, the adrenalin flows with the speed, the wind, that feeling of being one with that amazing power under me. All the stresses just melt away, and I'm in another world. I think it is the most exhilarating feeling you could imagine. Maybe flying might come close, but I don't know.'

'You do understand!' said Jo enthusiastically. 'I once told my Dad that if I could find a man as kind as loyal as my horse, I'd probably marry him tomorrow!' Realising what she had said, she coloured prettily. ' Well, perhaps....'

'I might hold you to that one day,' said David, and they both laughed.

'You're pretty good with horses yourself, David. Where did you learn?'

'On my Dad's place in Queensland. He only uses horses to work the cattle. A bit of a traditionalist! I have been on or around horses ever since I can remember.' He laughed. 'As a kid, I guess I found it easier to talk to horses than people. Still do!'

Jo noted that as David talked on about horses, he became more animated, and she found his good looks enhanced. *'Quite a guy really.'* They continued to chat, and Jo felt that they were starting to develop a closer relationship.

CHAPTER TWENTY FOUR

THE RACE

'Tell me,' said Jo, 'Are you going to enter the Walkabout Cup this year?'

'Well, hadn't given it much thought, but might be fun.' David said thoughtfully.

'Bet I will beat you!' Jo said laughing.

'How much?'

'Five quid, says I will beat you by 500 yards at least.'

'You're on!'

The day of the Walkabout Creek Cup dawned. There were several events on the program, the highlight being the Toolamulla Cup; a cross country race, twice around the town's perimeter, ending with a double circuit of the Imperial hotel and on to the finishing line. For the five previous years this had been won by Joanne Kingsley on '*Justa*'. The cup had pride of place on the mantelpiece at *Brolga Hills*.

There were ten entrants for the race, and as they headed out toward the starting line, Jo looked across at David. 'Good luck,' she called, 'you'll need it!'

He tipped his hat. 'Just have your money ready!'

Under starter's orders, the riders, and their horses waited impatiently. The horses whinnied in excitement. The starter's pistol rang out, and the race was on. Jo was quickest to start, Bob Stuart from Carton Downs followed, David not far behind. At the end of the first round, Jo was still leading, but Bob Stuart had been passed by David Wentworth, who was now only a short distance behind her. Jo encouraged '*Justa*' on. 'C'mon girl, don't let me down!'

Their positions remained unchanged, until on the third leg, around the hotel for the first time. David surged ahead giving her a cheeky wave as he passed. She pushed the mare faster, the adrenaline pulsing through her. This was living! She meant what she had told David, she never felt more powerful than moving with a speedy, willing horse under her. She was going to give him a run for his money. Thought he could beat her? She would show him!

Jo urged *Justa* forward, but she could never explain exactly what happened next. From flying along, the wind in her face; the excitement of the race, she felt the mare stumble and felt herself catapulted into the air, only to be stopped mid-air, crashing to the ground on her shoulder and head, her foot caught up in the stirrup, as Justa struggled to regain her balance. Startled by the unnatural weight on her side, she panicked and bucked and twisted to rid herself of the burden. When that didn't work, she took off at full gallop, dragging Jo, bouncing on the rough red dirt.

David Wentworth, was laughing as he pulled ahead of Jo. He heard her call out and looked over his shoulder to make sure she was not catching up, but to his horror, he saw the mare stumble, and Jo, caught by a stirrup being dragged over the stony ground. As he wheeled around, the terrified mare started to gallop off the track and into the bush.

David went after her and finally managed to grab the reins and bring her to a stop. He jumped from the saddle and quickly freed Jo's foot from the stirrup to lay her gently on the ground.

Her face was pale and covered in blood from a nasty gash on her head. Her left arm was twisted in an unnatural angle; she was breathing but unconscious. David crouched next to her, cradling her in his arms.

The thought that she might die was utmost in his mind, and the sudden realisation that here was the woman he had looked for and wanted all his life. He felt unaccustomed tears on his cheeks as he gently stroked her hair.

By this time, a crowd had gathered; the police, other spectators and Jack and Guy Kingsley had arrived, with Goldy, in a four wheel drive. Goldy quickly leapt down to examine her friend.

'Get her into the jeep and back to the clinic! Careful! Guy, you go ahead and call the Flying Doctor.'

'Jack, can you go and pick up Diana and bring her to the clinic? Sergeant, can you drive David and I back to the clinic?'

Within minutes they were at the clinic. Goldy kept a careful watch on Jo's airway, applied a pressure dressing to her gashed head, and gently splinted her arm. She made careful recordings of her vital signs, whilst Jo remained unconscious. David sat, white faced, at her side.

Within the hour a small plane was heralding the arrival of the flying doctor, and Jo Kingsley was on her way to hospital, her mother by her side. David and her father, took off by road for the distant hospital, leaving Guy behind to take care of things. 'I'm no good at this hospital stuff!' he announced. 'I'm more useful keeping things running at home. Dad will keep me up to date with what's happening with Jo.'

For several days, Jo's condition continued to cause grave concern. The doctors were worried by her failure to regain consciousness. Her skull had not fractured, but there was massive bruising and swelling and it had been necessary to drill burr holes through the skull to relieve the pressure. They had to give her a tracheostomy, so that a breathing tube could be inserted through her neck into her trachea, and attached to a respirator to pump valuable oxygen. Her blood pressure was dangerously low, and she had swelling in her abdomen. The doctors sent her up for a C.A.T Scan, which confirmed that she had a tear in her liver. The doctors then went into conference. There were two options. One for immediate surgery to suture up the tear, or two, to insert a tube into the artery supplying the liver, to block it with gel, to reduce the bleeding. Eventually, they opted for the latter and noted an instant improvement in her condition.

The doctors were pleased, but cautious. They warned that she was still seriously ill, and, her ultimate recovery would take weeks, if not months, and would take some rehabilitation before she could return to her normal pursuits. All that was dependent on her continuing to make progress.

Diana and Jack sat white and shaken by their daughter's side. David sat opposite. Jo's arm and shoulder had been set and were in a plaster cast. Diana reached across and touched him on the hand. 'How can we ever thank you David, for saving our daughter's life?'

'Anyone would have done what I did.' He said shyly. He could have added, *'There is something else, I love her, I didn't know how much, until now.'* But he didn't. As her parents slipped out for a coffee, David spoke softly to the doctor. 'I feel so useless! Is there anything I can do to help?'

'Just talk to her, about normal things. People can often hear, although they appear to be totally unaware.' After the doctor had left the room, David took a deep breath.

'Well young lady, I have to tell you that you scared me half to death when I thought I might lose you; and….it made me realise just know how much I love you.' He bent low over the bed, closing his eyes and kissing her fingers. 'and by the way, you made me lose the race!

Diana came back alone and David decided to go out for some air, but had only taken a few steps out of the room when Diana called him back. 'David! Come quickly!'

He ran back in time to see Jo, with her eyes open, moving her head gently from side to side.

'Oh thank God!' Diana was in tears, David took her in his arms for a comforting hug.

The nurses, then the Doctors, came in, sharing the happiness at Jo's improvement. Later, after the respirator and tube had been removed, Jo lay quietly observing them, then she said quietly, 'Mum, What's going on? Where am I?'

Diana stroked her head gently. 'You had an accident, darling. Don't you remember? You came off *Justa*, and she dragged you quite a way with your foot caught in the stirrup. David stopped her and got you off. If it hadn't been for him, you probably would not be ....' her voice trailed off as she choked back a sob.

David patted her awkwardly on the shoulder. 'It was just lucky that I was the one near you at the time.'

A shadow passed over Jo's face. 'Is my *Justa* okay?'

'Absolutely,' David reassured her, 'she just freaked out a bit for a few minutes, but she's just fine.'

Jo smiled weakly, 'Thank you. So, I guess I owe you five pounds do I, David?'

'No, I never finished the race.'

'But you were winning! Don't tell me you came back for me? I know how important it was to you to win!'

'Winning a race and losing you Jo! Doesn't sound much of a victory to me!' He kissed her gently on the cheek, and she found herself drowning in his gentle dark eyes. She couldn't resist teasing him. 'I probably wouldn't have come back for you, you know!'

'Oh, I think you might have. I'm really quite worth saving, you know!'

Once Jo was declared to be out of danger, Jack went back to Brolga Hills and a week later, Diana was persuaded to fly home when David opted to stay with Jo for the immediate future. In the days that followed, they both enjoyed quiet companionship, playing cards, or reading , and generally helping her to pass the time. He helped her with her rehabilitation, walking with her up and down the hospital corridors and stairs, or out in the garden. They talked a great deal, finding more and more that they had in common. This continued for some weeks, until one evening, Jo said quietly, 'When I was very sick, I imagined all sorts of funny things,' she paused. 'once I even thought I heard you say you loved me! Imagine!'

David smiled as he took her hand. 'That was no dream, Jo. I do love you. I think I always have. It wasn't until I saw you lying on the ground that day, that I really knew for sure. Tell me, do you feel the same?'

Looking into his handsome face, seeing his gentle smile and his soft dark eyes, and his obvious concern for her, Jo smiled back at him. 'How could I not? Of course silly! But I promise, I will beat you next time!'

David started to laugh, soon Jo joined in, and the nurses smiled as they heard the sounds of merriment from Jo's room.

About a month later, they both returned to Walkabout Hills, where David officially asked Jack for his daughter's hand in marriage, to which he happily agreed. The wedding was to take place when Jo felt well enough to walk down the aisle. 'I want to ride to my wedding on *Justa*,' she iinsisted. David assured her that would be the perfect start to their married life! Three months later, she managed just that. She and Goldy sewed a gold saddle cloth for *Justa*, and then helped by her brother Guy, she rode from the hotel to the church on the edge of town, where David, Father John, her family and friends celebrated their wedding. Nobody could doubt the love shared by the young couple. Jo was radiant in her beautiful gown and hooded cape. David looked so proud and so handsome in his tuxedo. Jack was almost as proud, and Jo's mother, Diana, shed tears of joy and pride

oooOooo

There was no racing for Jo for a long time, but it was always her intention to win that cup again – and to beat her husband!

Her opportunity the following year, with the repeat of the Walkabout Cup. Despite the doctors suggesting that perhaps it was a little unwise, Jo insisted she wanted to ride. 'I have to win my cup back!' she said. 'I have to beat David and win my five pounds back!'

She worked quietly with *Justa* for some weeks, until she felt confident that victory would be hers.

The morning of the cup dawned warm and clear. David was concerned about his wife, but knew he had no hope of discouraging her from riding. Once he saw how determined she was, he concentrated on his own preparation. In his own quiet way, he was just as competitive as she. He wanted that cup so badly.

As they drew up to the starting line, Jo felt a quiver of fear, as she recalled her last terrible experience. Once the starter's pistol rang out, all that was forgotten, as a surge of adrenaline sent her on her way.

Jo and David were neck and neck for the first two circuits. She gave him a cheeky smirk as she pulled slightly ahead. Good old *Justa!* As they began the final circuit of the pub, Jo was still slightly ahead. She glanced back to see David gaining fast on her left hand side. She urged her mount ahead. 'C'mon girl!' He drew level, only half a length between them. The finishing line was not far ahead.

Suddenly, Jo thought about her husband; his kindness and concern for her; how he had thrown the race before by coming back for her when she fell. She was almost overcome with emotion, and for just a moment, she eased her pressure on the mare. There was a flash as David passed her, and a roar went up from the crowd, as he flew past the winning post.

The joy and triumph on his face was evident, as he pulled up, and waited for Jo to catch up.

She leaned across to shake his hand, 'Congratulations,' she said, and was surprised. She really meant it.

Later she speculated that perhaps she could have beaten him, but it really didn't matter.

She had met her match and she was not going to jeopardise that for anything – not even the Walkabout Cup. It would be on the mantelpiece at *Brolga Hills* anyway.

CHAPTER TWENTY FIVE

THE DISAPPEARANCE

Goldy and Sylvia had been out on a station run, and arrived back in town in the evening. She called in to the pub to see her father. She saw her Grandmother sitting quietly reading in the lounge. 'Hi Grandma! Have you seen Dad around?'

'No darling, I haven't seen him since yesterday. I thought he might have gone out with you for a run.'

'No. Why would he?'

'I don't know, but nobody has seen him since yesterday, when he said he was going out for a little while. Maybe he went out to *Brolga Hills* to see Jack Kingsley.'

'Well I was out there today and nobody mentioned that he'd been there. Have you asked Suzi? She usually knows where he is.' Goldy felt a wave of anxiety.

'She doesn't know either love. She's as worried as I am.'

'Is his car here?'

'No, it isn't.'

'Perhaps he's broken down somewhere?'

'Kevin has been out ten miles in all directions but no sign of him at all. I think we'd better go see the sergeant first thing in the morning.'

'You're probably right, he's broken down somewhere, but he would stay with the car. He's too good a bushman to go wandering off.'

Early next day, Goldy put a call out over her radio. 'If anyone has seen my father, Danny O'Hara, from Walkabout Creek, or his vehicle, would they please radio in.' Nothing. She went down to the local Police Station to see Bob Paterson. The two policemen greeted her with a smile. 'What I can I do for you young Goldy?' asked the sergeant.

'Actually, I am looking for my Dad. I don't suppose either of you have seen him recently?'

'Come to think of it, no. I haven't seen him for a couple of days. Have you Brian?' said the sergeant turning to his young offsider.

'No Sarge. I haven't. I was talking to him the day before yesterday, but I haven't seen him since.'

Goldy felt tears threatening. 'I'm afraid something may have happened to him, an accident, or a snakebite. I just have an awful feeling!'

'I' m sure he's okay, but we will have a look around for him.' he said kindly.' Don't you worry, He'll turn up tomorrow!'

Danny O'Hara did not 'turn up', on the morrow, nor on any other day. He had simply vanished. A distraught Goldy rang her brother. He was equally concerned. 'Keep me posted Sis.' 'If he's not found in a day or so, I'll drive up. Chin up! I'm sure there is a perfectly good explanation. He'll be fine.'

A full scale search was launched. Every able bodied man, native tracker and policeman was out looking for the popular publican. Not a single clue was found for his disappearance.

Every station within two hundred miles was alerted, but no sightings were reported. The trackers followed his tyre tracks for twenty miles, before they disappeared into water and rocky ground. A helicopter was called in. Nothing.

'He *must* have had an accident!' cried a distraught Goldy to her Grandmother.

Clara was her usual calm self. 'Nobody knows the country around here as well as your dad. I'm sure he will be alright.'

Goldy went again to the police station. 'He might have had an accident or broken down somewhere!'

'No, we would have found some evidence, had that been the case,' said Bob Paterson gently. He paused, then sitting back in his chair, observed her solemnly. 'I have to ask you this. Do you know of any reason why your father might have staged his disappearance? Money worries; woman trouble? Was he depressed? Upset? Or ill?'

She shook her head. 'No Bob. Nothing. This is not something Dad would ever do. He would never just disappear like this!'

Next day, Sam arrived. He had managed to get a flight up in the police helicopter. Goldy ran to him. 'Sam! Something terrible has happened I just know it!'

Her brother held her tight. 'We'll find him Sis! We'll find him.'

Jack, Guy and their staff, including Charlie, David, united in their concern for Danny, searched tirelessly, using trucks, motorbikes and on horseback, for any sign of the missing man. Nothing.

It was evening, about four weeks later, Goldy and Clara were sitting on the veranda, when the police car pulled up in front of the hotel. Sergeant Paterson slowly unfolded himself from the driver's seat as Goldy ran expectantly down the steps. 'There's some news?' she inquired anxiously.

'Well, of sorts. We have found the truck; but no sign of your dad. I'm sorry.' Apparently the truck had been sighted from the air, over one hundred miles from Walkabout Creek, crashed and burnt out in a rocky outcrop, about two miles off any track. There was no sign of the driver, Danny O'Hara. The Sergeant told them he was calling in the detectives from the city.'Goldy, it is only fair to warn you, I'm afraid your father may have been a victim of foul play.'

Another week passed. A Tracker told the police, there was no evidence at all, that Danny had ever been in the vicinity of his vehicle where it had been found. He was not the one who had abandoned it.

Charlie took some time off and stayed in town with Goldy and held her whilst she wept, and for once, nobody said anything about his presence. Guy and Sam waited grimly at the pub, for some word from the police, about what what to do next. Finally a breakthrough! Just two miles from the pub, one of the local children retrieved a relatively new Akubra hat, which Suzi was able to identify as the one she gave Danny on his birthday. The searchers immediately turned their attention to the new area, and within days, six weeks after his disappearance, came the news they had all been dreading. Danny O'Hara's body had been discovered in an abandoned mine shaft, less than two hundred yards from where his hat had been found.

The forensic team flew in from Perth; the body was retrieved and flown out for an autopsy, as the detectives began their questioning.

The small town rallied around Clara and the two young people most affected. Goldy cried until there were no more tears, and Sam sat in stunned silence, as the reality of the tragedy unfolded. He rang his grandmother in England, to give her the terrible news, as Goldy clung to Clara. A stony faced detective faced them across the table in the dining room.

'I'm really sorry, but I'm afraid I have more bad news for you. The autopsy shows that your father was shot, through the throat, before being dumped down that shaft.' He let the severity of his words sink in, before he continued, 'This means, of course, that this is now definitely a murder investigation. We will want to speak to anyone who has had dealings with your father during the weeks prior to his death. We want to know if there is anyone who may have had a grudge against him, for any reason; any arguments he may have had; recent staff sackings or problems; anything anyone can think of. At the moment, we have nothing at all to go on. Your father seemed to be well liked in town, and everyone is very shocked. I'll talk to you again in the morning. In the meantime, just try to think about the things I have mentioned to you.'

The next day, the detectives continued their questioning. Sam told them of Danny's problems over the mining lease, not just with the Kingsleys, but also with the executives from Yellow Metals. Kevin told of Jim's sacking and arrest over the stolen bar takings. They discussed his relationship with Suzi. Goldy told them of the argument between her father and Charlie Wentworth, and how he had he wanted to marry her and how her father was strongly opposed to the match. Sam interrupted.

'You should talk to him; he has a record in Queensland. He killed a man in a bar fight.'

Goldy began to protest, but the detective ignored her. 'I'll get onto that. Do you know where I can find him?'

'He works out at *Brolga Hills*, for Jack Kingsley,' said Sam, 'He's head stockman out there.'

'Thank you, Mr O'Hara. You have been most helpful.'

The detective picked up his notes and his car keys. 'We will talk again. Now I think I will take a run out to *Brolga Hills,* and have a word with Charlie Wentworth.'

After he had gone, Goldy began to cry. 'Why did you have to tell them about Charlie's record? Charlie would never do anything to hurt Dad! Surely you don't think that Sam?'

Out at the station. Jack confirmed what they already knew. Danny O'Hara was very upset over his daughter's involvement with Charlie Wentworth. Guy went a bit farther. 'Charlie was having it off with her and Danny told him to stay away from her. Charlie was none too happy with him about it all! I believe he actually threatened him in the pub not long ago, but honestly, I don't think for a moment that Charlie is a murderer, but he will be down near the stables if you want to talk to him.'

The detective smiled tightly, 'Oh indeed I will, Mr Kingsley, I will. Perhaps you could ask him to drop in and see me in town later today. We've no real evidence at present, but this is a start. Thank you both. I'll see myself out.' He turned to go, then turned back to Guy. 'By the way, how did you feel about this mining lease?'

'Couldn't care much, one way or the other,' said Guy, 'but I 'll always back my father's decision.'

'Really?' Detective Ryan checked his notes. 'It was reported that you were very against mining and said, and I quote, 'Mining is tantamount to rape of the land' Did you say that?'

Guy paused, 'I might have said something like that. Just trying to get a point across to Sam O'Hara. He's my mate, but he's a city bloke, he really doesn't understand how we feel about our land out here!'

'Where were *you* the day O'Hara went missing?'

'Can't remember exactly, but probably here. I seldom leave the station these days. You can ask my sister.

Meanwhile, Sam and Goldy were talking about the investigation. Goldy was upset that there had been a suggestion that Charlie may have been involved in her father's death.

Sam was confused. 'I don't know what to think, Sis. I do know he was very upset when Dad told him to stay away from you. He does have a record of violence and I am sure the police will find out about his record soon enough. No point in pretending we don't know about it.'

Jack Kingsley sat in his office at *Brolga Hills*, his long legs stretched out in front of him, he rubbed his aching knee, as he listened intently to Detective Henderson. 'Sure, Danny and I had some serious discussions about the mining lease. I have been quite open with everyone about my feelings over it, but recently we seemed to have reached some agreement. Anyway, he and I were friends, been mates since we were small boys,' he said finally. 'You can disagree with a friend, but you don't kill him! Not over a hole in the ground!'

Guy who had been, sitting nearby, agreed with his father. 'Danny O'Hara was a good chap, nobody here would harm him. As Dad says, at the end of the day, it is only a piece of dirt!'

The detective changed tack. 'I believe you have a Charlie Wentworth working for you, Mr Kingsley? What can you tell me about him?'

'Yes, both the Wentworth boys work for me. Charlie is my head stockman. I've known him all his life,' said Jack lightly. 'Was at school with his father. He can be a bit hot headed, but he's no murderer! He was in a bit of strife a few years ago, back in Queensland, served time for manslaughter for killing a man in a pub brawl, I believe it was an accident, but the court disagreed. He has settled down since he's been with me. He's one of my best workers.'

'He's not always averse to the odd punch up.' Interrupted Guy. 'He has been rather at loggerheads with Dan for a while.'

The detective nodded. 'Thank you both again. I'll be in touch. Don't forget to ask young Wentworth to call at the police station. I'll see myself out.'

When he had gone, Jack Kingsley looked agitated. I don't like all that stuff about Charlie. You don't honestly think he would kill Danny do you?'

'No, of course not, Danny may not been one of his favourite people, but I don't believe he would kill him'.

Detective Henderson had not long been back in town, when Charlie turned up at the Police Station. 'Believe you wanted to see me,' he said as he dropped himself into a chair, 'I gather it is about Danny O'Hara. Dreadful business!'

The detective looked speculatively at him. 'You didn't like Mr O'Hara very much, did you, Mr Wentworth? I understand that he didn't approve of your relationship with his daughter.That must have been very upsetting for you?'

'That's true.' admitted Charlie, 'Well, it's true he didn't approve of me seeing Goldy, but I didn't dislike him at all. Quite the contary, he was a nice bloke. He went to school with my Dad and Mr Kingsley.'

'Yet you were heard on more than one occasion to threaten him.'

'Not seriously! He once said I would marry Goldy over his dead body, and I believe I said something stupid like, 'whatever it takes' but I would never.....' he broke off, jumping to his feet, 'Surely you don't think I had anything to do with this, do you?'

The detective ignored the question. 'Where *were* you on the day O'Hara disappeared?'

Charlie thought for a minute. 'I was fencing in the far paddock west of Brolga Hills, about a day's ride from the homestead. I camped out overnight; got back about four pm the next afternoon. That's when I first heard about him going missing.'

'Did anyone see you out there, fencing?'

'No, but my brother and my mate Doug saw me leave, and Doug was there when I got back. My brother had gone out to Milly Downs to see old man Astanov.'

'One more question Mr Wentworth, do you own a gun?'

'Not personally, but Mr Kingsley lets us use the station ones, to kill snakes, ferral cats, dingos and to put down injured livestock. There are always a .222 in the staff quarters.'

'You have a record in Queensland, do you not Mr Wentworth? Done time in jail?'

Charlie stared at him. 'Yes, but that was years ago and I've paid for it! What's it got to do with any of this? It's hardly relevant to Danny's disappearance! What happened in Queensland was an accident!'

The detective stood up, as he moved to open the door. 'It was not an 'accident', it was manslaughter, Mr Wentworth. I've already checked it out, and I'll decide whether or not it is relevant. Thank you for coming in. I'll be talking to you again.' The police were very thorough, following up on all the possible leads.

'What about the Aboriginal connection? asked the young detective constable.

'Very unlikely. I've spoken to the elders. Whilst they weren't happy about this girl, Suzi, they seemed to like O'Hara, and anyway, this doesn't look like a black feller's crime. O'Hara was shot in the neck before being shoved down that shaft.'

The detective paused, 'The sacked barman, Jim Malloy, was in Alice Springs that day, and s seen by up to a dozen people, so he's in the clear. We do need to track down those mining fellows who were here, and we need to look at the hotel register for the past six months, to see if anyone else of interest has been through here recently.'

'Already onto that!' said his colleague. 'The housekeeper, Sally Gregson, is organising that for us, as we speak.'

CHAPTER TWENTY SIX

CHARGES

The senior detective took a sip of his coffee, as he said thoughtfully, 'I think we may already have our man; 'A motive; opportunity; a weapon, and a record for violence. Mark my words, I think we will soon arrest our killer. But how to prove it! We need to check Charlie Wentworth, and check out his brother's alibi too. It is quite possible they were in this together.'

Goldy sat at the clinic with Charlie. He was visibly upset as he slumped, head his hands, at the table. 'The police have been asking me questions about your dad; about our relationship, the arguments we had. Sure I was upset with him, but I liked him and I would never have hurt him.

Apart from which, I know how much you loved him, and I would never do anything that would hurt you. I'm no murderer! You do believe me, don't you? They've even questioned David!'

'Of course I believe you darling, I know you could never do anything as dreadful as this.

Don't worry too much. They are talking to lots of people. They have even questioned Sam and me'!'

'Yes, but they know I have done jail time, and give a dog a bad name, and all that. I'm scared, Goldy! I swear to you, I had nothing to do with this!'

In Walkabout Creek, the police went back to *Brolga Hills* to check out the firearms.

As Charlie had told them, there was a gun found in the staff quarters, and it was were taken by the police. Although no bullet had, as yet, been discovered, the police were hopeful that it would soon be found.

'If we can match the bullet to the gun that Wentworth uses, we are home and hosed.' said Detective Henderson

'With repect,' said Sergeant Paterson,' it is all only circumstantial at this stage! We've never had any problems with young Wentworth, in the five years he's been here. Always seemed like a nice young guy to me. Keeps to himself a bit, but no trouble. Jack Kingsley reckons he a real decent bloke.'

'Be that as it may, it is pretty convincing to me. Let's bring Charlie Wentworth in anyway. You never know, he just might crack!'

'I swear, I had nothing to do with Danny O'Hara's death!' Charlie said desperately, as he sat in the police station. 'I love his daughter, but she's hardly going to want to marry me, if I murdered her father!'

'Save it for the judge.' said the detective, harshly. 'I suppose this was just an 'accident' too?'

However that afternoon, Charlie, appeared back at the clinic. The detective was not happy. 'I may not have enough evidence to arrest him yet, but I *will* prove it was him.' he growled, as he watched Charlie walk away from the Police Station.

The two mining bosses were identified, and interviewed by detectives in Melbourne. While they freely admitted their frustration with Danny O'Hara over the mining lease, they were shocked by the news of his murder, as well as being able to provide solid alibis for his time of death.

Later that evening, Charlie and Goldy sat together in her flat as they went through everything they knew about the case. 'Unfortunately that detective seems to believe that I am guilty.' said Charlie. 'He seems determined to prove me a murderer!'

'Darling, you're innocent, and all the determination in the world isn't going to prove otherwise.' she said, kissing him gently.

'I wish I had as much faith in the police force as you do. I think my previous experience has shattered my faith a bit. If only I could provide a watertight alibi for that day, I would feel a whole lot better!'

Goldy put her hand over his. 'They'll find Dad's killer eventually. I know they will. Just stop stressing darling!'

Later, after Charlie had returned to *Brolga Hills*, Goldy went to bed. She knew she would probably not sleep, but she needed to rest and to think about the events of the last few weeks. She finally fell asleep, dreaming of Charlie, and the times they shared their love. Very early next morning, Goldy awoke to frantic banging on her front door. She opened the door to Jo Kingsley.

'Oh Goldy,' she began in agitated tones, 'I don't know how to tell you', she sank down at the kitchen table, her face pale.

'It's Charlie and David. The police came during the night and arrested them! They have charged Charlie with the murder of your Dad, and David as an accessory to murder. I'm so sorry!'

Goldy thought she was going to faint. 'But how? Why? Surely you don't believe that they could do this, do you, Jo?'

'No, of course I don't. Neither does anyone else in my family. You should have heard my Dad pay out on that detective!' She then gave Goldy a rundown on the night's events. 'Detective Henderson and Sergeant Paterson arrived about 2am. They got dad out of bed and the detective said 'Sorry to disturb you Mr Kingsley, but we are looking for Charlie and David Wentworth. Would they be here, by any chance?'

Dad had motioned the two men inside, and Guy went down to the quarters to fetch them.

Later, as they both sat at the table, Sergeant Paterson just fidgeted uncomfortably, and said to dad, 'I'm sorry about this, Jack. Just doing my job.'

Jo haltingly told her the rest of it. 'The detective stepped forward and said to Charlie, 'Charles Wentworth, I am arresting you on suspicion of the murder of Daniel O'Hara. You do not have to say anything, but anything you do say may be taken down and used in evidence in court. Then he did the same to David, charging him with being an accessory.' Jo continued, 'Charlie just stared disbelieving as they snapped handcuffs them. They both were taken to the waiting police car, almost in a trance. My Dad walked with them, protesting all the time and he just kept saying 'It's ok, boys, this will be all be sorted out in no time.' 'But the car door slammed, and they took them away. Oh Goldy, What will we do?'

At this point, Goldy fell weeping into Jo's arms and the two women clung to each other like drowning sailors.

Once at the police station, Charlie and David were put into a small cell, and as they sat on the narrow bed, Charlie said quietly to his brother, 'How the hell is this happening? We are not killers!

It is all a mistake and by the morning it will all be sorted. They will realise that they have the wrong men.'

Later that morning at the police station, the sergeant let Goldy and Jo in to see them. As the couples hugged each other and cried, Charlie kept repeating. 'Just tell me you believe me when I say I didn't kill your Dad! They are saying I shot him with the gun they took from my room!'

Goldy held him close. 'It will all be alright. Of course I know you are innocent, my darling. You know I do!'

Fortunately for David, Yuri Astanov was able to provide the police with a sound alibi for him, for the said date, and he was reluctantly released, with a proviso that he not leave town for the time being.

There was no such reprieve for Charlie. That afternoon, after a reasonable lunch, he was again handcuffed, and driven to the airstrip for transfer to Perth in a police aircraft, on his way to the Central Law Court. The unreality continued.

When he arrived in Perth, he was transferred to a police van and taken to a courtroom for a preliminary hearing. It was over in a few minutes; the terse magistrate allowed no bail and he was committed for trial in two weeks. In the meantime, he was to be held at Fremantle Prison.

Still in handcuffs, Charlie was transferred to a large prison van outside the court. He sat on the narrow seat and looked around with interest, at his fellow passengers. Opposite him sat a big man, with a straggly beard, long hair and a dozen tattoos on his neck and arms. He was dressed all in leather and he glared ahead of him without speaking. Next to him, a wide-eyed dusky boy of indeterminate heritage, looked terrified, as he snivelled constantly, wiping his nose on his sleeve.

There was a sullen youth of about nineteen. He had cuts on his face as if he had been in a fight. He mumbled constantly, mostly expletives about the police. The man to Charlie's right appeared to be older and more relaxed than the others. He seemed to know the drill. 'Whatcha in for?' he asked Charlie.

'They say I killed a man, but I didn't'.

'No mate, I understand. 'Course you didn't. Just like I didn't bash the guy who wouldn't pay for the drugs he ordered! Keep tellin' yourself that and you'll be right. By the way, the name's Cody.'

'Charlie. G'day Cody.'

The van felt hot and airless. It smelled of sweat, stale air and something else. Was it fear? He didn't know. There were only high narrow windows, so there was nothing to see as they lurched their way to Fremantle. About half an hour later, they slowed down, the vehicle bumping over uneven ground, as they reached the prison courtyard. The van stopped, started, reversed, then came to a stop. The back doors opened and the men ordered out through a large door at one end of the large courtyard, and into a long narrow room with slatted benches down one side. They were ordered to sit.

The admission process was long and tedious. The exchanged their clothes for prison greens, one set of underwear, a pair of socks and a pair of ill- fitting brown shoes. They sat naked on their bench, to be called out one by one for a full body search in the middle of the room. As the guard donned rubber gloves, Charlie's sense of unreality, quickly became gross reality. This was all horribly reminiscent of his time in Queensland.

The Warden then read the prison rules, which Charlie barely heard. Cody, sitting next to him, said quietly, 'Stick with me mate, you'll be right.'

Obviously Charlie did not look as if he had been in prison before. Time enough to share that information later!

After the search, they were marched in single file through a self-locking door to the shower block, with their soap, toothbrush and toothpaste and a towel. At least the showers were clean and the water hot. Charlie began to feel better. 'I can do this for a couple of weeks,' he told himself.

Showers over, they were moved, once more in single file, across a broad expanse of flat ground within the inner perimeter fence of the prison. This fence topped with razor wire, whilst the outer wall was solid stone, with glass on the top, and guard towers at strategic points along its length. *Not much chance of getting out of here in a hurry*, thought Charlie.

To the left of the path there were some garden vegetable beds. 'Only prisoners with a special pass can work in the gardens, and those passes have to be visible at all times. The guards will only ask once, and then the prisoner can be shot!' the Warden growled.

Inside the grounds, an imposing building sat at right angles to the prison, with a large arched window. 'That's the chapel,' pointed out the warden. 'Services held every Sunday. By the way,' he added, 'if you look up at that window from the outside, you can sometimes see the ghost of a woman, the only woman ever hanged here,'

The men went through more locked doors, to the central corridor of the man prison block. Although well- lit by electric lights, there was little natural light, except from a central skylight.

They stopped in front of a large notice, the timetable for prisoners, which read as follows:

PRISON TIMETABLE
Fremantle Prison has a daily timetable which every prisoner is expected to obey:

MONDAY – FRIDAY REGIMEN
06.45 amWake up bell. All prisoners to be dressed and ready for
    unlock.
07.00 amUnlock and into yards for ablutions etc.
07.00 – 08.00 amRoll call, muster, breakfast in cell and return to
    yards
08.30 amPrisoners to work.
11.25 am onwardsWork parties to return to Divisions. (Time may
    vary according to Work Party).
12.00 middayRoll call, muster and lunch in the yards.
01.00 pmPrisoners return to work.
03.45 pm onwardsWork parties to return to Divisions.
(Time may vary according to Work Party)
04.15 pmRoll-call, musters, tea and lock-up.
11.15 pmLights out

WEEKENDS AND PUBLIC HOLIDAYS

07.45 amWake-up bell. All prisoners to be dressed and ready for
   unlock.
08.00 am Unlock and into yards for ablutions etc.
0800-0900 amRoll call, muster, breakfast in cell and return to yard.
11.00 amRoll-call, muster and lunch in yard.
04.15 pmRoll-call, muster tea and lock-up.
11.15 pmLights out.

NOTE

**PRISONERS ARE ALLOWED TO REMAIN IN CELL AT
WEEKENDS AND PUBLIC HOLIDAYS AS PER LOCAL ORDERS.**

Each man was then handed two buckets. 'One is for your
drinking water; the other is your toilet. Don't confuse them!' boomed
the guard, grimly. 'The toilet bucket to be emptied every morning.
You will be directed how and where to do that.'

Charlie looked down the wide corridor, noting the cell doors on
each side. He guessed there were about twelve on each side in that
section. He was shown into his allocated cell. As the barred door
shut firmly behind him, he heard the key turn in the lock. He looked
around in disbelief at the tiny space. No more than about two and a
half meters by two meters, with a narrow iron bed and a small table
and a chair. Barely room to swing a cat, let alone house a six foot
two man! There was a small barred window high above his head,
through which peeped a pale shaft of daylight. On the wall, someone
had scratched ' Frankie 1950-1962.' 'God help me,' he muttered. 'I can
hardly stand the thought of twelve days here. Let alone twelve years!'

When next he saw Cody, he muttered, 'So many hours in the
bloody cell. I'll go stir crazy in there!'

Cody grunted in agreement. 'Not exactly the Hilton is it!'

Goldy arrived in Perth two days later to see Charlie at the prison, but unlike the country prison, no physical contact allowed, so they could only look at each other through a small window. The love and longing they felt for one another, almost palpable.

As he protested his innocence, she again reiterated her belief in his innocence. Upset by his demeanour and obvious depression, she stayed a week before she returned to Walkabout Creek, having promised Charlie, that she would pass on his message to David to see that *Rufus* would be cared for, as long as necessary.

They corresponded regularly. Together they made plans for when he was finally cleared. She also sent him photographs of *Rufus*, of his horse, of *Milly Downs*, and one of herself.

'I am going to prove your innocence Charlie, if it's the last thing I do!' she promised him earnestly.

Jack Kingsley had contacted Charlie's family in Queensland, and equally convinced of his innocence, they promised to be there to support him through the trial. They also provided him with an excellent defence lawyer, Earle Dennison.

CHAPTER TWENTY SEVEN

CHASING A KILLER

On the day following her return from Perth, Goldy was reading the *West Australian* newspaper, when a headline jumped out at her which read: *'Vicious Killer on the Run in South Australia.' 'A young couple holidaying in the outback, dragged from their car, shot, and thrown down a mineshaft; the bodies were only discovered when the police found the couple's small dog barking at the top of a shaft. Their car was later found, burnt out a hundred miles away, in the Western Australia/South Australian border region.'*

She rang Earle Dennison. 'This happened just after Dad disappeared, this man could have been here around that time!' she insisted. 'Perhaps there is a connection!'

Earle was kind. 'My dear Goldy,' he said, gently. 'I think you're clutching at straws. Let's wait until they catch this fellow first.

Two weeks later, the police confirmed the arrest of one, Lyall Jenkins, a forty two year old Roo shooter from Streaky Bay, in South Australia. Jenkins had been charged with hijacking and murdering the young couple on a back track near the border. Earle rang Goldy.

'The police have questioned him about your father, at the moment he's admitting nothing, but I'll keep in touch with them'.

The lawyer also promised to let Charlie know of the latest developments. 'Lyall Jenkins goes to trial in two week's time, in Adelaide' he told Goldy.

For the first time since Charlie's arrest, Goldy felt a glimmer of hope. She followed the details of the case with keen interest. There were many striking similarities between the South Australian murders and that of her father's. A lonely road, unarmed travellers; burnt out vehicles, found a distance from the bodies; both victims shot and their bodies hidden in old shafts. The victims apparently, unknown to their killer.

'Only coincidental at this stage,' said Earle. 'Not enough to help for Charlie. I'm afraid, nothing short of a confession from Jenkins would be enough.'

Subsequently at his trial, Lyall Jenkins was found guilty and jailed for twenty years on each charge.

'What if I wrote to him?' Goldy asked Earle. 'He might just admit to killing Dad as well. After all, he is probably going to die in prison, so why wouldn't he clear Charlie?'

Earle thought it was probably a long shot, but he contacted Jenkin's lawyer and the prisoner agreed to answer a letter from Goldy. Goldy composed her letter and sent it off to Adelaide.

'I am, or I was, engaged to marry a wonderful young man called Charlie Wentworth.' she began, *'then three months ago, my father disappeared from Walkabout Creek, in Western Australia. He was later found shot and dumped in an abandoned mine shaft. His car was found burnt out, a long way from where he was finally found, Charlie was charged with his murder and jailed for twenty years.*

The fact is, Mr Jenkins, Charlie didn't kill my Dad, I know he didn't and I want to prove his innocence.

I thought that since you were in the area about the time my father disappeared, you might have some information which might help clear Charlie.'

Jenkins answered her letter in due course.

'Dear Miss O'Hara. What do you want me to say about your father's murder? You thought it might be nice if you could blame your dad's murder on me. Believe me, we are all innocent! Or we wish we were!' I am sorry, I can't help you. Anyway, good luck.'

Goldy rang Earle. 'Earle? It's Goldy O'Hara'. She told him of Jenkins' denial. 'What do we do now?' she asked tearfully.

Earle spoke carefully. 'Goldy, the weakest bit of evidence in Charlie's arrest was, what gun actually fired the bullet that killed your father? If we had the bullet, we might be able to prove that it did not come from the gun found in Charlie's room. If that bullet matched Lyall Jekins' gun, we would have conclusive evidence that Lyall. Which would prove that Charlie was not the killer. Other than that, I'm afraid I'm stymied. Jenkins is obviously not going to make a confession.'

He paused, sympathetic to the girl, so sure her fiancé was innocent. 'The police have been unable to find the bullet that killed your father, and after all this time, it is unlikely that they will. I'm sorry Goldy.'

Bitterly disappointed, Goldy went out to see Yuri. 'Why can't people see the truth? Charlie did not kill my father. You believe that don't you?'

He reassured her that he did not believe that Charlie was in any way involved.

'Unfortunately, what I think is not important.' He told her.

'It matters to Charlie and to me.' She said.

Goldy went down to Perth to see her brother and to tell him of the recent correspondence with Lyall Jenkins. He was sympathetic but had no fixed opinion one way or the other. 'Sis, if Charlie is innocent, the court will find that out. There isn't much we can do.'

Sam had almost finished at medical school and as Dr O'Hara he would be working at the QE11 Medical Centre, where he was doing some work placement at that time. Goldy joined her brother, and his girlfriend Sonia, for dinner that night. Sonia was a tall glamorous blonde, a medical student like Sam, whose elegance made Goldy suddenly aware of her own out dated dress and straggly hair. She felt relieved when the evening ended..

She took the next day to go and do some shopping, and to get her hair cut and styled. She felt better and Sam was very complimentary.

She rang Caroline Brealey at the Royal Flying Doctor base in Jandakot to ask if there was any chance of a lift home within the week. Day later, she took a call from Caroline at the RFDS; there was a plane returning a patient to Walkabout Creek in two day's time. Goldy was welcome to accompany them. 'Be at Jandakot at six am, on Wednesday.' instructed Caroline. 'See you then.'

On Wednesday morning, she caught a taxi to Jandakot to meet the RFDS crew. It was good to be with them all again. She told Caroline and Matt about Lyall's letter from Adelaide. What a relief to be able to unburden herself, especially to those, who, like herself, was convinced of Charlie's innocence. 'If only we could find that damned bullet!' she sighed. 'It's like looking for a needle in a haystack, I'm afraid, but we don't know exactly where Dad was shot.

'My guess is, that it would have been near where they found his body,' said Caroline.'Your dad was a big, powerful man. I don't think the killer could have dragged him around the countryside.

Anyway, what about his car? That was found nearly 200 miles away!'

'A vehicle can always be towed. I would have thought it difficult to track that far, over rocks and through water,' added Matt. 'Anyway, didn't the trackers say your dad had not been in the vicinty of his vehicle, when it was found?'

By the time she reached home, Goldy was quite excited. Kevin picked her up from the strip, and as they drove back into town she told him about the bullet.

'Goldy love, I know you want young Charlie to be innocent, but honestly, don't you think it is just possible that he did kill your Dad? The police seem pretty convinced you know.'

'Oh Kev! Don't say that. This might be my last chance to clear him! I've got to try! 'Well, I think that the bullet that killed dad, must be somewhere near the mine shaft where they found him. I just have to find it!'

A couple of days later, Goldie was in the Post Office, collecting the mail. Mollie Jenkins was in full flight about Danny's murder.

'I hear you're looking for the bullet.' She said. 'If you ask me, that's what those Aboriginal trackers should have been looking for. They can find anything those boys!' she lowered her voice. 'sometimes you wonder about them, they are so much cleverer at these things than we are!'

Goldie thought about what Mollie had said as she walked out into the street. She went to see Sylvia. 'Do you think any of the boys would be prepared to search for that bullet?' she asked.

'I think so, all them fellers really liked your dad. I'll ask around.'

Two weeks later, as Goldy sat in the small office at the hotel, paying invoices, Sally appeared at the door. 'Cuse me, love, but there's a young feller outside, says he might have found somethin' you bin lookin' for.'

Goldy hurried outside to the veranda. A young man she knew slightly, stood shyly on the steps. 'Hullo, Tommy isn't it?' he nodded.

'Yes Missus. Dey tell me you bin lookin' for the bullet dat done finish Mr O'Hara?'

'Yes, that's right,' said Goldy, hardly daring to breathe.

'I find dis in the wood on top of that old shaft,' he said, .'Maybe this will help?' He handed her a bullet.

'Oh thank you, Tommy. Thank you! '.

As soon as she could, she rang Earle Dennison.

'That's good news Goldy. Well done!'

'What shall I do with it now'?

'Just hang onto to it for the moment. I'll get onto the forensic guys and I'll get back to you.'

Later, Sergeant Paterson called in. 'Just had a call from Perth. They want you to hand the bullet over to me, with details of exactly where and how it was found, and by whom. Then I'll send it off to forensic .'

'This will clear Charlie, I just know it.' Goldie cried happily.'

Sergeant Paterson smiled. 'Well, we'll see Goldy. Thanks, I'll be in touch.'

The wait seemed interminable. Finally Earle Dennison rang. 'Goldy? I have some news for you. They've checked the bullet against Lyall Jensen's gun and I'm sorry, it's not a match' he paused, and Goldy heard a catch in his throat. 'It gets worse I'm afraid, they have found a match, but it is to the .222. The gun the police took from Charlie's room. I' m so very sorry.'

Goldy crumpled to the floor, the phone swinging uselessly from the wall. It was there, that Kevin found her later. He gently picked her up and gave her a strong brandy as he propped her in an armchair. 'Oh Kev,' she wept. 'I was so sure! I don't know what I can do now. I've only made it worse!'

'Nothin' you can do, love.' he said gently. 'Seems like young Charlie is guilty after all.'

CHAPTER TWENTY EIGHT

THE FAREWELL

Danny O'Hara's body was finally brought back to Walkabout Creek for the funeral. His family had thought long and hard about whether there should be a cremation and his ashes be returned to England, to be with those of his wife, or a burial. The reading of his Will provided the answer.

'I wish to be buried in Walkabout Creek, where I have spent some of the happiest days of my life.'

His Will provided no surprises. Everything, including his share of the pub, was left to to his two children, apart from small legacies to his mother, Sally, Kevin, Suzi, and ironically, Jim Malloy.

The funeral was held on a cool morning, in the little cemetery attached to the Catholic Church. It seemed that everyone was there. Father John conducted the service and Jack Kingsley gave the main eulogy, in which he described Danny O'Hara as 'one of the most decent men I have ever had the good fortune, to call my friend.'

Sam spoke of the love and support he and Goldy had received, even when they were both in England, after their mother had died so tragically in a car accident. Many of the congregation did not know what had happened to Suzanne, as Dan never spoke of his wife's death. There were visible tears, as Sam described his father's struggle to make a new life for himself, and of his gratitude to those present who had made that life so happy. He especially mentioned his grandmother, the Kingsley family, Suzi, Kevin and Sally. Sally sobbed out loud and Kevin blew his nose frequently.

The Kingsley family and Jo and David Wentworth, sat with the O'Hara family, and her grandmother held Goldy close as they both cried. It seemed unbelievable to her that she would never again see her father's beloved face, nor hear that gentle laugh. How she wished her Charlie could be there to comfort her. After the funeral, they all retired to the pub for the regulatory wake; drinks and sandwiches, which most did not feel like eating, but all agreed it was a mark of respect, so they met and were soon swapping stories about the kindness and good nature of Daniel O'Hara.

Charlie's trial was scheduled for September 10th. Sam and Goldy travelled down with David and the Kingsley family, and they were met at their hotel by Charlie's father Bob, and his other brother, Andrew. Charlie's mother, Rosemary, like Clara was too upset to attend, and they both remained at home. Bob and Jack were old friends since school days, and were both totally convinced of Charlie's innocence.

CHAPTER TWENTY NINE

THE TRIAL

The day of the trial dawned cool and overcast. Charlie was driven up from Fremantle in a prison van. He appeared in court in prison clothes and hand cuffed. The jury was sworn in and Justice Ryan addressed them in their duty.

He entered a plea of 'Not Guilty' and the case was handed over to the Prosecutor and the Defence Lawyer, Earle Dennison. In his opening address, the Prosecutor laid out the facts of Danny O'Hara's disappearance and death. He said he would provide evidence of motive, opportunity and the means to commit this heinous crime. Premeditated, well planned and an extremely vicious crime. He insisted that the accused must face the full wrath of the law.

In defence, Earle Dennison claimed that his client was guilty only of falling in love with the deceased's daughter, and of not being able to provide witnesses to say he was not in the vicinity of the crime on the day in question. Circumstantial evidence, he insisted, should not be used to convict an innocent man. Much of the following evidence appeared to be around the relationship between the accused and Goldy O'Hara.

Doug Wilson reluctantly related Danny O'Hara's conversation with Charlie out at Brolga Hills.

He said that he had heard Danny say that Charlie Wentworth would 'marry Goldy, over my dead body.' He then admitted that Charlie had said something like 'Whatever it takes.'

Jack Kingsley was called and gave a details of his relationship with the accused and declared his firm belief in his innocence. He spoke in glowing terms of the young man.

Guy Kingsley was called to the stand. He gave evidence of Charlie's quick temper and willingness to get into fights. The Defence lawyer was quick to challenge him. 'You do not like the accused, do you Mr Kingsley?'

'No, not particularly.'

The lawyer continued. 'It is true, is it not, that you, yourself, were at one time romantically involved with Miss O'Hara?'

Goldy held her breath, and Charlie looked Hard at her. *What was Guy going to say?*

'It is true that at one time I did have strong feelings for Miss O'Hara, but she preferred Charlie Wentworth'.

The lawyer persisted. 'So I would suit you, would it not, to have my client out of the way, so to speak?'

The Prosecutor protested. 'Objection, Your Honour, this witness is not on trial!' The judge agreed.

Earle Dennison acceded. 'Question, withdrawn.' He turned back to Guy. 'You and your father appear to have differing opinions of the accused?'

Guy looked directly at Goldy before he answered.

'I have already said I do not like Mr Wentworth, but having said that, I do not believe he would murder Danny O'Hara,'

He was then allowed to step down.

At the end of the first day, nothing seemed to have changed. Goldy ate little at dinner, while the conversation went round and round. She sought out Guy. 'I want to thank you for what you said today about Charlie not being a murderer. I appreciate that.'

He smiled. 'No worries. I honestly don't think he would have hurt your dad. Doesn't make a lot of sense really. Wouldn't put him in your good books, would it?'

She also talked to Charlie's brothers. They painted a picture of him similar to her own. 'Charlie was a kid who never hurt anything.' said Andrew. 'He used to pay me to put down any injured or sick animals.'

David laughed. 'I remember when he was a kid, he used to nurse sick calves and lambs in his bedroom! Drove mum crazy! Hardly a potential murderer'

'But there *was* that charge in Queensland,' she said slowly. David's face clouded. 'He was just defending me against a thug. It was a terrible accident. He never meant it to go the way it did. Honestly, Charlie is the gentlest person I know.' When called to give evidence, David reiterated those sentiments.

The next day the arresting detective was called to the stand. 'Yes, the accused had been cooperative. No, he could not establish an alibi. Yes, he did have access to firearms. Yes, Forensic had shown that the bullet which killed Daniel O'Hara did come from a gun found in Charles Wentworth's quarters on the station.' and 'No, there were no finger prints on the weapon, other than those of Charlie Wentworth .

'Call Miss Marigold O'Hara', boomed the Clerk of Courts. 'Call Marigold O'Hara!'

Goldy took the stand and the oath. Earle Dennison paused and looked at the pretty young woman before him. 'Miss O'Hara. would you tell the court please, what is your relationship to the accused?'

Goldy looked across at Charlie. 'He is my fiancé.'

'Your father did not approve of this relationship, did he?

'No, not really. Dad was not very happy about it at first, but he was coming around.'

'Speak up please, Miss O'Hara' said the judge.

Goldy repeated her answer

'On what grounds did your father disapprove?'

'He said that Charlie had no prospects; no money and nothing to offer me.'

'And yet, you continued to see him ?'

'Yes, I did.'

'Do you still intend to marry the accused?'

'Yes, of course.'

'Did the accused ever threaten your father within your hearing?

'No, never.'

'Is it also a fact, that when your father found out, he publicly said that you would marry Mr Wentworth, and I quote 'Over my dead body!?'

Goldy was flustered. 'Well yes, but that's just an expression and people say that all the time, it.....'

The Prosecutor interrupted her. 'Miss O'Hara. Did you not feel your father might have had your interests at heart when he warned you against this relationship?'

'I suppose he thought he was right, but he didn't really know Charlie. He heard some of the things some other people said about him.'

'Like what?'

'Objection, this is hearsay,' called Earle.

'Upheld" said the judge. Strike that from the record.'

'It would have made things easier for both of you without your father around...'

'Objection!' said Earle Dennison, loudly.

'Upheld', said the judge.

Finally, Charlie was called to the stand. There was a twitter of interest from the Press Gallery. The Prosecutor stepped forward and looked Charlie up and down, before clearing his throat.

'Mr Wentworth, I put it to you that you did not, in fact, like Daniel O'Hara at all. He certainly was a huge impediment to your plans to marry his daughter. Isn't that so?

Charlie straightened up, looked across at Goldy, and then looked directly at his accuser. 'That is *not* true. I *did* like Danny O'Hara. 223

Prior to his daughter's arrival in Walkabout Creek, we got along pretty well. It was sad that he didn't think I was good enough for her, but I intended to prove to him that I could make her happy, and that I could make something of myself, so that I could provide for her.'

'Is it true, that Daniel O'Hara ordered you to stay way from his daughter?'

'Yes.'

'Mr Wentworth, you intended to marry Miss O'Hara, did you not?'

'Absolutely!' said Charlie confidently.

'Did you feel that Daniel O'Hara might have been coming around to accepting your marriage to his daughter?'

'Yes. I believe so.'

'Mr Wentworth. Did you kill Daniel O'Hara?'

'No, I did not. I love his daughter. I would never do anything to hurt her, and she really loved her dad.'

'Is it true that you had an altercation and attempted to punch Daniel O'Hara in the bar of the *'Imperial Hotel'*

'Yes, so I am told. I don't remember much about it as I was pretty inebriated at the time.'

'Did you, in fact, actually threaten to kill him?'

'No, I don't think so!'

'So you never threatened Mr O'Hara, as other witnesses have said?'

'Not seriously. I may have said some of those things, but I certainly never intended t ....'

'Did you say that you would marry Miss O'Hara no matter what her father said?'

'Yes, I did say that.'

The questioning went on. It was endless. Then the Prosecutor said, 'Mr Wentworth, do you own a gun?'

'No,' he replied. 'I do not.'

'But you do have access to a firearm, do you not?'

'Yes, there is a gun in the staff quarters, on the station, for shooting snakes, dingo, wild pigs, ferral cats, and any wounded animal; steer, horse, dog, whatever.'

'And where is this gun kept?'

'In the staff quarters, in a gun cabinet there is a key on the hook beside the cupboard, anyone has access to it. People just have to sign it out.'

'Do you have a Firearms Licence Mr Wentworth?'

'No. My boss, Mr Kingsley, holds the licence.'

'You are not permitted to own a gun because of some previous trouble you had in Queensland. Is that not so?'

Charlie looked shaken. 'That's right, but......'

'What sort of trouble did you have in Queensland, Mr Wentworth?' interrupted the prosecutor.

His lawyer jumped to his feet. 'Objection, Your Honour. This question is irrelevant!'

'Upheld. Please withdraw the question!'

The Prosecutor looked disappointed, and a slight ripple of interest went through the court. 'Thank you Mr Wentworth, no further questions, you may stand down.'

The defence lawyer intervened. 'Surely my learned colleague is aware, that most young men working on stations have access to firearms? It's dangerous country out there. I am sure these guns are licensed. To this point, there is not one scrap of forensic evidence to link my client with the gun which killed Daniel O'Hara There were any number of people who had access to this gun.

After more winesses, more questions, the judge adjourned the case. 'We will hear the final summaries at 10am tomorrow morning.' Everyone stood up, and as the judge left the court, chatter broke out in the court room.

Charlie Wentworth, with his youthful physique, blonde hair and blue eyes, was fodder for the press and T.V reporters. They followed Goldy too. The constant questioning and flashing cameras, dissolved her to tears as she tried to hide between David and Andrew Wentworth.

CHAPTER THIRTY

THE VERDICT

Next morning, everyone was in court early. Charlie was led into the dock. Once the judge appeared, the summaries began. Firstly the Prosecutor rose slowly to his feet, his hands grasping the lapels of his black gown. He paced in front of the jury, deep in thought. He looked unblinking at Charlie. 'I believe that the Prosecution has provided undeniable proof that the accused is guilty of the murder of Daniel O'Hara. We have provided a motive: That the deceased was a serious impediment to the ambitions of the accused. He was strongly opposed to the marriage of his daughter. The accused had threatened the victim on at least two occasions, as outlined by witnesses. Opportunity?

Well there are twenty-four hours unaccounted for, by the accused. Plenty of time to kill Daniel O'Hara and dispose of his body, and his vehicle. I put it to you, Mr Wentworth, that you did *not*, in fact, like Daniel O'Hara and that you planned to murder him by shooting him, disposing of his body down the mine shaft; stripping of it of identification, hoping it would never be discovered. You then disposed of his vehicle, by towing it miles away and setting it alight. In due course, you could then achieve your objective, which of course was to marry his daughter.

You might even have got away with it, had it not been for the chance finding of the victim's hat, which led to the discovery of the body.

Later to the discovery of the bullet which we now know came from the gun to which you had access.'

He then appealed to the jury. 'Can there be any doubt of guilt, Ladies and gentlemen of the jury? The accused had motive; his desire to marry the daughter of his victim. He had opportunity; he *says* he was fencing, miles away; but cannot produce one single witness to collaborate this. He was certainly not at the station homestead, or surrounds on the day in question, and nobody can recall seeing him for some twenty four hours; and, he had the means - at least two guns, one of which was discovered in his room, after the murder. The bullet that killed Daniel O'Hara came from the gun used by the accused.

The defence would have you believe that the evidence is only circumstantial, but I put it to you, that the likelihood of all these things being purely circumstantial, is exceedingly unlikely. I rest the case for the prosecution, and ask that you find Charles Wentworth, 'Guilty of Murder in the first degree!'

Next Earle Dennison stood. He appeared relaxed and he smiled at the jury as he faced them.

'Members of the jury. I believe you are all reasonable people, able to see through all this circumstantial evidence the prosecution would have you believe. A motive? My client is a young, hardworking Stockman, whose only crime was to love someone, whose father didn't think he was good enough for his daughter. Not an unusual state of affairs for some of us, I would suggest! Hardly a motive for murder!'

There as a slight ripple of laughter. 'We have heard witnesses say, that Mr O'Hara loved his daughter very much, and was well on the way to accepting her choice of a husband.

The accused had no need to murder him! The young lady would hardly want to marry a man who killed her father! Opportunity? Surely, yes. He did have opportunity, but as for an alibi? Stockmen are, by the very nature of their work, often alone, sometimes for days at a stretch. There are no ready made witnesses out there. How can the accused provide an alibi, when his only witnesses were cattle, dogs and kangaroos?'

He paused and looked around the court room. 'Unfortunately, these animals cannot provide statements. Many station hands work alone on jobs such as outlined by the accused. My client has already told us where he was when Daniel O'Hara disappeared.

Nobody can attest to having seen him anywhere, during that time. Surely he would have been seen by someone while he was supposedly killing the victim, or disposing of his body, so close to town; or disposing of the vehicle.'

Earle paused, to let his words sink in. 'The means,' he paused, 'There are guns on many, if not all, farms and stations. The prosecution has produced the bullet that killed Daniel O'Hara, but they have yet to prove that it was Mr Wentworth who actually fired the gun.' He paused again, and looked steadily at the jury.

'All the evidence the prosecution has offered, has been entirely circumstantial. There *may* be circumstantial evidence which has cast suspicion on the accused, but, there is *no* forensic evidence at all, except that the bullet which killed Daniel O'Hara, came from a gun, which may, or may not, have been fired by the accused, which links my client with this murder! The police have found nothing in Charles Wentworth's possessions, to link him with any crime.

I beg you, look kindly on this young man. If you cannot find him guilty beyond reasonable doubt, then you must give him the opportunity to marry his young lady, and live a full and happy life, by finding him "Not Guilty".'

As the jury retired to consider its verdic, Goldy again took the opportunity to talk with Charlie's father and brothers. She was relieved that they appeared to bear her no malice over the present events. She and Sam had joined them for lunch several times during the trial, and even Sam appeared impressed, and began to voice some doubts that Charlie had, in fact, killed his father.

The Clerk of Court announced the return of the jury, and they all ran for the door. Judge Ryan observed them solemnly. over his gold framed glasses. 'Ladies and gentlemen of the jury, have you reached a verdict?'

'Yes, your Honour, We have.'

'How find you, the accused, Charles Andrew Wentworth? Guilty or Not Guilty of the murder of Daniel O'Hara.'

Goldy held her breath and felt her fingers pressing into David Wentworth's arm. She looked across at Charlie, but his face was impassive.

'Guilty.' Came the verdict. There was an uproar in the court room and Goldy buried her face in David Wentworth's coat. Charlie looked totally stunned, barely looking at Goldy as he was led from the court.

Sentencing was be announced in two week's time, and Charlie would be held at Fremantle Prison until that date. When the judge stood, so did the entire court, and there was a scramble of reporters as the court emptied.

The morning of the day of sentencing dawned. The court was packed. Judge Ryan finally entered the court, and taking his seat, ordered Charlie to rise. He looked at him for a couple of minutes, then he began.

'I have heard the evidence presented in this court, and the prosecuton has presented a very clear concise version, of what they claim, happened to Daniel O'Hara. On the other hand, your defence has been, unconvincing, to say the least. You have been unable to present any alibi. You admit to threatening the victim, your motive being to marry Miss O'Hara. You also admit to having access to the gun, which has been proved to be the one which fired the bullet that killed Daniel O'Hara. Whilst I could agree with the defence lawyer, that much of the evidence has been circumstantial, I feel there is no doubt that it has been proved that you had motive, means, and opportunity.

I believe the jury has made the correct decision. In view of your youth, I find sentencing difficult, but considering the seriousness of your crime, and the fact that it was premeditated and well planned, I am sentencing you to twenty years, with a parole period of not less than fifteen years.'

There were gasps and sobs. Charlie swayed on his feet, his face deathly white, as Goldy collapsed, crying into Jack Kingsley's arms.

Later, Goldy sought out Charlie's lawyer, Earle Dennison, who was as shocked as she was by the guilty verdict.

'We will appeal of course! I can't believe it!' he said. 'It's all circumstantial. They should not have convicted him!

Had it been a judge only, I don't think he would have been convicted, but a Jury often accepts circumstantial evidence as fact.

'I know he is innocent!' Goldy cried passionately.

'I believe he is too.' said Earle, 'but how to prove it!'

oooOooo

The entire population of Walkabout Creek soon knew what had happened, and even those who had supported Charlie in the past, agreed that this new evidence over the gun was pretty damning.

Goldy wept bitter tears. It looked as if Charlie was indeed lost to her. 'I just made it a whole lot worse by finding that wretched bullet. I was so sure it would prove his innocence!. He told me he didn't do it, and I believed him! I still believe him!' cried Goldy later, as she sat with Sam and Guy, in the lounge.

'Of course he's going to say that!' said Sam scathingly. 'He doesn't want to spend the next twenty years in jail!'

'But he's innocent, Sam. I just know it!

'Never trust a woman in love!' said Guy. 'Goldy, just because he's good in the cot, doesn't make him innocent, you know'

'Oh shut up Guy Kingsley! You wouldn't know a decent man if you fell over one!'

Goldy fled upstairs in a flood of tears and rage.Her grandmother followed her up, putting her arms around the distraught girl.

'You don't believe he killed Dad, do you Grandma?'

'No darling. I don't believe that for a minute. They'll prove he's innocent. You'll see.'

'Nothing will ever convince me that Charlie killed Dad! He is a good man and would never do anything like this!' Goldy cried passionately. 'Grandma, you know when you loved Grandpa Patrick, was he the whole world to you? Did nothing else matter to you? Did he make you feel as if you were the centre of his universe?'

Her Grandma nodded sadly, 'Indeed that was all true. My world began and ended with him.'

Clara held her close, Her own grief at the loss of her husband, and now her son, held quietly in her heart.

'There is nothing on earth that will ever shake my faith in our love. He makes me a better person, just by being himself. I know I will love him until the day I die.'

Clara gazed into space as she held her beloved granddaughter close. 'Darling girl, life has to go on, no matter what. Sometimes the time for that great love just isn't right. We just have to hope and pray.'

Downstairs, Sam was reproaching Guy. 'That was a bit rough Guy. Like it or not, Goldy says she is in love with him. Go a bit easy on her, mate.'

'Well the sooner she gets over him, the better! She needs to find a real man!'

'Like you, I suppose,' said Sam irritated by his friend's lack of sensitivity.

'Well, she could do worse, and I bet I could take her mind off that murderous little bastard!'

'That's my sister, you're talking about.' said Sam, slightly embarassed.

At the end of that week, Sam left for Perth. 'I've got finals in two weeks, Goldy, and there's nothing I can do here at present. Kevin, Sally and Troy can run the pub for now, and Grandma is here. We'll have to wait awhile before she decides what is to be done with it.'

Goldy kept working. She did not know how else to get through each day. Her clients were very kind and understanding towards her, and she was touched by their concern. Tadawalla came to see her, bringing a gift, two hand hewn boomerangs, some tiny wooden animals, and a shield. 'For you,' he said insistently 'I make 'em for you .'

Many of her tasks became automatic, as she tried to come to terms with the tragic events of the past few weeks. The only bright spot came when Sam announced that he had passed his final exams, and would be driving up at the end of the week to stay for awhile.

CHAPTER THIRTY ONE

THE AFTERMATH

After the trial was over, and Charlie began his sentence, David Wentworth, was offered the position of Head Stockman at *Brolga Hills* by Jack Kingsley. David, although devastated by his brother's plight, was happy with the arrangement, and quickly settled in to his new role.

A year into his sentence, after much soul searching, Charlie announced that he had decided to end their relationship. He spoke at length to his brother David, and asked him to pass his message on to Goldy

'I cannot tell her this face to face,' he said. 'I would lose courage if I looked into her face, but I want her to move on. It's going to be at least another twelve or thirteen years before I will even be considered for parole. Much as I love her, I can hardly expect her to wait that long. I may be very different when I get out of here. She might not even want to marry me then. I will have no job, no prospects, nothing. She is young and lovely, and she deserves a good life, with a husband and children, all the things I cannot give her. I have given this a great deal of thought, and this will be best for everyone.'

Goldy was heartbroken when David told her of Charlie's decision. Despite her tears and pleading, Charlie stuck to his decision.

Her letters went unanswered and he refused to see her or to take her 'phone calls.

Between helping her grandma with the running of the pub and her job, Goldy scoured old legal cases. She talked often with Earle Dennison, looking for loopholes, for avenues of appeal. All apparently, to no avail.

The people of Walkabout Creek were, as ever, kind and supportive; even those who were not as sure of Charlie's innocence, as was Goldy. Although she was relieved to find that nobody blamed her for Charlie's incarceration, those who seemed to think he was guilty, saddened her. She often talked to his brother David, along with Jo, who were both as sure as Goldy, that Charlie was not responsible for her father's murder.

Guy Kingsley called in to see her regularly, always the perfect gentleman. He seemed to have developed a different attitude toward her and was much kinder than previously. He brought several invitations from his parents to events at *Brolga Hills*, which at first, she refused. She could not bear to be out there,where there were so many memories of Charlie.

Guy was gently persistant, 'Come on Goldy. I know we might have got off on the wrong foot, and for that, I take full responsibility and I apologise. I am not really such a bad guy when you get to know me. Maybe we could start over again as friends. What do you say? Mum would really love it if you would come over sometimes. It gets pretty lonely out there for her sometimes, especially since Grandma died, and Jo and David were married. I spend a fair bit of time with Dad away from the homestead, and Mum really enjoys your company.'

Goldy could not help but be impressed by his sincerity. 'As long as you understand we are only friends and don't try to pull any of your stunts, Guy.' she told him.

'Absolutely! Goldy, I want to stress to you again, I don't believe Charlie killed your father. Although...'he laughed. 'I could understand someone wanting to kill anyone who tried to stop me having you, if, of course, you were my girlfriend!'

So Goldy began, once more to visit the *Brolga Hills* and renewed her friendship with Jack, and Diana, and developed a new relationship with Guy. Even to the point of him suggesting to her that sometime in the future, she should consider marrying him! She turned him down very scathingly, but he seemed not to be put off, and continued to be pleasant and charming around her.

Goldy threw herself into her work, determined to put everything behind her. Convinced that sooner or later, Charlie's innocence would be established. She kept writing letters to keep in contact with him, but he returned them all unopened, and would have nothing to do with her. She wept bitter tears and begged David to try to change Charlie's mind, but it was all to no avail.

Charlie's appeal was dismissed, despite all Earle Dennison's assurances. However, he said he would keep in touch with Goldie, but he advised her to leave Charlie alone. She promised, but insisted that if there was anything he needed, it was to be provided, and she would pay the bill.

It was now well over two years since she had any contact with Charlie. He had been right; she did want a family and a home. Neither of which she was apparently going to share with him. What had her grandmother said about it sometimes being 'the wrong time'?

As time passed, Goldy spent more and more time with the Kingsleys. Diana really loved her and was always trying to rope her in for some fund raising event, or just for dinner parties.

Diana made no secret of the fact that she and Jack would be delighted if Goldy were to marry their son! They were sure they would make a good pair.

However, Goldy had never quite forgiven him for his devious seduction plan, but she was also aware of his position in the community, and that he stood to inherit a substantial fortune from his parents. As it was, he presently held the position of station manager and Jack was anxious that he should settle down so that he and Diana could retire and go travelling in their retirement.

Her brother, Sam, continued trying to matchmake. 'Go on Goldy! He'd make you the perfect husband. You would never have another money worry in your life, and I know he has been totally enamoured of you, since the day he first saw you. Come on Sis! Do something for yourself for a change. You know Dad would have approved, he really liked Guy. Grandma would be pleased too I know.'

One Saturday, Goldy was at *Brolga Hills,* enjoying a pleasant day with Diana. Jack, David, Jo and Guy were boundary riding, repairing fences and looking for stray cattle. She and Diana were pruning the roses in the garden, when Diana stopped and looked at her.

'Let's go have some tea. There is something I need to say to you.' As they sat in the pretty sitting room sipping their tea, Diana confided.

'You know Goldy, Jack and I would be so thrilled if you were to become the new mistress of *Brolga Hills.* We could rest easy in our retirement if we knew you were here with Guy. I know he has asked you to marry him, and that you have turned him down, but he loves you very much and I think he always has. He's certainly not interested in anyone else! Also Jo is so very fond of you, she loves you like a sister you know. We used to worry about her and what would happen to her when Guy finally married, but with you here

I am sure she and David would be happy to stay on to help him run things'

Goldy didn't know what to say. She had never said anything to anyone, except Charlie and David, about her experiences with Guy, and most certainly not his mother.

She chose her words carefully. 'Diana, I love you and Jack and Jo and David. You have been my family since dad died, and I would love to be part of *Brolga Hills*, but I am not sure that I could ever love Guy, the way you, or he, would want me to.' She took another sip of tea. 'My heart still belongs to Charlie Wentworth; I guess it always will, I'm afraid. It would hardly be fair to Guy to marry him feeling like that about someone else!'

Diana lent across and held Goldy's face in her hands. 'My dear girl, there are many reasons for making a good marriage. Not all of them involving great love. Companionship, shared interests, respect, security, a sound future for your children. Let me tell you something, I have never told anyone before. I wasn't madly in love with Jack, when I married him. As you know, I was an air hostess. It was a great job, but limited future; for as long as the looks held out! I met Jack on a flight from Rome. He was good looking, rich, pleasant, attentive, and looking for a wife. I came here as a bride, and fell in love with the place.

I think Jack knew I wasn't as in love as he was, but, you know what? I now love him as much as it is possible to love a man. I discovered all the other qualities he possesses. He is kind, funny, loyal, protective, considerate, and he has never looked at another woman in nearly thirty years. Sometimes that crazy passion, we call love, can mislead us. Please, my dear, just think about it!'

Goldy felt confused and overwhemed by a myriad of emotions. She loved Charlie, there was no doubt about that.

229

She missed him so much that sometimes it became a physical ache, and she wept when she thought of their time together, of the loving they had shared, and how, now, he would not even accept her letters. It was as if he were dead, only he was not; just lost to her. She still wanted the things she had always wanted - marriage, a home, children, to be part of a family again. Diana was right. Life had to go on, but how?

She sought out David Wentworth, the nearest thing to Charlie she could find. She told him what Diana had suggested.

'I can't tell you what to do, Goldy', he said sadly. 'Charlie has made a decision not to see you and I guess he felt his reasons were sound. He was only thinking of you and your future. He thinks you have a right to be happy; if not with him, then someone else. Jo and I will support you whatever you do. I think that is what Charlie would want me to advise you.'

Several sleepless nights later, after discussing it farther with Clara, Goldy decided to go back to England for a while. She didn't want to stay there for ever, Australia was her home and whatever future she had, was there. However, a few weeks in the calm of Cornwall and her gran Tremaine's home, would certainly help her to clear her head.

She rang Sam and he was very supportive. Now that he had Sonia, he was painfuly aware of his sister's loneliness. Yes, he thought the trip would do her good, and at her request, he arranged the flight to London.

She resigned from the nursing post, after promising to be available part time, when she returned from England, until a permanent replacement could be found. She knew that would probably be a long time!

CHAPTER THIRTY YWO

A CORNISH RETREAT

Two weeks later, she arrived at Heathrow airport, and after a brief stay in London, caught the night train to Penzance. Anne Tremaine met her at the station and they drove the few miles to her home.

Despite her joy at seeing her granddaughter again, the meeting was a tearful reunion. The journey to Australia, so full of hope had become yet another tragedy for this little family.

Goldy soon adjusted to being back in England. She was enjoying her stay and had, as yet, no thoughts of when she might return to Walkabout Creek. She sat in the small parlour of her grandmother's cottage, looking out over the pretty garden, to the sea, watching some cheeky sparrows pulling worms from a freshly dug patch of earth.

On her lap was a bundle of letters, newly delivered, and she paused from reading to take in the peaceful view outside. One of the letters was from Sam, with news of his engagement to the beautiful Sonia. There was a long letter from Jo, full of news of *Brolga Hills*, of David, and importantly, of her pregnancy! All the local the gossip about Walkabout Creek, of her horse events and successes. She signed off with the message that they all missed her enormously, especially Guy!

Clara had written too, with news of the pub, the renovations and improvements. She enclosed a photograph of *Rufus*, just to reassure Goldy that David was caring for him. She sent love from them all, with a reminder to come home soon.

There was a scrawled note from Sylvia, with news of the clinic and all her patients. Goldy smiled as she read of some of the recent escapades of the community. Someone had been arrested trying to burn down the post office, apparently because the pensions were late one week! *Some things never change,* thought Goldy to herself.

The last letter was from Diana Kingsley, in her flowery hand with her usual chatty style. She was thrilled with the prospect of her new grandchild. As ever her news was sophisticated and full of fun. Her closing remarks resonated in Goldy's brain. '*Do think about what we discussed about marriage, my dear chld. You are far too lovely to spend your life alone. You always have us, but you need your own husband and children.*'

She did think about it. Certainly Guy was everything her father and brother claimed, but the memories of her time and love with Charlie seemed to push everything else into the background.

When she closed her eyes, she could see his warm smile and his blue, blue eyes, and at night she could feel his arms around her, loving her with his all consuming passion , but Diana was right. Charlie was gone. He had made it quite plain that he did not want her to wait for him. Had he not refused to see her, or even exchange letters? Indeed he was truly gone now, only a wonderful memory, but memories did not a future make.

It was true that Guy cared deeply for her. Had he not always told her that, since the day they met? He was a very attractive man, with a wonderful family; he was comfortably off with a secure future.

Undoubtedly good husband and father material, but he was not her Charlie. Diana said she coud learn to love him, but would that be enough?

She knew what her father would say. What would Gran Tremaine suggest?

Anne Tremaine was a wise old woman. 'I never give other people advice,' she said gently, in answer to Goldy's questions. 'I believe we have to chart our own course in this life. All I will say, is go with what is in your heart.'

On a fresh, windy afternoon, Goldy went walking along the cliff path near the cottage. She always felt at peace with the cliffs and the blue Atlantic ocean below. She loved watching the white spray crashing at the base of the cliffs, before throwing itself back into the sea, and hearing the scream of the seagulls overhead as they wheeled and fell on the wind currents, occasionally diving to catch a careless fish.She thought it was probably one of the most beautiful place on earth. No wonder her mother had loved it so much. From her viewpont, Goldy could see the fishing boats coming in from their labour, so far below they looked like models.

It was all so different from Walkabout Creek. Suddenly, she was overwhelmed with longing for the faraway place and the bush; for the smell of eucalypts and the melody of magpies. Time to go home.

On her way back to the cottage, she took the narrow path down past the little church yard and she sat for a while on the grass by her mother's grave. Suzanne had been such a lovely woman. Too young to die. Goldy wiped a tear away. *'Oh Mum, I wish you were here to guide me, to tell me what to do. You and Dad had such a good marriage, and I suppose you are together again now. Mum, you would have liked Charlie, and I know you could have talked Dad around, but now it's all too late!'*

How long she stayed there by the small church, she had no idea, but by the time she stood up to make her way home, dusk was falling. As she approached the house, Goldy was surprised to see a strange car parked near the front gate. It was empty, so she assumed her grandmother had visitors.

She walked slowly through the white wicker gate, up the path between beds of rampant colour, a myriad of flowers. As she entered the cottage, a large figure unfolded from an armchair – Guy Kingsley!

Her gran was smiling broadly. 'Well, isn't this a nice surprise? This nice young man has flown half way around the world from Australia, just to see you!'

By the time Goldy recovered from the shock, she found a voice, not entirely her own. 'Hullo Guy. What on earth are you doing here? There's nothing wrong at home is there? Jo? Diana? Is Grandma Clara is okay?'

'No, no Goldy, nothing wrong, except that we all miss you like crazy, but that can all be fixed if you will only come home!'

Anne Tremaine rose hurriedly. 'I'm sure you two have lots to talk about, so I'll just go and make us all a pot of tea!' She moved silently out of the room.

'What a lovely lady she is.' remarked Guy. 'Goldy, I won't beat around the bush, I have missed you more than I could ever have imagined. So I have come to ask you, most sincerely, to be my wife, and to let me take you home with me to *Brolga Hills*. The place just isn't the same without you. Say you'll marry me, please?'

Goldy thought about everything Diana had said.

She thought about the future, stretching out before her, bleak and lonely. Guy took her hesitation as refusal, and he clasped her hand in his.

'Honestly darling, I have loved you since the first time I saw you, and I promise I will do everything in my power to make you happy. I know it is Charlie you wanted, but he's gone, and in his place I will be the best husband in the world. Just say you will marry me!'

Goldy looked into his handsome face and saw a gentleness and sincerity she had never seen before. She took a deep breath and heard herself say, 'Yes Guy, I will accept your proposal and I would be proud to be your wife.'

His relief and pleasure were palpable. He kissed her gently, took her in his arms and then called out to Anne Tremaine. 'I think we need something stronger than tea! This beautiful lady has just agreed to be my wife!'

Anne embraced them both warmly. 'Guy told me he was going to propose, and I am so glad you have accepted. I know you will both be very happy. Now, you must ring your families! I am sure they will all be delighted"

She was right. Diana and Jim were thrilled with the news, and Goldy spoke to Jo and David. She sensed that David was a little subdued, but she understood. She spoke to Clara and then rang her brother. Guy was so happy to share his good fortune, and Sam was obviously delighted. Hadn't he always wanted the two of his favourite people to get together?

After dinner, Guy went back to his hotel near the harbour, despite Anne's invitation to stay. Goldy was standing in her bedroom when her gran came in to say goodnight.

'I'm glad that you accepted him Goldy. He seems such a nice young man and he can certainly give you everything your father wanted for you Sometimes, you know, we have to let go of the past, my dear, and go forward with our heads held high and make our own futures.'

Goldy stood at the window, watching the moonlight dancing on the water. 'Thanks Gran. I believe, it is the right thing for me at this time. I know my Dad would have wanted me to marry Guy. Perhaps Dad was right all the time. Guy will certainly provide me with security. I do believe he really cares for me. I guess it is now up to me to be the best wife I can be.' She kissed her grandmother goodnight and prepared to get into bed.

'Oh my darling Charlie, forgive me.' she whispered. 'You said this was what you wanted for me, but I didn't think it would be with Guy. Oh my darling, I hope I am doing the right thing.'

Next morning, Guy arrived early. 'I'm taking you into Penzance,' he said, 'I found a great little jeweller where I can buy you the best diamond ring in the shop! I didn't bring one with me in case you said no! Then we'll book our trip home. I thought a ship voyage might be nice, give you time to get used to the idea before you get back to Walkabout Creek. All the folks at home are so delighted!

They drove down to the town along narrow lanes with high hedgerows, and fortunately, not too much traffic. Goldy was caught up pointing out well known landmarks, like St Michael's Mount. Before we go home, I'll take you to Lands End,' she said. You can't come this far without going there!'

Guy was in high spirits and she found herself caught up in his euphoria. *'He really was an extremely good looking man, she thought, and really nice now he had lost that arrogant attitude'*

For all that he had been so demanding in the past, he now treated her with a deference and respect she found very refreshing. Apart from affectionate kisses and hugs, he made no moves on her at all.

He bought a beautiful ring in a small jeweller's shop in the main street, and as it needed a slight alteration to fit her slender fingers, Guy suggested they have a look around and have some lunch. Goldy wanted to buy a few gifts to take back to Australia, so they expored some of the little shops tucked away in the narrow streets of the town. She found a beautiful fully rigged sailing ship in a bottle, for Sam. The old man who made it was only too happy to show off his talents in his tiny workshop behind the counter. Goldy watched in amazement as he manipulated the masts and sails into an upright position with strong cotton and tweezers.

She bought a brass lizard for Jack, some lovely Cornish pottery for Diana, a warm wrap for Sylvia, a beautiful lace shawl for Clara and a magnificent porcelain horse for Jo. She found a model fishing boat for Kevin, and a Cornish doll, in full costume for Sally, and a brass dolphin for David. 'I'll get some perfume for Sonia, on the way home. I don't really think she's into souvenirs!'

Guy went into a travel agent off the main street, and soon had made arrangements for a cruise home, leaving in a fortnight's time from Tilbury, in London. Goldy was touched to discover that he had booked two single cabins for them. He certainly was taking nothing for granted. She wondered fleetingly if Diana had had some input into all this, but she wisely said nothing.

Guy decided it would be good to spend some time in London prior to their departure. 'May never get another chance,' he said, 'so I'd like to have a look around.'

Anne Tremaine was sad to see her grandaughter leave, but happy in the knowledge that she would no longer be alone. She liked Guy, his laconic, laid back manner made her feel relaxed and confident and reminded her of her late Australian son-in-law. His family had already opened their arms and hearts to Goldy, and she felt loved and reassured that she had made the right decision.

The young couple drove up to London, returned the hire car at Shepherd's Bush, and caught a taxi to Claridge's hotel, where Guy had again booked separate rooms.

They spent their days exploring the fascinating city. It seemed that everywhere had long queues; Madame Taussaud's Wax Works, Westminster Abbey, the Tower of London, where Goldy enviously compared her diamond with the Crown Jewels! The Natural History Museum, the Tate Gallery, the horse Guards at Whitehall, where

Guy was much taken with the magnificent horses when they went to watch the changing of the guards.

They spent their evenings at the various theatres, Covent Garden for the Russian ballet, Ella Fitzgerald at the Victoria and 'My Fair Lady'. They ate dinner at trendy bistros and Guy was unstintingly generous. Together, they walked miles through Kensington Gardents, Kew Gardens, Regent's Park Zoo and down to Buckingham Palace; travelled every direction on the London Underground, and went for a boat trip on the river Thames to Tower Bridge. Guy seemed unphased by all the activity and his enthusiasm was contagious.

Almost too soon, it was time to embark on their journey home. When at last, they found their way to the docks at Tilbury, Goldy was exhausted and more than ready to relax in the lounge, preferably with a long drink.

CHAPTER THIRTY THREE

THE JOURNEY

The ship was scheduled to sail to Australia via the Cape of Good Hope, South Africa. Their first port of call was Le Havre, in France, where they joined a day tour to visit Rheims, where, 500 hundred years earlier, Joan of Arc was burned at the stake in the town square. Goldy loved the old town with its pretty squares and open air flower and food markets. The magnificent churches and public buildings stood as testimony to the many hundreds of years the town had existed. There were trendy shops where Goldy indulged herself buying some expensive leather shoes.

A few days later, they sailed up the broad expanse of water into Lisbon, in Portugal.They only had a few short hours, but they went ashore, and were impressed by the scale of the buildings and by magnificent sculptures. On the edge of the harbour there was the magnificent monument to the explorers who had sailed from Lisbon over the past few hundred years. On a huge scale, it depicted the bow of a sailing ship and on each side were sculptures of famous explorers like Vasco De Gama, Christopher Columbas.

Goldy enjoyed her first experience of sea travel. There was plenty to do onboard and every evening had a floor show and a following dance which she and Guy thoroughly enjoyed.

He was so polite and charming to everyone on board that she began to see him in an entirely different light, and she and found it hard to imagine that he had once seemed so totally intolerable to her. He was the soul of courtesy and charm to eGoldy, and treated her with such kindness and consideration that she felt she was beginning to fall in love with him a little more every day.

It was not that she forgot Charlie, it was simply that she had moved him to a separate compartment in her heart, never to be forgotten, and always loved, as one does with a beloved who has died.

When they called into Teneriffe, in the Canary Islands, Goldy felt for the first time that she was indeed visiting an exotic place. The air was festive and the beautiful harbour gave magnificent views of the city, with its tree lined avenues, beautiful parks and trendy shops, with more than a touch of Spain. The sun shone warmly, and as the ship sailed out on the afternoon tide, everyone joined in the traditional farewell song, led by the entertainment crew.

The Atlantic ocean was an incredible blue, the weather glorious. As they headed south-east toward the west coast of Africa, they saw dolphins, seals, flying fish and numerous sea birds. They stopped for ten hours in Walvis Bay in Namibia, where they joined a short tour, of the nearby desert and the famous sand dunes, some of the biggest in the world. The main highway was a narrow road bordered by a few sparse palm trees, and Goldy laughed to see a road sign saying solemnly, 'Watch out for sand! There really wasn't much else! The endless desert gave way to sandy beaches and they saw flamingos feeding in the warm water.

Next port was Cape Town, South Africa. Goldy was enchanted by the beautiful city lying at the base of Table Mountain, a large flat topped mountain, almost perpetually draped in a tablecloth of white cloud. They went to the summit in the round cable car and were rewarded with an incredible view of Cape Town and surrounds.

There was a group of young Africans offering hand gliding from the top, but Goldy talked Guy out of that, very quickly!

Back on the ground, they went for lunch on the Victoria and Albert wharf, where a profusion of exclusive shops and trendy artifacts outlets, lined the arcades and streets. A group of musicians entertained them and boats of every size and type lay alongside the wharves. There was a lovely holiday atmosphere.

Goldy was struck by the huge divide between the white population with money who lived in beautiful houses in tree lined suburbs such as Camp Bay, and the township they visited just a few short miles from the city centre, which was nothing more than a giant slum. One tap in the middle of about four hundred homes, and an electric pole with dozens of wires leading off into small shanties, built of cardboard or tin. Despite the poverty, the people were friendly and welcoming, and Goldy saw one small boy happily playing with a homemade car constructed from an empty milk carton, with bottle tops for wheels.

They took a tour of the 'District 6 Museum.' This was a memorial to one of the most extensive resettlement programs in South Africa. Over 60,000 people were forcibly removed to a site 25 kms away. All their homes were bulldozed as being in a 'Whites only region. The museum had a plan of the district reproduced on the ground floor. There were notes and letters from former residents or their families, which gave an insight into the history of the area. The only buildings left were places of worship, and a community centre, still in use by those people to the present day,

'How much we have to be grateful for in Australia', she said quietly to Guy, who was sampling a homemade brew outside a hovel, watched by three wide-eyed children.

They sailed for a day and called at Mussel Bay, where they visited a small private wildlife reserve. They saw giraffes, antelopes, three elephants, and a group of rather tired lions, rescued from zoos and other private parks. There were also zebra, buffalo and a troupe of monkeys.

When they reached Durban, they left the ship and took a quick tour around the city, where they noted some very lavish colonial style buildings. The crowds and the hustle bustle of the markets, were really not their scene, so they joined a tour up to 1000 hills, where they visited a Zulu village and were treated to the spectacle of some traditional dancing. They spent a night in a luxurious Safari Park.

Although they shared a bungalow, Guy insisted that they sleep apart. Goldy was fast reaching the stage where she really wouldn't have minded if it had been otherwise, but he strongly stated that there would be nothing before they were married. When Goldy playfully chided him and reminded him of his earlier behaviour, he merely replied gruffly that, 'It is different now you are my fiancee, and things must be done properly.'

She asked him what would have happened if he had managed to get his own way with her back in Walkabout Creek. He thought for a moment and then said. 'I honestly don't know! You were always a challenge to me, and I'm glad we are doing this your way! It's so much better.'

When they returned to the ship next day, they looked forward to the last stage of the journey across the Indian Ocean to Australia. The last port was Mauritius, where Goldy delighted in the welcome from colourful dancers and musicians on the quay side.There was a large variety of shops and markets, but far less hectic than Durban. Goldy fell in love with a street which was almost completely covered over by umbrellas. Such a colourful and pretty sight!

Finally they reached Australia and they both felt overcome with nostalgia, as they sailed past Rottnest Island into Fremantle and smelt the fragrance of eucalypts in the air. Home at last!

Goldy's brother Sam was at the port of Fremantle to welcome them home, and to organise a private flight home to Brolga Hills.

The Kingsley and O'Hara families were delighted to welcome them both home, and Diana threw a lavish engagement party for the young couple. Jo and David were delighted, when Goldy and Guy reiterated Jim's insistence that they wanted them both to stay on and take a more active role on the station and, particularly, to take charge of the horse breeding program.

'We can move into the manager's house when you two move into the main house,' Jo said happily, 'especially when our new baby comes in a few weeks'.

Guy and Goldy's wedding was to take place six weeks later, in the Catholic church in Walkabout Creek. Before the ceremony, her grandmother, Clara took her gently in her arms. 'Are you sure about this, my darling?' she asked gently. 'I know you will always love your Charlie. Can you let that love go to be a good wife to Guy? He deserves that, you know.'

Goldy smiled, 'Yes Grandma, I can do this. I know Guy loves me, and I will be the best wife I can be. I will always love Charlie, but now it must be in memory only.' Clara gave her another hug. "God bless you child.'

Father John was in his element. David was best man, Sam the groomsman, Jo, the bridesmaid, and Jack Kingsley proudly agreed to give the bride away. Diana presented Goldy with a beautiful lace wedding gown, which she had ordered from Sydney. 'I always wanted another daughter,' she said tearfully, hugging Goldy tightly. 'and now I have one,'

Jack hugged her tightly. 'Welcome to the family, Goldy dear.' as he presented her with a diamond pendant and earrings set, which would have cost Goldy a year's salary! Her brother Sam, never stopped smiling all day. 'My sister and my best friend, all now one happy family. Dad would be so proud of you today, Sis. You look so beautiful.'

The large reception was held at Brolga Hills and it seemed as if everyone Goldy had ever met, was there. Sonia, now Sam's proud fiancee, flashed a large diamond ring, but insisted Goldy had scooped the pool with the handsome Guy, a thought perhaps challenged by Jo, as David also looked splendid in his morning suit.

With her usual generosity, Diana had included everyone in Walkabout Creek and surrounding districts on the invitation list. After the many sorrows over some years, this wedding brought much joy to the towns folk. Kevin and Sally were there, the bar staff, her health worker Sylvia and her husband; the police, teachers, shopkeeper, pastoralist families, everyone for a hundred miles around. The RFDS staff who could get there; Guy's friends from University, and Goldy's nursing friends from her orientation.

A welcome guest was Yuri Astanov, who presented Goldy with a beautiful bracelet, which had belonged to his late wife, Natasha. 'I cannot think of anyone who my Natasha would approve more, than you.' he said with a big smile.

There was one special guest, kept as a secret until the actual wedding day. 'Grandma!' cried Goldy delightedly, as she hugged Anne Tremaine warmly. Anne had been flown out from England by Jack Kingsley, and driven up from Perth by Sam and Sonia.

She was to stay with Diana and Jack until Goldy and Guy returned from their honeymoon, and then remain for a further month, before going to stay in Perth with Sam.

Anne was as charming, as always. She and Clara had immediately hit it off from the first time they met at Danny and Suzanne's wedding, all those years ago, so they were never short of things to talk about and thoroughly enjoyed each other's company.

Guy and Goldy drove the long trek to Port Hedland, and from there caught a plane to Hong Kong and then to Bali, for a month's honeymoon. Guy was the soul of kindness and generosity, and Goldy began to enjoy her married life. She thought of Charlie from time to time, but never being one to wallow in the past, she threw herself wholeheartedly into her new role, as Mrs Guy Kingsley.

David suggested that she should be the one to break the news of her wedding to Charlie, So with some trepidation, she rang Earle Dennison to tell him, and since Charlie would not accept letters from her, she asked him if he would let Charlie know. Earle was very understanding and promised to break it gently to him. 'I know it was what he wanted for you, but he will still be hurting. I'm afraid he will really think he has lost everything now, but you deserve to be happy, my dear girl. Not everyone gets a second chance.'

Within weeks of the wedding, Goldy was pregant. Guy was thrilled. 'I know you couldn't be that beautiful for nothing!' he enthused.

Diana was pleased, but said she wished they had waited a little longer before starting their family. 'You need time to get to know each other better.' Goldy felt sure they knew each other quite well enough!

Sally and Kevin, along with Troy, seemed happy running the pub, for Clara and after discussing it with her, it was decided to let them take over the lease for the time being. Clara expressed a wish to go south, to Kalgoorlie. In the meantime, Goldy visited weekly, to sign the cheques, and she and Sally had many good laughs together. She always kept her share of takings from the pub separate from Clara's, Sam's and the Gregsons, It was her little stash for a rainy day.

Suzi seemed to have disappeared from town. Sylvia said she had gone bush, with her 'husband'. She had occasionally been seen around with two or three little children. Goldy hoped she was happy.

CHAPTER THIRTY FOUR

THE NEXT GENERATION

Jo and David's daughter was born within weeks of Goldy's wedding. A little fair haired replica of her pretty mother. Her parents were delighted with her, and had many dreams about her future. Young Sarah Wentworth was destined to be a fine equestrian!! A baby saddle had already been ordered!

In due course, the Kingsley baby made his welcomed appearance, Daniel John Kingsley, the future heir apparent to *Brolga Hills*. A much loved child, young Danny was the centre of life at home, and a source of great joy to his grandparents. By the time he was two, he was riding his own pony with his cousin Sarah, under his aunt's careful supervision. Guy had a special saddle and helmet made for him, and the two children were often seen on leading reins, checking the fences with Jo.

Goldy watched them and smiled. Life was good. She was happy with Guy and pleased that David and Jo were so contented. She felt they were two very special people who really deserved the best life could give them She was happy to note that David had become so much more confident and outgoing alongside Jo. Although he was gentle, David was no pushover, and was not adverse to putting his foot down when Jo became a little too 'bossy', as he called it, and that she in turn, showed a great love and respect for him .

Guy kept his word to Goldy. He was a kind and considerate husband, even-tempered, generous and affectionate. The physical side of their marriage was very satisfactory, with his passion and commitment, complementing her own. As Diana had predicted, she found herself growing to love him more as time passed. She certainly loved him, but she was not sure that she was actually *in* love with him. Not in the way she had been with Charlie. But, she was expecting her second child, and was happy.

Although she still thought about Charlie, she had long accepted that he could never be anything but a lovely memory. She no longer yearned after the life they might have had, but worked hard to strengthen her marriage to Guy. She made the occasional phone call to Earle Dennison to see if there was anything he needed in jail. Assuring Earle that she would pay for it out of her own account, so Guy would not need to know. She had no wish to antagonise her husband, and this was the only secret she ever kept from him.

Another little boy joined the family in the Spring. Steven Guy Kingsley. Young Steven grew rapidly, a sturdy youngster, who in what seemed no time at all, was joining his father, aunt, cousin and brother, down near the horses. By now, Jack and Diana enjoyed their grandchildren so much, that they seemed loathe to leave on their promised travels. The house was large, so it was no problem having them there. It was really a blessing to Goldy, as no replacement had been found for her in the clinic, so she spent two days a week at work. Fortunately Diana was happy to care for the children.

Sylvia worked full time and only contacted Goldy in emergencies that she felt she was unable to manage. She was extremely capable and Goldy had every confidence in her ability.

When Goldy found herself pregnant for the third time, she was a little upset. Dr Morris had suggested that she go on the pill, to give herself a rest, but she had not made up her mind completely, and then found herself expecting again. Guy was thrilled. He adored his family, and spoke glowingly of - 'half a dozen kids'!

'He can have the next three!' Goldy confided to Diana one day, when she was feeling particularly large and cumbersome. All was forgotten with the birth of their daughter, Suzanne Diana Kingsley. She had Goldy's russett hair, and green eyes, and was a charmer from the day she was born.

Charlie Wentworth had now been in prison for more than seven years. Apart from his lawyer, his brother David and very occasional visits from his parents, he refused to see anyone. He kept very much to himself, and the other prisoners quickly learned to give him a wide berth. Cody was probably his only friend. From different worlds, the two men shared a mutual respect. Neither asked the other for any details relating to their incarceration.

Charlie took up studying Accountancy and Farm Management, in the hope that when he was finally released, he might be able to get a job on a farm as a manager. He still had his dream of buying a spread of his own, like *Milly Downs*, but he knew that the reality was he did not have enough money for such a venture. Apart from his beer money, he had saved every bit of his pay, in order to buy his dream, but it fell well short of what he would need. However, that dream kept him alive in prison.

He had a photograph of Goldy pinned up in his cell, and in his lowest moments, he would remember the loving nights he had spent with her, and the amazing woman that she was.

He had never lost that first fascination with her, which has only grown as he learned more about her.

He allowed himself to slip away into that fantasy world, where the walls of his cell faded away. At night, he would look through the bars of his tiny cell window, at the only sliver of sky in view; the distant stars, and when he heard the noise of traffic and police sirens, he dreamed of the dark velvet of the outback; of the ringing silence of the bush; the frogs, cicadas, and occasional Mopoke, that pierced that silence, and wondered what his life might have been with Goldy as his wife.

When he had first been arrested, he felt like a caged animal in the tiny cell that became his home. He raged against the world, refusing to cooperate, fought with other prisoners, earning himself loss of priviledges, and a short spell in isolation, and even contemplated suicide, until Earle Dennison managed to convince him that he was only making things harder for himself, and if he was ever to be considered for parole, he needed to behave himself. Earle supplied him with some extras to give a little comfort, but Charlie never knew they came from Goldy.

During those first few months, he had gained much comfort and encouragement from his contact with Goldy and from her letters. She was his world, and he lived for her alone. His longing to be with her was a physical pain, from which there seemed no relief. He loved her so desperately, and missed her so much. Finally, he convinced himself that she was entitled to have a life of her own, and not sit around waiting for him, and that dreamt of release. He decided he must let her go. He knew it would be pointless to suggest to her that this was best, so he decided that he would make this happen by refusing to see her, or have any contact with her.

David told him of Goldy's heartbreak over his decision, but he remained strong. She needed to have a life, not to share this twilight world of prison and misery. Nevertheless, he was gutted when told of her marriage to Guy Kingsley. In the darkness and privacy of his cell, he wept bitter tears.

He always asked Earle for any news of her, and later rejoiced to hear of her children. He wished they were his, but he was happy for her. 'She'll make a great little mum,' he told Earle.'I know that I made the right decision for her!'

oooOooo

Goldy was sitting on the veranda of the pub one Saturday afternoon, when she saw an old man with a white beard climb out of a very weather beaten truck. He raised his hat to her, and she recognised Yuri Astanov, from *Milly Downs* .'Hullo Mrs Kingsley. What news of my friend Charlie Wentworth?

Terrible business. He would never hurt your father; not my friend. He is a good man. I miss him very much.'

'Me too. I agree he is a good man,' responded Goldy, 'and I know how much he used to enjoy coming out to see you.'

'Ah yes, he has a special feeling for *Milly Downs*, yes?'

'Yes, indeed he does. For you too, I think. I know once he dreamed of buying it from you?'

'He did, but I was not yet ready to sell.'

'There's no way he could afford it anyway now.' She said sadly.

The old man smiled sadly. 'Perhaps you would come out and see me sometime? You could perhaps bring Charlie's brother, David? I need a little help.'

'Yes. Perhaps we could come at the weekend. How about next Sunday?'

'That sounds just fine. I will look forward to that. Goodbye Mrs Kingsley.' He raised his hat again as he disappeared into the bar.

The next weekend, as agreed, and with Guy's blessing, Goldy and David drove out to see Yuri Astanov. *Milly Downs* was as enchanting as she remembered. She felt nostalgic as they crossed the creek near the lake and drove up the hill to the homestead. It was small, but neat and Goldy noted that Yuri had placed a vase of wildflowers on the kitchen table. He had organised a small afternoon tea for them, including an apple cake, which, he proudly said, he had baked himself.

Yuri and David seemed to have developed a sound rapport, and Goldy noted they were soon discussing livestock and other problems on the station. Goldy took the time to look around the small garden next to the house. Everything was so neat and tidy that she could almost forget that the old man lived alone. By the time they left for home, they had made definite plans to go back. David to repair some fencing, and Goldy to bring some cuttings for the garden.

So a routine was developed, whereby once a month they spent the day at *Milly Downs*. Sometimes Goldy took the children who loved to swim in the lake, Yuri often told them stories about Russia and Poland, and he taught Daniel how to whittle a piece of wood and make a flute out of it. Often they took Rufus with them and he loved the lake as much as did the children.

Many weeks after their first visit, Goldy sat with Yuri watching the children playing cricket with David.

She remembered Charlie saying that there had been an accident in which Yuri had lost his wife and child. She gently asked him about them, and saw a pained shadow pass across the old man's face.

'Yes, it was very sad. One time, the rain, she just kept coming, and my wife, she wanted to go to town to get some supplies. It was my son's ninth birthday and she wanted to get some candles for the cake. I told her it didn't matter, but she wanted everything to be so good for him. I tell her to wait for me because I had to move some cattle to higher ground, but she does not wait. Together, they get in the old ute to drive to town, but the water it is across the road,' he indicated the small flowing stream, just below the house. 'She thought it would be okay, but the current, she was too strong and they were washed away downstream. There was no chance for them and they drowned.'

He wiped away a tear as he continued. 'For so long I wished I had gone too, but life is to be lived, even when we don't want it. I'm sure you know how that feels.'

Goldy took his hand and squeezed it. 'I am so sorry Yuri. You must miss them very much.'

He nodded, 'But to see the children here, it does my old heart good. You understand?'

'Yes, of course. We will come whenever you want us to.'

On the drive home, Goldy confided in David that her first date with Charlie, had been a picnic at *Milly Downs*. She felt very nostalgic, and found tears were near the surface. 'I wish Charlie could be here!'

David was very sensitive to the occasion, and he was always so supportive.

CHAPTER THIRTY FIVE

FIRE

Fire! Fire!' the cry rang out across the stockyards at *Brolga Hills*. Jack and Guy ran outside. On the horizon beyond the the paddocks, the sky glowed orange in the evening light. The water trucks, always in readiness, stood near the stables. Jack quickly barked orders to the stockmen.

'David! Take the ute out and see exactly where it is! Doug, Casey, you get those trucks started! Jim, you get some of the boys and check out where those new cattle are. If necessary, drive them down to the creek! Guy! Get those hoses going! Turn on the pumps and water down the roof and verandas! Water down all the outside of the house! While you're at it, give Sergeant Paterson a call, to keep him up to date with what's happening out here! Diana! Goldy! Quick as you can! You make sure the women and kids are ready to evacuate if necessary. The fire is coming from the east, so the road should be safe into town.Then load up some blankets, torches, water, and food for the children. Be ready to go if I give the word.'

Goldy helped Diana organise the staff women and their children. They were all gathered on the veranda, their eyes wide with fear.

Her own children, and their cousin Billy, sat quietly each clutching a favourite possession. Danny and Billy had their horse books, gifts from Grandpa Kingsley, Steven had Charlie's old dog, *Rufus*, held firmly by the collar, and Suzanne clung lovingly to her Raggedy Ann doll.

The fire was burning fiercely. The boys reported it was still some twenty miles from the homestead, but a stiff breeze was driving it directly toward them. David and Jo went to the stables to check on the horses.'What will you do with them them Jo?' asked Goldy, anxiously.

'Well, *Justa* and *Misty* and four of our best mares will all get into the floats,' she replied, 'The rest will probably have to take their chances. David says we will just have to release them if the fire looks like reaching us. That's the only hope they've got I'm afraid.'

Some of the cattle in the home paddock were becoming restless as they smelled the smoke. The horses too, were agitated. Jo and David loaded the mares onto two floats; Guy loaded four of the foals onto a small trailer behind the truck. 'If it comes to the worst , I'll take the four wheel drive, the trailer, the dogs and our kids and Billy. Jo will take one float, one of the boys can take the other, and you, Goldy, can take the truck with as many women and children as can fit on, plus the other foals. I'll send one of the boys with you, and we'll meet in town. Dad and Mum have their own car, so I'll just check what they are doing!' He bent and kissed her quickly. 'We'll be okay, sweetheart, just taking precautions.'

It was with a sense of unreality, that Goldy heard Jack issue the order to evacuate. The smoke was thick and acrid, and the flames were now clearly visible, as the fire devoured everything before it. Everyone did as they had been instructed to do. There was no panic as the women and children were loaded into the waiting vehicles.

'Go with Daddy, and look after Billy. Mummy will see you all in town at the hotel.' she kissed them quickly, as Guy started the engine and pulled out of the drive. She went in search of Diana. 'Are you coming Diana?' she called.

'You go along, Goldy, I'll wait for Jack We'll follow you in the car, if it gets too bad here! There's another truck ready to go, if one of the guys can drive it.'

'Doug will take it, I am quite capable of driving our truck into town,' called Goldy, jumping into the driver's seat. 'Hold on everyone! We're off'!'

It was a nightmare drive, down the rough track that passed as a road into Walkabout Creek. The smoke was now so thick, it was difficult to see more than a few yards ahead. Many of the people in the truck were coughing violently, and as the wind changed direction, sparks flew ahead of the main blaze, starting small fires. Goldy was relieved that her family was in front of her. She had every confidence in Guy, to take the children to safety.

The wind change was very evident; there were outbreaks of fire alongside the road, and as she rounded a corner, Goldy was forced to swerve violently, as a burning tree crashed down onto the road. For the first time, Goldy felt afraid and wished she had kept David with her. Some of the children in the cab, began to cry. She felt like crying too, but she jollied them along, and they were all singing raucously by the time they pulled up outside *The Imperial*. To her great relief, she saw that Guy had already arrived with the children the foals and the dogs. Jo was there with horses.

One of the horses had panicked, fallen in the float and cut itself quite badly, but that seemed to be the only casualty and Jo was coping admirably with that. Sally and Kevin were busy unloading the truck and making sure everyone was comfortable and settled. The mares and foals were taken around to the back of the pub, and tethered on the small square of lawn. The dogs frolicked happily in the back garden.

Guy appeared at her side. 'Have you seen Mum and Dad?' he asked, looking around anxiously.

'Your mother said she would stay with your father and leave with him.' she told him.

'Guy! Where are you going?!' she cried, as he jumped back into the four wheel drive.

'To get my folks! Can you give Jo a hand to see to that horse until David can get to help her? She's some nasty cuts there that need dressing. Thanks darling! ' he shouted out of the window, as the tyres squealed and he took off in a cloud of dust.

Most of the townspeople had gathered at the pub. They all watched fearfully as the orange glow grew brighter. Sergeant Paterson observed with an experienced eye. 'Unless there is a wind change, that fire will go through here, for sure! If that happens, the safest place will be in the old cellars under the pub.' He turned to Sally. 'Mrs Gregson, do you have the keys to the cellar? If so, I suggest you unlock them now, and take the children, and the old folks, downstairs, just in case.'

With them safely settled in the cellars, Goldy paused on her way to see if Jo needed help with the horses. As she stood on the veranda with Sergeant Paterson, she said quietly, 'Bob, do you really think we are in danger?'

'I'm afraid so, Goldy. We haven't had a fire this close in over a hundred years, according to the locals. Most of the Aborigines left town hours ago; that can't be a good sign! But you never know for sure, what a fire is going to do. So let's not panic yet! The old pub is a good solid stone structure. 'What is the water situation like here Kev?"

We've two bores out the back, with pretty good pressure, Sarg'. I'll get onto those and wet down as much as I can!'

'I wish Guy hadn't gone back out there, Bob.' she said quietly. 'I have a bad feeling about it. That road was hell coming in, I hope to God they will be okay.'

'The Kingsleys have been running cattle out here for over four generations. There aren't too many men as good in the bush as Jack and Guy Kingsley.' he said, patting her on the shoulder.

Kevin and Troy had managed to rustle up some food and drink for everyone, and Sally found more blankets. Soon most of the children were asleep. Goldy checked on her three and her niece, and found them sleeping, all wrapped up in one big blanket, with *Rufus*!

She thought of Yuri Astanov at *Milly Downs*. He should be safe as he was well south of the fire, and not in any direct line at present. She sat on the veranda and watched the approaching fire. She prayed for Guy and his parents.

She thought about Diana, and what she had said about growing to love Jack. That love had grown to a point where she was prepared to risk her life, rather than leave him to secure her own safety. She thought about Guy. Would she be prepared to risk her life for him?

Suddenly, she knew the answer. She went looking for Clara. 'Can you get someone to pop down and give Jo a hand with that injured horse? I'm going to help Guy.' she told her. 'If anything happens to me, I want you to make sure that David and Jo know I want them to care for our children.'

As Clara protested, Goldy said gently, 'You would have gone for Grandpa Patrick in the old days, wouldn't you?'

Clara nodded, as she embraced her, 'Take care, my darling. God go with you.'

Goldy jumped back into the truck and headed out toward *Brolga Hills*. Her eyes were stinging from the smoke, and the trees along the track were burning like beacons. Several times she had to take evasive action, veering off the track as burning branches fell from above, when her way was blocked by fallen timber. She was about half way out to the homestead when she came across a large tree which had crashed across the track.

As she pulled up, she recognised the front of Guy's four wheel drive, stuck under the tree, one end of which, was burning. She quickly clambered out and ran to the vehicle. At first she could see nothing, but as her eyes became accustomed to the darkness, she saw three figures, motionless in the jeep. Guy was in the driver's seat, a nasty gash on his head; she was not sure if he was unconscious or just in shock. Next to him, Diana lay sprawled like a broken doll across the seat. Behind the front seat, she saw Jack lying on the floor, his leg twisted under him. As she called their names, Guy stirred. 'Goldy? Where the hell did you come from?'

'Never mind that! Quick! Help me get your Mum and Dad out of this thing, before the fire reaches the petrol tank!'

Guy slowly crawled out of the vehicle; Goldy, tried to wake Jack, as Guy gently lifted his mother free of the wreckage, and carried her to the truck. Jack was harder to extricate. He was unconscious; his leg appeared to be stuck under the seat in front of him. No matter how hard Goldy tried, she could not free him. Guy seemed suddenly to snap into action. He grabbed a tyre lever from the back of the vehicle, and bodily dismantled the seat. As they pulled Jack from the floor, the fire reached the back door, and as they laid him flat in the back of the truck, the jeep burst into flames, and as they backed off, it exploded in a fireball of orange and red.

Goldy quickly turned the truck around, and headed for town as fast as she dared. She still had to negotiate the burning trees and logs, but somehow, having cheated death so closely, she felt confident they would be all right.

When they reached town, she went straight to the clinic, where she was able to assess their injuries. Although Diana and Jack both had fractures, they were fully conscious and their injuries, although severe, were not life threatening.

Goldy alerted the flying doctor, and suggested that due to the fire and smoke, daylight would be soon enough to evacuate them.

Providing of course, that the town was still on the map in the morning! She gave Jack and Diana something for their pain, splinted Jack's broken leg, Diana's two arms and left ankle, then put thirty stitches in Guy's head where he had hit the windscreen. When she had finished, she threw herself into Guy's arms and cried with relief.

'What on earth made you decide to come back?' he asked wiping tears from her grimy face.

'I just knew I had to be with you,' she sobbed. 'I knew I couldn't lose you and that you needed me there. Don't ask me how, I just knew!'

He kissed her gently. 'Thank God you did, otherwise we would all have been charcoal by now! Dad's car stopped, about five miles from the homestead; couldn't get it going again. They were going to try and sit it out, but they never would have survived.' As they went back to the hotel, arm in arm, Goldy organised for some of the men to go to the clinic and carry back her in-laws on stretchers. Sally put them in the dining room. 'They can easily be taken downstairs to the cellar if necessary, but it's quieter for them here.' she announced.

Later, with hot cups of tea in hand, Goldy and Guy sat quietly on the veranda. Guy stood up and anxiously scanned the horizon. 'I do believe that wind has dropped, and if I am not mistaken, it has changed direction!' He called out to Bob Paterson, and the two men, cautiously checked again, before letting out a whoop of delight. The wind had indeed changed. Turning the fire back on itself.

Next morning, shortly after breakfast, the RFDS plane buzzed the pub. Goldy raced down to meet it. 'That fire has certainly burnt out a large area!' said the young pilot. 'We flew over *Brolga Hills* on the way in; it looks pretty bad and you've lost some stock, but I think at least some of the homestead may be okay, but we couldn't see too much out there for the smoke!'

Soon Jack and Diana were safely loaded on board, bound for hospital. Both now well aware of their injuries, and although obviously shocked, they were lavish with their praise for their daughter-in-law. Dr Ben Morris, merely smiled and said 'I would expect nothing less from our Goldy, but he gave her a hug all the same and said quietly. 'Well done, Sister, well done!' He checked Guy's head wound; gave him the all clear, and within minutes, the little plane taxied down the runway and was soon lost in the clouds.

'I need to go home.' said Guy. 'I have to see what the damage is. There will be stock that need seeing to; probably quite a few to put down, if they are badly burnt, and the water to be sorted out. Jo and David have already gone to see how our horses fared.' He looked so desolate that Goldy put her arms around him and kissed him gently.

'We'll go home together.' she said, 'Grandma Clara will watch the children, and I'll come back to town tomorrow. Sylvia can handle any minor burns.' Guy buried his face in her hair. 'I don't deserve you, my brave girl, but I love you and I'm so glad you're my wife. Thank you for last night.We all owe you our lives.'

As they drove out to the station, it was evident how close the fire had come to the tiny township. The logs were still burning, and the air was thick with smoke. They had to take several detours en route and when they came to the burnt out Jeep, they got out of the truck and walked across to it. It was now just a blackened wreck of twisted metal. They both stood somberly looking at it, and Goldy shivered as she remembered the terror of last night. Farther on, they saw the burnt out shell of the Kingsley's car. Guy was right, they would not have survived.

As they turned into the gateway of the homestead, Goldy braced herself for the inevitable losses ahead. Through the smoke she could hardly believe what she saw. The homestead stood welcomingly in the weak morning light, apparently untouched. Jo waved cheerily from the house watching over a makeshift holding paddock, where several horses grazed contentedly on the green grass of the manicured front lawn, the remaining foals frolicking happily beside them. On the veranda, fire weary stockmen stood up to greet them. 'G'day boss! What kept ya?' said Doug, as he shook Guy's hand.

Guy looked around increduously. 'This is amazing! How on earth......?'

'Luck and hard work! The men just about emptied out the swimming pool! They managed to keep all the horses near the house, and then the wind changed at the last minute, and the fire burned back on itself. 'Fraid the stable block's gone, but the staff quarters are okay, a bit singed on the end, but it could have bin a whole lot worse. We've lost most of the fences on the east side, and stock losses are pretty high. The ones by the creek are okay, but some of the others weren't so lucky.'

'Are there many still out there that need putting down? Inquired Guy, anxiously.

'Yeh, I'm afraid there are.' said Doug. 'We was just havin' a break before we go back out there.'

'I'll pick up a gun and some ammo and I'll join you.'

Doug looked doubtful, as he looked at Guy's bandaged head. 'You sure, boss? You look like you need to take it easy for a day or two.'

'I'll rest when the work's done,' he said grimly.

'I'll get busy and cook up a feed for when you get back.' said Goldy, 'Come on Jo, I'll make us a cuppa.'

`Some of the cattle were relatively unscathed, and were driven to the west side of the property, where there was still water and feed for them. Others were badly burnt and had to be put down. At the house, Goldy heard the shots ring out, and her heart ached for her husband. As the weary men trooped into the kitchen, Goldy served them a hot breakfast of bacon, eggs, sausages, tomatoes and hot buttered toast, washed down with strong coffee.

As they ate, they told stories of their adventure. Guy proudly describing his wife's action in saving him and his parents from certain death on their way into town. 'Why didn't you guys go with everyone else, when Dad gave the order?' he asked.

Several of the men looked uncomfortable; finally Doug spoke. 'Well, it's like this, Guy . Some of the men here, have been with your dad for near on twenty years. This is the only home we've got see, and we were damned if we were going to see it go up in smoke! As for the rest of the boys, well we are pretty partial to life here in Brolga Hills.'

'We are greatly indebted to you all. Thank you, on behalf of the entire Kingsley family.' said Guy, choking back his emotion.

'Was it very awful out there?' asked Goldy later.' As Guy sat wearily at the kitchen table.

'Pretty terrible. We had to shoot a couple of hundred head of cattle, not to mention quite a lot of widlife, that couldn't outrun the flames. Kangaroos, dingos, possums, bandicoots, rabbits, some emus. That fire must really have been travelling. I am really upset that I have lost my little bay mare too. She must have got separated from the others and panicked. At least the rest are safe, the dogs too. Thanks to the boys.'

Within days, the station was buzzing with activity, as the rest of the staff, and the children, returned from town. Axes and saws rang out, as repairs began, and new fences appeared. There was a sombre moment when a stockman from *McDougall Park* Station called in to tell them that the homestead there, had been completely destroyed. They were thirty miles east of Walkabout Creek, and it was a stark reminder of how close they had come to disaster. The manager, Jim Walsh, had suffered severe burns and had been flown to Perth. His recovery, very much in doubt. Guy offered to send some men over to help drive their remaining cattle down, so they could at least have feed and water, whilst their land recovered.

After the loss of stock and feed, one of the least pleasant results of the fire, was the increase in snakes and other reptiles seeking shelter, food and water, away from the burnt out bushland. In the first week, Dirk, usually unfazed by the reptiles in the bush, was obliged to kill several large King Brown snakes, in and around the house. There were also four or five dugites, all potentialy lethal. Goldy kept a careful watch on the children.

One morning, about a week after the fire, a shout went up from the staff quarters. Doug, who had been repairing the burnt wall of the building, lifted up a piece of tin, and came face to face with an angry King Brown, some fifteen feet long! Before he could take evasive action, he was struck on the forearm, as the reptile pumped a lethal dose of venom into him.

Goldy, in town at the clinic, heard the crackle of the radio, and heard Guy's anxious voice calling the RFDS. 'Emergency! This is Brolga Hills station. We have a snake bite! Large King Brown! Requesting immediate assistance and evacuation for one, Doug Drummond!'

As Goldy listened, she heard the RFDS answer. She did not know the doctor on line, but the advice he gave was assured and calm.

'A plane will be on its way immediately; in the meantime, the usual first aid measures should be applied Pressure bandage above and below the bite, splint and rest the limb, keeping the bite site below heart level. Above all, keep the victim calm. Do not give alcohol! Be with you shortly! Over and out!'

Goldy knew that neither the clinic or the station carried antevene for snake bite. She had asked about it before, and Dr Morris had told her that the antevenene had a very short shelf life; was very expensive, and was generally well out of date when it was required. Good first aid measures, and quick evacuation were the only answer. Meanwhile, at Brolga Hills, the entire staff had turned out to clear the small strip of debris, so the aircraft could land safely. Guy worked frantically with a bulldozer, to push the heavier logs to one side. Just as he finished, they heard the drone of the RFDS Beechcraft, which was soon on the ground. Doug was administered the antevenene, stretchered, and loaded into the aircraft.

Within ten minutes, he was on his way to hospital. Yet another amazing feat from the Flying Doctor!

Life slowly returned to normal. Jack and Diana were relieved to be home, but Jack confided in Guy that he was now anxious to retire to the property they had bought in the Perth hills. Once they were well enough, they intended to go South and leave the station in the capable hands of their son Guy and his wife, and their daughter, Jo and her husband, David Wentworth.

Doug Drummond made a good recovery, although he had weakness in his arm for the rest of his life. The hospital said he was very lucky to have been at the homestead when he was bitten. Had he been out in the bush, he probably would not have survived.

Sadly, Jim Walsh from *McDougall Park* station, did not recover from his burns and died in hospital three weeks later. A stark reminder of the potential disaster of a bush fire.

CHAPTER THIRTY SIX

BUYING A HORSE

The stock numbers were slowly recovering, and the first rains brought green shoots to the surface, leaves to burnt trees, and cooled the parched landscape.The new stables had been built, and David was organising for himself and Jo to go Sydney, to buy that coveted stallion. Guy was unable to go with them, much to his disappointment, as he had to run the station, especially since his father was still not completely recovered from his injuries.

Goldy remembered her conversation with Diana, when she, Jo and David were at the stables looking at their latest acquisition, a beautiful filly bought at the yearling sales in Perth, a few months earlier. Diana had remarked, 'She's certainly lovely, but I thought you two were looking for a stallion?'

'Of course!' said David. 'But we still haven't found what we're looking for. This stallion has to be something really special, if we are to improve the blood lines up here'

'Yes', added Jo. 'He has to have good conformation, stamina, spirit, ability, intelligence. David and I are planning to going east in the future to see if we can pick up something there. We are determined to get him in the end!'

Goldy laughed. 'You sound just like your brother, and I guess Guy always get what he wants in the end?'

'Always! Haven't you learned that yet? ' Jo joined her laughter.

David and Jo were away for about three weeks, as they hunted for the best stallion they could find. Guy sent them off with a list of instructions. 'We don't want a thoroughbred', he told Jo, 'too fine boned, lacking the stamina needed for droving cattle. Something strong, with good stamina, good confirmation; big hearted.'

Although Jo and David saw many magnificent horses, the did not find what they wanted. They went to Adelaide, Sydney and outback Queensland, looking at Quarter horses, before finally following up a lead in the Snowy Mountains of Victoria, where a legendary old horse breeder had something that sounded interesting.

Here they found exactly what they were looking for. A magnificent stallion, which, prior to his capture, had been runnng with a herd of mares, in the high country. He was about four years old. At 16 hands, of good confirmation; strong, spirited and intelligent. They saw some of his progeny and Jo was delighted. She and David explained to the owner what they were planning, with their own breeding program.

'We have some really good mares, that I bought in Adelaide, but trying to find the right stallion to get what we want, has been pretty near impossible. This boy looks exactly what we've been looking for!' David enthused.

The weathered old man, leaned thoughtfully on the gate, as they watched the horse prancing around in the yard. 'His dam was one of my best brood mares; a brumby, but she's had some really great foals. I put her to an excellent quarter horse, my neighbour owned, and that colt was the best I've ever bred; got stamina, strength, speed, but the blighter escaped and joined the wild horses. I've been trying to catch him for nigh on two years.

I finally did get him back, but I'm getting too old to break horses these days, can't manage him, but he is a beauty! In my youth, I would never have parted with him.' The old man had a faraway look in his eye. 'Too smart for his own good that one!' He'll need a strong hand to bring him into line,' he warned.' My boys don't have the time or the patience to give him. He'll make a magnificent horse for the person who can handle him and gain his trust and respect.' He watched Jo carefully as she caressed the horse's neck. 'Do you think you are that person, Mrs Wentworth?'

'I reckon I am. Been breaking in horses with my Dad, since I was a kid. My brother and I never had a horse we couldn't handle, and my husband is a great trainer. We'd really like to buy him. What do you call him?'

'Well, I call him *Dibs*, but his name is actually *Diablo* - Devil.' the old man chuckled. 'I'll be sad to see him go, but he needs to be worked. You two seem to know what you're about. I think you'll do fine! Come up to the house, we'll sort out the price and the paperwork.'

He shook hands with David, then Jo, and the deal was done. After parting with a sizable cheque, they organised transport to the west for their new purchase, and then flew home.

'Wait until you see him!' Jo enthused to Guy. 'He is just magnificent!'

Three weeks later, the stock transport truck arrived to deliver *Dibs* to his new owners. Their parents, Together with Guy, Goldy, and the children went down with Jo and David, to supervise the unloading.

Dibs was indeed a magnificent animal. He was dapple grey with a dark mane and tail and four white feet.

'He's got socks on!' announced young Danny.

David laughed. 'My grandad had a little rhyme about white feet, Danny. He used to say, "One white foot, try him; two white feet, buy him; three white feet, buy him for your wife; but four white feet, run for your life"!'

Guy joined the laughter. 'I don't know about that, but he is pretty spirited, and will take some training, I'm sure! In the meantime, you kids had best keep away from him.'

Guy looked enviously at *Dibs*. 'What a beautiful animal!' he breathed. 'What I wouldn't give to be the one to train him.'

'Never mind Guy,' said Jo kindly, 'I fully intend that you and I can work with him when David is busy.'

Secretly, she would have been more than happy to have David train him altogether, but Guy was still in charge at *Brolga Plains*. She loved David and the way he related to horses, his gentleness and understanding, in contrast to Guy, who although he rode very well, always seemed to try to dominate. It was one of the few things about which she and her brother disagreed.

Some evenings, Jo watched David as he stood at the fence talking to the big stallion. *Dibs* initially eyed him with caution, but having decided he was no threat, approached the gate and nibbled at an apple or carrot; nuzzling him and allowing David to pat him.

Over the next few weeks, David developed a sound relationship with *Dibs*, until he and the horse seemed to really understand each other. It made Jo smile to see the stallion looking out for David, in the early mornings when he always spent an hour or two, working with him.

Daily, either Jo, David, or Guy worked with *Dibs*.

As an observer, it seemed to Goldy that Jo was right about Guy needing to dominate him. He spent many hours with *Dibs*, around and around the sandy training ring, on the end of a lunge rope. He finally put a bit in his mouth and a saddle cloth on him, and eventually a saddle. *Dibs* did not take kindly to the weight on his back, and bucked and pig rooted until he was exhausted and in a lather of sweat. Guy and Jo had strong words, but he would not back down.

Goldy watched the battle of wills between man and horse with growing concern. Although Guy had a sound knowledge of horses, he lacked understanding and she often thought he was a little too impatient. He did not like to be defeated, and more than once, she saw him lose his temper with the stallion, and take a whip to him in anger.

She noted that Dibs responded far better to Jo and David's more persuasive methods, but when she raised the matter with Guy, he was unconcerned. 'Jo and David are too soft with him. He's coming along slowly, he just has to learn who's the boss around here! He'll be okay. He's too smart to keep fighting me. He'll be fine!'

A few days later, Dirk climbed into the saddle; only to be thrown off immediately. Three more times, he attempted to mount the stallion. Twice more he came off. The third time, he managed to circle the ring twice, before *Dibs* suddenly pitched him off against the railing.

Guy was furious, and raising his whip, he hit the horse hard, across his neck. As *Dibs* turned away from him, he struck out with his back legs, catching Guy a savage blow to his head. He dropped like a stone, and lay unmoving, as the horse stood trembling, in a lather of sweat, on the far side of the ring.

Goldy, watching from the kitchen window, ran screaming from the house. 'Jo! David, Doug!

Get that horse out of there, and help me with Dirk!' But as she reached his side, and lifted his head, she knew he was already dead. His neck was broken and the front of his head smashed. As she knelt in the red dirt, she let out a terrible cry, echoed only by the screeching cockatoos, high above in the gum trees.

CHAPTER THIRTY SEVEN

A TERRIBLE DISCOVERY

The men carried Dirk's body to the homestead, while his wife, parents and sister clung together in disbelief, as they laid him gently on his bed. His children looked on in shocked confusion.

Later, David quietly spoke to Jo. 'What's to be done with that horse Jo?' he asked. 'Jack wants me to shoot him?'

Jo hesitated for only a moment, between her tears, before saying. 'No, David, It wasn't a deliberate attack; it was an accident; a response to the way Dirk was treating him. He doesn't deserve to die. Leave it with me. 'She thought about the times Dirk had taken a whip to the animal, or shouted at it in temper. 'No David, I don't want Dibs destroyed. Can you put him in the yards behind the stables for now, we can decide what's to be done with him later on. Just keep him away from Mum and Dad, Goldy and the children for the time being. Please darling, Just take care of him'.

David agreed and he promised he would care for *Dibs*, until a decision could be made.

The entire community was shocked by the death of Guy Kingsley. His father became an old man over night, and his heart broken mother retired to her room, an emotional wreck. His sister and her husband worked hard to keep everything running smoothly, despite their own distress.

A grief stricken Goldy gathered her family to her, as she tried to make sense of the horror.

Explaining to the children was difficult, especially three year old Suzanne, who announced, '"Dibs" was naughty to kick Daddy, wasn't he, Mummy? Will Daddy come home soon? We are all very sad 'cos he's gone away.'

Then there was the question of the funeral. Jack wanted his son buried on the station.'We've had Kingsleys on this place for over a hundred years,' he argued. 'He belongs here with my father and grandfather.' He went to see the local shire president, Boyd Brown.

'It's not that simple any more, Jack. We now have to get permission from the Minister for local government.'

'Well then do it!' demanded Jack.'No son of mine is going down to the city for burial in one of those huge anonymous cemeteries. My son belongs here, with his family!'

Boyd promised to do what he could, once the body had been returned from the Coroner's department in Perth. 'Routine after any accidental death,' he told Jack.

Eventually the permission for the burial was granted. One warm spring morning, some weeks after the accident, Guy Kingsley was buried under the big ghost gum tree, on a green slope near the western boundary of Brolga Hills. Jack, David, Sam, and Doug were pall bearers, Goldy, Diana and Jo held hands as they walked bravely up the small incline with Grandma Clara and the children. Little Suzanne's chubby little legs struggled to keep up, but she refused to be carried. The stockmen brought up the rear of the sad procession.

For his family, the tragedy of his sudden death had hit hard, and they were all in a state of shock. Unable to fully believe, or accept what had happened.

Father John conducted a short service, but his words were lost to his wife, who heard only a steady drone, as she choked back her tears, standing with Jack, Diana and Jo. The three united in their grief. Father John tried to offer a few words of comfort to the family, and then they all walked back to the homestead.

Goldy felt shattered. She asked herself had she perhaps not loved him enough? Was this some kind of punishment on her? She wept bitter tears.

The family's lawyer arrived from Perth, for the reading of the Will. There were no surprises. Guy have left everything he had to Goldy, and anything he would have inherited to be held in trust for their children. She was to receive a generous cash settlement.

Goldy was devatated by the loss of her husband. As Diana had predicted, she had grown to love him more than she would ever have thought possible. The thought of a future life without him was unbearable. Yet again she had lost someone she loved. She gently refused Diana's offer of help, as she went to their room to pack up his clothes and personal belongings.

She cried as she folded away his shirts, and pressed his sweater to her face, inhaling the vague fragrance of him which lingered there. So shattered was she, that she decided to leave his desk for another day.

It was a couple of weeks later when she braced herself to go through his personal papers. There were the usual formal things. An Insurance policy. Pedigree papers for some of his horses; vaccination papers. A packet of letters, photographs, Passports, cheque books and bank statements.

She was surprised to fnd an envelope, tucked away at the back corner. It was addressed to *'My Wife, Goldy Kingsley. To be opened only in the event of my death.'*

Inside was a letter attached to a formal looking document. She sat at the desk, the late afternoon sun streaming through the window. She read the letter first, written in Guy's strong hand.

My darling Goldy.

I have loved you with my heart and soul, since the first time I saw you in Walkabout Hills. I love the life which we have; as I love the beautiful children whom you and I have created.

Hopefully, before you read this, enough time will have elapsed so that I have been able to demonstrate my love for you, so that you will have had many years of happiness with me.

Always remember, my darling, that I have loved you, more than life itself, and please try to find it in your heart, not to hate me. I don't know whether you will ever be able to forgive me. There can be no excuse, but no matter what I may have done, or what lies I may have told; I love you with my heart and soul, as I have every day of our marriage.The last thing I ever wanted to do was to hurt you; but once the deed was done, there was no turning back

The attached is the exact truth. I want this to be revealed on my death, whenever, or wherever, that may occur.

Yours always

It was signed in his large strong hand
Opening the folded document, Goldy's horror grew with every line she read.

To Whom it may concern

I, *Guy John Kingsley*, solemnly swear that what I have written here, is the truth pertaining to the disappearance and murder of Daniel O'Hara. I, and I alone, am totally responsible for his death.

Danny O'Hara's plan to mine the property was totally abhorent to me. The land at Brolga Plains is my heritage, and that of my children. I love it with a passion, almost as great as that which I have for my wife, Goldy.

My father tried to persuade him to abandon his scheme, but he was determined to go ahead. Due to his friendship with Dan, my father refused to seek advice about lodging a legal challenge.

On the day of Dan's disappearance, I was doing a routine windmill check at Solly Creek, on the back road out of Brolga Plains, when I saw him driving out, presumably to see my father. I stopped him, and we talked about the mining lease. We started to argue about his proposed operations.

He told me that he intended to persuade my father to sink two shafts, not far from the homestead. I was very angry and I pushed him in temper; he fell backward, striking his head. I swear I never intended that to happen. I knew at once that he was dead and I panicked.

I tried to make it look as if someone had attacked and robbed him. I removed all identification, including a wallet, a silver cigar case, and a fob watch, all of which can be found wrapped in a cloth, in my safe. Then I took my gun *from the back of my car, and I shot him through the neck, and pushed his body down a nearby mine shaft, where it was later found.*

As for his vehicle, I towed it for over one hundred miles across country, through rocks and water, before setting it alight and crashing it into rocks. I then drove home and a week later. After wiping it clean, exchanged the gun, a .222, with the one kept in the staff quarters, usually used by Charlie Wentworth.

I thought that there was little chance that the police would ever find Danny or look for a firearm, but if they did, the it was almost certain that Charlie would use that gun in the meantime in fact I made sure of it. Asked him to put down a steer, so any finger prints would be his. This was necessary to avoid detection, and it was logical to throw suspicion on him, because of his very publc falling out with Danny O'Hara, over his wish to marry Goldy. He had been heard threatening Dan, and I knew he had a police record for manslaughter in Queensland, so it was very easy to discredit him.

I guess I never really thought he would get twenty years, and for that I am sorry. I admit to wanting him discredited, and out of the way for a while. I wanted to marry Goldy myself. She has always been the one and only woman for me, and I knew that at that time she had developed very strong feelings for him.

It is my prayer that my wife can, in time, forgive me. I am so sorry for what happened. I swear I never meant Danny O'Hara to die. He was a good man, and I liked him.

His son Sam has been like a brother to me since we were teenagers. I beg his forgiveness also.

I am making this statement, so that on my death, before I meet my Maker, I will have confessed my sin, and tried to right a terrible wrong.

To my beloved parents, if they be still alive, I am so sorry for the pain this will cause you. Please forgive me. To my sister Joanne, I can only say how sorry I am to bring this shame on the family.

I hope I have been a good son, brother, husband and father. God knows I have tried.

May God have mercy on my soul'.

It was signed , Guy John Kingsley, and dated the day after the bushfire, in which he nearly died.

Finally she put the paper down. Almost blinded by her tears, she found the key to his safe, and unlocking it, found the package, wrapped in a blue cloth. She opened it slowly. There was the wallet, and the memories came flooding back, as she held the silver cigar case, with her father's initials on the front, and inside the loving inscription she had ordered 'To the best Dad in the world. Love Goldy'.

The fob watch was there also. The one her brother Sam had given him, also for his fifty fifth birthday.

Goldy thought her heart would break, as she went in search of Jack and Diana. How to tell them that their beloved son, and Jo's big brother, was, in fact, a murderer? Her own husband had murdered her much loved father! She simply handed the letter and package to Jack.

They sat numbly together, as the terrible truth began to sink in. Finally, Jack rose wearily. 'I'd better get David in here, then we must call the police,' he whispered. 'Charlie must be released as soon as possible, poor devil!' then he broke down as he and his wife wept in each other's arms.

Slowly it began to dawn on Goldy. Charlie was innocent! He would soon be free! But then she cried again, as she recountered her husband's terrible confession. 'I so want them both to be innocent!' she sobbed.

For David, it was a bitter sweet moment. His brother would be free, but his wife and her family were devastated. Goldy, whom he loved and admired, was inconsolable.

'David, how can this happen? I cannot believe that my husband would do this terrible thing! Not the Guy I know and love. What am I to tell his children?'

CHAPTER THIRTY EIGHT

FREEDOM

At Fremantle Prison, Charlie was contemplating his upcoming freedom. Earle called in after speaking to the judge and ringing the prison governor. Charlie was told to be ready for release in the morning. He was shocked when he was told that Guy Kingsley had confessed, in a letter, to the murder of Danny O'Hara.

'Why for God's sake?' he had exclaimed. 'and why frame me? I know he wanted Goldy, but this is unbelievable!'

'I guess we will never really know,' said Earle, 'although he did say the murder was not deliberate. The main thing is, you are free!'

Charlie made sure she saw Cody before he left, to tell him his good news.

'Well I'll be damned,' said Cody. 'You really were telling the truth when you said you didn't do it! I'm glad for you,'

Charlie shook his hand. 'Good luck Cody, maybe we will meet again one day.'

On a warm spring morning, the heavy doors to Fremantle Prison swung open, Charlie Wentworth emerged, blinking into the bright sunlight. There were no words as David stepped forward to hug him . Arms around each other's shoulders, the brothers walked out to the car park.

When at last emotion subsided, after their first exchanges Charlie said quietly, 'How's Goldy coping with all this? Is she okay?'

'She will be, once the funeral and everything is over. She is very glad you are free at last, but as you can imagine, she is in a state of shock at present. I am sure that she is looking forward to welcoming you home.'

'I don't think that I want to go back to Walkabout Hills just yet. I thought I might go home to Longreach for a few weeks. Catch up with the folks. I think the Kingsleys will need some time to come to terms with all this before they see me. They need time to grieve for their son, and Jo for her brother. My freedom has come at a terrible price for them. Goldy too. Don't forget she has lost her husband, and the children, their father.'

David looked thoughtful. 'I appreciate your sentiments but don't know that is necessarily so, Charlie. You are the one who has been so terribly wronged, not them! Anyway, I've booked us into a hotel for the next couple of days, then, if you still want to go home, I'll organise a plane ticket for you. Unfortunately, I can't come with you, as I am needed at *Brolga Plains*. With you and Guy not there, old Jack really needs a hand.' He is not coping at all well at present. Losing Guy in the accident was bad enough for him, but this has really knocked the stuffing out of him. I can't help but feel sorry for him. He's a good man is Jack Kingsley.

Back at Walkabout Hills, Goldy waited in nervous anticipation. As David Wentworth's station wagon pulled up at the homestead, she took a deep breath. The door opened and David stepped down, with a cheerful wave. Heart in her mouth, Goldy waited for Charlie, but as the minutes passed, she realised with sorrow, that he was not coming.

'I'm sorry Goldy,' said David softly. 'Charlie didn't come; he couldn't face you all, not yet.' He put his arms around her. 'Maybe later', he said gruffly. 'He's gone home for a while. I guess, he has a lot to think about.'

For Charlie, to be home with his parents, and brother Andrew, was very comforting. There was something wonderful about being in his boyhood home, in his old room. It was all so far away from his last few years in prison. Within weeks, his eyes began to lose their haunted look; his smile less strained, his conversation less guarded. His mother's home cooking put some meat on his bony frame. He began to look forward to each new day with an enthusiasm not felt for a long time. He rode daily with his brother Andrew and relished the feel of the wind and sun on his face.

A couple of months later, the postmaster handed Charlie a letter. He looked in surprise at the envelope, not recognising the flowery writing, but it was postmarked 'Walkabout Hills'. He tore it open quickly, and with growing interest, took in the contents.

P.O Box 10, Walkabout Creek W.A

My dear friend Charlie,

Your brother David was here recently with your wonderful news. I am so very happy that at last you are to be free. I always believed and hoped, that this would happen one day. Nobody who knows you as do I, could possibly think that you could do this terrible thing.

I am sad because of the way that this has happened for you, and the sorrow for Miss Goldy, that her husband has been the cause of all this unhappiness, but, in my experience, life is often sad, before it improves. This I have found to be true over my long life.

I do not know what are your plans right now but I have an idea that might just suit you and me both. It occurs to me that you might like to come here for a while to help me. I cannot pay so much, but I think together we could do much to improve Milly Downs and make it good like in the old days. What do you say? I am well. but getting very old. I find it very had to look after Milly

Downs these days. Your brother David and young Goldy have been so good to me while you have been away, but with Guy gone, they will not have time to help so much. Please think about this most seriously and let me know,

Your affectionate friend, Yuri Astanov

Charlie thought long and hard. He was not ready to go back to *Brolga Hills.* Not to face the ghosts of yesterday; nor to see Goldy. Go to Milly Downs? Why not? It was still his most favourite place on God's earth. Maybe, one day he might return to *Brolga Hills,* but that was all in the future.

He went inside to see his father. 'Got a minute dad?' Bob was going through accounts at his desk, a job he hated. He was always grateful for an interruption. 'Sure son, take a seat What's on your mind?' He picked up his discarded pipe, relit it and walked around his desk to flop onto the old leather sofa.

'Well,' Charlie began slowly, 'you and I have talked before about what I can do with my future; especially now, and we both agree that there isn't really much for me here. Andrew is more than capable of running this place for you and I really want to do something for myself. So what do you think about this?' He handed Yuri's letter to his father, who read it without comment, then folded it and handed it back to Charlie, as he drew a long breath on his pipe.

Eventually he spoke. 'Well son, I hate the idea of you going back west.

This will always be your home, I hope you know that, but it might be a good place to make a new start. If I remember rightly, Milly Downs was the place you once hoped to buy wasn't it?'

Charlie nodded.

'Maybe this would be the next best thing, hey?' His dad continued cautiously, 'and what about Goldy?'

Charlie shrugged. 'I will always love her, but I guess that was all a long time ago, Dad. We are two very different people to the two young dreamers who fell in love. It seems like a different world, a different lifetime. She has three children, now she is a widow. She owns part of *Brolga Hills*, and I have absolutely nothing! Who knows?'

He turned away abruptly and gazed out across the garden to the dry bush beyond. 'Perhaps one day I will be able to see her without feeling that someone has ripped my heart out, but not yet. I just don't know how I feel about anything anymore Dad.'

Bob observed him shrewdly. 'You know, son, I have learned in life that the only things I have really regretted, are the things I never tried. If this is what you need to do, give it a go son. We are always here if you want to come home. You both deserve that chance.' He started to feel the emotion rising in his throat, threatening to overwhelm him. He stood up suddenly and patted Charlie roughly on the back. 'You had better go tell your mother, but be prepared for tears.'

Rosemary Wentworth did shed tears for her son, but she agreed with her husband that this was the right thing to do, and she set about preparing for his departure.

Charlie wrote back to Yuri, accepting his offer.

A week later, he was on a plane back to Perth, where, with a bank draft from his father, he bought himself a second hand utility and took off next morning for Walkabout Hills.

Charlie hadn't told anyone, apart from Yuri, and his brother David, that he was returning, and he had asked both of them not to spread the news. He wanted to slip back into his life there, with as little fuss as possible. David reminded him that Goldy may have to be told, as she was a frequent visitor to *Milly Down* He agreed.

The drive north was a sheer joy to him. The clear blue sky, the long grey/green bush stretching as far as the eye could see, and the occasional red rocky outcrops, were balm to his soul.

Along both sides of the road, there were wildflowers, all the way to the horizon. Pink and white Everlastings, Banksia trees bent almost double with blossom, purple Geraldton Wax, White Smoke bush, and farther north, clumps of Spinifex grass and the red and black of Stuart Desert Peas. A frantic Emu, darted erratically in front of him, before peeling off into the scrub. He stopped frequently to stand on the edge of the bush, breathing in all the familiar smells, the sheer cleanliness of the air, mingled with eucalyptus.

He watched idly as a Wedge tailed Eagle floating high above on a thermal. 'Free like me.' He whispered, feeling intensely happy. A big red kangaroo watched him curiously from a nearby rock, turning and hopping rapidly out of sight.

Meanwhile, Yuri was waiting excitedly for Charlie's arrival. He had contacted David to ask him to bring Rufus, now a very old dog, out to the station, to be there when Charlie arrived. When Charlie pulled up in the utility in front of the homestead, he sat for a few minutes, enjoying the familiar landscape.

CHAPTER THIRTY NINE

BACK TO MILLY DOWNS

Finally, he stepped out into the bright sunshine and had walked only a few steps when he saw the old dog, sitting on the front steps. At first, the Rufus barked at the stranger, but Charlie crouched down and called softly 'Rufus? Here boy!' The dog stopped barking, he paused for just a moment, then flew down the steps, yelping with joy as he jumped up at Charlie, almost knocking him over as he licked his arms and wriggled with excitement. Charlie buried his face in the dog's greying fur, and there was salt on his cheeks as he hugged his beloved pet. 'I didn't think you'd remember me, you're a funny old thing. Oh Rufus, my Rufus!'

Yuri appeared at the door, smiling with pleasure at the dog and his master. 'Hullo there,' he called. 'I told the dog you were coming. Welcome Charlie, welcome home, my friend!'

As he watched Yuri move carefully down the steps, Charlie noted how much the old man had aged. He stepped forward to shake his hand but found himself in a bear hug. Untangling himself from Yuri and from the still ecstatic *Rufus*, he felt warm tears on his cheek. 'It's so good to see you both my old friends.'

'Come.' said Yuri, 'We must have a drink to celebrate!'

Two hours later, the men sat on the veranda, Charlie sipping his beer, Yuri his Vodka, and chatting as old friends do. The dog lay across Charlie's feet with a look of pure contentment on his old grey face. They sat, watching the sun, a huge golden orb, sinking into the purple horizon.

Next morning, early, David Wentworth arrived to welcome him back. 'Good to see you bro!' The two men hugged warmly. 'You too, Davey boy! How are you? You look as fit as a Mallee bull, mate! Married life must agree with you! How is Jo?'

'It sure does. I love my Jo, she's great, as are all the people out there on *Brolga Hills*, but you know that Jack Kingsley has said there will always be a place for you there,' said David. 'We would all be happy to have you on the station.'

'No mate, no need for that. I will be very glad to stay here at *Milly Downs*. Anyway, I don't want to be at Kingsley's just now. I don't want to see Goldy; I couldn't bear it. Tell me,' he said hesitantly, 'How is she? How is your poor wife, Jo? How are Jack and Diana? Are they coping with losing Guy? And what about the children?'

David shook his head. 'I guess they are all coping in their different ways, but it has been tough on them all, but especially hard on Goldy, what with the kids and everything. They are good little nippers, but it is hard for them to understand. I don't expect you to feel sorry for Guy, after everything that's happened, but I do feel for the family.'

Charlie nodded. 'Jack contacted me as soon as he knew the facts. He wanted to know how he could ever make up for what Guy had done to me. Poor devil, I feel for him. He's such a good bloke. No good wallowing in the past. I'd like to go back one day, maybe, but first I need time to get used to my freedom. I guess it is a very different world from the one I left behind.'

'With, or without you at Brolga Plains, Charlie,' Jack had said, 'I can never forget what my son did to you. There will always be a position here for you if you want it. It is the very least I can do for you!'

Charlie had written back to Jack, to explain his decision about *Milly Downs*. He asked him not to let Goldy visit him for the time being, and he promised to keep in touch. Jack felt sad, but he understood.

A month after his arrival at *Milly Downs*, Charlie had settled easily back into station life. He quickly adjusted to his new role as the manager and moved into the small weatherboard house with Yuri. He and Yuri had always had a companionable relationship, and the old man's quiet conversation helped Charlie to regain some of his confidence. He laughed more easily and began to enjoy his life. He still avoided going into town for fear of meeting Goldy. He did not yet feel ready for that encounter.

Word soon got out in town, that Charlie Wentworth was the new manager of *Millie Downs*.

In spite of Jack having told her that Charlie had asked that she not go out to see him, Goldy sought out David. 'Will you take me out to *Milly Downs*?'

David paused, then sighed. 'Goldy, you know I can't do that. Charlie doesn't want to see you at present.'

'Why doesn't he doesn't want to see me?' she repeated.

'I'm sorry Goldy, but you need to remember, the last time you two met, you were engaged to be married. He only gave you up was because he thought that best for you. Now he is free, but very conscious that this has only come about because of Guy's confession.

He appreciates that Guy has been your husband, and that you obviously cared very much for him. He doesn't know how he would cope with seeing you at the moment, and he doesn't want to cause you, or himself, any more distress. Give him time, please, Goldy.'

'He must really hate me!' she said miserably.

'No Goldy, that's not true. He just needs time to get used to everything. He'll come around in his own time, I promise. You'll see, if I'm not right.'

Goldy was tempted to drive out to *Milly Downs* anyway, but David dissuaded her. 'You're not being fair! I've already told you Goldy, just give him time!' he insisted. She slowly began to accept that Charlie did not wish to be part of her life, so she put her energy into her growing family. She frequently asked David how he was getting on.

She missed her visits to Yuri, but she was determined not to upset Charlie, so she kept away. Then, one day, quite by chance, she bumped into him on the post office steps. She was shocked but pleased to see him, and after a few slightly hasty words, they went their separate ways.

Charlie was happy to see her, but it seemed to him that she had been embarrassed to see him. He could not have known, or even imagined, how her heart turned over at the sight of him. Nor how much she longed to give him a hug. He felt sad as he reflected on how different their life might have been had it not been for Guy's deception. He tried not to think about her at all, but if he was honest, she was seldom out of his thoughts and he now carried his precious photograph of her in his wallet. He discussed her with no one. Not even his brother.

Then out of the blue, Charlie received an invitation to visit *Brolga Hills*, ostensibly from Jack and Diana.

At first, he was reluctant to accept their invitation, but David was adamant. 'You can't avoid them all for ever, bro.' he said kindly. 'You have done nothing wrong. Quite the opposite! Come on, Jo and I will be there too to support you.'

Once the ice was broken, he soon became more comfortable at *Brolga Hills* and an accepted part of life there. Nobody mentioned Guy's role in Charlie's absence, and the children took to him almost immediately. He soon became an important part of their world, taking on the role of friend and mentor, a constant source of fun and information. However, it still appeared to him that Goldy was cool and that she often avoided him.

Eventually Jo had to make a decision about *Dibs*, their beautiful stallion, that had inadvertently brought about Guy's death. After speaking with David and then Goldy, she went to see her father to discuss it with him. At first he was angry that she had disobeyed his instruction to have the animal destroyed, but after some thought, he had to agree that it had indeed been an unfortunate accident, for which *Dibs* did not deserve to die. He also, reluctantly, acknowledged that Guy's treatment of the stallion had inadvertently contributed to his own death, but he requested that the horse be kept away from Diana. She was still struggling with her son's death.

Armed with Jack's tacit approval, Jo handed the stallion back to David to continue his training. Thus their breeding program was back on track.

CHAPTER FORTY

AN UNEXPECTED GIFT

About three months after Charlie's first visit, Goldy stood watching him through the window, as he helped young Steve to unsaddle his pony. Jack moved to stand by her side.

'Goldy, there is something I need to say to you.' he said seriously, as she turned to face him.

'Please my dear, sit down.' She sat, wondering where this was going. He continued, 'Goldy, Diana and I could not love you more if you were our own daughter. You were a loyal and loving wife to our son, and you are a wonderful mother to our grandchildren. Guy, sadly, is gone, but you are still young and alive and you deserve to be happy. We both know, that in the beginning, it was Charlie you loved, and whom you planned to marry.'

Goldy opened her mouth to protest,

'No, no, don't deny it!' said Jack putting a hand on her shoulder. 'If you still feel for him as you did then, I want you to know that you have our blessing'. He kissed her gently on the cheek.

Goldy could feel tears threatening, 'Oh Jack, thank you for that, but I really don't think he feels that way for me any more. It has been such a long time. He made the decision a long time ago that he did not want me anymore.'

Jack smiled his quiet smile, so like Guy's. 'My dear girl, Charlie loves you. I see it in his face every time he looks at you.' He gently took her hand.

'Don't let happiness slide away. Grab it with both hands. Frankly, I can't think of a better role model for my grandchildren!'

oooOooo

Yuri and Charlie often had their evening meal together. Yuri liked to cook, almost as much as he liked to talk about his early life in Russia, and he often entertained with songs and verses. Over the months they were together, Charlie grew increasingly fonder of the old man. Yuri, in turn, enjoyed the younger man's company. They had quite heated debates on the way the world was, or should be. They exchanged philosophies and they laughed together a great deal.

One cold evening, as they sat together in front of the fire, talk turned to families. Yuri encouraged Charlie to talk about his parents and his brothers. He was interested in all Charlie's thoughts. He asked so many questions, that Charlie felt he knew his family better than he did! 'Do you have any family left in Russia?' He queried.

'I have no family anywhere, any more.' Yuri said sadly. 'When my Natasha and I came to this country, we had so many dreams. We were going to have many fine sons to work our land. Maybe make us rich, yes! Sadly, we only had our one little boy, Vassili, but no more. Then, as you know, I lost them both. Does seem very hard at times does it not?' He laughed. 'Now I have only you and your dog! But that is ok. Maybe my boy would have grown up like you. He had the fair curls, and the blue eyes, just like you.'

Charlie agreed that it was hard. 'Me, I will probably never have a wife or children.' He said sadly.

Yuri laughed. 'That is up to you my young friend. You should marry Miss Goldy and you could have fine sons too!'

'Not possible any more Yuri.'

'But you still love her, this Miss Goldy?'

'You have to ask? You know I do Yuri! She has always been the only woman for me.'

Yuri puffed on his pipe, 'Then you must have faith in that love. Love will always find a way, but you have to leave the door open, yes?'

Charlie nodded. 'Yes Yuri, but it takes more than love sometimes. I have nothing to offer her and she now has so much. I could hardly keep her on my salary!' After a nightcap, the two bade goodnight, and Charlie and *Rufus* went to bed.

With the onset of the wet season, the creek was now flowing swiftly over the crossing on the track leading up to the homestead. Charlie had gone out very early to move the cattle to higher ground. Accompanied by his ever faithful *Rufus*, he was running later than usual as he headed back to the house for breakfast. Most mornings, the two men ate breakfast together while they ran through the plans for the day

Charlie was surprised to see no smoke drifting from the kitchen chimney, no smell of the usual roasting coffee. He gingerly walked into the house. The kitchen was cold and empty; the fire dead in the hearth. With a feeling of foreboding, he called out. 'Yuri? Are you there?' The question hung heavy in the silence. He walked through into the main bedroom. Yuri lay on his back on the bed, a sweet smile on his weathered face. In his hands he held a photograph of his wife and son, but his faded blue eyes saw nothing. Charlie felt for a pulse, but he already knew the old man was dead.

He felt the tears pricking behind his eyes and a lump rose up in his throat as he sank slowly to sit on the bed next to Yuri. 'Goodbye, old friend,' he said softly. I will miss you.' Then he covered Yuri's face and gently closed the bedroom door.

Yuri Astanov was buried in the Catholic cemetery. Father John said he wasn't sure whether Yuri was Jewish or Russian Orthodox, but he said he felt sure Yuri wouldn't mind. Considering how much of a loner he had been for so long, there was a good turnout for the service. Charlie and David were both very sad, as they walked with Yuri's coffin to the small cemetery. Goldy was devastated at his loss, and shed copious tears for the old man who had been such a comfort to her over the long years of Charlie's imprisonment.

Charlie and David took it on themselves to search for any legal documents required by law.

They could find no Birth Certificate, but his Citizenship records showed his place of birth in Poland, and that he was eighty three years old. They also found a letter detailing that the Deeds for *Milly Downs* and his Will, were in the keeping of a law firm in Perth, Spencer and Hodges. Charlie made a note of their address and contacted them in due course.

Until other arrangements could be made by the Solicitors, Charlie chose to stay on to care for the property. 'Maybe the new owners will keep me on as manager,' he said to David. 'Otherwise I am going to be looking for a job.'

'Jack Kingsley will always give you a job, you know that.'

'Yes, and it would be really great for me working there, when Goldy would be my boss and she owns half of the bloody property, where I would be a station hand!'

David blanched at this uncharacteristic burst of anger, and said nothing.

Apart from letters from his parents, Charlie seldom received mail, consequently he rarely called at the post office. It was on one of his infrequent visits to town, that he was accosted by the Mollie Jenkins, the postmistress. 'Good morning, Mr Wentworth! Don't you ever collect your mail?

There is a very official looking letter waiting for you. If you come back with me now you can have it. It needs a signature.'

Curious, Charlie followed her back to the post office to collect the said letter.

'Aren't you going to open it?' asked the always nosy Mollie.

He muttered something unintelligible, stuffed it into his pocket, and made a hurried exit. Once home, he made himself a coffee and sat down to read his mail. His amazement grew as he read the first, a letter from a solicitor in Perth.

Dear Mr Wentworth,

> *We wish to advise you that under the will of the late Yuri Astanov, of Milly Downs Station, Walkabout Creek, in the state of Western Australia, you are the sole beneficiary of his entire estate This legacy includes the property of Milly Downs Station, which is freehold, {meaning that there is no mortgage held over it.} There is also a sum of money, and a portfolio of shares, at present held by the Commonwealth Bank. Once any outstanding bills are paid, this amount of approximately $100,000 will be forwarded to you. If you wish, we would be happy to act on your behalf to arrange the transfer of the Deeds to Milly Downs to you.*

> *Please contact us at your earliest convenience, so that we may expedite this matter as soon as possible.*

We are enclosing under separate cover, a letter from Mr Astanov which he wanted you to have, together with his bequest

Yours faithfully etc.

Charlie then opened the enclosed, hand written in Yuri's flowery hand, his heart thumping at the implications of Yuri's generosity to him.

My dear Charlie.

That you are reading this means that I have already left you and gone to meet my God, and my beloved wife and son I know that you are the one person in this world to whom I can leave my beloved Milly Downs. Safe in the knowledge that you will care for it as I have tried to do.

Hopefully, you will be able to marry your lovely Goldy, now that you too, are a land owner!

I wish I could be with you to share your happy future. I will be there in spirit at least.

Please can I tell you, that you have brought much joy into this old man's life since you joined me You have indeed been like a son to me. If my gift can bring you some happiness, then I die a very happy man. Thank you for your friendship.

Please, remember me sometimes, as you sit with your family.

I am forever, your friend,

Yuri Astanov.

As Charlie sat with the letter in his hand, he felt wet tears on his cheeks as he thought of his benefactor. Then collecting *Rufus*, he drove across to *Brolga Hills*. Firstly, he went to find David to tell him of his good fortune. David was delighted. 'Good old Yuri!' he exclaimed. 'This is wonderful news Charlie. Just think, now *you* actually own *Milly Downs,* just like you always dreamed, all those years ago!'

'Pity I had to lose Yuri in the process. I really loved the old man, you know. He was more than a friend to me, and he never stopped believing in me, but it never crossed my mind that he might leave *Milly Downs* to me!'

'I know that Charlie, but he loved you. You were more than just a friend to him. He had no family, so I guess it makes sense that he chose to give it to you.'

'Keep it to yourself for the moment will you David? I have some things to sort out.'

David looked hard at his brother. 'Would that have anything to do with the beautiful redhead up at the homestead?'

'Might do, Dave, but I'm not saying anything at the moment.'

CHAPTER FORTY ONE

THE MEMORIAL BALL

With Clara gone down south to Kalgoorlie, Sally and Kevin Gregson, together with Troy, had done a great job running the pub since Danny's death. So, they approached Goldy to ask if she and Sam thought Clara would consider selling out to them. Clara was reluctant to sell, but she agreed to a long leasing contract, which they all decided was a good idea and it was readily settled.

As a parting gesture, Goldy suggested they open up the ballroom and have one massive party a masked ball! – 'The Kingsley/O'Hara Memorial Ball', no less!

Goldy paid for a well known city dance band to come up for the weekend, and Sally and Kevin organised the catering. Sam and Sonia agreed to pay for the drinks, and Goldy and Jo organised some ball gowns to be hired, for those who did not have anything suitable. Jack promised to arrange for Clara to come up for a few days.

Diana volunteered to bring up a large assortment of masks from the city with her. An open invitation was sent out to everyone in town and those from the surrounding stations. All the staff from everywhere were welcome, and whilst the dress was advertised as 'formal,' nobody was too clear about what that meant, so it was really 'Anything Goes day!'

'I just want everyone to have some fun, after all the sorrow there has been over the past few years,' announced Goldy.

With the help of some local girls, and the boys from the station, the chandeliers were taken down, washed thoroughly; the bulbs replaced, and returned to pride of place above the newly cleaned dance floor. Sylvia and Goldy made new drapes for the windows and everything was in readiness for the ball. The small charge, per head, was to be donated partly to the RFDS and partly to finance a modern fire engine for the district.

When the night finally arrived, there was great excitement. Sally and Jo had arranged flowers throughout the ballroom, and it looked spectacular. Goldy was very disappointed that Charlie had declined the invitation, saying that he did not, as yet, feel comfortable in attending social outings. Sadly, she remembered, how he had loved to dance all those years ago.

As she and her brother did a last minute check on the ballroom, Goldy felt very emotional. 'Oh Sam,' she whispered, 'Wouldn't Dad have loved this?'

Sam put his arm around her a gentle hug. 'I'm sure he approves,Sis, wherever he is.' he answered, with a smile.

Goldy was at the hotel early to see to any last minute arrangements, and as the guests began to arrive, she was delighted to see how much trouble people had gone to, in order to make the night special. Many of the women had made lovely ball gowns and their husbands and boyfriends were equally smartly attired. Even some of the stockmen arrived in moleskin trousers with fancy shirts, and many availed themselves of Diana's masks! Diana herself looked magnificent, if still fragile, in a silver gown with pink rosebuds around the hem and neck, her blonde hair piled high, as she acted as hostess with Goldy .

'She looks like someone from 'Gone With the Wind'!' remarked Sally. 'What a beautiful woman she is!'

Jack Kingsley, now silver haired, was as elegant as ever, in a tuxedo, led two of his favourite ladies into the ballroom. Diana on one arm and Goldy on the other. Goldy had opted for a shamrock green dress, which almost matched her eyes. She wore her red hair up, interwoven with green velvet ribbon. Joanne and David Wentworth made a handsome couple, as she looked radiant in sky blue. Sam and his new wife, looked dashing, she in dark blue taffeta, and he in a dark suit with a shirt to match Sonia's dress. Sally was in a pretty pink gown and Kevin was dressed up in a pale suit, complete with a bow tie! Troy turned up looking like a river boat gambler!

Dr Ben Morris arrived with his wife, and Caroline and Matt Brearley, all looking very elegant. The now retired police sergeant, Bob Paterson and his wife Betty, suitably attired, accompanied by senior constable Wilkins, long since transferred to another post, with his wife, Madge. The postmaster, John Jenkins and his wife, Mollie, made an impressive pair.

When the band started to play, the dancing began and the old pub had never looked better! So many beautifully attired couples whirled around the dance floor.

It was after supper, and the dancing had just started up again. Jack Kingsley smiled at his daughter-in-law. 'Would you indulge a lame old man in a slow waltz, my dear? Goldy smiled as she rose to her feet. 'Delighted Sir!' she said as they walked onto the dance floor.

They had completed a couple of circuits, when a tall masked stranger in an elegant suit, cut in. 'May I?' Smiling Jack stepped back.

They had done a circuit of the dance floor when a familiar voice said, 'Hullo, beautiful lady.'

'Charlie!' she cried delightedly. 'I didn't think you were coming. What a lovely surprise! I'm so glad to see you!'

'I wasn't sure if you would be, but I couldn't miss a chance to dance with the beautiful Goldy O'Hara! I think I can just about remember how to do this!'

They danced together as easily as they ever had, and when the Cha Cha was announced, the clock seemed to turn back to a happier time, until he said, with a mischievious grin, 'Would you care for some fresh air Madam?'

Laughing, they went out onto the veranda, where they stood gazing up at the velvet sky. He breathed in deeply, taking in the smell of the open air. 'There was a time when I thought I would never be able to do this again,' he said quietly, 'It is so wonderful to be back. You must come out to *Milly Downs*,' he told her. 'Yuri and I made lots of changes before he died. I actually persuaded him to paint the homestead! Must be the first lick of paint for twenty five years at least.'

For a moment he looked very sad. 'God I miss him, Goldy!'

'I know you do,' she said sincerely. 'So do I. He was so good to me after you went away. He never lost his faith in you. We both knew you were innocent. Do you ever think of that day you and I went out there for our picnic. I remember that was the first time I had ever seen the bush at night. It was so beautiful.'

Charlie laughed gently. 'Will never forget. It was one of the best days of my life. You have no idea how often I re-lived that when I was in prison! I used to think about things like that . Do you know that I could hardly see the night sky from my cell. That was one of the hardest parts of prison life. My happy memories of you, were all that kept me from going completely crazy.'

'Charlie, I am so sorry...'

He cut her off. 'Not your fault, Goldy. None of it.'

'I would have waited for you Charlie, only you made it very clear that you didn't want me to.'

'Ah Goldy, it seemed for the best at the time. Anyway, look at you now. Three beautiful children, a comfortable life. Much than I could ever have given you. Life hasn't been so bad for you has it?'

'No, but there hasn't been a day when I haven't wondered how you were.'

He seemed about to say something, but changed his mind and laughing, pulled her back into the ballroom. 'Hey, they're playing another Cha Cha! Come on, it's my favourite.'

Jack and Diana smiled at the couple as they stepped onto the dance floor, and Jo gave Goldy a cheeky wave, as she danced away in David's arms. Goldy felt happier than she had for a long time.

Everyone voted the masked ball to be the greatest social event ever seen in Walkabout Hills, the main topic of conversation for some weeks to follow. There was even talk of making it an annual event, so great was the support it received.

In spite of their relaxed conversation at the ball, Charlie made no further efforts to speak to Goldy, on anything but a casual level. Any hopes that she might have harboured on rekindling their relationship, soon died away, and sadly, she resigned herself to the fact that she would have to live with her memories only, from then on.

CHAPTER FORTY TWO

RENAISSANCE

One afternoon, Charlie was walking young Steve around the lawn on his pony, when Jack wandered across from the house. 'How's it going Charlie?' he asked casually. 'Settling without Yuri?'

'Yes, thanks, Jack. Life is pretty good over there, 'though I miss the old boy.'

'How wonderful that he left *Milly Downs* to you.'

Charlie looked shocked. 'How did you know? Surely David didn't tell you?'

Jack chuckled. 'No, of course he didn't. You forget, there isn't much that goes on in Walkabout Creek that I don't know about. I'm on the Shire Council, and I see all the land sales and transfers in the district. I am really pleased for you Charlie, and, I haven't said anything to anyone, not even my wife!'

'Thanks for that Jack. You have been so good to me since I came out of prison. It can't have been easy for you, and I really appreciate it. One of the things I have really enjoyed, has been coming over to see you all at *Brolga Hills*, especially the kids. I love your grandchildren, there's a kind of inordinate goodness and purity about them, isn't there.?'

'Yes. There is.' Jack acknowledged. 'Maybe one day you will have some of your own. You are still a comparatively young man, Charlie. Perhaps now you are a man of means, you should think about getting married one day. I can strongly recommend it!'

Charlie gave him a quick glance, but Jack's expression gave away nothing.

'I would love to get married, Jack, but I don't think it is any secret that there has only ever been one lady for me, and I am afraid she is lost to me now. I'm sure you would agree?'

'I wouldn't be so sure, young man. I have it on very good authority that things may not be as bleak as they appear. Have some courage! Nothing ventured, nothing gained, so they say! You might just be pleasantly surprised.' Jack slapped him lightly on the back, then chuckled as he walked back into the house.

Goldy saw them from the lounge room window, and she turned as Jack entered the room. 'You look very pleased with yourself. What have you been up to?'

'Actually I have been discussing matters of courage with Charlie.'

She looked puzzled. 'What sort of 'matters of courage'?'

'Why don't you go and find out,' he said smiling at her.

She gave him a sideways look as she walked quickly toward the door.

She went over to where young Steve was quietly grooming his pony, under Charlie's direction.

'Hi there boys. How's it going? You are riding much better, Stevie, don't you think so Charlie?'

Charlie looked across the pony's back at her, and as their eyes met, she felt her heart give a flutter. 'Yes, he's doing very well.' Charlie said quietly, not taking his eyes off Goldy.

Together they walked the boy and pony back to the stable, where Charlie helped settle him down and gave him a feed. Goldy then said gently. 'That's very good Stevie. Now go and see Grandma and she will give you something to eat.'

'Thank you Charlie!' called the child, waving gaily as he ran off.' See you *Rufus!*'

'You're welcome Stevie ' replied Charlie, laughing. 'He's a good kid, Goldy. Going to make a cracking horseman one day, that boy of yours.'

Standing near him, Goldy said, 'I can't believe how good you are with the children, Charlie.

Thank you. It has really made a difference to them since Guy…,' she couldn't say it, not to him.

'No worries. It's not hard. They are lovely kids,' he said gruffly. 'Just like their mother.' He took a couple of steps away, and took a deep breath, before turning back to face her.

'Goldy, I've really missed you. I used to feel so good when I was with you.'

She smiled sadly, 'I know. I feel the same.'

'Really? I didn't think you really wanted to talk to me anymore. You've been pretty quiet since the ball.'

'I thought you wouldn't want too much to do with me, after everything that has happened. If you hadn't met me……'

Charlie grabbed her hand and pulled her closer. 'Goldy, if I hadn't met you, I would have been so very lonely. You gave me so much joy and happiness in that short time we had together, I would go through it all again, just to have that!'

'But it was because of me that you spent all that time in prison! I really thought you would hate me!' Goldy began to cry quietly.

Charlie put his arms around her shaking shoulders. 'Goldy, Goldy. I never stopped loving you for one single minute. When things were a bit tough in prison, I used to look at your photograph, then I used to shut my eyes and think of you. I would remember your lovely face, your happy laugh, and then anything was bearable. Your warmth, your love, were always so special to me. The hardest thing in my life was sending you away. I didn't want you to wait for years, and then perhaps discover that you didn't want me anymore. Prison changes a man, you know.'

'Charlie, how could I not want you? I have loved you since almost the first day we met. You are the best thing that ever happened to me. I know I married Guy, and I won't pretend I didn't grow to love him, but if you had been here, or even said anything, I would not have looked at anyone else – ever!'

He pushed a lock of hair back off her forehead. 'I know it's been a long time and so much has happened, but do you think,' he hesitated, 'do you think we could give it another go? Maybe there is still a chance for us?'

'Oh Charlie!' cried Goldy. 'My own dear Charlie! I thought you would never ask!'

She smiled up at him through her tears, all the years were swept away, as he kissed her gently and wiped away the tears, as he held her close.

'Oh Charlie, it's been so long. I am so sorry for everything.'

'I have already told you, my darling, that you have absolutely nothing to be sorry about.

All I know is that you always believed in my innocence, and you are still my beautiful Goldy. What happened was not your fault. Just the knowledge that you believed me, has kept me sane all these years. I think I love you more now than ever!'

He kissed her again, this time with passion, which she returned. 'Goldy, will you marry me?' he said quietly, as he held her close. 'I have the home of my dreams to offer you now, which I will tell you all about in due course, and I do love you so very much.'

'Yes, Charlie, my own love. With or without a home, I will marry you, and I promise I will love you for the rest of my life.'

'How do you think the family will cope with all this?' he asked, nuzzling her hair. 'What about the children?'

'The children all love you Charlie, and as for the rest of them, nobody blames you for anything. Quite the opposite, Jo, Jack and Diana have already given their blessing!'

They kissed again, then Charlie smiled. 'C'mon then, let's go tell the family.'

Hand in hand, with Rufus ambling beside them, they turned and walked across the lawn to the homestead.

oooOooo

BIOGRAPHY

Jane Paul was born in England and travelled extensively throughout much of the world, both as a child with her parents, and later as an adult.

Her early life was spent as a ballet dancer in Australia and Europe. When a severe illness ended her career, she returned to Australia, and trained as a registered nurse in the 1960's. This role took her to some of the more remote areas of Australia.

Jane has been writing since she was a small child, editing a school newspaper, and writing children's stories. She published her first book in 2015 – 'The Waterfall Gods' was based on her family's history is Sri Lanka.

Since retirement, Jane has been travelling again to Europe and Scandinavia, gathering material for more books.

Her novel, 'Walkabout Creek' had its beginnings when Jane worked as a remote area nurse; some of her experiences are recreated in the book. A sequel is planned.

In her spare time, Jane enjoys her children and grandchildren, music, books her dog and cat, and drinking good wine with her friends, She intends to wear out, not rust out!